For those who live in the shadows,

For those who fight when hope seems lost,

For those who are still standing - bruised, battered but still burning with life,

This is for you.

WHISPERS

THE WHISPERS SERIES BOOK THREE

within the WORLD

S.K MAY

Trigger Warnings

Gore, Death, Murder, Assault,
Bullying, Flashbacks of Abusive relationship,
Explicit Scenes and Language,
References to substance abuse

CHAPTER 1

3 MONTHS AFTER LUCE'S DEATH

Roman

My wolf was eager to meet Mimi. It wanted to speak with her, smell her, touch her. It needed to mate; it needed her. He was becoming ravenous with desire. Larissa wanted to give Mimi time to adjust to London before I spun her world with the revelation that wolves exist. Not only a wolf, but an Alpha, and she would be my Luna, helping to run our pack, or rather, every pack within the United Kingdom.

Larissa was numb to the world of pain since the loss of her sister. I didn't want to bother her, but on the night of the full moon, he grew impatient. He wanted her now.

Larissa came down to the gym as she had done since coming into all those powers that night. I taught her control and how to use her magic without casting spells. We focused on using the right amount to prevent her from losing control. Her face was the same as usual, tired and drained. She had lost her spark.

"Morning, Larissa," I said with my usual pep.

"Do you *have* to be so cheerful?" she grumbled, walking over to take the gloves and slide them on.

"Always! Today is a grand day. Do you know what it might be a grand day for?" I asked her. I had lost all sense of normalcy with my wolf eager for its mate.

"What? Having a mate that actually gives a shit about the loss you have suffered?" she mumbled while I fastened the gloves to her tiny wrists.

"How about finally meeting your mate?"

Her gaze found mine, and she froze. Her olive skin turned ghostly white, telling me she had completely forgotten.

"Fuck, Roman. I forgot. I am *so* sorry, I ha—" I pressed my finger to her lips.

"It is fine. You have been a little out of it."

"It's not an excuse, Roman. You have been waiting for Mimi. I saw the way you locked eyes at the wedding, and I have just been in a haze. Sorry. I *can* say you made an impression; she asked who the hunky man beside Nik was."

My wolf whined. "She asked? What did you say?"

Larissa laughed as she poked my chest playfully.

"That's not funny. Do you know what it's like to have a mate and wait to claim her? My wolf is going crazy, and tonight is the full moon, and it seriously just wants to go to her." She tilted her head to the side with a wide grin on her face. "Not fair."

"Today is a light day at work. Come and take me to lunch, and I'll introduce you. I promise."

My wolf howled with delight. It would finally be able to meet her and see her, and maybe touch her. My nerves amplified at the thought.

What was I going to wear?

Larissa

"I'LL SEE YOU SOON, LARISSA," THE VOICE THAT HAD BEEN haunting my dreams for months now spoke. I rolled over to find the bed empty, yet again. I sat up and cuddled my knees, the loss of Luce hit me again. Nik hadn't been the same since the witches attacked. It had been a year since my mother's death and six months since Luce. He had locked himself in his study, poring over books, scrolls, and whatever documents he could find, looking for answers. He blamed himself for what happened, but I blamed myself. I sighed as I rose from my bed.

I dressed myself in bike shorts and a black crop and wandered down to the gym. Nik distracted himself with knowledge while I focused on my power. After I killed those witches, their power came to me. I didn't quite understand how, but I thought it might have something to do with the linking spell. I honestly had no clue, but I would figure it out eventually.

The hardest part was processing the guilt of killing all those witches. The darkest parts of my mind warned them to leave; it gave them the chance before taking their lives. I should feel *more* guilt, but I don't, and I doubt that I ever will. It was me or them; that was how Roman worded it. I pushed the door open to see Roman setting up the bag, and I walked over, wrapping my arms around his waist. His warmth seeped into me as he turned in my arms and stroked my hair.

"Hey, pretty girl, what's going on?" he whispered into the top of my head before he kissed it.

"I feel like I am living in a daze. Nik barely comes to bed anymore. Every day is filled with the same shit, and I feel like there is a clock above my head slowly ticking down to my death. I don't want this life anymore. I hate living like this. I want my mate back; I want to feel normal again." I huffed in frustration as he took my hand, wrapped it, and put the gloves on.

"I know it seems bad at the moment, but trust me—" My thoughts drifted to the fact that we were due to move into our new home on the weekend. A roar echoed above us, and Roman sighed and shook his head. "Get started. I will be back in a minute." He stormed off upstairs. I stayed still, listening to the slam of the door and the shouting that followed. Their voices were muffled, but I could hear what they were saying clearly enough.

"Nik, enough of this bullshit!" Roman shouted at his brother.

"Roman, fuck off," Nik snarled in response.

"No, you can get the fuck off your high horse. Go downstairs and be with your fucking wife before she dies."

"She is *not* going to die. I won't let it happen."

"Nik, stop fooling yourself. We know how this ends, she knows how it ends. She just wants her mate; she is grieving. Have you forgotten that it's been six months since she lost her sister and one year since her mother died? She shouldn't be alone today. Have you thought about that?" I could hear the pleading within his tone, he wanted his brother to see reason.

Silence filled the space between the brothers, and a tiny creak could be heard as I believe Nik collapsed onto his chair, followed by a thud from Roman on the couch.

I could no longer be here. I needed air. I unwrapped my wrists and headed for the door. The person I needed had abandoned me.

The elevator beeped as I rode it, tears running down my cheeks. Katrina wanted to protect me from this. I was supposed to grow old and die. I never should have moved to London; Richard was right.

Forgetting that it was the start of winter, I snapped my fingers, and my clothing switched to pants and a warm jacket with a beanie, I sprinted out the glass door. I heard Bodhi shouting behind me, my personal guard. I ignored him, focusing on the road before me. I ran through the crowds, but the noise in my head wouldn't stop. The constant thought that I would die, the constant dream that haunted me, the constant need for my mate who rejected me at every turn. He had barely touched me since that day.

I stopped when my watch beeped at me. I glanced down. 'Time to rest.' My heart beat a little faster than usual, my legs ached while I glanced around. Bodhi kept his distance, understanding that I needed space. I didn't even process where I had been running, but when I stopped to take in my surroundings, I realised I was in front of Luce's and my old apartment. I dropped to my knees as sobs left my body. I wrapped my arms around myself and squeezed tightly, aching for any sort of comfort.

Both my mothers and my sister were gone. There were no graves. Their bodies had dissolved into dust, lost to the earth. I stared at the façade, remembering the day we drove up. We'd had a small argument after sitting in the car together for so long. Luce was petrified of her future starting. More tears fell. The future she no longer had; her bright future, gone in a blink. I got up to continue my run, hoping to shake off the ache lingering in my chest. I didn't even know where I was headed, but I needed to just keep going. I needed to not think about the pain, to feel something other than loss.

My phone rang, and I saw Nik's number flash across the screen. I threw my phone to the ground and screamed. Now he was calling me, and not when I needed him months ago? I picked up the broken phone.

"Fuck," I muttered to myself while Nik prodded our bond, but I forced him out. He did not get to disturb my time right now. I ran harder and faster than I ever knew I could. I stopped in front of Refresh Marketing. I watched Travis and Alina gossiping and laughing through the window, and I glanced down at my clothes, snapping my fingers once again, changing my attire to its usual sophisticated and sexy style. I walked over with a smile while holding fresh coffee for them. Magic had its perks.

"Good morning." I beamed at them, hoping they would cheer up my foul mood as they had been for months now. They helped me to smile through the fog that had permanently taken residence in my head.

"Ah, here is our favourite billionaire." Travis winked as he glanced behind me. "Oh, he looks mad." I observed the way he perved on my mate, his mouth salivating. There was no denying how sexy the man was, but his personality needed work. Thousands of years later, and he was still a jerk.

I peered over my shoulder to see Nik entering the building, and I snorted before turning back to them. "He can be mad."

"Is the make-up sex better than the actual sex?" Alina asked, her eyes twinkling as she watched my husband's every move.

"Need to have sex to know that," I mumbled, Nik's hand landed on my back. His touch set my body on fire, yet I shuffled away from him. I didn't need any temptation right now; I wanted him to know how mad I was.

"Larissa, I need to speak with you." I took a sip of my coffee. "Now," he ordered, his voice stern.

I rolled my eyes as I stood up straighter, turning toward him. He held up his hand while anger vibrated through the bond. A silent warning to not start this now in front of others, which only made me want to start it, to show everyone how much of an asshole he could be.

I cleared my throat. "I will see you guys later. Enjoy your coffee," I said before moving toward the elevator.

Nik walked behind me, shaking his head at any person who dared to enter. The doors closed.

"It's interesting how you want to talk when I have been ignored for months, and now you storm in—"

In a flash, he slammed his hand into the emergency button and spun around, his lips crashing against mine. My back found the wall as he ground his body into mine. My body exploded. I had missed his touch and the comfort it brought to my body.

"Nik," I moaned as his mouth trailed kisses along my neck and down my jaw. His fangs grazing against my skin sent shivers through my spine. I hated him, but I craved his touch.

He chuckled, sniffing the air like a predator catching the scent of his prey. "Careful, Larissa, or everyone will smell how badly you want this, even with how much you hate me right now."

The one benefit to our bond: he would sense just how pissed off I was at being abandoned by him.

"Do *you* not deserve that hate?" I asked him breathlessly while his hand travelled down my body, grabbing the material around my breast and ripping it to reveal it to him. His teeth sank into my flesh as I groaned. His fingers found my underwear, ripping them apart in seconds as he circled my clit. My head banged against the wall, my body shuddered from the overwhelming sensations that tore through me. I had missed his touch; I had missed *him*.

"I deserve every bit of it and more, but you deserve to know just how much I need you." He glanced up, his blue eyes brighter than usual. "I love you so fucking much." His finger pushed inside, and I felt myself tightening. "You feel so fucking good." He groaned, the sound making me moan louder. "I need to taste you." He got on his knees, tearing my dress to shreds.

"Nik, did you have to?" I muttered, annoyed that my clothes were now in pieces.

"I watched as you made clothing appear out of thin air before. You can do it again."

I chuckled as his tongue licked my wet pussy. It ached for him against all reason.

"You taste so fucking sweet. I could eat you all fucking day." He lifted my leg over his shoulder, holding me in place. My hands scrambled for somewhere to hold while he feasted on me, his tongue dancing around my clit. I moaned louder, he said, "There's my good girl. I want everyone to hear you moan my fucking name."

"Nik!" My body rode his face, chasing the sensations of his tongue. He chuckled and delved deeper into me. "Nik!" I screamed as the orgasm tore through my body, threatening to tear me in half at how good it felt to be touched after so long.

He stood up, licking his lips before kissing me. My hands fumbled with his pants, aching to feel him inside me. He lifted me and pressed me into the wall. His kisses were forceful and electrifying as his hand grabbed my hair and pulled my head back. His teeth sank into me once again, moaning as he thrust inside, filling every inch of me.

My eyes rolled into the back of my head while I bounced on his cock. He growled as I chased my next release. I grabbed his hair, yanking his head to look at me. I felt his body shiver from the force of it.

"You are so fucking tight," he groaned as his hands moved to my hips, holding me in place as he thrust in faster. His fingers digging into my skin brought the balance between pleasure and pain. "Fucking perfection. Look at me. I want to watch you come on my cock."

I did as he ordered. Staring into his eyes, my walls tightened against him before he changed his angle. My body came undone, and I screamed in pure euphoria.

Nik followed not long after as the siren for the emergency button began to beep. I laughed and glanced up at the cameras with a smile. I had completely forgotten. At least Travis and Alina would have had a show. I knew they were able to watch them, and I knew they would have after seeing Nik's mood when he entered. I pulled the button out and snapped my fingers to fix my torn clothing before I spun around to glare at Nik. He leaned against the wall with his arms crossed, a look of satisfaction on his face.

"I am still fucking pissed off at you." I pointed at him to prove a point, forcing all my anger through the bond.

"Even when you are angry, you look marvellous bouncing on my cock. Those sounds are locked in my memory bank. I shall never stand in this elevator without thinking of those moans coming from your beautiful mouth."

My cheeks flushed at his words. "You are so dirty, and just because we fucked does not make up for you leaving me alone."

Sadness crossed his features; he was speechless. The elevator beeped for my floor. "Run along to work now, wife." He winked at me as I walked to my office. Today would be a long day.

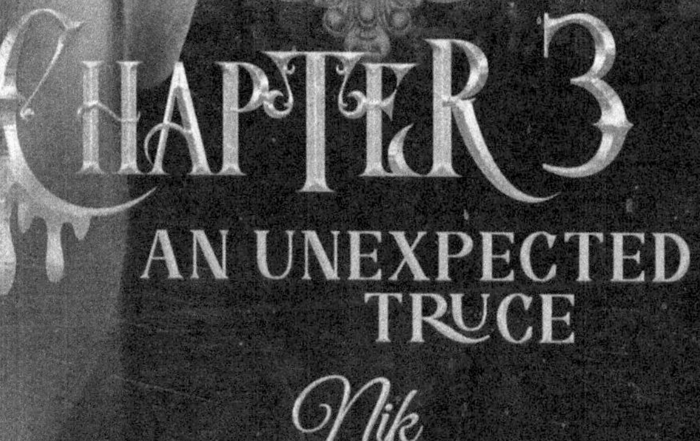

CHAPTER 3

AN UNEXPECTED TRUCE

Nik

Flashback, January 3rd, 2020

'Breaking news! Russia has dropped a bomb on the United States. They have declared war. The president has declared war on Russia, as North Korea has rallied its troops.'

I spun my head to look at Aurora, her mouth open in shock. We had seen so many battles in the past. We were waiting for something to happen. Reports had been talking about it for months, maybe even years. Time became harder to keep track of.

"Nik, what do we do?" Aurora asked, her eyes glued to the television.

"Hold all my calls," I said bluntly to my receptionist, Laura. They were the same words she'd heard for months. I sighed, staring into the vast space of my office. Roman was right this morning, I had been abandoning my wife, my mate, for too long. I held onto the singular focus of figuring out how to break this curse. I had never felt more powerless in my life than I did that night. The night her sister made the ultimate sacrifice for her. Larissa was right, they were sisters, and they would do anything for one another.

After we discovered Katrina's grimoire, I scoured through it for hours, but there were no notes on what she had done to recreate Liyana. Or how to break this fucking curse. I could feel it in my soul that her time was coming to an end. I had to stop it because this time felt final, and it was unnerving to know that I may lose her forever.

I read through all the notes on the gods, curses, and even witches, but since the destruction of Juliet, no witches dared come near me. Larissa had more power than any person on earth; she could literally snap her fingers and kill someone, but the darkness between us grew. My bloodlust grew stronger, and my monster fed off it. Every drop of her blood infected me, and I couldn't escape it. I should not have drunk from her earlier, but it called to me.

"Sir, I know you said no calls, but Daniel Wright is here to see you," Laura's meek voice sounded through the intercom. What the fuck did he want?

"Send him in," I responded curtly as I took a seat at my desk, quickly cleaning it to hide any evidence of what kept me up most nights.

Daniel entered with his air of sophistication; his hair slicked to the side as if he still lived in his century. With that signature smirk on his face, he thought he was better than me, but he never would be. Without me, he would not exist today. My blood created the entire vampire line. I stayed seated with my hands clasped together, leaning back in my chair to show that I did not care for his appearance today.

"I see the formalities are gone," he muttered as he took a seat, unbuttoning his navy suit jacket that he paired with denim jeans. The man had no fashion sense. He fiddled with the thick golden rings on his fingers.

"What do you want?" I snarled at him.

"Nik, I thought we were friends," he said slyly as I smelt his anxiety over our conversation.

"You threatened me over a year ago. You sided with Duzi, and you threatened my mate with this witch bullshit. Shall I continue? Because that is just in the space of three hundred and sixty-five days."

He snorted and shuffled in his seat. "Yes, I have done all of that and quite possibly more, but…" he paused as he ran his hand over his slicked back hair, "Duzi has gone too far."

I laughed. He was switching sides. "You want to backstab the man who helped give you more power. That means one of two things; you are here as a mole, or you realise that Duzi is an absolute fucking power-hungry dickhead."

He pulled on his collar. "Or I discovered who *you* truly are."

I kept my body still. I had had conversations like this in the past. My response was always important, and so I had to be stoic. There was an uncomfortable silence between us.

"Duzi ordered that I investigate Larissa and Katrina Solis. I scoured through their history and noticed there was no father. So, I asked around and found various other sources that helped me slowly piece it together. The day of your wedding, it all clicked into place. Her father is neither human nor witch. I stayed to hear more of the conversations between your complicated family circles. I traced your history back further than ever as I found small pieces of you in every single culture around the world until the very start." Daniel stood and bowed his head, taking a knee before me. He took a knife from his pocket as he sliced his hand.

.   .   .

"With blood as ink, our vow is sealed.

To honour this, until the end.

So let it be, through pain and joy.

Our pact is forged in sacred space."

I stood. A blood oath to a god's son? He was serious. I walked around and licked the blood from his hand to seal the pact between us.

"Remus, I apologise for my past actions. They no longer reflect the person that I am."

I growled at him. He had no right to use that name. He would now be my little *pet*; I would use him for everything that he had. This was exactly what I needed to make my day better. I reached behind for the phone on my desk and pressed the number one.

"Larissa Dankworth," her melodic voice sounded through the phone. A small smile spread over my face as I heard her use her married name.

"Get up here, we have a visitor."

"Nik, I am about to see Julian and Stuart. Can it wait?" she pleaded, trying to remain professional within our working environment.

"Bring them up, it cannot wait." I hung up the phone. Daniel hadn't moved from his knees. I walked over to my bar and poured myself a glass before warming two glasses of blood. I needed to compose myself and my inner beast before we spoke further, and I wanted Daniel to have a clear head around my mate.

"Sit up," I ordered, handing him the glass of blood as I sat on the couch in the middle of my office. I sipped my blood, feeling Larissa get closer with every passing second. Daniel sat down opposite me, his heart beating faster than it should. "Do you regret your decision?" I asked him, crossing one leg over the other.

He shook his head. "No, I have no doubts, but I honestly fear your mate. From what I have heard, she has more power than imaginable. She is a young witch, and I want to be sure that she has control of her magic rather than her magic controlling her." His voice wavered as he spoke, his fear evident.

I chuckled before taking another sip, the flavours dancing on my tongue. "She will have control."

"Can you promise that?" he asked as the door opened.

"We give each other control." I stood as Larissa walked over, her eyes trained on the man who had threatened her in the past. Her eyes glowed for a moment before she wrapped her arms around my waist. I could feel a disconnect after I left her to deal with her grief alone, but our love had no barriers to break it. I kissed the top of her head as the slight anxiety she felt melted away.

"Do I want to know why this asshole is here?" she asked, crossing her arms, and I took note of Stuart and Julian doing the same. She had the ability to influence people without meaning to, and I wondered if she could access that through our bond. I nudged her and motioned toward them. She cleared her throat and focused her breathing to allow the control to dissipate. Stuart and Julian shook their heads, confused about what the hell had just happened.

"Let us all sit down." I cleared my throat as I sat down, but Stuart and Julian stayed standing behind Daniel while Larissa sat down beside me. The couch creaked under our weight, and I remembered the time I fucked her, or rather, she fucked me on this couch. She was a vision. She shot a glare at me. "Daniel has sworn a blood oath after discovering my true identity. He will provide us with information on Duzi."

"I-I will…not be…doing that," he spluttered, finishing his blood in one gulp. He went to move, seeming to gasp for breath.

"You will do exactly as your Lord states, or I will rip your lungs from your fucking throat. You do not get to threaten my existence only to swear a blood oath and not provide details on anything." Larissa's voice echoed a dark threat.

Larissa's power filled the room before my own throat tightened. I placed my hand on hers, settling her instantly.

"I thought you had control of her. A fucking human thinks she can threaten me. I swore an oath to you and not to your peasant witch." As soon as the words left Daniel's mouth, I knew they might be his last.

"Larissa," I growled in warning, hoping she would be able to control the influence of her power. She relaxed into the couch as I moved forward. "You understand that under the blood oath, my secrets are now yours, and if you spill them, it will result in your instant death." Daniel nodded his head. "Good. Now that you understand that, Larissa is the daughter of Pluto. She is a demi-god. She is more than just an ordinary human." His mouth dropped open in shock. "The recent influx of her power is due to Juliet attempting to kill her. Larissa won the fight, not without losses, but she inherited the coven's magic. We are not sure why she has more power than normal, but I assure you, she has a hold on it."

"Wait, you killed Juliet?" He scratched his chin, his eyes flicking around the room as he stood. "Duzi was working with her. *He* had planned for Juliet to kill Larissa."

"He what?" Larissa lunged forward, and I grabbed her, pulling her back to the couch. "I will fucking kill him."

Daniel, Stuart, and Julian all wore similar expressions as their brows drew in confusion. I dragged her into the bathroom and slammed the door shut. My monster was feeding off her anger, and I had let her process these emotions without me. Her actions were all my fault. I grabbed her, pulling her back against my chest and holding her tight. She continued to fight against my hold.

"I have you, my principessa." Her mood shifted as tears began to fall from her eyes. "I am sorry. I should have been there for you. This is my fault, and I am sorry. I should have protected you from the pain, but I left you alone to process it alone. I fucked up, but I am here now. I need you to understand that I won't leave you again." She stopped fighting me before she spun in my arms and kissed me, her eyes still filled with all the tears she refused to let fall. I wanted to hold her, but I had to return to find out more about our enemy.

"Just give me a moment. I will come out. I promise."

I kissed the top of her head and left her alone as she asked.

"She is fucking dangerous, and you want me to tell you everything about Duzi?" Daniel walked toward the door. I could smell his fear of a 'peasant witch', as he called her.

"That hit from Juliet ended in the death of her sister. Her sister sacrificed her life to save Larissa. She has every right to be mad and dangerous, as you say. If Duzi had left well enough alone, it never would have happened. You will tell me fucking everything." Daniel went to stand near the couch, but Stuart and Julian forced him to sit down.

"He will kill me!" Daniel exclaimed with wide eyes.

"So will I, but the only difference is, I will enjoy it a lot more than he would." His throat bopped from the threat as I made my eyes flare. "Understand?"

He nodded, exhaling slowly. "Duzi is working his way through some of the oldest vampires to gain favour with them. He wants to overthrow you."

"That is nothing new. What else?" The door to the bathroom opened, and Larissa came out wearing different clothing. She no longer looked professional, but more like her casual and relaxed self. I smiled as the floral black dress clung to her sexy body and perfectly outlined her breasts. She glared at me with a sly smile.

"The witch deal? How did that work when he wanted a registrar but made a deal with Juliet?" I asked, wanting to know how he made the deal to spare her.

"He swore her clemency; she would be spared if she helped. He would spare her entire coven." I felt the lick of Larissa's magic as Daniel relaxed slightly. She was using her influence on him, making his tongue a little looser.

"It wouldn't have been possible to hide that many witches. How was he planning to do that?" she asked as she made herself a drink before handing one to me. Her question made sense.

"He influences everything. Nik has been gaining influence in the business world, but Duzi has been doing it in other ways. He has been gaining favour with some of the richest and most influential vampires. Vampires who don't know who Nik is."

"Did you tell Duzi the truth about my life?" I asked him, knowing he would try to spin it for his personal gain.

"No, as soon as I discovered the truth, I came straight to you. He can't know the truth. Nobody can know the truth." Daniel was right about this. Stuart and Julian glanced at each other.

I cleared my throat. "Gentlemen, you are aware of my age, but you do not know the whole truth. I am the father of all vampires. I started the existence of our kind. It is important that this information does not leave the room, understood?" They nodded, barely reacting. I still had some influence, I hoped.

"Smart choice. What is Duzi's next move?" Larissa asked as she fiddled with her glass. The bond alerted me to her feelings of being on edge. She feared another attack. I rested my hand on her thigh.

"That, I am not sure of, but he is working closely with the human Stacey."

"WHAT?" Larissa and I shouted in unison.

"That fucking bitch. I will kill her. The fucking werewolf attack was from him, wasn't it?" Daniel nodded to her question. He had been trying to kill her for a while.

"When's the next attack?" I demanded. I feared the next one might end her life. Fate had intervened a few times, but I doubt she would again.

"That, I don't know." I grabbed Daniel by the shirt and lifted him into the air.

"You will return to that piece of shit and find out, do you understand me?" my voice bellowed as Julian and Stuart bowed their heads from the power I exuded.

"That is fine, but I cannot lie to him about the information I found out." I smiled at him as I moved closer. His body relaxed as I worked my way into his mind, influencing his entire existence.

"Daniel, you will forget who I truly am except when you are in my presence. You will remember the blood oath. You will continue to work for Duzi and inform us of his comings and goings. Do you understand?" I compelled him to ensure his silence. With the blood oath and my compulsion, I knew it would be safe.

"Yes, I swear." He stood, moving toward the door as Julian and Stuart sat on the couch.

Before he left, I called out to him, "You will also stop all your human trafficking from this moment on. No more harm will come to virgins, no more harm will come to any person. It will cease from now on. If you worry about income, I will provide some until you find alternatives."

Daniel opened his mouth to speak but stopped and bowed his head as he left.

CHAPTER 4
THE GODLY TRUTH

Larissa

"DO YOU HONESTLY THINK YOU CAN TRUST HIM?" I ASKED, turning back toward Nik. He glanced toward Julian and Stuart, who were still in the room. He didn't want to have this conversation with them present. I understood because they would have their own questions. He sighed and sat down, and I moved to sit with him.

"So, do we call you daddy?" Julian asked, a small smile playing on his lips, his playful nature coming to the front. I giggled. Stuart seemed more reserved.

"No, you will not call me daddy. I am Nik or Lord Dankworth."

"Sorry, daddy." Julian winked in my direction, which caused laughter to erupt from my mouth. Stuart continued to glance between Nik and me.

"Ask it, Stuart," Nik ordered with a sigh, knowing what question would be asked.

"She is Aurora, she is…how is she alive? I am at a loss for how this all works. I knew Aurora before you met her, remember that we met at Oxford—it was how our business partnership started and…" I could feel his anger over being lied to. Julian and Stuart were polar opposites. Nik looked at me, and I tapped into a little part of my magic to dissipate his anger slightly. We were a good team when I was not being ignored.

Nik sighed. "Did you want to explain it, or shall I?" he asked as his eyes met mine. I glanced back towards the men that I had partnered with. They heard that I was the daughter of a god, and they heard that Nik founded Rome thousands of years ago.

I shrugged. "Aurora was a reincarnation, as am I…kind of. It is hard to explain. Nik and I have been fated mates since what year exactly, Nik? The fall of the Roman Empire?"

He nodded, standing to pour himself another drink.

"He made a deal, and *we* have been cursed ever since. I live for a time, before dying, not long after meeting him." I dared not explain the whole truth to them. They just needed the basics.

Stuart tilted his head, his eyebrows knitted in confusion, "So, Aurora is you, and you share the same memories?" His voice trailed off with a hint of uncertainty. His eyes raced between the two of us.

"Not quite." Nik chuckled. "Either way, she is Aurora. What other questions do you have?" he asked, sitting back down and crossing his legs, his hand resting on the small of my back.

I rolled my shoulders, shaking off his touch. He had not earnt the right to touch me in this manner. I was still mad at him.

Stuart and Julian continued to ask questions about Nik and his life as well as what they could do to help with Duzi. He asked them to keep an eye and ear on Daniel, and anything they heard about Duzi and his possible plans. They left as Nik turned toward me, putting his arms around my waist and pulling me against his body.

I pressed both hands against his chest, taking a step back. "This does not change what…the way you just…I am hurt, Nik." I clicked my tongue, spun on my heel and left his office.

I rode the elevator down, feeling his frustration through our bond. It wasn't directed at me; I could sense it was his own actions. I blocked it out. I had enough work to focus on, plus the information about Stacey. I rode the elevator down to Travis and Alina, hoping they would have answers about our supposed friend.

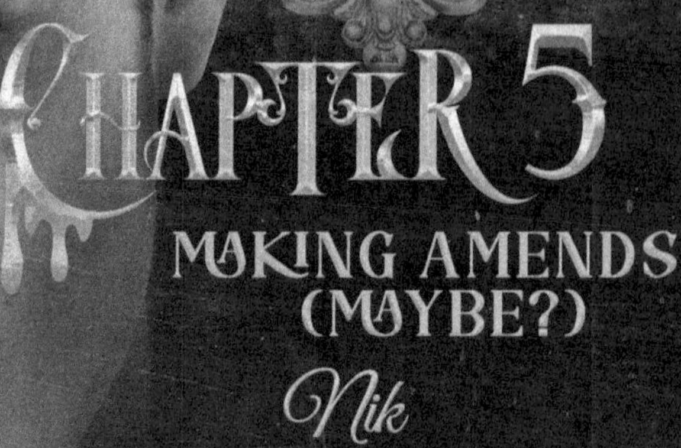

Flashback, January 4th, 2020

"Nik, I have asked my family to get on a plane and come here."

*"Sounds good. I shall organise some accommodation for them,"
I said as I left Aurora alone to deal with that. I had more
important things to worry about. People were making moves I
did not agree with.*

Larissa still grieved her losses, and I hadn't been
supporting her. I cut my work day short to show her just how
much I was sorry for ignoring her during her time of need. My
receptionist yelled after me, reminding me of the meeting with
Leo. I knew he would understand. I had another meeting on for the
day thatI didn't care. Larissa had to be my priority, and I needed
her to know that. I ignored Laura and strolled toward the elevator.

We were due to move into our home on the weekend, but I
wanted to surprise her. I had paid the men more than necessary
to work longer hours to finish ahead of schedule. My focus had
to be on her. I had to fix my mistake. I picked up several items
before unlocking the door to our new home. It was beautiful, an
absolute masterpiece.

The double-door entry had coloured lead lighting, and I imagined the sun would reflect through the glass and create beautiful shadows on the white walls. She picked white for the entrance, stating it made the room seem grander, and she was right. I entered the living room; the couches were covered in white plastic to protect them. The television was installed on the wall, and bookshelves covered the remaining walls, with a fireplace in the corner. There was another quiet space by the window with a built-in couch that Larissa had declared her quiet corner. I smirked at the idea of her lying there, reading a book in next to no clothing.

I ventured into the kitchen, which she had requested I have no input in its design. It was difficult, but I was grateful that I listened. The kitchen was phenomenal. Two massive chandeliers were centred in the ceiling rose, creating patterns on the ceiling that matched the rose. The double stove was surrounded by an arch with a black-tiled splashback. The counters were white and grey swirled marble, timeless and sophisticated against the white shaker-style cabinets. The island bench had a rather large triple sink, each having its own function. I pulled on the door to the pantry, hidden as if it were a cupboard. She had designed this to perfection. It would be a chef's dream, having access to everything they need. My mate, my perfect mate. She was always right.

My steps echoed on the cherrywood floorboards while I walked into the large dining space. The table was ridiculously large, with a mat to cover the opulent sixteen-seater table. Certainly not needed, but if it were any smaller, it would seem out of place in this large space. I clapped my hands, and the fireplace roared to life, warming the room that I would bring to life with my love for her. I checked the time on my watch. Roman would arrive shortly with what I needed.

My phone began to vibrate. "Larissa, what is it?" I asked her, sensing apprehension through our bond.

"Where are you? I came up to get your signature, and Laura said you were gone. You left in anger, apparently."

I chuckled. "I had another matter to attend to. There was no anger, I assure you. Bring the documents home."

"I've told you not to call it home. It is a penthouse, a halfway house until our home is ready," she mumbled into the phone. I could picture her eyes rolling.

"Larissa, I am standing in *our* home." My voice beamed with pride that we had done it with minimal arguments – the kind that usually tear normal couples apart. I wouldn't lie that I missed the version of her that was easy to please. I rather enjoyed her passion, her fight, her voice, but her complacency made decisions so much more efficient. I noticed the line was quiet. "Larissa?" I queried, hoping that nothing had happened to her.

"I am still here, Nik. I am just shocked." I heard a knock behind me, and I glanced over my shoulder to see Roman walking in, holding a massive wooden box. I pointed to where I wanted him to place it. He winked and dropped it with a loud bang. "What was that?" she asked, and the noise echoed through the foyer.

"Nothing, just testing the strength of the bed that I will fuck you on later," I said, her anger flaring at my failed distraction. Sex this morning would not heal the wounds we had, but angry sex always had more passion. My cock hardened a little in my pants as I thought about eating her pussy on the kitchen table.

"Nik!" she shrieked down the phone.

I cleared my throat. "Finish up, and Andreas will bring you here."

"I need an hour to finish."

"That's fine." It would give me enough time to put the finishing touches on her surprise. "I love you."

Larissa hung up the phone to avoid responding, her own form of *screw you*. I rather enjoyed this childish action, but I had told her that she would no longer be allowed to kick me out of our room when we lived in this house. She'd begrudgingly agreed.

"Brother, what are you doing randomly staring into nothing?" Roman asked before I spun around with a smirk on my face.

"I was honestly just thinking about the fact that I cannot wait to live here with my mate." A pang of sadness hit me as the voice in my head echoed, *Until she dies.* Larissa had spoken about the voices in her head, but I had yet to tell her the truth that since Luce's death, I had my own.

"Ah, there is my brother, back from the haze that he has been living in."

"Yeah," I mumbled as he slapped me on the back. I clapped my hands together. "Let's get down to business." I ordered him around, sprinkling the rose petals in various places, and rushing around to light candles. I wanted her to know just how much I screwed up and how much I was sorry. I wanted her to see the love I had for her. I was dealing with my demons alone and abandoned her, when we should have battled our demons together.

CHAPTER 6
THE PHONECALL

I FINISHED WORKING THROUGH THE PAPERWORK BUT MY thoughts continued to drift to Stacey. Why had she betrayed me at the retreat? Why was she behind all this? She spoke about being in love with Nik, but surely it was more than this. She had no magic. I never sensed it…Unless she had more than I thought possible and could mask herself. I had the power to do that, but Stacey always seemed boring, plain, simple. Now I was starting to overthink everything. Had I missed the clues? I reflected on the time I opened up about being mated with Nik and that I would die, but she brushed it off. I thought about the other times when I told her things, and she would scoff or roll her eyes. I slammed my fist down before I peered over at my phone. The phone I had magically restored.

I picked it up, my finger hovering over her name, contemplating the idea of calling. Would she pick up? Or would the number be disconnected? *Do it*, the voice whispered. I inhaled deeply as I pressed the button. The phone trilled.

"I wondered if you would ever have the guts to call me." Her voice sounded through the speaker.

I waited for a moment to gather my thoughts; I didn't expect her to answer. "It was never about the guts. I just believed you were more chicken and would have gone into hiding." Her witchy laugh came down the end of the phone. It made my skin crawl. How had I never guessed that she was this evil and manipulative?

"I played you well; the caring friend, the shoulder to cry on, with sly, underhanded remarks. You trust too easily, Larissa. You were warned that London would lead to your death."

My memory returned to that day when I told her about Richard and his warning that terrified me. I closed my eyes, feeling a tear roll down my cheek.

"Do Travis and Alina know?" I wondered. I wrote a note to remind myself to ask Nik to compel them for the truth.

"God, no. They are oblivious. They never even figured out why I wanted their blood. They assumed it was for protection of some sort. Stupid fucking vampires. They have no clue. Duzi had a brilliant plan until I realised that I could find another ally more powerful." She spoke with such conviction while I wracked my brain over who this ally could be. The only person stronger than Duzi was Nik, but he hadn't spoken about any deal between them. He spoke about her obsession with him, but never a deal. I wrote another note.

A knock at the door broke my focus. "Stacey, what is your plan?" I asked her, waving Nik's receptionist into the room. She smiled, placing a white box in front of me. I rolled my eyes and mouthed a thank you to her.

"My plan is your death. It is destined to happen. You want to know the best part, Larissa…?" She paused, and I swear it was for a dramatic effect. "This time, you won't be brought back. This time, it is final. Katrina fought to break the curse, but never realised that to break it, she had to sacrifice an aspect of the curse to stop it. Have you clued in yet, Larissa?"

It wasn't making sense. Mum said we were never supposed to meet, but Stacey was telling me something completely different. I was more confused about this curse than ever. "No, I haven't, Stacey. Can you clue me in?" I snapped back at her, hoping she would reveal something.

She laughed. "Nothing will stop your inevitable death, Larissa. Sacrifices can only be cancelled out by another sacrifice." The words rang in my head as I wrote them down. They seemed important. I didn't understand it now, but I had a hunch they would be important in the future.

"At least I know one thing for certain, Stace."

"What's that?" she said with an awkward laugh, not expecting this.

"I will see you in hell."

"Oh, you are funny. Perfect Larissa, ending up in hell. I doubt that."

"You clearly don't have everything figured out, then. My father is the King of Hell." The line went quiet, the beeping tone alerting me to how much I had her worried. I smirked as I put the phone down. I had won this round for now. My hands were shaking from the adrenaline as my magic tickled just underneath my skin, like I could feel it trying to escape.

I called Roman, who had been helping with control since Nik left me on my own.

"What's up?" he asked, his voice slightly on edge.

"I just spoke with Stacey and I-I...I..." I fumbled over my words while the magic intensified, my brain filling with darkness as the screams of the dying witches returned.

"You are losing control. Remember what I told you, find your focus. Think of a memory, a person, an emotion, and focus on it. Let that fill your mind to block out the rest. You control the magic, it does *not* control you." I smiled as he quoted the words to me. He had explained that he repeated the same mantra when he turned into a wolf. He revisited the pain that he and Nik felt when they first transformed into beasts. The challenges of control and how they gave power to their inner beast, thinking that was the way to control it. Only to discover it led to less control. They were beasts, and, therefore, incapable of reason. Magic was no different; it grew stronger with emotions. I had to focus on something other than the anger or sadness that radiated through me.

"How are you going?" he asked softly as a beeping sound registered through the phone. Nik was trying to call me, but he hadn't noticed the strength of my emotions over the last couple of months. He had blocked them off for his own selfish needs.

"Better." My heart rate slowed, the prickling slowly abating. "Much better. I will learn control one day, yeah?"

"Larissa, you have mastered control of a volatile magic very well. I have trained many beasts in the past, and none have regained control on the edge as quickly as you. Take comfort in that. Your power is shared, and you need to remember that. You've mated with Nik, which means you gain strength from him, and your magic will take parts of him." I closed my eyes, guilt eating away at me. Nik's monster had become more erratic as he struggled for control, and the more magic I used, the worse it would be for him. I exhaled while my body shivered from the excess adrenaline. Nik was forcing me to contact him.

"Roman, I must go. Nik is calling in a rather forceful way," I mumbled with another shiver bursting through my body.

He chuckled down the line. "I will speak to you later, Larissa. Remember to focus." The line beeped to signify the end of the call. Nik forced his way through my block, reactivating the full strength of the bond.

"Alright, already." I dialled the phone, and Nik answered as soon as it rang. "I was speaking with Roman. What's wrong?" I felt his anxiety simmer down.

"I'm sorry, Larissa, your magic just…" He paused before asking his question. I wondered how it affected him. "What happened?" His serious tone had returned like nothing had affected him.

"I called Stacey and—"

"You did what?!" he shouted down the phone before I could finish. His growl echoed, and it was almost like I could hear it beside me. My body trembled, wanting to submit to him. I shook it off. "We shall speak of this at home. Andreas is on his way up to collect you now." I giggled. "What do you think is funny?"

"I honestly thought you would have flown here to come and collect me." I leaned back in my chair.

"Oh, trust me, I thought about it." He chuckled down the line as he breathed out in relief from the lightened mood.

"Pity Andreas is coming up. I haven't been flying for a while. I think I almost miss it." The phone went quiet. "Nik? Nik? Are you there?"

"I will see you soon." The call ended as a smirk played over my face. I tapped the phone to my chin. The man who had been ignoring me for months, who had fucked me in an elevator a few hours ago, was now flying to take me to our new home.

He arrived within ten minutes, gliding into my office wearing a pair of jeans and a cream-coloured jumper. The colour made his eyes seem brighter than usual. He leaned against the frame of the door with his sexy sophistication, his eyes taking in every piece of my body while it tingled with delight.

"Just because I spread my legs this morning in a moment of weakness, it does not mean that I will do it again." I paused, my next words bringing on emotions I had buried. "You hurt me, Nik." Tears fell down my cheeks as he looked over his shoulder. I was the last one here. He didn't want anyone else to hear our conversation.

"I know. I fucked up on a grand scale. I hurt the person that I love the most in this world because I was so focused on trying to save you. I screwed up. I might be thousands of years old, but it doesn't mean that I am above trivial human mistakes."

"Nik…"

"I know, I know. You said in the past that you don't want half a life with me. You want a whole life. I just want to give you that, but…" The elevator buzzed behind us, the cleaner arrived, and Nik sighed. "We can finish this discussion at home without prying ears. Please?" he pleaded.

I glanced at the dress box in the corner, deciding to ignore it for now. I stood up and started to pack my bag, knowing I had done as much work as needed today. Despite having no experience in marketing, and the drama of my life—I had been absent from work more than *at* work—I was nailing this job. Since the retreat, we had become a team. We worked together, conversed, and had daily meetings to discuss changes. The office no longer had an autocratic management style. We all participated in the goal of excelling. Nik took the bag from my hands while we walked toward the elevator, his hand hovering on the small of my back as my skin tingled from the absent feeling. My body wanted his touch, and I slowed my step to feel him, even for a moment. It brought warmth to my system, reminding me of what he did to me. The door to the elevator slid open, and as we stepped inside, Nik wrapped his arm around my waist, pulling me close to his body. I leaned my head on his shoulder and sighed.

"I missed you more," Nik whispered into my hair, kissing the top of my head just before we arrived at the roof.

Flashback, January 5th, 2020

"Aurora, you're stupid sometimes. Leave it alone." Her family failed to see reason as she wanted to fly them personally. I told her it was not safe and that she should accept her losses. She was immortal, and they were bound to die. I had no time for her childish behaviour.

LARISSA HESITATED IN HER ACTIONS TOWARD ME. HER HEAD WAS telling her one thing while her body wanted my touch. I would do whatever she wanted. This morning, we craved each other. I had not felt her skin or tasted her sweetness in so long that I had to have her. Larissa's own desires couldn't be stopped, either. Even as we flew home, her emotions flicked between love and anger. I only hoped that when she saw our home, it would dissipate a lot of her anger. That she would understand why I had abandoned her when I showed her what I had discovered. The feel of her body against mine calmed the thoughts of her impending end.

"Close your eyes," I whispered into her ear as I made the descent. My feet landed on the paved ground before Larissa's heels clacked. I let her go and stood back, allowing her to find her footing. I spun her around, rubbing her shoulders. "Time to open." I leaned down to kiss her neck, smelling her intoxicating scent while my body vibrated with delight that she was mine.

She gasped as I moved to stand beside her, watching her beautiful face light up with joy at the sight of our home. Her eyes flicked over the stone exterior, at the flowers that crept up the entry, and the lead lighting in the door. I moved forward and pushed it open, gesturing for her to enter. I watched her slow movements as her head rotated, taking in every single feature of the home that we designed together. We mixed modern with old Victorian features, but the chandelier in the entrance made a statement. It was bigger than a car.

"Nik." Her voice was so soft as she flitted through the house. I waited, leaning against the wall in the entryway, listening to her shoes clack on the timber and tiled flooring. "Holy shit, the wardrobe!" she screeched. She had never been a real girly girl, but her love of shoes meant I had to make a few alterations to the original plans. She stopped at the top of the stairs, her face lit up with happiness, her smile beaming with sheer delight. "You made it bigger," her voice echoed through the space, filled with elation.

"I had to." I pushed myself from the wall and walked to the bottom of the stairs, watching her long, toned legs take one stair at a time.

"Oh, why is that? I don't have *that* many clothes," she quipped.

"I believe it is due to your ever-growing collection of shoes."

"You need to have a pair for every occasion and in every colour." She shrugged, flicking her hair over her shoulders.

"Of course, my principessa, which is why by expanding it ever so slightly, I ensured there was plenty of space for them. My love must have everything she needs." I moved closer to her when I felt her sadness. I closed the space between us, putting my arms around her. "What is it?" I asked, tilting her head to see those beautiful green eyes.

"Nothing. It's nothing." Her voice was so quiet while she buried her head into my chest. I knew.

"Larissa, it is not going to happen this time. I won't let it."

"You can't say that. You know it…" She paused. "We have to figure out what is working against us."

"I know, princess, I know, but we should enjoy tonight. At least for a while. I have a surprise for you." I took her hand, placing a gentle kiss against her soft skin, and led her into the dining room.

"Oh my god, Nik," she gasped. Candles lit up the space, creating a romantic glow, and the roses around the room gave off their floral scent. Rose petals covered the floor surrounding the picnic area I had set up for us. Food sat steaming beside the fireplace, which covered Larissa's face in a warm glow, but her tears shone brightly. I never meant to hurt her. I pulled her into my arms and held her tightly to my chest, pushing every inch of love that I had for her through our bond.

"Wait." I pulled the box from my pocket, handing it to her. She opened it quickly, holding it up as the candlelight sparkled against the diamonds.

"What is this?" she asked, turning around.

I clasped it around her neck. "I bought a star for you. Our love is as infinite as the stars in the night sky."

She picked it up, pressing it to her lips, then stared at the eight-pointed platinum star with an emerald in the centre to signify how she held my universe together.

"I will cherish it," she whispered. "Wait, you bought an actual star in the sky and named a star after me? I can't believe it."

"I wish I could take back how much I neglected you for my own selfish need. I never meant to hurt you in that way. Words cannot describe how sorry I am for that. You are my everything; you give me purpose, and I left you alone when you needed me the most. You have lost your entire family, all those that you love, and I couldn't even give you comfort. I did this to say sorry, to show you that I would do anything for you."

Her breathing was erratic as I kissed the top of her head. "I have to know, Nik. I have to know what you left me for. Don't leave me in the dark. Tell me everything."

CHAPTER 8

ONE ROMANTIC SURPRISE

Larissa

NIK SWORE HE WOULD TELL ME EVERYTHING AFTER DINNER. HE cooked a three-course meal. The bruschetta entrée had the flavours dancing in my mouth. I had not tasted tomatoes as fresh as these in years. Nik mentioned that most of the vegetables were from the garden out the back of the house. The main course was chicken scallopini, and I devoured it before putting my fork on the plate.

"Nik, you cannot fill me with food all night and avoid speaking to me."

He chuckled before licking the sauce from his knife. "I am aware, Larissa. I wanted to avoid a hangry mate." He stood, offering his hand as I slid my own into his, the familiar warmth filling my body. "We need to go for another flight to the penthouse, all my notes are there."

I groaned, my stomach aching from too much delicious food. The idea of flying now was less than ideal as bile filled my throat. I wanted answers, and despite his secrets in the past, he was willing to give me everything that had kept him holed up in the office for months.

"We don't have to."

I shook my head. "Nope, let's go. I want answers. You haven't ignored me for this long for nothing." I took his hand, moving to walk back through the foyer, but Nik stood still. "Um, this way?" I asked, confused by his lack of movement.

"Wait, I want to show you one more thing."

I sighed.

"I promise, one thing."

I nodded while Nik pulled out a blindfold from the back pocket of his black jeans. I rolled my eyes. "I hope this isn't some kinky thing." He laughed as I spun around, and he covered my eyes, fastening the blindfold behind my head. He planted soft kisses along my neck, inhaling my scent. "Did you miss this?" I asked.

"Yes. I would often sneak in while you were sleeping to watch you and smell you."

"That doesn't at all sound creepy," I mumbled as he led me through the house. I held my arms up, feeling for anything.

He cleared his throat. "Yes, it is, but when I walked in, your heart rate changed, and you would fall into a deeper sleep. My own body relaxed from the sound and smell of you. I may not have been around you; I may not have given you physical comfort, but I was always there," he whispered in my ear.

"I don't understand. Why did you never wake me?"

"Larissa, I heard and felt every tear, every emotion. You were physically and emotionally exhausted. You needed the rest. If I look back now, I wish I did." His voice broke, filled with emotion that he was trying to keep contained within his façade. I spun around, lifting the blindfold to see his blue eyes glassy. I touched his cheek, wiping away a tear that trickled down his face. I thought he had blocked me out. I thought he had abandoned me. But he was always there. He felt it all and more. My heart ached at the pain that lingered between us. I swallowed before taking a deep breath.

"It's in the past. We can try and move past it."

He pulled the blindfold back down with his signature smirk.

"Surprise time." Nik sounded way too cheerful, and I listened as a door opened and a gust of cold London wind hit my skin. I shivered but not for long, once Nik wrapped a cloak around my shoulders. He took my hands. "Slowly, slowly," he whispered, the temperature dropping while my teeth began to chatter. "Feel behind you for the chair." My hand touched the smooth fabric. "Good girl, now sit down." I ran my fingers further before plonking my behind on the seat. It moved backwards.

"Argh!" I squealed in shock. Nik's laughter filled the air before his warmth landed beside me. His arm slid along my shoulder and pulled me closer.

"You can take the blindfold off," he said, his voice soft against my ear, making the hairs on my body stand up.

I slid it off my eyes to see the entire backyard lit up; the trees and rose bushes covered in lights. Many of the plants may have been devoid of leaves, but it was a sight, one that I would always remember.

"Look up." I watched his finger slowly rise toward the sky as a shooting star flew across the darkness.

"Wow." I gasped at seeing this rare moment.

"Need to make a wish." He closed his eyes, muttering to himself softly. "I've made one."

"I thought you wouldn't need to make one because you have everything you need." I chuckled as he tickled me playfully.

"You are everything I need and more. That will never change, but I still want things." He glanced back up at the sky. "The moon looks beautiful tonight. I remember the night after you spilt coffee on me. It was a full moon. All I could think about was that I had to see you again. You came to the window of that run-down apartment and watched the sky for a while. I could have watched you for hours."

"I remember that day. I was thinking of you and everything you made me feel. It was as if a piece of the puzzle had finally fallen into place. For the first time in my life, I felt whole."

Nik's eyes found mine in the dark, and his thumb rubbed my cheek. "You will always be the piece that makes me whole. In every world, in every universe. You are the light that brightens my darkness."

"I love you, Nik."

"I love you, too, Larissa." He kissed me, soft, gentle, and so loving as I leaned into his body. "Let's stay for a little longer."

Flashback, January 7th, 2020

"Nik, you are so callous." Her tears fell to the floor.

"It is the only thing that has kept us alive this long!" I shouted at her.

"Sometimes, I hate you." Her voice was low.

"Sometimes, I feel the same," I said as I walked away from her. Aurora insisted on sacrificing herself for her worthless family. I didn't care. She would come back to life.

I dreaded showing Larissa the study and the multitude of notes I'd compiled on how to break this curse. We knew it had something to do with never meeting one another, but we had yet to figure out how that played into everything. We flew back to the penthouse, and as I unlocked the study, Larissa entered slowly, her eyes flitting through the mess scattered everywhere. She picked up an empty blood bag and raised a brow at me.

"I warned you it wasn't pretty." I leaned against the wall, watching her intently while she ran her fingers over the documents, reading and piecing it all together.

She became fixated on her mother's grimoire, stopping when she read a particular sentence, the same sentence that spoke to me: *Blood must have blood.* It felt relevant, but I couldn't figure out how it worked. She closed off her emotions through the bond, her powers now making it easier to do so. It was an attempt to protect herself. Or me. She sat on the desk and observed the wall of red cotton strings, linking prophecies and theories.

I pushed off the wall and headed over to her. "According to Greek, Roman, and even Egyptian mythology, curses have a common thread that whatever starts them is what ends them. Malignus wanted my father's spear to bind the curse because it had powers that he wanted access to. I never knew that Roman had it this whole time. For our curse to start, I..." I paused to prepare myself. "I had to sacrifice your unborn child." Larissa shifted slightly, glancing at the floor and crossing her arms over her body. She may have forgiven my past mistakes, but it didn't make my actions disappear. "The hard part is we can't sacrifice another baby because you are not able to conceive, and the one time you did, I figured out that you were never going to bear any children in the future. We can't sacrifice a child that you will never have."

"So, in other words, I'm screwed. I thought you said you had good news." There was a hint of laughter in her voice.

"Yes, but all curses have back doors. I am still trying to figure it out. Katrina never wanted us to meet. She discovered one way to end the curse, but we can't undo the fact that we have found one another. We have consummated, and we have drunk from one another. It is hard to break that bond when it is this established." The whisper of voices returned to my head, telling me to be quiet, telling me to stop speaking with her. I shook my head.

"What is it?" she asked, running her hand over my back.

"Since...since Luce's death, I have heard them," I said, attempting to explain what I had been avoiding for a while.

"Heard what?"

"The same whispers that you have. Someone telling you to do things, horrible things." I stared up at the ceiling. "It's them. The gods. They want...Fuck, I don't even know what they want. They only wish to take the one person that I need to survive. Larissa, I don't think you understand. Before I met you, after Aurora's death, I had given up. I didn't want to exist anymore. What was the point of living only to spend limited time with my mate before holding her dying body in my arms? I have lost you so many times that I was becoming numb to it. I dreaded finding you again, but...but with you, I *have hope*. You woke something inside me again. You brought back my hope, and you made my heart beat again. This time, it is forever. I can feel it. This time, we find our happiness; Katrina would have made sure of it. I just need to figure out how. What else did she put in you or put with you to break the curse?"

Larissa wrapped her arms around my neck, crashing her lips against mine before she touched her forehead to mine. "Nik, I feel it, too, but we need to be prepared for anything. We can't put all our eggs in one basket, and we can't assume we will win. All I can feel is this invisible clock counting down. I told you on our honeymoon that you are the key to breaking this curse. It is something you have to do. I want you to promise me, and I am serious, that when I die, you need to let me go. Don't fight me, let me go. We are bonded in ways that I will never understand. I can feel your heart beating, I can sense you, we are intertwined, and I don't think the gods planned for this level of closeness. I think they fear it. They know we are close, but they want to put a wedge between us to push away the chance of discovering the truth." She spoke the truth, but the thought of letting her go was not one I wanted to entertain.

"I can't promise that, Larissa." The very thought of it was breaking my heart.

"Do you trust me?" she pleaded, grabbing my hands and pulling them close to her body.

"With everything I have."

"Then trust me now. Promise me that you will let me go. Promise me that you will move on in whatever capacity that is. Hold me in your heart." She pointed to it, pressing her finger against my chest. "Hold me right here, then let me go. I'll always be yours. The love I have for you is monumental, it defies logic and reason, but I know that you have to do this."

I moved away, turning my back to her, staring at the wall that had kept me from her.

"You know you are asking me to let all this go. You want me to destroy all this, my research, to ensure your survival."

"I'm not asking you to stop looking for a way out. I am asking you to move on after I am gone. Stop waiting for me to come back and do something that *you* want. Do something you have never done before. Promise me, Nik." Her green eyes were pleading with me, begging me to do something for myself.

I sighed, tears falling from my eyes. I had to give this to her; she was right. We had been searching for centuries, and we were the closest we had ever been. Could the curse really be as simple as letting her go? Holding her in my heart but letting go of ever having her again?

"I promise, Larissa, I promise." I nodded, my voice deflating in defeat.

CHAPTER 10

DANCE WITH THE DEVIL

Larissa

AFTER SEEING THE WORDS IN MY BIRTH MOTHER'S DIARY, *BLOOD demands blood*, it all started to make sense. I made him promise to let me go because I knew the truth, and it was tearing me apart. I had to hide this from Nik. I told him I had a meeting early and snuck out of our home, meeting Andreas as he leaned against the car.

"Where are you sneaking off to?" he asked with a sly smile.

"Drive me to work, please." I spoke bluntly. I didn't have time for games. He glanced over my clothing as I snapped my fingers, and my attire changed. I slid into the car, my emotions scattered, but I had to hide it from Nik. He could never know. It would break his heart if he did.

The car ride seemingly took longer than usual. I rode the elevator to the empty floor; empty because the previous tenants had moved to a bigger location. There was only a table with a couple of chairs in the middle of the open space. I locked the door and magically sealed the room. My hands were shaking with nerves, knowing I was about to summon my father. I snapped my fingers as the gold bowl appeared, and I pulled out Katrina's grimoire. It was her spell, after all. I had filled it with the necessary ingredients already, so it only needed my blood. I set up the black candle and cut my hand, holding it over the bowl and watching my blood drip into it.

"Pluto, Lord of Shadows, ruler of the deep,

I call to you from the silence where lost souls sleep.

Guardian of the unseen, keeper of fate,

Come forth now, let us communicate.

Bestow upon me your wisdom and might,

As I summon your presence this night."

The room shook.

"Hello, daughter. I certainly never expected to see you again. At least not for another couple of months."

I sighed. "Cut the bullshit. I have to know the truth. I read Katrina's grimoire." A chair slid across the floor, hitting the back of my legs as I plonked down.

"What do you think you know?" he asked while he took a seat, crossing his legs in his black and red pinstriped suit.

"A blood sacrifice must have blood. He sacrificed my baby to bring me back. My blood must be spilt to end it as a baby grows inside the mother's blood." A smile spread over his wicked lips. "But it doesn't make sense. Katrina said we were never supposed to meet."

He cleared his throat as he stood, walking toward the window. "Humans are blissfully unaware of the tyranny of the gods. You, my dear, are a pawn. Katrina found the back door to the curse, and she brought you, Liyana, back for it to play out again. You weren't meant to meet Nik, and if you died having never met, the curse would have broken as blood would have been spilt, but..." He clicked his tongue and turned back toward me. Sadness crossed his features as he looked anywhere but in my direction.

"Please, I have to know. Stacey made it seem like Katrina missed something, but I know she wouldn't have. You've never lied to me. You're just a fucking asshole." I baited him.

He laughed as he prodded my magical seal to break out into the world. Anger took over as I looked at his leg and snapped it. He fell to his knees, panting, before his red eyes focused on me.

"Glad to know you have inherited my darker attributes. Also Stacey is uneducated pawn." His leg healed, clicking back into position. "The day Elizabeth died…Do you remember the day?"

I nodded. "Yes, quite well. Why?"

"Elizabeth knew what had to happen. You were kept in this bubble, shielded from everyone. The pills blocked the aura of your magic. The town was spelled, but you just had to go and cut your finger on the gate latch, didn't you?"

"What?" I shouted in shock; this couldn't have started from that.

"The moment your blood hit the floor, you never stood a chance. They tasted your future, the power you were destined to have. They couldn't fully sense you yet, but they tracked down Elizabeth and demanded that she hand you over. It was rather convenient timing that your sister and your mother fought that day." He winked.

My mind raced, going back to that moment. She wasn't scared to die. She had no fear. She was only scared for me. "Wait, what? You manipulated Luce? How? Why? And wait, my mother died to protect me?"

"Yes, they knew, but couldn't see you yet. It's why the fire didn't burn you. The spell was cast to keep you safe, with the mixture of your own power cocooning you."

"But…" My brain threatened to explode.

"Wait, impatient daughter, I'm not done." He snapped his fingers, filling the table between us with food and coffee. I snorted and rolled my eyes. "Larissa," he growled in warning.

"Sorry." I giggled, remembering his ridiculous rules while I was his hostage.

"The moment you left your small town, you were easier to sense. The more magic you used, the easier it became, and then that night…"

I touched my neck, remembering the feeling of it being torn into. "The same night you felt me."

He nodded and sighed, popping a grape into his mouth. I would never understand why gods were always fascinated with fruit. "The more power you came into, the more you became a threat to them."

"Why? And why did you allow me to access all my magic, then? I don't fucking understand. It's like you are only telling me half-truths. I mean, why can I only heal sometimes and not all the time? I know I am human, but I have a god's blood, and Katrina could heal herself. This does not make any sense." I huffed in frustration, my elbows banging on the table.

"Your family bloodline was gifted magic by the gods. The original Solis did many things for them, and they returned the favour, granting your family power. It was never what the witches claimed. You were either an elemental or a spellcaster. Your blood just had power, and Katrina discovered this. She tapped into the untouched potential, and when our blood interlinked, your magic became greater than she or I thought possible. It became even greater than the god who promised to help break the curse. That's why she has been pushing for you and Nik to meet. She wants your power returned to her. As for the healing, that is more complicated. When you tap into the god power, you can heal. When you use standard magic, you are just human. How do you distinguish between the two heights of magic? That is not something you need to concern yourself with."

"Wait, you knew about me?" I asked, disregarding all the other information he told me. All the notes in Katrina's grimoire made it seem like he had no idea about me.

"She never spelled me. I…I cared for your mother. She was something else. I held your mother's hand as she birthed you into this world, or rather, in the underworld. I blessed you, and I was one of those who cast the shield over the town to keep you safe."

"What the hell? You knew she was trying to break the curse. The day she died, you sent Nik and Roman to get her. Why? If you knew where she was."

"Oh, Larissa. So much to learn. I wanted to warn her that the god was close. And besides, I have a soft spot for Nik."

"You taunt him," I quipped back in confusion.

"He makes it so easy being so broody and filled with pain." He crossed his arms in the same manner that Nik often did. I had to stifle the laugh threatening to escape.

"That's just evil."

"Uhm." He waved his hands in the air as a reminder of who he really was.

I started to laugh as his face softened.

"So, the gods are the ones pulling the strings." I finally felt like I had some semblance of an idea about this curse.

"Ah, god, only one. They want your power."

"And the only way to get it is for me to die, with my blood being spilt?"

"Nik has to be the one to spill your blood. Only then will the blood sacrifice be broken."

"And my magic?"

"Will return to them, or, if you're smart, you spell it to return to the earth from whence it came. Witches have the choice, for magic to go down the bloodline or to return it to the earth."

"Who is it? Who's the god?"

"I can't reveal everything, sweet daughter. Time will reveal all. The question only remains: What will you do when your time is up? Could you give up your life for his happiness?"

"She's giving me these dreams, isn't she?" He nodded as he sighed, his body shivering.

"I fear our time is at an end, little one. Don't be a stranger. I have enjoyed this little chat. I told you from the start, I only wanted to keep you safe."

It wasn't a lie, he had. He said Nik didn't understand everything. My magic grew more unstable. I realised I truly didn't care where it went. I only cared that Nik had to kill me. He had to undo the sacrifice, even though it would destroy him. I felt Nik poking at the bond. I would never be able to look at him knowing this. I wouldn't be able to continue every day.

"Wait! Two more questions," I pleaded with him, and he nodded.

"Why did you get the witches to help you on the day of my wedding? And why Malignus?"

"Malignus is simple. I suffered losses that you will come to understand one day. I couldn't bear the thought of keeping my name when it had been the cause of those I loved. I lost my spear and wanted to become the creature they believed me to be. I became the definition of evil. It was them. As for the witches, I hoped that they would be able to take some of your magic, which would in turn…" He shivered.

"Someone is stopping you from answering." I turned my back, knowing that this god was watching me at this very moment. I wanted to cry. I wanted to scream, but I couldn't. I had to show strength, to prove to this sadistic person that I would win despite all the cards being stacked against me. I spun back to my father before blowing out the candle. "Take my memories. Take this away. Return it when I need it most. I will never be able to hide this from him."

"Your love for him astounds me. I will, Larissa, on one condition." He held up his fingers as he walked over.

My body tingled. Nik was trying to find me. "What?"

He smiled while Nik kicked at the door, and then Malignus snapped his fingers.

CHAPTER 11

WHAT SECRET IS SHE HIDING?

Nik

Flashback, January 7th, 2020.

"Roman, I tire of her. I truly think I am beginning to hate her. Is this part of the curse?"

"Maybe. Or maybe you should comfort your mate." My brother ended the call suddenly.

I woke to an empty bed, Larissa nowhere to be found. She had blocked off the bond. I dressed myself and rushed down the stairs to see that Andreas was gone. I flipped out my phone.

"Where is she?" I growled down the line.

"She went to work. She stated she had early meetings," he answered in a quivering voice.

"She lied." I checked her calendar. I made a point to know every meeting she had. There was no early meeting. "Has she exited the building?" I asked, hoping that maybe it was slightly true, and she only wanted to work to avoid thinking about the curse.

"No, not even for a…" I hung up and flew to work without a second thought. I hoped that it was nothing, that she simply wanted to work, but I could feel her magic buzzing through the bond. She was using magic and a significant amount of it, but her emotions were blocked. I hated how she could hide them from me, but I had done it to her for months. I landed at the front of the office and raced into the building; her floor was empty. Not even her scent lingered. I closed my eyes and focused on every noise in the room. There was no trace of her. If anybody had taken her, I would have received a call by now. No, she was here. I stepped into the elevator and noticed a void on one of the floors. If she had to do magic, it would be in the empty space. I jumped from the elevator and ran down the stairs, my heart thumping in my chest, the monster wanting to be let free to find her.

The door refused to budge, but I felt a flicker of her. I kicked at the door continually as Larissa's emotions returned slowly through the bond. One final kick and I burst into the room. Larissa stood in the middle of the dark area. It only had a table and two chairs sitting opposite each other.

"What were you doing?" I asked, curious as to who the other person was that she spoke with.

"Just thinking about the potential of this space." Her face lit up, but it didn't reach her eyes.

I doubted her. I felt her magic, her anger, and her sadness just before I burst into the room. Those emotions disappeared in seconds, and they were replaced with almost a sensation of being numb.

"Larissa, don't lie to me," I warned her, feeling my eyes flare.

"I'm not. I thought about expanding this area. I just couldn't focus. I didn't sleep much last night."

I wrapped my arms around her waist, pulling her against my body, her arse rubbing on me. My cock hardened instantly. I smelled the crook of her neck, loving the way she instantly relaxed my body. I spun to see her face, those green eyes now glowing. I twirled the red strand in her hair. A reminder of the day she lost her sister and took in more magic.

"You used magic. What did you do?" I spoke softly, even with my anger radiating beneath the surface. Something seemed to be wrong, and I didn't want to provoke her temper.

Her brow creased as confusion filled the bond. "I...I didn't, did I?" She glanced around but I noticed no physical evidence of spells, but the smell of magic lingered in the air. I tilted her head, searching her face for any signs, but saw nothing. I pulled her into a tight embrace. We both knew what was coming, and we were powerless to stop it.

"Maybe I was possessed again?" she pondered as she took a step back to look at the room. "I can feel my magic and someone else's, but I...I..." Her body shivered, but she wasn't cold.

"Come on, let's go and get something to eat. We can talk more about how you shut yourself off last night. I feel like you discovered something but didn't want to reveal it." I took her hand in mine and placed a gentle kiss on her soft skin. She smiled as we strode toward the elevator.

———

Breakfast was quiet. She barely spoke, and her attention seemed elsewhere. Last night revealed just how much the gods may have been involved in this. Juliet had been using them, or rather they had been using her. I tried to track down the witches that were left from the coven, but it almost seemed like they had disappeared completely. I leaned back in my chair watching her movements; she was angelic, the light surrounding her brightening the entire space between us.

I reached over the table for her, my touch distracting her from her thoughts.

"Hey." Her voice was soft and melodic, and I smiled at the sound of such a simple word.

"I am hungry for something else." I winked at her, wanting to feel her skin on mine, wanting the sensation of our bodies touching, the tingles and satisfaction it brought me to feel her. Her heart raced at the thought. "Shall we finish up and head somewhere a little quieter?"

She nodded, putting her fork down and heading for the door. She had become accustomed to me paying now, and barely fought the idea, even before we joined our bank accounts. She still spent less than what I did. Her only expense was another pair of shoes every now and then.

I would buy her more clothes and jewels, and bags. I may have bought her another car. My main project would be completed soon, and I couldn't wait to reveal it to her. I had been working on it since she found that apartment all those months ago. We walked slowly to my office. It had the space, and she would seal the room to avoid my receptionist, Laura, hearing anything she shouldn't. I wanted to enjoy taking my time with her today. I wanted to show her just how much I loved every inch of her. The thought was driving me insane with lust, and I could smell Larissa's desire increasing with every floor we passed.

I strode with haste toward the office, Larissa's heels clacking on the floor as she followed behind me. Her heart rate increased the closer we got, and my fangs itched to taste her, knowing the blood would be flowing faster than usual. I pushed the door open, watching her sexy body strut into the office, her tight arse and perfect curves, even down to her toned legs. This girl had no faults. I am sure others would disagree, but to me, she was an angel.

"Sometimes you are creepy when you stare at me like that." She chuckled while she leaned against the back of the couch.

I pushed the door closed, loosening my tie. "Why is that?"

"Because I honestly never know if you are going to eat me, figuratively or literally." Her brow creased.

"Oh, Larissa, I will always gladly eat you in whatever way I can." I shimmied out of my suit jacket, wanting to be able to move freely, to twist her body in whatever direction I wanted, to please her. "I have an issue," I said as I unbuttoned my shirt. Larissa's eyes lit up with desire as she took me in.

"Oh…" She cleared her throat, shaking her head for some clarity. "What is that?" Her eyes drifted to my cock, already hard and waiting for her. She licked her lips, her hands twitching to touch me. I stood far enough away to enjoy the stroke to my ego and to tease her a little.

"You are clothed." I unfastened my belt, pulling it from my pants in one long pull. Her eyes widened with delight as she snapped her fingers. Her clothes disappeared in a second, and she put her wrists out.

"I think I have been a bad girl. I might need some punishment for my wicked ways." She bit her lip, a combination of nerves and exhilaration rushing through the bond.

"You have never been tied down, have you?" I asked her, swinging the belt to grab the other end and pulling it quickly to make a whipping noise. She jerked a little, and I could smell just how wet she was.

"No, no, I haven't, and it terrifies the hell out of me, but seeing you right now, holding that belt, I want it." Her eyes sparkled as her nipples hardened. Literal perfection.

"Come here, then," I ordered as she kicked her heels off. "No, with the shoes on." I quirked my eyebrow at her, wrapping the belt around her wrists and pulling it tight. She gasped, but her eyes pleaded for more. I watched her body erupt in goosebumps. "Be a good girl and lie down on the couch for me."

She spun around, I smacked her arse, the sound echoing through the office. I admired her perfect curves and the swell of the mark from my hand on her arse. I groaned, watching her lie down on the couch, her entire body spread out for me. I wanted to take my time with her and love every single inch of her body. I removed the last of my clothing, stroking myself slowly, her eyes laser-focused on my cock.

"You want to taste it, principessa?" My voice was hoarse as I imagined her lips around it, the warmth of her mouth taking every single inch of my cock until it hit the back of her throat. I groaned as I climbed atop her, kissing her delicious lips and inhaling her scent. "You are so fucking beautiful, wife." She wrapped her legs around me, and I could feel the heat radiating from her pussy. I wanted to be inside her, to feel her tightness around me.

"Nik," she said breathlessly as I nibbled her neck, making my way down her body. My cock would have to wait because my mate needed to be pleasured first. I took her nipple into my mouth while my hand grabbed the other one, kneading it exactly as she liked it.

"Fuck me," she groaned, her hands reaching for me.

"Nope, hands up above your head, please. No touching until I say you can touch."

"Yes, boss," she purred before I kissed her lips harder, the sound of her voice driving my monster wild with need.

I returned to her body, kissing, licking, and nibbling down every single inch of her, every act causing her to lift her pussy with need. I could hear her arousal dripping onto the couch. I would never have this cleaned again if it meant I could smell her desire for me every single fucking day. I growled as I sucked on her clit, and she loosened her legs, giving me more room.

"Mmmm, just like that, Nik," she whispered, her voice soft and gentle.

I ran my finger up and plunged it inside, and she mewled with need. The sound needed to be recorded for my personal use whenever I wanted it. I inserted another finger as her pussy tightened; she was close. I moved faster as she rode my hand like a toy before she screamed in pleasure. The best sound in the world. I pulled my fingers out, licking her juices off them, enjoying the taste of her sweetness.

She sat up quickly, forcing my head back down. I chuckled and gave her what she wanted, wrapping my arms around her legs and licking her, moving my tongue in the ways she loved.

"Oh, Mr. Dankworth, you are naughty." She chuckled, growing wetter by the second. I had to taste the other part of her. I needed a fix. I know I shouldn't, but I wanted one. She came on my tongue before I moved up her body, licking the sweat from her abdomen.

"How badly do you want it, principessa?" I asked her, rolling my cock around her entrance. She tried to move her hands, but I forced them back down. "No, you wanted this, so no touching." I held onto her hands as I slid inside her. "You feel so fucking amazing, Larissa, taking every single inch of me and begging for more, aren't you?"

"Yes," she moaned, wrapping her legs around me, forcing her heels into my arse for more. I grabbed a pillow, putting it under her, lifting her slightly as she gasped. "Oh, god, yes."

"No gods here, sweetheart, only demons." I thrust harder, maintaining my rhythm, feeling her suffocate my cock with every single thrust. I slowed down a little, kissing her lips and moving at just the right angle. I wanted her to come at the same time as me. I lifted her leg, kissing down her neck, causing a small cut with my fang, enjoying the taste of her blood. "Come with me, my love."

She nodded as I covered her moans with my lips, a growl escaping my chest.

I spun her around, laying her on top of me. Her pants filled the room as a blanket appeared.

"Sometimes, I wonder why you never tire of me," she said as I stroked her hair, "the same girl for literally centuries."

I lifted her head to stare into her delicious green eyes. "You are the most perfect of all versions. Nobody will ever compare to you, Larissa. I told you it became monotonous with the others, but with you, I am constantly guessing, and constantly being challenged, and I would prefer that every single day for the rest of my life. You are my mate, and I cannot wait for our life together."

"I love you, too…" She paused, holding my gaze. "Remus."

Hearing her say my name, I hadn't heard a version of her say it in centuries, sent a thrill through my body. I pulled her into my chest, holding her tight. I closed my eyes, hoping with every single part of me that we would defeat this curse, so I could enjoy my entire life with the perfect woman in my arms. I never wanted to be parted from her ever again.

Chapter 12

PLEASURE WITH PAIN

Roman

It had been three months since I was introduced to Mimi, and she seemed adamant about avoiding our bond. I knew she felt it, I could smell it every time we were close. I didn't understand why she pushed me away.

I rode the elevator to her floor, using the excuse of having a meeting with Larissa to sneak legitimate time to see her, rather than stalking her in the dead of the night, which I did anyway. At least my wolf had calmed down. Being in her presence kept him contained, and he no longer wanted to rip out someone's throat.

I held the roses in my nervous hands, my body tingling with excitement, but dreading another rejection. If only I could make her see that we were mated and meant to be together. I now understood why Nik grew impatient with Larissa and her refusal. At least Mimi had not sought the arms of another man to avoid her obvious attraction to the fine specimen that was her mate. The elevator beeped, and I strolled out the doors, I heard the women collectively gasp at the sheer size of me. Nik had more than enough vanity for the both of us, but I would never deny that I was just as hot as him.

Mimi had her caramel hair swept from her face, her brow creasing slightly, and her lips parted as she mouthed the words she read in her head. I watched as she brought the pen to her lips, nibbling on it before highlighting a passage. She stopped suddenly, registering the sensations in her body now that I was near. Her beautiful eyes slowly rose, meeting my own as a smile crept over my face. Her body lit up as she grabbed a bottle of water, taking a quick drink, her hand shaking. I listened to her heartbeat increase as Larissa opened the door, watching the interaction between the two of us.

"Roman, how are you?"

"I missed my sister-in-law." She rolled her eyes. "Hello, Mimi."

"H-hi, Mr Silvia."

"Mimi, you can refer to him as Roman, it is not disrespectful." Larissa glanced at me with a weak smile, knowing the longer she took, the harder it was to be away from her. Larissa's eyes lit up. "Mimi, could you please fetch Roman and me a chilled juice from downstairs?"

"Any flavours in particular?" Her tone was filled with annoyance.

"I know Roman likes tropical. I'll have the same, actually."

She grabbed her purse and walked away.

"Why are you sending her away?" I asked, unable to tear my eyes away from Mimi's perfect body.

Larissa didn't respond for a few seconds before moving closer. "If you are quick enough, you might be able to ride the elevator down. A few moments to speak to one another. Better run, Alpha." She tapped my arse as I moved with haste toward my mate. Any opportunity to spend time with her. Any opportunity to speak with her. My heart thumped in my chest, eager for another smell of the magnificent creature that owned my heart.

I stepped inside the elevator, stopping the doors from closing as Mimi froze in place. She moved to one corner while I stood in the other. I peeked a glance at her, her smell filling the small space; jasmine. I wanted to bottle it up and pour some over myself.

I cleared my throat. "How are you enjoying working for Larissa?" I asked her, hoping the small talk would lead to something more.

"Yeah, good, fine, great." She fumbled her words, and I smirked.

"Mimi..." I paused, struggling to find the right thing to say without creeping her out. "I..." I shook my head. "I would like to take you to dinner sometime." I waited. "Of course, that is if you are interested. Sorry, I shouldn't assume. That wasn't a question. Would you like to have dinner with me?"

Her face flushed with embarrassment as she shifted her feet, her eyes looking anywhere but at me. We had barely spent any time together, we barely had the time to get to know one another, a few moments here and there. I stood before her like a creep, asking her to dinner.

"Mr. Silvia, I...I...I can't." The doors beeped open, and as she prepared to run for the exit, I stepped in front of her. I could see her desire, I could feel it, smell it. Why did she insist on fighting this attraction?

"Why?"

"Par...don?" Her voice broke.

"I asked why?" I persisted, wanting an answer on why she denied how she felt.

"A lady is allowed to say no."

"You said can't, you didn't say no. Which is it, Mimi?"

"It's both. I have no…no…no," she cleared her throat, "no interest in you romantically."

The doors to the elevator closed as I pushed the top button, giving us more time to discuss this in the tiny space.

"Now we both know that is a lie." I took a step closer, her hand connected to my face in a swift slap. I didn't expect that.

"Ow!" My eyes flared at the touch of her soft skin against my own.

Her heart thumped harder, her desire growing with every beat.

I took another step.

"Don't, Roman." Her tone was angelic as she whispered my name softly and so perfectly. I had to hear it again. My wolf whined in agreement.

"Why not?" My own voice was soft to match hers.

"I can't." She shook her head, her eyes staring at the floor.

I wanted to see them. I needed to gaze into them to feel whole again. I lifted her chin slowly before seeing her perfect features so close. Her eyes darted to my lips as she licked her own. I had to take the shot. I pressed her against the wall. I moved the hair from her face and pressed my lips against hers.

The touch was euphoric, and my cock hardened instantly. My Luna, my queen. She didn't fight me. A small moan left her throat before I dropped to the floor in shock, pain rushing through my lower body.

"You kneed me in the groin, what the hell?" I strained.

She pressed the button frantically, desperate to leave the confined space. "I told you no. I can't, wolf."

I could feel her pain as she said those words. She was conflicted, but how did she know my secret?

CHAPTER 13
A MEETING WITH DUSTIN ZIMMER

Larissa

I SMILED, WATCHING ROMAN CHASE AFTER HIS GIRL. MIMI WAS A strange girl. She would open up, talking and laughing, but then she would shut herself off instantly. I narrowed it down to her young age. She may have been nervous. I wandered over to the breakroom, knowing Roman would try to entertain her for longer than usual, and I needed a coffee.

Stuart and Julian had asked for more mock-ups of recent designs, as they did not like the team's work. They kept asking me to design them, but that was no longer my job. I ran the company. I dealt with the finances, the meetings, and the delegation. I missed drawing and designing, but I had no choice. Nik appointed me the official owner with all the paperwork in my name since our marriage. I never would have to ask him for money or permission. It was solely my company. It felt wrong, almost unnatural, but I would adjust. This was my life now.

I pressed the coffee pod into the machine, pushing the button to froth the milk as I stretched out my neck from the fuck fest on Nik's couch yesterday. My body ached from all the bending, but I wanted more.

I had another meeting in ten minutes, but no idea who this person was. Mimi stated they had been eager for a meeting.

Dustin Zimmer. I asked a few contacts, but nobody knew of him. Even Nik was at a loss, and he knew most people in the tiny country we lived in. Nik's primary focus right now was investigating what happened to the world and how it had been hidden from him.

I sat back down at my desk with my coffee, flicking through my calendar, taking in the next few weeks of bookings and meetings.

I knew my life would be short thanks to the constant dreams that taunted me, but I couldn't give up hope. I couldn't let it control my life. A knock broke my concentration, and I glanced up to see a familiar face.

My magic prickled with vengeance, my hatred overwhelming me as I stared at the man responsible for my sister's death. My mobile rang, and I glanced to see Nik's name flashing on the screen. I only saw blood, the whispers wanting to bathe in his, to rip him to pieces for what he had done to me and my family. I used my magic, pulling him into the office and slamming the door shut behind him. My phone continued to ring, so I threw it against the wall.

"I don't think your mate will be happy with that." He sat down in the chair opposite my desk, crossing one leg over the other.

"Do you think it was wise to come to my office after what you did?" I barely recognised my own voice, my magic taking full control of my body. I watched it seep out of me and surround Duzi, wanting to suffocate him, to reduce him to a pile of dust as he had done to Luce. I realised only I could see this when Duzi remained oblivious. My office phone rang and I knew it was Nik.

"Nik is waiting," he said, his voice a taunt.

"I don't answer to him. What do you want?"

"I want your mate. I want him to stop his investigation."

"Go speak to him yourself."

"No, I rather like the idea of seeing his mate."

"You just made your biggest mistake, Duzi. Do you think this will scare Nik and get him to back off? It will only push him to find the answers. You also forget your little deal with Juliet made me stronger than you could ever imagine."

An invisible noose wrapped around his neck, pulling him back off the chair as I spelled it to rise in the air. He gasped for breath, scrambling for the rope he couldn't touch. The whispers grew louder. I stepped closer, lowering him, replacing the noose with my hand and squeezing tight with every inch of my supernatural power. I could feel his blood pumping between my fingers. I dug my nails into his neck, watching some of his blood leak down onto his suit collar. A hand landed on my shoulder, and I turned to see Nik's crystal blue eyes staring at me.

"Let him go, principessa," he whispered, his hand on mine, the one wrapped around Duzi's throat. "He isn't worth it."

"He has to die for what he did. He killed Luce. He needs to burn as Juliet did."

"I know. I know he does. Let him go, Larissa." He stroked my cheek, logic replacing my vengeance as I shook my head. Duzi dropped to the floor.

"Why thank you…Lord Dankworth," he said between coughs as the adrenaline rush stopped, my body filling with nausea.

"Get the fuck out of here now!" Nik bellowed, standing between Duzi and me. I wondered if he did it to protect me or that piece of shit. I fell to my knees as bile rose in my throat, and I vomited from the sheer power I had used. The only downside to using so much power was that my body sometimes struggled. I never understood why, when my father was a god.

"This isn't over, Nik." His warning rang in my ears while my anger spiked.

I stood back up, slamming the door shut before he had a chance to scamper away. "I will say this once, and you will hear me. If you so much as touch one hair on his body, I will fucking kill you. I don't care what you do with this information, I want you to know that I will fucking rip your limbs from your body while keeping you alive before I rip that pathetic excuse of a heart from your chest. I will relish in your demise, knowing that I have removed a plague on this city." Nik's hand on my lower back was comforting, and a calmness enveloped my body. His touch brought the anger back under control.

"You heard my mate, Duzi. It is in your best interest to leave." Nik's voice was contained, and I wondered why he appeared so calm. Duzi left in a flash, closing the door behind him. I placed a supernatural block around the room to prevent any other ears from hearing.

"What the hell? Why did you stop me? He deserves to die!" I yelled, wanting to know why when I was so close to removing an enemy from this world.

Nik sat in my chair, leaning back with a smirk on his face. "Oh, he really does, and I must say, you've never looked sexier than you did protecting me," he said, scratching his chin.

"Don't try and flirt your way out of this. Answer me."

"We have Daniel. We need to know Duzi's contacts before we can stop his *plague* on this city. You know I am right. He will die, but not now, not yet. I will make sure you are right beside me as we…What did you say you would do again? I rather liked the sound of that, but I do worry that maybe my monster has influenced your purity a little too much."

I sighed, sitting opposite him. "I don't want to kill. I…I lost control."

"I know, beautiful, I know. It is fine. You were a vision, and as much as I was worried, I couldn't be prouder of you. Let me do the killing. My soul is already marked. I won't bring you down to my level."

I snapped my fingers as a glass of wine appeared in my hand. "Don't judge me," I said before taking a sip. My hands shook as Nik pulled out his phone. He would sit with me for a while, and I was grateful for it. I needed him near me as the whispers still picked at me to hunt him down. They wanted Duzi's blood, and I would get it, despite Nik wanting to protect my purity.

CHAPTER 14

THE DEALS AND THE STALKERS

Nik

Flashback, January 9th, 2020

"I am tired of your bullshit, Nik. It is always what you want. I have no life. I am going, and you can't stop me."

I had to keep her safe. Aurora was my mate, even if it felt like something was missing. It had become a norm for our relationship. She came back and it was almost like the spark was gone.

Duzi seemed to be amping up his threats. He wanted me to be scared, to stop investigating the truth. I refused to give in to the pathetic excuse of a man that he was. The more he pushed, the harder I tried. I would discover the truth.

Larissa had been all jumbled up since she attacked Duzi. Every part of me wanted her to rip him to pieces, but it would only end worse for her with another trial. I also needed him alive to find the breadcrumbs he had left behind. She had a few meetings off-site today, and Andreas and Bodhi were ordered to stay by her side the entire time. I never wanted her without a guard. I swung side to side in my chair while I looked out at the expanse of London below. I held the glass of blood to my head, the smell bringing forth the inner monster. Roman could sense how close he was to the surface. The leash was fraying at the edges, and I worried about who would be the target of my rage when he took over.

"Sir." Laura's voice rang through the intercom. "Mr. Wright is here." I finished my drink in one gulp and sat up straighter.

"Send him in. Thank you, Laura."

"You're welcome, sir," she quipped, friendlier than usual.

Larissa told me I had to be nicer to her, so I started small and noticed a slight change in her attitude. She no longer seemed to regret coming to work. She was more punctual and completed tasks with more efficiency. I smiled at just how intelligent my mate was. I fixed the cuffs on my navy suit and stood, making my way to the door. Daniel was required to check in with any information he discovered.

Daniel entered, and I listened to his heart thumping away. He was nervous. Even though he had sworn allegiance, he still feared me. Good. He should be scared. I wanted him dead, but for now, he had some use. I motioned for him to sit on the couch as I poured us each a glass of whiskey. He wore jeans and a black polo shirt, no suit or work attire. It was odd.

"What is with the casual attire, Daniel?" I asked, handing him a glass of whiskey, noticing his shaking hand accept it. "What is it?"

"You threw me into a lion's den. I have had to lie the entire week and pray that I wouldn't lose my head. You are a prick."

I smirked before I sat down, taking a sip and watching his demeanour soften slightly. He exhaled a deep breath before finishing the glass. "What news do you have for me?" I wouldn't lie, I rather enjoyed seeing the man who threatened me on numerous occasions sitting before me in a puddle of sweat. This was probably the influence of my asshole father, who loved seeing people on their knees before him.

"Duzi is not aware of my betrayal." He winced in pain; pain inflicted through the vow when he thought something untoward. My inner monster purred with delight.

I cleared my throat. "Please, continue."

"He has been in contact with Leo, Benjamin, Theodore, Demetrius, and even Richard." My ears pricked up at the last name mentioned.

"Richard, the same Richard who oversaw Shaftesbury? The one who kept an eye on my mate since a babe?" My anger rose, thinking of his betrayal. Daniel flinched.

"Y-yes."

"What did he want?" I demanded. I knew the other names; some I had turned in the past, and Demetrius had even been my ward centuries ago. They were all my allies, but why had they met with my enemy? They all knew why I hated the man, especially Richard, for what he did to his mate.

"He is trying to get your closest allies to switch sides."

"With what offer?"

"More wealth and power, as well as…" He paused, scratching the back of his neck and glancing toward the door.

"As well as *what*, Daniel?" I stood, my fists clenching as Larissa prodded our bond, feeling the influx of rage surging through my body.

"As well as the promise of killing you and removing you from your seat of authority." Daniel's body sank into the couch. I could smell his fear as the door to my office flung open. Larissa's eyes flared from the anger I radiated. She looked between both of us before rushing over and placing her hand on my chest.

"Daniel, get out now!" she yelled at him without looking over her shoulder. He scurried from the room, a roar escaped my throat. Her soft hand stroked my face, bringing peace to the monster inside. "I'm here, Nik, I'm here. What is it?"

I needed blood, I needed to work out this frustration. I took her face in my hands, kissing her harshly. I needed to feel anything but the pure hatred spreading through me. I rushed to the wall, her body slamming into it. I paused, looking into the green eyes that brought light to my soul. She had no fear, nodding in understanding of exactly what I needed. I grabbed her dress, ripping it in half, exposing her black lacy bra and silky underwear. I groaned at the sight and the smell of her arousal. My fingers wrapped around her throat, pulling her closer. "I'm not going anywhere, Nik, I'm right here."

Her words snapped something inside me. My fingers tightened, eliciting a smirk from Larissa. She wanted this badly, her inner demon screaming for release.

"You're mine," I growled, my words echoing around us.

"Always. What are you going to do about it?" Her voice was laced with seduction and need. She was so *fucking* sexy.

I pressed harder, pushing her against the wall with more force, my other hand tracing down her soft skin. Her breathing hitched slightly while I played with the top of her underwear, swiping my finger down and over, feeling her wetness soaking through. I hooked my fingers into the bottom, ripping the fabric and smelling her need. My dick had never been so hard, wanting to bury itself inside her warmth. My thumb circled her clit as I watched her nipples harden. I wanted to sink my teeth into them.

"Oh, Nik," she moaned, I slipped a finger inside. Listening to her mewl with need was driving me crazy.

"That's my good girl. Come for me so I can lick up that sweetness."

"Holy fuck." She groaned as I forced my tongue into her mouth, her body responding by riding my hand, chasing her orgasm. I felt her walls tightening, and I picked up my pace. She finally screamed in euphoria. "*NIK!*" Her legs faltered before I threw her in the air, wrapping her legs around my neck, and pressing my mouth to lick up her juices.

My tongue started slowly. Larissa gripped my head and the wall tighter as she forced her head back, hitting it softly. She chuckled before I increased my pace, wanting to feast on her delicious taste. It danced on my tongue as I delved deeper, wanting to consume her.

"Nik." Her voice was breathless. "Oh my god."

I smirked, stopping for a moment. "Do you need a bre—" I was barely able to finish my sentence before she forced my head back between her legs.

I nibbled on her clit.

"Yes, yes, yes, please, more," she begged.

"Hurry up and come on my tongue so I can fuck you like you deserve."

"Just stop talking and finish the job, then." She taunted and I groaned in frustration, increasing my pace, her desire covering my entire face. I never wanted to clean myself. Her legs tightened as her screams echoed through my ears. The most amazing sound, one that I would never tire of.

I threw her once more into the air, her giggles filling the room. In that small amount of time, I removed my belt and unfastened my pants, allowing them to fall to the ground before catching her. I hovered her over my cock. It throbbed with need, my lips finding her mouth.

"How do you taste, principessa?" I asked Larissa, a needy sound filled the room.

"Nik, stop talking and fuck me already." She bit my lower lip, causing blood to spill into her mouth. I hissed, thrusting inside her, filling her as she whimpered not from pain but from the pleasure of hitting her sweet spot.

"Oh, you asked for it now. I won't be gentle. Be careful what you wish for." I slowly slid out before pushing in harder and faster, making her body hit the wall. She moaned, loving the sensation. "Liking that, are you? I hope you are ready for more." As I teased her, pulling the entire way out, she slapped my cheek, her eyes flaring with anger. I dropped her onto my length, placing my hand on the wall as I plunged deeper into her. Her magical sounds filled my ears like music to my soul. I glanced up to see the vein in her neck bulging as my fangs elongated; they needed more of her. I grabbed her hair, forcing it to the side before I pierced her soft skin. Her walls tightened as the ecstasy spread through her body, filling the space between us. I increased my pace, chasing my own pleasure while her pussy wrung my cock of all it needed.

Larissa's orgasm tore through her body, and my own followed soon after. I licked her wound, laying her down on the couch, and covering her with a blanket before I pulled my pants back up. Larissa shivered. I took a little too much blood from her. Her skin appeared pale. I moved the hair from her face.

"Rest, my love. I'm sorry." She barely would have heard my words before falling asleep.

I stepped outside to finish my conversation with Daniel. He sat on the couch, waiting for us to finish, staring at the ground. He would have heard.

"I apologise, Daniel, I needed a moment. Let's speak in this office." I motioned for the conference room.

He walked with trepidation, his heart pounding. He was afraid, and rightfully so. He sat as far away from me as possible, and I smirked.

I sat, still able to smell Larissa's sweet scent on my skin. "Which allies has Duzi been speaking with?"

Daniel cleared his throat and looked everywhere but at me. "Richard..." I grasped the table to keep my cool. "Mike and Julian."

I thumped my fist onto the table. "How long?" I spoke through bared teeth. Larissa still slept soundly, so I needed to calm myself before I tore Daniel to pieces and hunted down the others next. "Did they agree?"

"Richard refused to help after he saw what Duzi did to Luce. Mike agreed, and Julian said that he needed more persuading."

"Persuading, as in what? What can he offer?" I asked. I had to focus. I exhaled deeply, focusing on Larissa and her love. The taste of her on my lips helped calm the monster. Her pussy tasted like...*concentrate*, Nik.

"Money. And he has stated he has access to a witch who can

perform particular spells, and she will grant three wishes." He avoided glancing in my direction.

"Do you know the witch's name?" I wondered who had that kind of power, since Larissa destroyed Juliet's coven, only leaving four of them alive. They transferred their power to Juliet, which had since been absorbed into Larissa. If it weren't for her father's blood, she would have died.

"It started with S. I thought she was a human initially. I can't remember it, but it was a definite S. Maybe Sarah, Sienna, Stephanie…"

"Stacey." Larissa appeared in the doorway. "Please tell me it isn't Stacey."

"Yes, it was Stacey." Daniel beamed with happiness at remembering, not noticing Larissa's eyes flaring with rage. The girl who obsessed over mating with me and tried to kill my wife because of it. She was a witch!

CHAPTER 15
WE CAN'T. I CAN'T

Roman

I stood outside Mimi's apartment, watching her move between windows while she spoke rather animatedly into her phone. My wolf was eager to listen, but I couldn't betray her trust. Something seemed to be blocking the spark between us. I felt it, and I knew she did as well. From her eyes on the day of the wedding to the simple touch of her warm skin, which erupted in goosebumps. Lightning lit up the area as her eyes shot out the window, finding mine. She hung up and disappeared.

"Fuck," I mumbled to myself. I was standing in a dark corner watching her like an actual stalker. This wasn't going very well for me. I understood why Nik told me to let it happen naturally. I had no idea what I was doing. I never had this before. I should have listened to him. "Fucking hell."

"Are you stalking me now?" Her beautiful voice wafted through the air as I dragged my eyes from the floor over her long legs, covered in black pants. She had her arms crossed over her body, having forgotten a jacket. Her breasts were on full display, and I wanted to bury my head between them.

"I wouldn't say stalking, more watching from afar to make sure you are safe." I rubbed the back of my neck. Why do I lose all reasoning with her?

"Leave me alone. Final warning, wolf." Her words contained venom, but it wasn't reciprocated in her emotions. She spun around and walked back to her apartment.

"You can't utter a warning of that magnitude and not feel it inside. What are you involved in, Mimi? What are you scared of? I know it's not me; the mate bond would never make you feel fear," I asked her, moving closer. She stopped, and my fingers ached to feel her skin, to touch her, to mark her as mine.

"Roman, please. We can't, I can't." Her voice was soft, barely a whisper, as I stepped around her. I lifted her chin to look into her beautiful eyes as her jasmine scent surrounded me.

"Why? Tell me why, Mimi. You can't fight this. The gods put us together for a reason. You can't fight your fate."

"I can try, and I will." Her stubbornness made me smile. I loved her fight.

"Maybe ask your boss how that worked out for her."

"Screw you, Roman. Just find another mate. Go prey on some other girl, go stalk someone else. I reject you." Her words made my wolf whine, but they didn't hurt my heart.

"You said the words, but there was no meaning behind them. A rejection only works if you mean it." She pushed past me, toward her door. "Mimi, just tell me why," I pleaded with her. I could feel her hesitation.

"They will never accept it," were her final words as she made her way inside. I listened to the lock click into place. "You are a monster."

"You don't mean those words. I'm not giving up, Mimi." A small smile spread over her face as she held her hand up to the glass, but moved it away once the door behind her swung open. A man appeared, glaring at her.

"Get upstairs now, we aren't finished." She hung her head, and I wanted to rip him in half for talking to her that way. She expected me to walk away, but how could I do that now? She needed me. She was in trouble, and I had to protect her.

CHAPTER 16

THE ANNUAL CHRISTMAS BALL

Larissa

I was looking forward to tonight, but also worried about the outcome. Nik had been wary since discovering that some of his allies had been approached to betray him. He planned to speak with Stuart and Julian tonight. My nerves were all over the place, my hands shaking as I applied my eye shadow.

"Roman, you have no business being at the Christmas celebration. You don't work for any of my companies." Nik's phone was on loudspeaker

"Hire me for a night, then. Security, just something, brother, please." I smiled at his eagerness.

"Roman, I told you to stop stalking her and to let it happen naturally." Nik pinched his nose while shaking his head at his brother's persistence.

"I can't. I refuse to let it happen naturally. She tried to reject me."

I spun around. "What? When?" I asked him, moving closer to the phone.

"A couple of days ago." Roman sighed, sounding defeated.

"Roman, you went to her apartment again, didn't you?" I crossed my arms.

"I don't need to see you to know the face you have right now. Yes, I went there. Somebody else was there, and he gave me bad vibes. Like *real* bad!"

I rolled my eyes and waved my hand at Nik. I watched him leave the room, perving on his arse as he did. He glanced over his shoulder at me, knowing what I was doing.

I stared at my jade green wrap dress as it hung up in the bathroom. The dress clung to my every curve, accentuating them, and I could not wait for Nik to see me in it. I walked into our wardrobe to grab a pair of heels, putting them on the bed. I listened to Nik growl at his brother for not listening to him as I picked up my vibrating phone.

UNKNOWN

Time is ticking, Larissa.

I knew it was Stacey. She wanted to mess with my head, but I refused to let her. This wasn't going to be my end. I would defeat this curse. Nik and I would get the ending that we deserved.

Nik continued to argue with his brother on the phone. I could understand Roman's eagerness, but he would only end up pushing Mimi away more than anything. I returned the robe and pulled on my Spanx and bra before walking back to the bathroom to grab my gown. The jade green sparkled in the light; it was stunning. The colours were very Christmas, as the golden thread wove its way through the green in different patterns to the bodice. It screamed *Larissa*. I smiled while I slid into the gown before feeling Nik's hands on my back, zipping it in place. I glanced up in the mirror to meet his crystal blue eyes. A smile crept over his face.

"Hello, principessa." He kissed my cheek, and I returned a smile.

"I love you, Nik."

"As do I, my beautiful wife. Are you nervous for tonight?" he asked as I spun in his arms, straightening his matching green bow tie.

"I am always nervous about being in a room filled with people. I will never not be nervous about that. I am glad that I get to speak to more than just the people at Refresh, though."

Nik cleared his throat as unease filtered through the bond. "About that…" He grabbed my hands and planted a soft kiss against them. "I will be speaking to Julian, and I would like you there. I need a quiet room."

"You want a dampening spell, why?"

"Duzi approached Julian to switch sides, and I won't have it. I need to question him about it and remind him not to cross me. There may be some violence."

"May?" I questioned, knowing Nik well enough to know that meant there would one hundred per cent be violence.

"I want to be positive," he quipped. I rolled my eyes.

"Is Roman coming?" I asked him, wondering if his big brother wore him down. He avoided looking at me. "Nik, he needs…"

He placed a finger against my lips, halting my words. I exhaled, waiting for him to answer. His phone buzzed as he pulled it out, and he mouthed 'one moment'.

I slipped my feet into my heels before making my way downstairs. Our house was beautiful. I couldn't love it more. It reflected old-fashioned and modern architecture. I ran my hand down the oak balustrade, taking each step and listening to the sound echoing through the foyer. I had never felt more at home. I felt whole.

Nik sped down the stairs to join me, taking my hand and leading us outside. He opened the car door before joining me in the back seat.

"Andreas, drive and close the binder," he ordered, his eyes flashing between red and blue. My magic prickled at my fingertips, but it wasn't from me.

"Are...are you pushing me to use it right now?" My voice wavered. The bond between us continually changed and adapted, but I had never experienced anything like this in the past.

"I was thinking about how it will look when you cast that spell later, and I wanted to taste your blood while you used it."

"Nik, *don't* do that again. The sensation was unnerving, and I don't want you to have any influence over this. Understood?"

"Yes, I promise, but I do need a drink. Where would you prefer?"

My body tingled. I wanted to feel his fangs sink into my skin, to hear him drinking part of my soul. He groaned, feeling my emotions flick between the bond. "Fucking hell, Larissa."

His lips crashed against my own, the feel of him setting my body on fire. I wanted him. I pushed him back, lifting my leg and straddling him. I was incredibly grateful that this dress wasn't tight. I deepened our kiss, nibbling his lower lip as his tongue massaged my own. He groaned before his lips travelled down, along my jaw and down my neck. He paused to smell the crook.

"All mine," he mumbled as his teeth sank into my skin. I moaned, giving him more access as his fingers ran along my underwear. "So fucking wet and ready for me." His hands fumbled with his pants as I magically made my underwear disappear and lowered myself onto him. It didn't matter how many times we had sex or in what positions, it always felt the same. The feeling that we couldn't live without one another, that we wanted each other more than reason. He licked the wound as it closed, my own need to taste him grew as I rode him, chasing two different highs. "Do it." He struggled to get the words out as he threw his head back to give me access.

I bit into his neck, feeling the metallic taste turn sweet. I whined in delight with another orgasm shuddering through me, filling me with a euphoria that I never wanted to end. Nik grabbed my hips, thrusting himself harder and deeper into me. I loved being filled with every single inch of him. He roared as he finished, and I collapsed onto him as his hand lay on my shoulder. We caught our breath before he helped me off him.

Nik fixed his suit as Andreas rolled the divider down slightly. "We arrived five minutes ago. I drove around the block to let you finish. Let me know when you would like me to head back."

I laughed out loud while Nik scowled. I had forgotten we weren't alone. Nik handed me a wipe to clean myself quickly as I magically made my underwear reappear. I fixed my hair with the snap of my fingers before helping Nik with his tie once again.

"Ready when you are, handsome." I winked at Nik, feeling the power of our blood running through our bond. I was an addict, and he was my drug.

Chapter 17

CONFRONTATION

Nik

Flashback, January 10th, 2020

More bombs were dropped. Asia had been obliterated by a nuclear weapon. The fallout would last centuries before the area could ever be inhabitable again.

Aurora stood up. "That's it. I am going to get them." I rolled my eyes at this discussion again.

"No, you are not. Sit down," I barked at her while I took a sip of my whiskey.

"You are a fucking asshole."

I helped Larissa from the car, then we posed for photos on the red carpet. Our names were shouted from all directions. She'd made a name for herself as the head of one of the most sought-after marketing companies in London. I had no hand in it, and I could not be prouder of her. The lights, although annoying, showed off her true beauty with a smile that could light up a room, and eyes that could make you fall to your knees in adoration. The red part of her hair shone brightly, a sign of the power that coursed through her veins. I no longer feared losing control of my monster because she would always be with me. Our life may have been tumultuous, but this was our destiny; we were always supposed to end up here, in this moment, with this soul. Every day that passed, I lived more like this was our life than contemplating her end.

She glanced up with a smile that made her eyes sparkle, concern flashing between us.

"Are you alright?" she asked, her brow creased slightly. I ran my finger along her creased brow before kissing her forehead.

"Nothing could be more perfect. Let's head inside. They have enough photos of my beautiful mate." I waved to the photographers as she chuckled. She had adapted to this life as if born to it.

We entered, and she held out her hand, greeting various people before a man stood before her. She beamed as he introduced his wife.

"Nik, this is Mark. We had an interesting conversation at the retreat. He told me how he knew that we would always end up together." She rubbed Mark's arm while staring at me lovingly.

"Oh, this Mark." I held out my hand, shaking his. "Thank you for speaking to my wife that day. I know you probably had questionable glances from fellow workers."

"Larissa proved herself more than once, and I am grateful for the opportunities she gives every single one of us. She shares the workload and ensures that people's talents are used in the best ways. She was born for this role."

I pulled her close to my body. "Yes, she was. She is remarkable."

She looked up at me and wrapped her arm around my waist. Her heart was full, making me smile. "I hope you enjoy your night, Mark. We need to continue greeting our guests. Thank you."

He bowed his head as we walked away. Larissa and I moved about the room, speaking to a multitude of employees within our company. She was now a co-owner of Dankworth Industries. I had full control of all aspects, but she now owned a piece of it. I had never done this in the past, but this goddess made me do things I never imagined possible. No other version had ever wanted more, whereas Larissa pushed me further than I ever expected. I saw Stuart and Julian appear, and Larissa stiffened from the emotions that filtered through our bond. She followed my eyes to see him, a small growl escaping my lips.

"Nik, do it properly. I will ask to speak with Julian, you find a room, and I will join you." She would find me through our bond. She walked over, hugging Stuart and Julian as I ventured into various spaces before finding a small conference room. It was perfect. I locked the other doors and waited, feeling for Larissa, wanting her to arrive with Julian. It didn't take long for her to enter with them both.

Her magic wafted through the room, blocking the sounds from outside. They looked between both of us, and Larissa used her magic to calm their nerves. I motioned for the men to sit down.

"Stuart, you are not needed. If you want to leave, you are welcome to go. I only need to speak with Julian."

"We go together, you know this, Nik. What is the meaning of this?" Stuart asked as his heart beat faster, his nerves apparent as he shuffled in his chair.

"It has come to my attention that Julian has been speaking with Duzi, seeing what he has to offer." I watched Julian hang his head in shame. He dared not look in my direction as Stuart stood up.

"So, what if he did, Nik? He is allowed to question the motives of our Lord. He is allowed to seek help from others." I was taken aback by his statement, never expecting it. Larissa turned her head to the side, even she pondered his words.

"Yes, you are correct, you are allowed to question the motives of your Lord. You are allowed to see if something else is out there. But we both know that Duzi speaks with a poison that will destroy the very fabric of society. What could the man possibly offer to make it worth our long friendship?" I stood, my rage increasing with every second, and Larissa's eyes flared at the sensations.

"You are the creator of our species, but all you care about is this fucking human." Julian stood and pointed at me. "She is dangerous. Tell me I'm wrong, Nik. Is she not more powerful than any person can comprehend? She is a ticking time bomb." Larissa gasped at the words from someone she considered a friend.

"Julian." Her voice broke as her eyes watered.

"Am I wrong, Larissa?" he turned to her and asked, his voice pleading with her for the truth.

"I have never harmed you. I have never sought to harm any person. Those I killed were trying to do the same to me. I am not evil. Why would you even doubt that when you… You've spoken with me at length." As I watched the interaction, I saw that Julian was scared of her, but why?

"Who told you she was dangerous?" I queried, but I knew the answer. He couldn't kill her, so his next plan was to smear her name, her reputation. That would hurt her more than any physical attack. He knew this. I slammed my fist on the table. "You believe that fucking asshole over me? Over us? Why? What has he promised you?"

"Don't answer him, Julian," Stuart warned him as I noticed him stepping back toward Larissa. My head and heart were at war as my monster wanted to rip them both apart, but Larissa pushed through patience, wanting this to go well.

"Duzi told us that her blood contains a power we could never dream of, and it's how you grow stronger. It's why you keep her all to yourself and won't share it. You can compel other vampires, and you can control light and shadows because of her. We only want what is fair."

Larissa screamed as Stuart wrapped his arm around her. She wasn't prepared. I knew she could handle herself, so I barely moved, not wanting to aggravate them further. Larissa's eyes locked onto mine as we spoke to one another without words. She nodded.

"Stuart, Julian. I don't know what Duzi has told you, but while my blood *is* powerful, it has never given Nik what he was born with. You know this already. He is the father of vampires. He is a demi-god. He has powers in his own right, and that will never change. You can't believe any words out of Duzi's mouth. If you drink my blood, you will die. This was his way of removing another off the map who refused to accept the new alliance. Please, believe me. Don't do this. You are friends, you have always been amazing. Don't let his words poison you."

I stood frozen in place as I contemplated whether I wanted them to actually drink from her. It would be one less stress, one less alliance I wouldn't have to worry about backstabbing me. Stuart held her tighter as Julian turned her head. I couldn't let this happen.

"If you touch a single hair on her head, I will *fucking* kill you. I will tear your arms from your body. I will break your legs in a hundred different ways. Then I will feed your body to werewolves."

Julian turned, his eyes red and his teeth hanging over his lip. Stuart looked at me, his eyes flaring. Why was Larissa not using her magic? Why was she not fighting?

"STOP!" she shouted, pushing them off her with a force that made even my own body stumble slightly. "THAT'S enough! Don't you see this is what he wants? Duzi wants people to fight, to distract us from what he is trying to do. He wants to create a divide, but there is no divide in vampire ranks. It has to stop. You do this, and you give him the power. You get nothing but death. If you don't believe me, here…" She cut her finger, holding it up to them both. "If you don't trust that Nik and I are lying, have a drop. Take it and die. I would never lie to you. I would never be dishonest or try to do something for another's gain. I don't want to lose you both. I enjoy our banter, our business, but I won't lose you to *him*. He is not worth the trouble, trust me. He ordered those witches to harm me. He wanted to kill me to hurt Nik. Now he wants to attack in any way he can, but this won't hurt me or Nik. It will only end with *your* death. If you don't believe me, drink. Do it!" she yelled, making them jump in fright. She wanted them to understand that these were their only options: trust us or die. I held still, waiting for them as they looked back at me, then at each other, their unease evident.

"We have known each other for centuries. I would never lead you astray. Yes, I have let things fall behind. Has my attention been elsewhere? Yes. I wanted to be with my mate. She needed me, and for the first time in my life, I needed her. She completes me more than I would ever dare admit to anyone outside of this room. She gives me peace from the demons of my past, the pain that I caused, the people I selfishly killed. She makes me remember the point of life, and I won't let Duzi destroy what beautiful things are left in this godforsaken land. It's why we are fighting to find the truth, to bring peace back to the entire world." I sighed as their eyes returned to their normal colours.

"We only want to protect the world from him, not destroy it." Larissa licked her finger as I strolled over, running my tongue over the cut to make it heal.

"Why does her blood not have the same effect on you?" Stuart asked.

"I am ancient, and I can eat anything." I moved the hair from her face and kissed her. "Do I have your allegiance or not? Tell me now!" I ordered, and they both dropped to their knees and hung their heads.

SEX APPEAL

Roman

WHEN NIK AGREED TO ME ATTENDING THE CHRISTMAS celebration, I dressed myself in a suit faster than I ever had in my life and I drove like a madman to the event. I had to see her. I had to know more. Mimi was mine and I wouldn't lose her. I saw what the loss did to my brother, and I couldn't, I refused to even consider that. She didn't get to reject me. She was born to be my mate.

I entered the bathroom after seeing Larissa walking with Stuart and Julian; they were up to something. I fixed my bowtie and glanced over myself in the full-length mirror. The suit fit me perfectly, showing off my muscular frame, and my hair was pulled back into a ponytail. I would be hard to resist. I closed my eyes and told myself to focus. I had to speak to my inner wolf to remind him to keep calm. A wolf-out would only push her further away.

I stepped from the bathroom, sensing she was close. I scanned the area, seeing her standing at the bar with a glass of champagne in her hand. Her caramel hair was pinned off her face on one side, and my cock hardened at the sight of her tight —and I mean *tight*—black dress, hugging her curves deliciously. My wolf howled, wanting to bury himself inside her. Her eyes moved through the crowd, raising her glass and smiling before they stopped on me. I watched her breathing hitch, her chest heaving at the sight. She looked away, avoiding what I was doing to her body. Her desire coursed through my body. She wanted me, and I wasn't going to stop until she got me.

I strolled over to her, leaning on the bar beside her.

"Fancy seeing you here." I beamed at her as she cleared her throat.

"I thought I made it clear that there is nothing between us," she snapped, avoiding eye contact, instead nodding and waving at others who glanced her way.

"You say that, yet I can smell just how much you want me. I bet your panties are soaked just thinking about me buried deep inside your tight pussy."

She gulped, her bright hazel eyes meeting mine. The pull toward her was strong as she moved closer.

"Fuck me, Roman." She huffed in frustration.

"Yes, that is the aim." I chuckled, and she hid a smirk on her face. I was wearing her down. I needed her to realise that there was no escape.

"Roman, I told you, I can't." Her voice was soft, barely a whisper, as she continued to deny her feelings.

"Tell me why. I can help you. We are mated, Mimi. You can't stop this between us. We are born to be with one another. I'm yours and you are mine. What is holding you back? Is it the wolf? Or something else?" I asked, her eyes meeting mine at the mention of something else. "Mimi, are you in danger?" I had to know after seeing the man at her apartment the other day.

"I can't tell you," she growled at me, taking another sip of champagne.

"Why not?" I pushed for more. I had to know the answer.

She scanned the area, searching for something. "Not here, it's not safe."

"This is my brother's party, of course it is safe."

"If you think that, you are naïve." She slid her hand into mine as we ducked through the crowd, into the disabled toilet. She locked the door while my wolf was jumping with glee at the feel of her soft skin wrapped in mine.

"Do I need to be worried about being alone with you?" I quirked an eyebrow at her, but she turned her back on me. Her skin was shining under the light, and I reached out, running my finger down her spine. Her head fell back. "What scares you so much that you can't let yourself want this?"

She turned around, her eyes filled with desire. They flicked to my lips, and I pushed her against the door, crashing my lips against hers. She moaned as I lifted her, feeling her legs wrap around my waist. I needed her, and I wasn't letting her go now. She was *mine* and always would be. Her tongue searched my mouth like she needed this as much as I did. I paused, running my hand over her soft cheek, and she nodded, giving me the only message I needed for this to happen.

I perched her on the bench, reaching up under her dress, running my finger over her and feeling just how much she wanted this. I needed to taste her. I had to bury my head between her legs. I moved to get on my knees.

She grabbed my hair, pulling my head up to look at her. "No, just fuck me, Roman. I don't need foreplay. I have to feel you, and I have to do it now before I lose all my courage." My wolf growled, wanting to know her sweetness. I didn't care, I just wanted to be inside her.

She pulled me against her lips, and then I moved them to her jaw, nipping down her neck as I struggled with the zipper on my pants. My cock was already beading with my seed, wanting her. I didn't care for protection. I would mark her as mine tonight, and she would never be able to resist me again.

"Roman." She moved as I thrust roughly inside her. We both needed this. The months of putting it off, the months of teasing. She threw her head back, but I caught it before she broke the glass. She wrapped her arms around me, her heels digging into my arse. "Harder." Her voice was hoarse as I pushed myself deeper inside. She squealed in delight. "Yes, fuck me. Give me all of you, fuck me, Roman."

I drove myself to the edge, where my wolf threatened to take over. I pushed her legs wider before bracing on the wall beside her head. I grunted with every thrust, giving her every single inch of my shaft. I wanted to cover myself in her. I ached, never wanting to be away from her, as we both felt the bond partially snap into place.

I smiled. "You are mine now, Mimi, until the day you die."

She screamed during her orgasm, the bond filling with pleasure as I finished inside her, filling her with every part of me.

I stood back, moving the hair from her face. "You don't get to reject me now, Mimi." My fingers ran through my seed that spilled out of her. "I am inside you now and forever."

She opened her mouth as screams echoed through the hall. "No!" She glanced at her watch. "It's too soon. No!" She jumped down, pulling her hair into a ponytail and running from the bathroom.

What the hell just happened?

As Stuart and Julian agreed to be spies in their dealings with Duzi, swearing their allegiance to Nik and me, a cold draft suddenly fell over the room. My magic ached, and my head pounded.

"Nik." My feet felt heavy, my legs were jelly as he rushed over, grabbing me. "Something's wrong." The spell dropped as screams filled the hall outside. He put me down on the table, moving to run outside the room. "Nik!" I shouted after him.

"I've got this. Stay here until you find your feet. Stuart, Julian, are you coming?" he asked them as they glanced between us. Stuart moved to sit beside me as Julian made his way to Nik. The door closed behind them, and my body shivered with a sensation unknown to me. What was this? What was outside that door? I had to know.

I pushed myself from the table, storming towards the door to see what was outside. The moment I crossed the threshold, the stench of blood and the sound of screams filled my senses. My eyes scanned the room, looking at the bloody bodies that lay on the floor. Holding back a scream, I saw a monster running towards me. I froze, and the world seemed to slow down. The creature had no hair, no features, just grey, pale skin covered in bluish veins. These were the vampires that Nik spoke of, the ones who let their monsters take over. Stuart roared as he moved before me, his face contorting.

I saw Nik fighting a group of them, and my magic tingled as I pushed Stuart out of the way, my hands alight with fire. I would burn all these fuckers to the ground. A monster charged at me as I shot flames, burning it alive as it screeched, its body turning to ash.

Stuart stayed close while Nik sped his way over with Julian, forming a circle around me.

"Nik, let me loose." I could feel my darkness forcing its way out, wanting to be part of the carnage. It wanted blood. Nik's eyes were glowing red, his face and mouth covered in blood.

"Larissa." His voice was filled with warning. I hadn't used this much power since Luce's death. I had been wary, only using small amounts, but the bloodshed got worse as they tore through the innocent humans and vampires around us.

"I can't just stand here. I've got this!" He nodded, and I raised myself from the floor, allowing the magic to flow through my entire body, filling it completely with fire, ready to explode. My eyes flared with anger as I forced out my own type of control. "Everyone, get down." I barely shouted, controlling every person as they dropped to their knees.

I shrieked, forcing the fire out over the entire room, keeping the innocent people protected and burning the monsters alive. I screamed, feeling every part of my soul filling with a darkness that would never wash away. A darkness that was in my blood, but I didn't care anymore. I hid from myself for so long, but I was Larissa *fucking* Dankworth, and I would destroy them all. I watched the creatures' bodies writhe in pain, screeching at their ultimate demise. My body lowered to the floor as the last of the monsters dwindled to ash.

I felt depleted, weak, but alive. I stumbled, but Nik swept me off my feet, holding me against his chest.

"You did it, Larissa. You saved them all." My heart ached for those who didn't survive, for those I didn't get there fast enough to save.

"I need to heal the others. I have to help them." I tried to move, but he held me down with his stare. His blue eyes were filled with warning and love as he rested his forehead against my own.

"My love, my beautiful mate. Stuart and Julian are already sharing their blood with those they can save. You did it. Close your eyes and rest. You are still half human, and using that much magic can hurt you."

"Nik!" Roman's voice boomed as he ran over, holding Mimi's hand. "Is she okay?" he asked, kissing my cheek.

I turned to look at him. "Hi, Roman."

"Hey, you." His voice was soft as he moved hair from my face, his brow creasing. "Her eyes."

Nik glanced away, wanting to avoid the conversation.

"I am going to take her home. We can discuss it later."

"How is Mimi?" I was too dazed to think about what could be wrong with my eyes.

"I'm here, boss. I can't say the same for the others." Her voice was filled with sadness as her eyes brimmed with tears.

"Roman, get her home, please. Take care of her." He nodded,

kissing my forehead before whispering something in Nik's ear. They nodded before Nik's hold on me tightened.

———

I woke the next morning still feeling depleted. My sleep was filled with the sounds of the monsters' screeches as I burnt them alive. I sat up, rubbing the sleep from my eyes and stretching my arms. I stood up and made my way to the bathroom, and when I looked in the mirror, the first thing I noticed was that my eyes had a thin red ring around the pupil. There was also another strand of bright red in my hair. Every time I touched that magic, it changed another part of me. I turned on the shower, letting the water cool my body as a rush of air hit me. Nik's arms wrapped around my waist, the tension melting from his simple touch.

"Nik..." He reached before me, grabbing the shampoo and massaging it into my hair. "How many survived?" I asked him, feeling his erection poke my arse.

"Enough, Larissa, don't focus on who you could have saved, focus on who you *did* save, and that was over a hundred people. They are alive because of you. That's the only thing that matters. Do you understand me?" The stern tone of his voice made me not want to question him.

I nodded as he rinsed the soap from my hair, grabbing the coconut and vanilla body wash, cleansing my skin from the sins of yesterday. His touch gave me comfort and filled me with desire as I rubbed my arse against him. Nik groaned with a small chuckle.

"Are we a little eager, Mrs Silvia?" I giggled, rubbing myself on him while he grasped my breast, rolling my nipple between his fingers. His other hand caressed my arse before his hand landed firmly against my cheek with a small sting.

"Nik," I pleaded, needing to feel him inside, needing to feel anything that he would give me. His hand ran down my body as he toyed with my clit, rubbing small circles over it. I leaned against him as he spanked my arse again.

"My naughty little wife, tell me, have you ever had somebody between these two sweet cheeks?"

I shook my head. I never thought about it. "Not today, Nik. I just need to feel you deep inside me. I want to feel your fangs sinking into my neck. I want to hear you slurping on my blood. I need you, please," I begged him, knowing he would calm the noise in my head.

Nik spun me around, lifting me as I wrapped my legs around him. He sped to the bedroom, throwing me onto the bed, making me bounce along the mattress. He climbed over me, his large figure looming, his eyes flaring red with need. I pulled him down, kissing him with everything I had. I licked his lips, and he groaned.

"I love you, Larissa." His voice was hoarse before he kissed down my body, lifting my legs over his shoulders as his tongue licked up and down my wetness. I wanted more. I wanted to take control. He stopped, glancing up. "I can't read that. What are you thinking?"

"I want to ride your fa—" I barely finished my sentence before he sat me on top of him. I chuckled at seeing his eyes and fangs flaring.

"Ride my face, my principessa." His words made me melt as I lowered myself, feeling his tongue. I moved slowly, riding his face while his hands reached up, groping my breasts. I moaned, increasing my pace as his tongue and mouth attacked my pussy. He growled, and my toes curled, needing that sweet release. "Good girl." His words were my undoing, and I screamed in pleasure. He tossed me into the air before grabbing me and dropping me onto the bed. "My turn," he muttered as he thrust inside me. He lifted my legs up to his shoulders, pinning them to his chest. He twisted my body as he roared, before lifting me onto his, wrapping my legs around him. His eyes flickered as he fought for control with his monster. I lowered myself onto his hard cock, grinding up and down. His teeth sank into my neck, drinking what he could as I mewled at the sensations coursing through my body.

"Bite me," he groaned moments before I sank my teeth into his neck, feeling the horrible taste slowly replaced with a sweetness. We climaxed together, a low rumble escaping his chest before, letting his head fall against me.

"Come find me, daughter, I need to see you." My father's voice flitted through my head, but I pushed it away, holding Nik close to me.

CHAPTER 20
GODS AND THEIR PETTY WAYS

Larissa

NIK FELL ASLEEP NOT LONG AFTER, EVEN THOUGH HE MAY HAVE stayed awake most of the night. He needed the rest, for once. I snuck into the gym in the penthouse, locked the door magically, and cast a summoning spell, watching my father appear. His black and red pinstripe suit and red pocket square stood out, his eyes flaring red, and his entire being exuding power.

"Ah, my beautiful daughter. I see you got my message."

"Yes, I did, Malignus. I'm assuming the more blood Nik and I share, the easier it is for you to communicate with me?"

He clicked his tongue. "You are correct, indeed. I am so glad you inherited your mother's brains."

"Same. I would be a psychotic asshole otherwise. What do you want?" I asked him.

"What's with the attitude?" He walked around the room, his hands behind his back.

"Why would I not give you attitude? Did you forget my kidnapping and torture?" I crossed my arms, shaking my head at him.

"Oh, shoot, I forgot." He snapped his fingers, and pain filled my head, the memories flooding back. The memories of what was to come.

"Holy shit, I have to die…" I bent over, hurling the empty contents of my stomach from the shock. "Wait, why are you wanting to see me? What horrible news do you have to tell me this time?" I wiped my mouth, grabbing a bottle of water from the fridge in the corner and a towel to clean up the mess.

My father sat down on the edge of the boxing ring and crossed his legs. His face was sombre, no cockiness or arrogance, almost like he dreaded what he had to say. He sighed and patted the space beside him. For once, he wasn't the monster that I had come to know. He was someone else. He almost seemed like a dad scared to break his daughter's heart.

I sat down beside him, and he took my hand. "I want you to know that I never expected this to happen. I loved your mother. It was the reason I kept her soul alive in the dungeon. She revealed the truth, and I am powerless to stop it. I might be a god, but my powers are weakened from the betrayal centuries ago. I fear this might be why."

He stood and rubbed his hands over his face. "I am not a perfect person, and I have never been. You are caught in a conflict that is centuries old, and it is over the most trivial thing in the world. I love my brothers, and I had the best relationship with Jupiter; we were thick as thieves. He ruled the skies while I ruled the underworld. We spoke daily, as I can speak through spirit, as can you with your ability to control. You're welcome. I felt abandoned, being given this power and never able to walk the earth and be among the humans in their prime, rather than dealing with their torture. Jupiter created an object for me, the *Golden Chalice of Divinity*. It gave me the ability to walk the earth and be among humanity. I would travel with Proserpina, my wife at the time. We loved it, and we had never been happier. We longed for a child but had yet to be blessed with one, so we sought help from my brother's wife, Juno, who was the Goddess of Marriage and Childbirth, and asked that she bless us with this chance. We waited, and nothing happened. Then my brother came to visit. He accused me of wanting to create an army to overthrow him and his power. I was aghast; I never had any intention of harming my brother. I loved him as I love him still. He took back the *Golden Chalice*, told me I was no longer worthy, and forbade me from ever stepping foot as a whole being on the earth again." I opened my mouth, but he raised a finger. "I am in spiritual form. I possessed James, which is a workaround. I siphoned some of your power to do it. Back to the story, please."

He cleared his throat. "Jupiter melted down the chalice and turned it into a spear, handing it to Mars for his loyalty. I was not aware at the time that Nerio had created the rumours. She wanted a battle, she craved it. She is rather manipulative and strategic. Mars and Nerio were never happy in their marriage, but we were not allowed to split. I summoned Mars to ask him why his wife had sought this. Mars is the son of Jupiter, and I helped to raise him, teaching him my strategies and skills. He was intelligent and incredibly tactical in all he did. He wasn't aware of his wife's actions and apologised, promising to speak to his father. I never heard anything more until Juno came to see me. She spoke of a prediction. I would have a child, and they would be a darkness on this world. Their power would disrupt the cosmos and cause the land to be destroyed. I was enraged at the nonsense, demanding she allow us to conceive. I was so filled with anger that I didn't see Nerio in my realm. She murdered my wife, Proserpina, to ensure I could never have the chance of procreating." He hung his head and shook it.

I walked over and wrapped my arms around his waist. "I am sorry, Pluto. I am truly sorry for all the hurt you have endured." He returned the embrace, kissing the top of my head.

"I am sorry, Larissa. My past is the reason for your death. Sit down, the story isn't over yet." I sat back down and waited for him to continue. "Mars was enraged at his wife for committing this act, and he sought comfort in a beautiful maiden, Rhea Silvia. She had sworn to be a vestal virgin, but her love for Mars was strong. She conceived two sons, Romulus and Remus. Nerio wanted them dead for his adultery. He protected her, but not before Nerio cursed her to be the wolf that we know her as today. Nerio created the first werewolf family. She banished Mars from ever seeing them or being part of their life."

I gasped. "You cursed Nik on purpose, because of your own anger. It's why you asked for the spear—it was the chalice that gave you the chance to walk on the earth. When Nik refused or couldn't find it, you were enraged and punished him as retribution for his father's crimes. But Mars never did anything. Wait, if you and Jupiter are related, then you are Mars's uncle, which makes Nik my…Please tell me you are joking."

Pluto shook his head as a small smile crept over his face. "Mythology isn't exactly what they have always believed to be, Larissa, but ancient stories that have been twisted through time. Jupiter and I were never brothers in the biological way. He is my *best friend*, but we have always considered each other brothers. You are not related to Nik, I can assure you of that. Now, back to Nik's father, Mars. Exactly, he never did anything against me. He should have punished his wife. He should have banished her or stripped her of her powers. Instead, he allowed this whole situation to happen, and now the only child that I have is destined to be slaughtered by the gods."

"But…" My brain clicked into place. "I am the power that will disrupt the cosmos. The darkness, the voices, it all makes sense. I never asked for this."

"Juno didn't realise when she blessed Katrina that this would happen. She wants to undo her mistake. You must die so the power will be returned to the gods."

"They don't deserve this power. They deserve nothing. They sit in the fucking sky, watching us like we are nothing. They will not touch my power." My magic tingled along with the anger that flooded my system. I had to control myself or Nik would be alerted. I shut the bond down momentarily.

"I know, Larissa, I am aware. You are so innocent in this. You are being punished for Nerio and her bullshit pettiness. You forget we are still human at heart. We may be divine creatures, but we have weaknesses."

Tears flooded my eyes. "I have to die to stop it all, don't I?" My father nodded. "I used too much power yesterday; it's why you are here today, isn't it?" He nodded again, hanging his head. I walked aimlessly around the room. "Can we stop this? Hasn't enough blood been spilt? Katrina, Elizabeth, and…Luce."

He quirked an eyebrow with a sly smile on his face. "Elizabeth is in heaven with Katrina, their sacrifices earnt them a ticket to the clouds. Luce, however, is being well taken care of." He winked, but before I could decipher his meaning, he continued, "When you die, your powers are passed onto the next generation, but you have no children and are not able to procreate. Sorry about that. That was my pettiness, the not being able to have children. I wanted to ensure that Mars felt my pain over his seed dying eventually." I rolled my eyes. "Your power returns to the gods that gave you the blessing, which is Juno, unless…"

"Don't leave me hanging now."

"Witches can give their powers to whomever or whatever they wish. I cannot intervene too much, or they will know. You must figure this out for yourself."

"I hate riddles, you know that, right? I have a strong dislike of riddles."

"Your stubbornness is from me, and I won't apologise for it. The more power you use, the more you piss off the gods, the quicker your death will happen."

"Yep, my death where my mate must kill me. The dreams make sense now. I see her silhouette at night. She calls to me."

"Larissa, I can only make you one promise: this isn't the end. I want to apologise once more."

"You didn't know." This many apologies were not necessary.

"No, for the witches. I may have helped Duzi and Juliet along. I hoped that she would strip you of your powers, and it would stop the vendetta from the gods against you. I hoped that you would be human, and they would let it go, and just maybe..." I put my finger to his lips.

"We both know that it wouldn't have mattered to them. They made up their minds from the day I was born that I had to die. Nerio will get what is coming to her, I promise, Father." It was a bold statement and one that I would hold myself to.

"I have to go now," he said with sadness.

"Wait, may I ask one favour?"

He moved the hair from my face, staring at me like I was the most precious thing in his life. I probably was; the child he longed for but never got to know. The child he loved from afar as he stayed trapped within his own personal hell.

"Anything for you." His eyes flickered to brown, something I had never seen before.

"Don't take my memories. I want to tell Roman. I have to tell him what his brother is going to endure. I have to make sure he is there for him in whatever he needs. Nik will lose it. He has dreaded his monster ever harming me. To stop this curse, he has to do exactly that, and it will rip his soul in half. He won't survive without his brother."

"You are to go there this instant, tell him, and once it has been told, the memories will be gone. Understood."

"Thank you, P-Father." I spoke the words we both needed to hear. He never planned this life for me. Circumstances were out of his control, and he never saw all the pieces until it was too late. Fate had other plans for my life.

CHAPTER 21

THE PROMISE

I WOKE TO BANGING AT MY DOOR. I RUSHED DOWN, OPENING IT TO see Larissa. She was drenched from head to toe, and I pulled her inside, watching her shiver, her eyes filled with tears.

"What are you doing? It is storming outside. Are you insane?" I grabbed her a towel, wrapped her in it, and pulled her into my warm body.

"I don't have a lot of time. I need you to hear me, and I need you to understand that you can't say anything, especially to Nik. Promise me, Roman, with everything you have, you must promise me."

Her eyes pleaded with me. "I-I promise you." She exhaled in relief.

"I have to die to break the curse. I have to die. It is the only way for it to stop. I don't know if I will come back or not, but…" Her voice broke. I lifted her chin to look into her eyes.

"But what?"

"Nik has to kill me. The blood that was shed when the curse started at the death of my baby is the same blood that must be spilt to break it. Nik *must* kill me. It is complicated and messy, I know, but it *has* to happen. Do you understand me?"

"Larissa, we will find another way." The idea of her dying, it made my heart sink. She had been in my life for centuries. How could I let this happen without trying to find another way?

She groaned. "There is no other way. Everything has led to this moment. Pluto told me everything, and it has to happen for it to stop. I need you to trust me. It has to happen."

"You can't expect, after centuries, that we would just let you die, that we would let this happen."

"You can and you will. It must happen, but I need you to understand and promise that you will be there for Nik. I need to know he will be looked after. It will destroy his soul. He will lose himself by doing the one thing that he has never wanted to do. It will crush him, but it has to happen. Please, I need you to be there to bring him back to the light. Don't let him lose control, don't let his monster take over. Promise me, Roman," she sobbed, her face covered in tears as her eyes twinkled brightly.

"I promise, Larissa." She grabbed a knife and cut her hand, grabbing mine and doing the same.

"Words are cheap. Swear to me, Roman, before I lose my memories. I can't keep this secret from Nik, but you can." She brought our hands together, binding them in invisible golden string.

"I swear to you that I will be there for him, and I will not tell him anything that was spoken about today." She forced a letter into my hand, her eyes telling me its importance without any words being spoken. I nodded.

She let go, and her body sank to the floor. She glanced around the room and looked up.

"What am I doing here?" Her memories were gone, but the remnants of the spell still lingered in the air.

"You were caught in the storm and ducked in here," I said, my heart and my wolf whining at the lie.

"Oh, right. Can you drive me home?" she asked.

"Absolutely, I'll get dressed," I said softly with a weak smile.

I took each step slowly, filled with dread. This secret would destroy my brother and me, but I would do it for Larissa because I loved her. I closed my bedroom door, thinking of the pain that was coming for us. Nik wanted his death before Larissa, but if he had to kill her this time, he might actually try to end his life.

CHAPTER 22

A TRAITOR IN THE MIDST

Nik

Flashback, January 10th, 2020

"I am an asshole? I am trying to keep you safe. They had their chance."

"You truly are the monster that everyone thinks you are. There is no saving you. I almost believe that you deserve this curse. You don't deserve me." She stormed away as I shook my head.

"You are my curse!" I shouted after her. Needing some air, I flew into the sky for clarity.

I woke feeling refreshed, but noticed that Larissa was not beside me. I reached over to the cold side of the bed before finding my phone. There were no messages. I could feel her, though. I sensed she was no longer in the house. I sat upright as a small growl escaped my lips. How had I not felt her? I closed my eyes, focusing on the bond. She had forced me out and thrown up a shield. What could she be hiding?

I grabbed my phone as Roman's name flashed across the screen. This wouldn't be good.

"What is it?" I asked, getting to the point.

"I've got her. Nik, she had another episode. She kept talking about nonsense. It didn't make sense. She is safe, though. I am about to drive her home. Do you think it was from using too much power?" His voice sounded off, but I couldn't place it. Why did he seem to hesitate before every word?

"I don't know, she is blocking me. Tell her to stop it. Are you bringing her back, or do I need to come and get her?"

"We are already in the car. She is asleep, so I won't wake her."

I sighed in relief knowing that my brother would always keep her safe.

"Thank you, brother. I'll see you soon."

I clicked the phone off before hopping into the shower. She had used so much power last night that it still thrummed through our bond. I needed to use the excess energy, as sex did not help like it normally did. Sex always helped to remove the power from my system, but the sheer force that she used needed a little more. I sped around the penthouse, cleaning and fussing around while I felt Larissa getting closer. She had woken up, the bond now fully open. My heart was lighter knowing she was unharmed. I cooked her breakfast as she rode the elevator.

I stood, waiting as the doors swung open. She jumped into my arms, wrapping herself around me, and burying her head into my shoulder. I inhaled her scent, and her body relaxed instantly at my touch.

"What happened, princess?" I asked her, walking over and sitting her atop the kitchen bench beside the warm breakfast. I heard her stomach grumble as she giggled. She glanced at the breakfast beside her, but my hands stayed glued to her sides, powerless to move. I had to keep touching her to know she was safe, that she was okay. These possessions terrified me. Who had the power to control someone as powerful as her? A pit of despair continued to grow inside. Something was coming, we could both feel it. I didn't know what, but it wasn't good.

I thought back to her promise on our honeymoon, that whatever happens, to let her go. Could I really let the love of my life go? She was different, *we* were different. It seemed like this version truly was my soul mate, the one I was destined to be with, but an invisible force wanted to keep us apart. Larissa's hands touched my face as I met her gaze, her stunning green eyes with a thin red line, showcasing the power that radiated inside her.

"Where are you?" she asked, her brow creasing with concern as her thumb stroked my cheek.

"I'm here, I promise. Do you remember anything from this morning?" I let her go as she rubbed her hips where my hands had been gripping a little too tightly.

"Not really, it is really fuzzy, which sounds consistent with what Roman told me. I suppose one day, these things will make sense." She reached over, grabbing a piece of bacon. I listened to the crunch as she bit into the overcooked piece. She enjoyed them like chips.

"Yes, let's hope they will. Eat." I stepped back as she slid off the bench, grabbing her fork and digging into the food. I motioned for my brother to follow me.

We entered the study, and I closed the door, locking it to be sure that she wouldn't enter and interrupt the conversation. Roman walked over to the cart, grabbed a glass, and poured a scotch before downing it instantly.

"Roman, that is a little odd, even for you. What is it?" I observed my brother curiously.

"Nik, I…My brain is exploding. When will this stop? When will it all make sense? She kept speaking about Pluto, not Malignus, but his actual name. Can we summon him?" he asked, pouring another glass and finishing it in one gulp. "And things with Mimi are strange. She knew that an attack was about to happen. Nik, she is mixed up in something."

"Wait, how? I barely had any inkling until Larissa dropped the shield after the conversation with Stuart and Julian, who promised to stay loyal. At least for now, but I have a few more people to speak with or I simply go to him and cut his fucking head off. If only he wasn't in charge of the council."

"Why not call an emergency meeting and overthrow him? You told me to reveal my heritage and take control. Why not do the same? People would follow you if you revealed yourself to be the first. Okay, it will put a huge target on your back, but loyalty to the father of vampires would be strong. It would stop the manipulation, and, if he was removed, imagine the power of taking back the world. Imagine showing everyone that we can live again. We won't have to hide on this tiny fucking island."

I scratched my chin, pondering Roman's words. Was it time to take control and reveal my truth? What would the consequences be? He spoke the truth about Duzi—it would stop the support, which is what we wanted, but he would ramp up his attacks on my mate, and the thought of losing her this time made my body shiver with worry.

"Think about it, Nik. Christmas is next week. Plus, you have to deal with the deaths of all the men and women who died during that attack. Are you handling the death notices, or have you delegated it to the authorities?"

"Both. Authorities have informed the families, but I will be speaking to them and offering my support and financial assistance if needed. Can we go back to Mimi and why you think she had a hand in it?"

"There were a few things that she said that made me think. How we can't be together. She knew I was a wolf; she says *can't* be with me, not won't, as if it is against a code of some sort. Last night, she gave in to desire, and it was magical, and the bond clicked into place slightly, she hasn't fully accepted the mate bond yet. I don't think she understood what she did last night. When we finished, she literally looked at her watch and said, 'No, it's too soon.' The monsters attacked not long after. Nik, could she be…"

I watched my brother's hesitation over saying the words that could implicate her; words I would have to take into consideration, but I hoped my brother knew that I wouldn't kill his mate, even if she had committed treason.

"The People's Revolution. They want to show the world what kind of monsters vampires can be. Could you ask Bodhi?" He hung his head. I walked over, placing my hand on his shoulder and squeezing it slightly.

"Brother, I promise, even if she is, she will not be judged. You just found her, and I won't have my brother lose his love." I turned toward the door. "BODHI!" I shouted, moments before he sped up the stairs, a grin on his face. He had come into himself rather well, and I couldn't be prouder of him and the way he had protected my mate when I had all but abandoned her.

"Yes, Master. How can I serve you?"

"Have you ever heard of a Mimi…" I looked at my brother, unaware of her last name.

"Shit, I don't know." Roman opened the door quickly. "Larissa, what is Mimi's last name?"

"Mimi Rose Virelli," her melodic voice called back. Bodhi's face dropped.

"Yes. She worked closely with my family. She is part of The People's Revolution."

"Fucking hell!" Roman roared, storming from the room.

"Roman," I growled in response, chasing after him. "You can't and you know it. You will make the situation worse."

"What situation?" Larissa appeared wearing tight black shorts and a crop top. She was preparing to work out, and those clothes made my desire flare, and her eyes shone brighter.

"Mimi is a fucking traitor," Roman grunted whiles he paced the room.

"No, she isn't. She is so sweet and innocent."

"That's the point," Bodhi added. "They plant people, and they take on a façade to lower your defences and reveal secrets that you never intended."

"What? But…" I walked over to my mate, putting my arm around her waist, feeling her skin touch mine and needing to be deep inside her. I pushed the thought aside. Not appropriate right now.

"She doesn't know we are aware, so we can use it to our advantage. For now, Roman, go about your business stalking her…I mean, keeping an eye on her. Bodhi, I want a detailed report on everything you know about the Virelli family, and Larissa," I turned to her, "go do your workout. I can't handle the power thrumming between us. We either fuck, feed, or fight because I am on edge and I need a release."

"We could always do all three." She bit her lip.

"On that note, I'm off, brother. I will keep you updated." Roman stalked from the room, and Bodhi left us.

I twirled her beautiful hair in my fingers. "What shall we do first? I have time before I must speak to the families."

Her eyes glowed red. "I'll leave that up to you, my sexy mate."

I threw her over my shoulder, smacking her arse. She squealed in happiness.

CHAPTER 23

GIFTS FOR CHRISTMAS

Nik left after we thoroughly worked off our excess energy. The man was a stallion, and I would never tire of the never-ending orgasms he gave me. I wanted to go with him as he spoke to the families of those who died last night, but he recommended I leave it alone to avoid any questions that couldn't be answered. I understood, even if I didn't agree. I was some of their family members' boss. I leaned my head against the glass of the penthouse. We were driving home later today after he finished, and we would begin preparations for Christmas. I wondered what he had planned. He said it would be a day to remember. Christmas hadn't felt the same since I lost Mum. It just seemed like another day, another reminder of the family I had lost.

I distracted myself, opening my laptop to respond to emails and organise a new schedule. We lost Mark and his wife, and his children were now orphans. I only hoped that they had more family to take them. I told Nik that they should be given enough money for schooling and anything else they needed, and he agreed. Losing two parents was hard enough; they didn't need to worry about financial stability later down the road.

I could feel his heart break with each conversation. He had

already spoken to ten families and had another ten to go. I slammed the laptop shut, refusing to sit there.

"Bodhi!" I yelled out seconds before he sped over, appearing before me. Startled, I held my chest. "You don't have to do that. You know you scare me every single time."

"Sorry, Lady—" I glared at him. "Larissa." I had spoken to him about not using formality when we were in private. I knew it to be a form of respect, but still, I hated being called Lady Dankworth.

"We are going shopping. I have to get out of the house, and I need to buy something for Nik. I'll send him a text letting him know, but we are going out. Organise Andreas or whoever else you need." He nodded as he pulled out his phone. I could feel that Nik was with another family.

ME

I am going shopping. I love you.

NIK

Be safe. I'll join you if I can.

I clicked the phone shut, snapping my fingers and changing my clothes. Even the use of this minimal magic felt wrong. What could it possibly mean? I would bring it up with Nik. I'd never had this feeling before my possession earlier in the day.

I turned back to Bodhi. "Ready?" He nodded and motioned for the elevator. I grabbed the keys to my car, my wedding present from Nik, and we drove to Oxford Street, the best place for high-end fashion. I sped through the city, loving the sound of the engine purring. I parked the car, noticing the paparazzi were out in force today. I had forgotten about them.

Bodhi glanced at me, and I smiled. I kept my head down before turning the car back on and heading towards Regent Street. It would be highly unlikely that they would be at this location; they knew where to find those of interest, and it wasn't at Regent Street.

"Smart choice, Larissa, you look good in anything." I rolled my eyes at him.

"Don't suck up to your boss, please," I said with a chuckle. "Let's shop."

I scanned the area, noticing that nobody was around and feeling better about it. We walked through the stores, enjoying the old architecture and the general happiness of those around us. I walked into the various shops, buying clothes for Nik and me. It felt in bad taste to spend money, so I began to purchase items for children, asking them to be wrapped up and placed in the car.

Nik had barely any Christmas decorations for the house, so I decided to start our collection. I wanted there to be some hype at our house. We needed to make our Christmas special. I found a golden angel to place at the top of the tree. It was breathtaking. Her golden wings shimmered in the light, and her dress sparkled with LED lights.

"Are you joining us for Christmas, Bodhi?"

"I don't believe I have been invited," he said, watching the people around us.

"I am inviting you. Join us. I know you have no family, and I want us to form our own little family."

His smile reached his eyes as his entire pale face lit up. "I'd love that, Larissa, more than anything. My family never believed in Christmas. I am loving this fresh start." He beamed with joy, and I felt a little sad knowing that he had such a limited childhood.

"I know what you mean," I muttered, reflecting on how much had changed in my life. A cloud loomed over my head. My family were dead, but the love I had for Nik made me feel whole, and it was hard to explain. We were two puzzle pieces that fit together, and despite the trauma that tainted our relationship, the hardships and the losses, it didn't stop or affect the love we had for one another. It was twisted, but that was our love, and I wouldn't change it.

I paused before leaving the store, looking at a necklace. It was a heart that had a key in the middle, making it whole. The young male assistant walked over. He smiled as he pulled it from the cabinet, handing it to me.

"It's stunning. I love it. Can we personalise it?"

"In what way?" he asked as he pulled out a notepad. I smiled as I drew what I wanted. He nodded. "I'll need a deposit."

"Done." I paid the amount and left.

Bodhi and I returned to the car. I stopped as I put the last bags in the back seat. "We are going past the children's home to deliver these gifts. They deserve to feel special, even if for a day."

———

Bodhi drove to the children's home. I walked into reception, and the stone-faced woman with the most amazing resting bitch face turned her nose up at me.

"Oh, look another uppity is here. Come to look at adopting for Christmas, only to return them as a dog no longer of use?"

I gasped in disgust, raising my brows as Bodhi growled. I put my hand out to stop him, staring him down. He lowered his head in submission.

"Hello, I am Larissa Dankworth. I just purchased a whole bunch of gifts for the children. I wish I could adopt them all, but it's not possible for me at this moment. Possibly in the future." I had thought about maybe adopting with Nik to fulfil our dreams of raising a child. "They have been wrapped in pink and blue paper, and labelled with appropriate ages. I wanted them to feel loved and like they hadn't been abandoned. I am aware it isn't much, and they deserve so much more, but I have seen horrors these last two days. I wanted to do something good." I could feel Nik approaching as he flicked into the bond. I had texted him what I was doing.

The lady changed her tune as her face softened.

"Do you have enough money for a Christmas feast? I would be happy to pay for this as well, and continue to do so every year if it meant they knew the spirit of Christmas even if for a day."

Nik stood beside me, pulling me into his side and kissing my head.

"Always try to bring light to the darkest places," he whispered. "We both needed this." The stress of the day was evident on his face, his eyes lacking their usual spark.

The receptionist walked over to Nik, bowing her head and offering her hand. I rolled my eyes.

"I am Trish. It is an honour to meet you, Lord Dankworth. We would be happy to accommodate whatever you wish. How many presents did you have?" she asked, no longer paying attention to me, but rather to my husband, who loved the stroke to his ego.

"I have fifty presents, twenty-five girls and twenty-five boys. Is that enough?" I asked her, trying to pull her focus back to me.

"We have thirty children, so that is perfect. Did you want to bring thirty in?" Her eyes lingered over Nik, taking in his large figure.

"Larissa and I will give you all of them to hand out as you see fit. Maybe the others could be used for spare gifts for the common area." He stared at me, and I smiled, his eyes brightening with love and devotion.

"Yes, Lord and Lady Dankworth." I walked away to grab the presents. Bodhi stepped in to help. We walked them inside and Nik wrote a cheque for ten thousand to pay for a Christmas feast. He left my card to be called if more money was needed. I chuckled as he joined me in the car, while Bodhi was squished in the back seat.

"Comfy back there?"

"Not funny, Lady Dankworth."

Nik laughed as he sped through the streets, driving us home to our mansion. The car ride was silent, but he held my hand the entire time. The bond filled with despair and regret at the events from the ball. The hurt would hit him hard, and he would never talk about it. This was Nik, stoic, but I only hoped he would open up, even if slightly, as he had in the past.

CHAPTER 24

WHAT COULD GO WRONG AT CHRISTMAS LUNCH?

Nik

Flashback, January 12th, 2020

Duzi came to see me. I wondered what this pathetic person wanted. I sat down to order some food.

"Nik, we should take control. There are whispers in other parts of the world. The humans are hopeless. We can be their saviours."

"Duzi, we live in the shadows. They will stop eventually." At least I hoped they would. Duzi didn't have the resources to do what he had planned.

I was grateful for the Christmas break; it was needed after the last week of fielding press interviews and ongoing questions about the night the monsters attacked. I still had no clue who let them in, as the security footage had been tampered with. The only small piece of evidence we had was Mimi, and Roman would not let me speak to her just yet. He was trying to gain favour with her. He wanted her to understand that we were not monsters, as she was raised to believe. It was *not* going well. As Roman said, it was fighting and fucking, but no resolutions. Larissa begged him to bring her to Christmas dinner. She hoped maybe her softer nature, her light, could break down the barrier so Mimi could see we were not what she thought we were.

I stared at my laptop, at another threatening email from Duzi, telling me to stop. I had started whispers that I wanted to overthrow him, and that I would call for an emergency meeting soon. He had every reason to fear. Roman was right. We couldn't hide who we were, not anymore. We had to take back control and we would.

Knock, knock.

I looked up to see Larissa wearing a red and green Christmas dress. She had gone a little overboard with the Christmas spirit, but the house had never been so lively, even with past versions of her.

"Can I sit on your lap for a wish?" She winked. I could smell the food cooking from the kitchen. She had planned a four-course meal for only a few people, but the joy on her face was unmistakable, and I wouldn't break her heart.

"Oh, you can do whatever you want on my lap." I winked back as her cheeks blushed slightly, her thoughts thinking naughty things as I laughed and shook my head.

"Don't tease me when you know we have no time, knowing that Roman has heard us having sex on a few occasions is just bad taste." She ran her finger along my desk, making her way over as her eyes drifted over my impressive body.

"He could always join us. Don't forget you shared us in the past." I reminded her, thinking back to those few times. It brought the three of us closer.

"That was the old version of me that did whatever she could to *please* you." She emphasised the words with finger quotations. "This version is creeped out by sharing brothers, even if you are both way too fucking handsome." She climbed onto my lap as I sniffed her neck.

"Do I smell like Christmas?" she asked, pulling back.

"No, you smell like mine." She rolled her eyes, swatting my chest playfully. "You're nervous." I registered her feelings with her deep sigh and the emotions that flooded the bond.

"Slightly. I just hope Roman has convinced Mimi to come. I hope that we can get her to see that they are wrong, or a least a little misguided, in their thoughts of you. Not all of you are monsters. I just wish people saw that. Maybe I am naïve," she mumbled, turning away from me.

I pulled her head back to see her face. "Larissa, you have a kind heart and a beautiful soul, but you are most certainly not naïve. Mimi will come around. Roman can be quite charming."

She laughed. "I remember. I fell for it."

"Did you, though? Or was it just to avoid the magnitude of what you felt for me?" My signature smirk returned. A small smile spread over her face. I could make her laugh every day with my cocky attitude.

"Your ego is atrocious."

"And yet you love me for it."

"Yes, I do. I think I would love you a little more in a Santa suit, though. You should climb down my chimney and Ho, Ho, Ho yourself into our bed tonight." Larissa chuckled at her poor attempt at a joke.

"Oh, Larissa, I would do anything to Ho, Ho, Ho my way inside you." We snorted together as the doorbell rang. "My brother always has the worst timing," he grumbled as we both stood up.

"I had better go and check the arancini balls, anyway. They have to cook for the right amount of time, or they will be ruined."

"How did I get so lucky with a sexy wife, with big brains, an incredible body, and insane skills in the kitchen?"

"You have a big dick." She winked, swaying her arse as she walked away. I burst out laughing. Sometimes she blew my mind. I waltzed down the stairs, opening the door to Roman and Mimi. Her face was covered in a scowl, but Roman appeared happier than ever. She pushed herself inside, scoffing as she took in the interior.

"She is a firecracker. I love it," Roman said, slapping his hand on my shoulder. "Where is my sister-in-law?" he asked "Larissa!"

"She's in the kitchen. Don't disturb her. Something about arancini balls."

"Cooking up a storm, I see. I hope she made her brownies, those are pieces of art. They should be on display in a fucking museum." He pushed past me, and I was left in the foyer with Mimi.

"I am here for him. I don't care about you or your concubine. I will be polite to Larissa because I truly believe she has been fooled by the monster inside. I only hope to convince her to see the truth." She crossed her arms, glaring at me as if I would yield to a lesser creature like her.

"What truth is that, Mimi?" I asked her as I leaned against the wall, inspecting her features. She spoke words of hate, but her body showed no signs of the same. No increased heart rate, no hatred seeping from her pores. I doubt she even understood what she was supposed to hate. She had been fed lies about my kind probably since the day she was born.

"You are the monster, and the day that you are rid of this earth will be the best day for humanity. Your kind should never have been created."

"Mimi, do you know the beginning of our kind?" I queried, wondering what she knew exactly.

"It was a demon cast out of hell to torture the innocent and spread its seed." Her eyes were filled with such passion that I worried whether Roman would ever be able to convince her.

"Mimi, I am afraid you are severely misinformed. I shall leave you to your preposterous thoughts while I join my family for dinner. You are welcome to join us." I walked away from the woman who, were she not mated to my brother, I would not hesitate to rip her heart from her chest and eat it for breakfast. Larissa appeared with a look of concern, so I smiled to appease her. She would have felt my anger through our bond.

"First course is ready." Her voice rang out as she dished it up. Roman handed Mimi a glass of wine. She flung her caramel hair over her shoulder as I poured a glass of whiskey for myself, noticing that Larissa already had a wine in her hand. I sat at the head of the table, and Larissa sat beside me, with Roman on the other side next to his mate. Bodhi took a seat beside Larissa.

"Mimi, how are you liking London?" Larissa asked, her way of breaking the tension in the air.

"It is not what I expected, but I found some areas to love." Her statement left nothing more to add. Larissa clicked her tongue, raising her brow in an exasperated way. She expected a little more, and I wouldn't allow my mate to be spoken to with such disregard. I put my fork down; it clattered against the plate.

"Mimi, I understand your opinions, and I respect that we have different ideas on certain things. I also respect my brother enough not to kick you out of my house for being rude to my wife. You can hold your opinions and still be a nice person..."

"Nik," Roman growled in warning, but I raised my hand to him.

"Roman, I understand the need to protect your mate. Maybe she should be better educated in being a nicer human being," I snarled at him.

"Enough!" Larissa shouted. "It is Christmas. I can respect that Mimi is guarded, and she has every right to be that way. Can we not just have a nice family fucking dinner? I slaved in the kitchen to cook for us, and I won't have it ruined with passive-aggressive comments or conversation. That goes for all of you, do you understand me?"

We all nodded in unison, whether on our own accord or from Larissa's ability to control our actions. She smiled and picked up her fork, continuing to eat.

CHAPTER 25

WHY CAN'T IT BE SIMPLE?

Roman

THIS HAD TO BE THE WORST DINNER OF MY ENTIRE LIFE. THE snarky comments and the evil looks between Mimi and Nik. Two people I loved, two people I cared for deeply, and yet they hated one another. I knew Mimi had an internal conflict because of who I was, but the bond overrode those thoughts. Her need to be near me, her need for my touch, would always prevail. I reached under the table, placing my hand on her leg as a form of comfort. She looked at me, a smile spreading over her face. I loved this woman. She held my heart. I only wished she would accept what we had. I could understand Nik's pain now, especially when I thought about how Larissa picked me to fight the bond with Nik. Mimi continually told me she was rejecting the bond, but she didn't understand that she had to feel it inside her heart for it to take effect.

Larissa was dishing up dessert, so I took the moment to escort Mimi outside for some fresh air.

"Are you glad you came?" I asked her, pulling my jacket off and draping it over her tiny frame.

She pulled it to cover herself further and shook her head. "You can't force a relationship between your brother and me. His kind caused the end of the world to happen. His kind is an abomination. I will never accept him." The words hurt, they stung, knowing that before Nik became a vampire, he was a wolf like me.

"Mimi, you need to understand that there is more to Nik's story than what you know. I wish you could understand that vampires are not the monsters that you believe them to be. Your perception has been twisted to suit a narrative. Have I ever made you believe that I would harm you? I turn into a wolf when the moon is highest in the sky. I can also turn on command, but the idea of harming you…it kills me. Monsters are not black and white; we had no choice in what we became. That choice was taken from us. Stop seeing the world through a small lens and open yourself up to see the beauty in all of it. Mimi, I love you. I know you feel the magnitude of my love for you. Just please understand that monsters are not always monsters."

"You are asking me to reject everything I have ever been told. You are, by definition, my enemy, and you are asking me to trust you."

I threw my hands up in frustration. "For fucks sake, Mimi, why did you come tonight? Why are you here if it is so hard for you to accept the truth?" I asked her, wanting to shake her body to bring some sense to this conversation. She remained quiet as realisation dawned on me. "You are here for intel on my brother. That's all this is, isn't it? You don't give a damn about me or being near me; you are here for him." I ran my fingers through my hair.

"Leave," I ordered her.

"What?" she gasped.

"Leave, Mimi. I won't have you here harming two people that I love. Leave now!" I growled at her, and she didn't wince. She didn't move away. The bond never allowed partners to be scared of each other's inner beasts, knowing that they would register them instantly. "Come on, Mimi. You are not scared of me. Can you not believe the words that I tell you?"

She hesitated, glancing between the house and me as she fought for control of the thoughts running through her head. I grabbed her, lifting her and wrapping her legs around my waist.

"Stop thinking and just feel." I kissed her, pouring everything I had into this kiss, wanting her to feel everything that I felt for her. She groaned as she ground her body into my groin. My wolf howled, wanting to bottle her scent, her desire filling our senses. "Stop fighting me, Mimi," I whispered against her lips.

"I can't flick a switch and change my upbringing overnight. Stop asking the impossible, Roman. I know what I feel for you, and I cannot find the words to explain it, but I feel like if I don't see you, I will die. I feel like I could stop breathing, and the idea of hurting you causes me even more grief. I love you, Roman, but I've told you, we would never work."

The world grew silent as I listened to my brother and his wife dance around the kitchen. I wanted that. Why had the gods given me a mate who only saw me as a monster?

CHAPTER 26

START OF THE NEW YEAR

Larissa

IT WAS THE START OF THE NEW YEAR, AND I DREADED GOING INTO the office. It had been two weeks since the attack at the annual Christmas party. The media had been swarming with the idea that vampires had too many secrets and they had to be revealed. Society was reeling from the monsters that were attacking daily. Whoever had control of the monster army had them tearing through random areas daily, killing whomever they wanted. They were the creatures that you read about in books, the horrors in the dark.

The elevator beeped to my floor, and I took a sip of my coffee before stepping out into the eerily quiet office space. We had lost half of our staff from that night, and I worried about finding replacements. People were wary of my magic. I was deemed dangerous despite Nik telling everyone who mattered that I was harmless. Flicking the lights on, the office felt cold. I truly had no idea what to expect as I strolled into my office and sat down. The computer beeped to life, and I entered my code. I hadn't spoken to Mimi since the awkward Christmas encounter and doubted she would return to work. She had been planted as a spy, and the idea that she had given others information about me or twisted real facts made me feel sick.

I sipped my coffee before I heard the elevator beep to life. I stood up, watching Mimi walk out, her skin radiant, her eyes bright, and a bounce in her step. Perhaps she had spent the night with Roman. She plonked down at her desk, dropping her bag with a loud thud.

"Good morning, Mimi." I watched as she picked up her pad and walked into my office.

"Morning, Mrs. *Dank*worth," she said, emphasising the first half of my name.

I raised my brow at her. "Mimi, do we have an issue with you being here? Because I will happily replace you. I decided to give you the benefit of the doubt and let you stay despite knowing that you are part of The People's Revolution. Those who I am pretty sure are behind the slaughter of your co-workers."

Her mouth dropped open. "Lar-Larissa, I didn't want that to…"

"Save it, Mimi. It happened, you knew about it, and you refused to tell anyone to stop it. What was the aim of it? Kill Nik, or just kill people for the sake of it?"

"We wanted to remind people that they were dangerous."

"Who? Humans or vampires? Because from where I am sitting, you are more dangerous than them."

She hung her head in shame. "How did you overcome your hate?" she whispered as she took a seat at my desk. I eyed her suspiciously, even though she didn't give off any bad vibes. *'Trust her,'* the voices whispered. They had not led me astray so far, so I listened to them.

"Mimi, it is complicated. A spell was cast to protect me from Nik. It sounds bad, but I promise it isn't. Nik and I are fated mates, destined to be together, but a curse has always ended my life early, before bringing me back and repeating the cycle. My mother discovered a way to break the curse, to keep me safe, but it meant I had to hate vampires, and I did. I hated them more because of a misunderstanding. Now I understand that they aren't all evil. There are good ones and bad ones, just like humans. They decide who they are, they don't allow the monster to take control. They can, but they choose not to, and that's the difference. Humans choose to be evil, we choose to kill. Vampires make the conscience choice to be better than what they are thought to be. The problem, Mimi, the biggest problem for you to overcome is to see beyond the hate. If you can't do that, you need to learn to let Roman go. He deserves someone who can love him completely."

"But I…I do love him. I know he would never hurt me, I can feel it inside."

"That's the mate bond. Roman isn't evil. Get him to turn in front of you, see his darkness, see his monster. Then come back and tell me what you felt, tell me your thoughts." I wanted her to see reason, but I doubted it would happen so quickly.

"That's not the only issue, Larissa." She picked at her fingers, raising one to her mouth and pulling off the dead skin with her teeth.

"What's the issue, Mimi?" I sighed, hoping for a moment that I was breaking down those walls only for them to be put up once again.

"I can't hide from them. They have resources, they will find me, and they will kill me. I can't be with Roman. Every day that he stalks me is a day closer to them discovering the truth of…"

"What truth?" I reached across my desk for her, a form of comfort as she slid her hand into mine.

"That I love him with every part of me, but I can never betray my family," she sobbed. I stood to comfort her, but she grabbed her bag and ran before I could reach her.

"Mimi!" I called after her, knowing better than to chase her. She had so much going on in her head. I could understand those emotions, that internal conflict that seemed to never stop. I pulled out my phone to text Roman.

ME

Not that I agree but keep an eye on Mimi today.

ROMAN

Are you implying that I stalk her?

ME

Not implying, I am flat out saying it. Today, I give you permission to actually stalk her from a safe distance. Don't go to her unless she asks, please Roman.

ROMAN

Anything for you Larissa. Xx

————

The rest of the day was a blur. I sorted through marketing deals and resumes to hire more people. It seemed to be never-ending. I wouldn't be able to make it stop, even as strong emotions flooded the bond. I hadn't seen Nik for two days. He had been out and about with vampire business, planning a coup against Duzi. I worried about what that would mean, but it had to happen. Another surge of emotion had me getting to my feet and riding the elevator to his floor.

Laura appeared to be sinking into her chair, looking terrified. I gave her a small smile as comfort before I burst into the office, just as Nik slammed his fist onto the desk.

"Whoa there, wrestler. I am sure it isn't the desk's fault," I said, putting my hands on my hips as his red eyes met mine.

"Mate," he called out as I walked over. I rubbed his shoulders, feeling his body relax against my touch. "I missed you." He sighed, grabbing my hand and bringing it to his lips.

"Were you successful?" I asked him as I continued to melt his stress away.

"I think so. Tomorrow will reveal all. I don't want you anywhere near the meeting tomorrow. Do you understand me? There will be blood, there will be a massacre. Duzi won't go quietly."

I spun the chair around before I grabbed his face, forcing him to look at me. "Did we not say our vows to one another? Did we not promise to be there for one another, whatever was thrown our way? You don't get to decide to leave me out of it. I was born to be in it. I am going with or without your permission." I let go of his face, his blue eyes sparkling with desire and adrenaline.

In a flash, I was on his lap, my legs around his waist as his lips crashed against mine.

"I want you safe," he whispered against my lips as he nibbled, running his fangs down my neck as my breathing hitched. My legs clenched together with need. I wanted to argue and fuck him at the same time. He chuckled, feeling my emotions flit between anger and desire. "Oh, Larissa, I will never tire of the way I make you feel."

I grabbed his hair, pulling it back. "Neither will I." I kissed him again.

"Fuck, I have a meeting."

I looked down at his erection. I wanted to prove something to him, to be in control of his beast. He shook his head. "No, Larissa."

"You always take care of my needs, let me take care of yours. I am feeling particularly naughty today." I got on my knees, pulling the zipper down on his pants, pulling his hard cock out and running my tongue up the length.

"They will smell your desire and know you are here."

"Oh, Nik, I can hide that and yours. Just don't move," I whispered as I slid underneath the desk, pulling his chair in and getting comfortable, casting a shielding spell over both of us.

Laura's voice chimed through the intercom. "Your eleven am meeting is here."

Nik groaned as I wrapped my lips around his cock, pushing it further into my mouth. "Holy fuck, you are unbelievable, Larissa." He cleared his throat to compose himself. "Send them in."

I giggled. "Don't move now, Nik, your dick is at my mercy." I slid it all the way in until it hit the back of my throat, making him shift in his chair. I licked around his knob, tasting the tiny bit of pre-ejaculation. I moaned at the taste of him. My other hand massaged his balls as he spread his legs wider, and his hand came under the desk. I ignored the conversation around me while Nik forced my head further onto his cock. I was so turned on, I could feel how wet I was. I groaned, my throat vibrating against his shaft as he twitched to control his position. I nibbled and licked, running my tongue up and down, sucking on his balls and enjoying the sensations. My hand involuntarily slid down, moving my underwear aside and touching myself for my own relief. I moved at a quicker pace as Nik's other hand came over, taking control of my head bobbing up and down on him. I could taste more of him, but could feel him holding himself back due to the meeting. It only made me more determined to make this powerful monster come undone with my mouth. I sucked harder, moving my hand while working the top of his cock. He gasped. I could feel his balls twitch, he was close. I quickened my pace as he grabbed my hand, forcing his cock to the back of my mouth, his cum squirting down my throat. His body relaxed, and I licked my lips. I went to tuck him back in, but he swatted my hand away.

"Thank you, I will be sure to look into those issues for you," he said as he finished his meeting. He pushed himself back, his eyes flicking between their red and crystal blue.

"Barely holding yourself together, are you, Nik?"

"Oh, fuck, you are such a naughty girl." He lifted me onto the desk as he got on his knees, ripping my underwear as he kissed up my leg. "The worst part was feeling you touch yourself. That is my job. Only I am allowed to make you come, and right now, I want it on my tongue. I hope you are ready, principessa."

His fangs sank into my thigh as his fingers plunged inside me. He didn't take much, pulling himself away from the urge to feed. "Fuck, your scent is intoxicating." His tongue licking all the wetness that continued from the way he touched me.

"Nik," I moaned breathlessly, grabbing his head and pressing it harder against me. My orgasm grew, curling my toes. My legs tried to move, but he forced them open wider with a growl. As his tongue delved deeper, I screamed. "Yes, Nik!" My body shuddered from the intensity of his tongue.

As Nik stood, I noticed his cock was still hard. "Sometimes your stamina is a blessing and a curse." I paused between each word, trying to catch my breath.

"You started this. I hope you are ready to be thoroughly fucked." I giggled as he wiggled his eyebrows.

"Oh, Nik." I reached up, pulling his tie and smashing my lips against his, tasting myself on him. I moved my legs around him, helping him find my entrance as he pushed himself inside. My eyes rolled into the back of my head as he thrust in harder and harder, our skin slapping against each other. "Oh…oh…oh…oh" were the only words I could form as another orgasm tore through me. My body wanted to collapse, but Nik pulled me off the desk and spun me around.

"We aren't done yet, my beautiful golden rose." He thrust inside as if he would die if he couldn't be as close to me as possible. My walls pulsated against him, tightening with the momentum. "You are so fucking tight. That's it…take every single inch of me, principessa."

"Nik, I need…"

"Oh, I know what you need." He twisted us into a new position, causing my body to tremble. My toes curled as another orgasm escaped my throat, filling with room with the sounds of my desire. Nik roared as he put his hands on either side of my body. "That is one for the memory books." He spun me to look at him as he moved the stray hairs from my face. "That sneaky act will never happen again. Do you understand me?"

I rolled my eyes. "Yes, Lord Dankworth."

He kissed me with a smirk on his face. "You will be the death of me, Larissa Silvia."

"Yes, I will, but I'm worth it." I winked at him as he pulled me into his warm embrace.

CHAPTER 27
THE END OF DUZI

Nik

Flashback, January 12ᵗʰ, 2020

"Duzi wants us to come out of the shadows and take control of the world." I stroked my chin, telling Aurora of his plan.

"I think it is a great idea. You should be the face of it. Nobody could resist your charms. It is perfect. Tell Duzi that you agree." We were finally on speaking terms.

I BARELY SLEPT. INSTEAD, I SAT UP LIKE A CREEP, WATCHING MY love sleep, her naked frame wrapped in blankets. The most precious thing in my world. Today would be intense. I had garnered enough support to overthrow Duzi, but I couldn't be sure of the outcome. In the world of political espionage, you never knew what could happen. My phone buzzed.

ROMAN

> Whose head are we ripping off today? I need to let loose

ME

> Oh brother, I don't think I need a wolf present. You know despite my love for you, we are still mortal enemies.

ROMAN

That's only because I can kick your arse any
day of the week.

ME

Want a quick spar?

ROMAN

See you in 5.

I got up, grabbing Larissa's phone to let her sleep a little longer. She needed it. The dreams were intensifying; she refused to speak of them, but we both knew they were serving as a warning. I walked down to the gym, one of the places I rather enjoyed in our new home. I dressed in a pair of shorts and a tank top before stretching my aching muscles. I knew Roman was close when I heard him howl in the distance. I scoffed at his arrogance. The door burst open as his fur slowly turned back to skin, with steam coming off him.

"What's with the theatrics?" I chuckled, stepping into the ring.

"Come now, we are both nothing if not theatrical. We may differ in other areas, but we both know that our egos can fill a room." He snorted, then joined me in the ring.

My brother was taller, more muscular, but I definitely had the better looks and the brains. He was all brawn. He rolled his shoulders and held up his fists as I charged at him, tackling him to the floor. He wasn't prepared for the speed attack.

"Oh, you sly dog," Roman muttered as he got his breath back.

"Isn't that you, brother?" I asked him with a wink as I spun around. I heard Roman charge at me, so I flew into the air.

"Oh, that's cold...like your dead heart." Roman jumped, grabbing my feet and pulling me toward the ground. The ground shook from the impact of our bodies. We laughed, rolling around on the floor together.

"Are you going to talk to me about why you need to kick some arse today? Or is it just one word starting with M?" I asked him as we lay beside each other on the ground. I listened for Larissa's stable heartbeat in the distance.

"Yeah, Larissa told me about the conversation between her and Mimi yesterday. Tell me, brother, why couldn't we have easy mates? We really pissed the gods off, didn't we? Have you ever wondered why?" he pondered as he sat up and looked around the room.

"Come on, it's probably because Father cheated on his wife with our mum. Or something stupid along those lines."

"True, they are pettier than humans." I nudged my brother, and he sighed. "I know everything will sort itself out. I just wish it was easier with Mimi. She told me she loves me, but it's her family and the fear. How do you overcome fear that is so ingrained?"

"Come on, Roman, there is one person who understands that the most, and we both know what she would say."

"Thanks for waking me up," her voice croaked as she stood wearing one of my shirts. She walked into the room and sat between us. "What are my two boys doing this morning?" We wrapped our arms around her, pulling her to the ground. She laughed as her legs flung up in the air. We snuggled into her, the warmth and love she exuded gave both of us a feeling of peace that couldn't be explained. "Roman," she turned toward him. "Mimi will come around, I can feel it."

"I know, Larissa, it's just at that stage where I can't see the light at the end of the tunnel."

Larissa wrapped her arms around my brother. "I promise, Roman. I will happily cast a spell to make it work between the two of you."

"Isn't personal gain against the witches' code?" I quipped in her ear, taking a nibble out of it.

"Considering I am going to die young, it can't hurt." The room fell silent before we all laughed. I wanted to remember this moment. I wanted to burn it into my brain. Roman and I held her tight between us, knowing that her end would come eventually. Until then, we would live in denial.

———

I brought Larissa along. It would be better to know exactly where she was rather than her sneaking in with her invisibility magic. Roman waited outside, in case I needed any backup. I had enough men to hopefully convince others on the fence to join me and overthrow Duzi from his position of power and influence.

"Would you stop fidgeting?" Larissa whispered as I reached for her hand. This would either end the way that I wanted, or it would end in blood.

"Sorry, I have never been this nervous. These are emotions I haven't had for hundreds of years. I have always been the strongest in the room, and I am the strongest in this room, but men have never questioned me. This is new, and I am not a fan of it." She squeezed my hand.

"Oh, Nik, it will be fine. You are the literal king of all vampires."

"Yes, I know, and I am bringing my human queen to be slaughtered. Fucking brilliant. Why do you have to be so bloody stubborn? You could have transitioned, you could have fucking stayed home, but no, you want to be by my side at the most *dangerous* meeting in vampire history."

"Nik, we are in this together. Sorry that I am not complacent like the other versions. Here I was, thinking that you might like me better than them. I guess I was wrong." I rolled my eyes at her remark.

"Don't start, Larissa," I growled in warning.

"I have one question. Are there any people that I shouldn't kill? Not that I am aiming to kill, but more so if I lose control and burn everyone alive. Do you have a list of people that you want protected?"

I glared at her as a joking smirk covered her face.

"I do not find you funny."

The doors swung open as all eyes turned toward us. I smiled, as did Larissa, who stayed close, our hands fused together. She bowed her head out of respect for those who believed they were above her station. In my eyes, she was above all of them. She was a demi-god.

"Ah, Lord Dankworth, thank you for gracing us with your presence!" Duzi bellowed from the other side of the room. Everyone dispersed knowing what this was about. "Shall we get to it? I already know the truth."

My gaze met Daniel's, who looked at the ground. He was unable to betray me from the blood oath. He had been feeding me intel on all the men that Duzi had been meeting with and what they were offered. It helped to counter those offers with more tantalising offers from me.

"I do not know what you speak of, Duzi. I thought this was

nothing more than the monthly meeting of the Lords." I smiled with my usual cheek as my eyes flashed red.

"Nik Dankworth, you won't win this. I have more power than you can ever comprehend."

I looked over my shoulder at Larissa. She nodded, giving me all the permission I needed to step away and get started. She had become my rock somewhere along the way, my everything. She was never dependent on me. I had become dependent on her.

"Ladies and gentlemen of the vampire court. I won't bullshit you tonight, unlike my counterpart, who is known for his sly underhanded dealings and his manipulations. Yes, I have used some of those tactics, but I never use them to benefit myself. I use them to help a cause. I have never abused the powers that were given to…" I stopped myself. Was Roman right? Should I announce my true identity to the room? I glanced back at Larissa, who kissed her palm and blew it toward me. She would be right there, no matter what decision I made.

"I take that back. These powers were not necessarily given to me. I was cursed centuries ago at the destruction of Rome. I made a deal with the god, Pluto, to save the life of my love, and I was cursed to become this monster. I am the *first of all* vampires. I am sure that you may not believe me. I can prove it, but I want you to hear my words as I tell the truth. I am Remus, the son of Mars and the first she-Wolf to walk the earth. Werewolves came first, which is why there are so many similarities between us. It is why we have mates, why we become linked, why we crave destruction. Was I aware of what my deal would give me? No." I locked eyes with my beautiful principessa, her green eyes shining with pride and adoration. I pointed toward her. "I did it for love, and I would make the mistake every single time. Love and emotions are what give us power. They are what keep us alive."

I sighed, shaking my head to formulate my next words. "Duzi has threatened my mate on countless occasions. He recruited witches to attack her, which caused the death of her sister. She is innocent in all of this, and she always will be. Duzi has lied about the truth of the world. It exists. It wasn't destroyed as we were made to believe. We no longer have to stay in London, we can travel and see the world. We can search for long-lost family. The world is no longer covered in darkness. Step into the light with me, brothers and sisters, let us close the divide. Duzi has to answer for his *long* list of crimes. Let's make sure he pays."

A few jeers could be heard around the room, but it didn't appear positive. Larissa pushed positivity through the bond as I forced a smile on my face. Duzi stood, trying to appear taller, and I heard a snort from the corner of the room. I shot a glare at Larissa, needing her not to draw attention to herself. But even I had to admit, the way Duzi walked now, it was comical, with his short stature and constipated face. He sauntered before the crowd, nodding his head at everyone.

"Duzi, stop trying to grandstand and get to the point. You will physically never measure up to my size. Speak your truth."

He chuckled. "Ah, young Nik. Lord Dankworth. The man who believes he knows more than he does. Your lies are hilarious. You believe you are the first vampire to walk this earth? We all know the truth, and you are not that man. Do not listen to his stories about the gods. They don't exist. There has never been any actual proof of them, and never will be. All of you know the person that I am, you know that I care for each of you so much." He held his hands close to his chest as I rolled my eyes. Larissa's magic flared at the insult to her mate. The bond between us grew deeper with every passing day.

"Nik's mate is the daughter of Katrina Solis, the *dangerous* witch who could kill us with the flick of her wrist. She did not think of us as people, and Larissa has shown the same disregard—"

"Careful, Duzi, this is between us. Leave my mate out of this," I threatened, my monster desperate to rip him in half. He wanted to dance in his blood for every single word that came out of his mouth.

"Look at him. We know the sacred bond between vampire and mate. He twisted the law for his benefit when she killed a vampire with her powers."

"Do *not* twist the facts. You know that she had no part in that. Her pure blood killed him. His choice to drink from the mate of another was far worse than the purity of her blood."

"She was not your mate. She had not been marked."

"She verbalised it, but she wasn't comfortable receiving the mark. She feared my kind, and I was patient. Patience that is now wearing thin with you."

Duzi growled. "I want to fucking kill you, you maggot." He spat the words at me.

I laughed at his words as saliva came from his mouth. "Oh, Duzi," I clicked my tongue. "Duzi, Duzi, Duzi. You are a fool. Do you not remember how you were turned? I showed leniency when you tricked a vampire into turning you. I allowed you to live despite your malicious actions towards Valerie." A growl echoed as I took note of Richard behind me. "Your time has come to an end." I felt a shift within the room. Larissa had leaked small amounts of magic to persuade those on the fence. I smiled at her over my shoulder. "Larissa may be a witch, but she has never harmed any person who has not harmed her. She is kind and innocent, but her actions are not on trial here. Yours are. Are you going to admit the truth?"

"You are preposterous. What fallacy are you referring to?"

"You cut us off from the world. The world still exists. How did you do it?" I pushed my compulsion out, persuading him to reveal the truth.

"I…I…Don't try to compel me." The room gasped, and I held my hands up in mock defeat.

"You caught me, I wanted you to spill the truth. I told you I am the first. I have more powers than you could ever comprehend. Admit the truth, do we not agree?" I made eyes at every person in the room as they whispered amongst themselves.

"Compel him!"

"Do it!"

"We deserve the truth!"

Shouts came across the room, and Duzi, for once, looked terrified.

I strolled over to him. "You heard the crowd, now tell us the truth."

He turned his eyes away, but I grabbed his head, forcing him to admit the truth. I registered fear through the bond as I turned to see Larissa cornered by two vampires who were baring their teeth at her. I moved to protect my mate, my love, when she shook her head, her eyes filled with emotion, warning me to stop. I tilted my own, every part of me wanted to tear them apart, and Larissa could feel it. I glanced back at Duzi, noticing the smug look upon his face. He planned it, he wanted to reveal my monster, to show just how dangerous I could be in this moment to protect her. I straightened my shoulders, feeling Larissa relax and feeling a rush of magic through our bond. She had removed the threat to her. I smiled at myself. I worried, but she was stronger than I wanted to admit.

I spun back toward Duzi. "Distractions and attempts to prove anything won't work. You will answer me, and you will *fucking* answer me now." I raised my voice, pushing forth my power, causing him to fall to his feet, as did everyone else in the room. Duzi appeared terrified. Sweat beads rolled down his forehead, and he was frozen in place.

"Duzi, tell the truth, what do you know of the world?" I asked, my fangs elongating. They wanted to rip into his throat, to taste the victory of his submission.

"Y-yes, the world still exists. The bombs didn't destroy everything. Only one nuclear bomb was deployed in an area of Asia to stop the dictator. I can't remember his fucking name, but it was to stop him. He wanted to bomb everyone, but Russia, America, and parts of Europe agreed that a message had to be sent. Every other bomb was just a standard bomb, but the damage was astronomical."

"But how did you pull it off? And why?"

"When vampires made their existence known to take control, not all countries rolled over like London. They fought, and because of our weakness in the sun, they won. When I heard of this, I refused to go back into the shadows. It was our time to rise. It was why I convinced you to be our mascot. Girls were fawning over the idea of being mated with creatures that looked like you." A small stroke to my ego never hurt. Larissa scoffed. "A group of us compelled politicians and military personnel to turn off radars, convincing them the world was dead. News slowly spread, and the power of whispers took over. It wasn't hard. We destroyed outside communication and kept our control in the United Kingdom. We rule it all, and it is fantastic. Humans now bow to us instead of us hiding in the shadows."

"But acid rain, that wouldn't be possible if the bomb was so far away. That doesn't make sense, how—" How did a meagre man such as him manage to do this, while I knew *nothing* about it.

"We paid and compelled people to drop it. We used drones in the sky and dropped it on rainy days."

"But we could smell it. That's not possible."

"Yes, we would drop it high enough that our scents would register it before it started."

"You kept humans trapped in this world for what?" My anger rose. They didn't deserve this. I had been humiliated. I fell for this. I fought for peace that we didn't need.

I grabbed him by the throat, lifting him into the air. "You don't deserve to fucking live. People were tormented, people lost loved ones. You cut the world off from supplies."

His maniacal laugh echoed through the room. "What hurts more, Nik? The fact that you didn't know or the fact that you weren't involved?" I threw him into the wall.

"We are done here. Take him to the dungeons under the courthouse, where he can await sentencing. He will reveal who his accomplices are and who has been compelled."

"This isn't the end, Nik! I will kill you and your precious fucking mate."

"Oh, shut up with your empty words. You are a waste of space." I waved him off, watching him be escorted out of the room in chains. Chains that rendered him human and powerless.

I peered around the room at all the faces waiting for answers. "We will rebuild. We will restore peace, and we will speak to the outside world again. You are dismissed." Everyone filed out, touching my shoulder and bowing their heads as a sign of respect. I smiled at each and every one of them. Larissa walked over, her thoughts as muddled as mine.

"I see you are just as scattered as I am. What are you thinking?"

"Aurora."

"What about her?" I questioned, but deep down, I understood. She flew into a radiation cloud, or at least that is what I saw before she fell into the ocean to never be recovered.

Did she truly die that day?

CHAPTER 28
THE UNANSWERED QUESTIONS

Larissa

Nik was quiet the entire drive home. He stared out the window, while Andreas glanced back at his master with worry in his eyes. I shrugged, not knowing how to comfort him. He saw her die, right? I wouldn't have been born otherwise. She was a vampire. Was she shot out of the sky? Did she do it to herself? Katrina set out to break the curse because of Aurora's death, because they were friends. My head ached as I rubbed my temple. When we arrived home, Nik exited the car and disappeared into the house.

I could sense his head scrambling for a reason, for an answer that I knew we would never get. I left him alone and warmed up some leftover food for dinner. My phone vibrated, and I only then noticed the five missed calls from Roman.

"Hey," I said softly into the phone to avoid Nik hearing. I shook my head at myself, remembering that it wouldn't matter.

"Thank fuck! What the hell happened? I haven't been able to reach you or Nik. I have been worried sick. I thought he was dead. I thought you were dead. Bloody hell, Larissa, a simple fucking text would have been nice. I almost wolfed out on a girl at—"

"Roman!" I shouted over his ramblings. "Roman," I said again, ensuring he was listening as the line went quiet.

"He won. Duzi has been arrested, but he discovered that the world has never been radioactive." My mouth opened and closed a few times, lost for words.

"Larissa, I don't need to be your mate to know something else happened. What is it?"

"Aurora," I whispered, barely able to say the name of one of the multiple versions of me.

"She's de—" He stopped, realising exactly what the rest of us did. "How the fuck did she die?"

"I have no idea, and it freaks me out. I shouldn't be here if she's still alive, but if there is no radiation, how did she fall into the ocean? Nik saw it, but...he hasn't spoken to me since he had the same thought, and I am not brave enough to approach him when I can feel his emotions flicking between anger and sadness."

"Larissa, go to him. I'll come round, but you need to talk to him. You have no idea just how much of an effect you have on him. Just your presence calms him. Go!" he pleaded.

"Fine," I muttered, hanging up the phone and tapping it against my chin. I stared up at the ceiling to where Nik would be sitting, probably mumbling to himself. I warmed up a cup of blood and climbed the stairs, my heart beating faster with every step. I knocked on the door and was met with silence. I could feel him inside, though, so I pushed it open. Head buried in his hands, his hair was dishevelled, and his clothes were ragged. This wasn't the Nik that I and everybody else knew. I put the cup in front of him and sat on the black leather couch in the corner.

"I just can't comprehend it. If she did live…but I'm pretty sure she is dead. Or was it just psychosomatic pain? Is that why it never hurt as much as the others? We had barely found each other before I lost her again, but Aurora had no strength, no voice, no fire to her, almost like she was devoid of emotion. Did I miss something? Did she take her life, and I was clueless to see it? I became complacent because you always came back, you always stuck to me like glue. This…" He peered up, and his eyes made me gasp. They were the brightest I had ever seen them. They were also filled with tears. I hardly saw Nik cry or feel worthless, and here he was, feeling everything.

"Nik…" I stood up and walked over, and rubbed his shoulders. "They were stuck in a loop, *Groundhog Day*, they were just as sick of it as you were. I'm sorry." I cuddled him, but he shook me off and stood up.

"You have nothing to be sorry for, Larissa. I sought to end it after Aurora. What was the point if I lost you? If my heart broke into a million pieces *every single* time. This time is different because I know you won't die. I know this time is the life we deserve. I finally have hope that we will have our happily ever after…especially when you transition." He smirked and licked his lips

I rolled my eyes at him and pushed him away playfully. "I am still sorry for causing you this pain. We *will* have our happily ever after." The words seemed hollow. I didn't believe them. Something was coming, and it would *not* end well for us. I glanced at the ceiling, at the gods who would be looking down on us. The figure who plagued my dreams drew closer with every passing day.

"Let's go do something fun." I grabbed his hand and led him out of the dark room filled with devastation. I wanted to do something happy with him, something to make him smile.

"Shopping?" he asked, quirking an eyebrow at me.

"I do need another pair of shoes."

"Yes, your only vice."

"My only one?" I questioned, knowing I had more than one.

"The only one that I see." He spun me into his arms and bent me down, finding my lips in a passionate kiss. "I love you, Larissa Silvia."

"As do I, Nik Dankworth." That would never change. He had my heart, every single piece of it.

CHAPTER 29

IT IS TIME

Larissa

I WOKE WITH AN IMPENDING SENSE OF DOOM, EVEN THOUGH I HAD a dreamless sleep. My body knew something was coming. It felt on edge, prepared for an attack that could appear at any second. Nik still slept beside me, his breathing calm and controlled as I rolled over to look at the peacefulness of his face. I kissed his cheek, and he mumbled in Latin, making me chuckle. I moved away to shower for the day before me. The water did nothing to ease the anxieties that plagued my mind. I wiped away what I could before dressing myself to head to work. Nik had been up late; the news of Aurora had thrown him a little bit. I mixed up some pancakes, cutting my finger and allowing some of my blood to drip into the bowl before mixing it again.

My body shuddered, responding to Nik waking up as I heard the floor creak. The worst part of fixing up our old house was that it would always have creaks. Thankfully, I lived with a monster and wouldn't have to worry about one attacking. I had my protector.

His arms were suddenly around my waist, sniffing my neck with his signature groan. He nibbled my ear. "You know you are *mine*, right?"

I chuckled at his possessive nature. I turned in his arms, staring up at his beautiful face and the way his blue eyes looked into my soul, laying me bare within his arms.

"Good morning, principessa. Why didn't you wake me?" he asked, holding me tight.

I put my hand on his cheek. "You looked peaceful, and you came to bed late. I wanted you to rest. I cannot imagine the darkness that plagued your mind last night. Did you want to talk about it anymore?" I asked him as he leant into my touch, closing his eyes briefly.

"No, I don't wish to talk about it further. I don't need to think of the past when I have the future in my arms." He smirked as he moved hair from my face. I rolled my eyes.

"Don't be all cutesy to distract me. What are you doing today?" I asked him, pressing gently against his solid chest and moving away from him.

He groaned as he slid onto the bar stool. I pushed a plate toward him before making him a bloodcino. I enjoyed the normality of our morning despite Nik being thousands of years old. His face only showed his adoration while I took care of him. He hadn't had this for some time, and he enjoyed being looked after. His sole focus used to be me, but now, he knew he didn't have to worry. I had my independence. I had my power. But that would never stop his possessive nature. He pulled my chair out so I could sit beside him.

He chuckled. "I love our life, Larissa Silvia. You are perfection."

"Oh, shut up and eat your breakfast. We have another day of taking over the world. My plan for marketing domination, and yours is unlocking the secrets that Duzi has hidden from us all. I cannot wait to see what *we* do with it." His eyes lingered on my breasts as I waved my hand in his face.

"Your boobs look amazing right now."

I adjusted my top. "Oh, really, what are you going to do about it?" I said seductively.

"Bury my head between them and sink my fangs in, enjoying the feel of your flesh in my face."

I snorted, taking a big bite of my breakfast. "Eat your food. I have a meeting with a possible new investor. By the way, how would you feel about Refresh relocating to another office? A fresh start without the reminder of the losses we have had."

"You mean, you would no longer be just a few floors away?" he said with mock surprise.

I laughed. "Oh, Nik, we live together, and we constantly feel each other's presence. We are mated on another level. We could do with a little more space." I nudged him playfully.

"You are right and it would stop my constant struggle to ride that elevator, get on my knees, and eat your pussy under that big desk of yours. I thoroughly enjoyed that session in my office. It's all I can think about. You are something else, Larissa. But I will give you Sophia's number. She helped us find that apartment for you."

"Oh, yes, please." He pulled out his phone, shooting a text through for me. "Thank you. I need to get dressed." He reached for my hand. "Nik, I have a lot to do today, and you had enough sex last night." A boyish grin appeared on his face as I ran up the stairs with happiness in my heart. I pushed aside the anxieties that told me today was the day. I grabbed my pills from the counter, my hand shaking as I looked in the mirror at myself. I had to take them; they protected me from the gods and their influence, but why should I hide today?

'Don't take them, you need clarity, it's the only thing that will help you to survive the day.' My father's voice rang through my head.

Bile rose in my throat and I ran to the bathroom, emptying my stomach of the pancakes I had just consumed. Nik sped up the stairs. "What is it?" he asked with concern on his face.

"Nothing. They just did not sit right. I'm fine." I brushed my teeth, staring at my tablets and the warning that played in my head. I spat out the yuckiness in my mouth as I glanced up, seeing Shaftesbury in the mirror; the café and my home before it was destroyed. Somebody was talking to me. I couldn't do this. I threw the tablets at the glass with force, shattering the mirror as the images disappeared. The glass broke into smaller pieces, landing on the basin and the floor around me. I saw blood trickling from a cut on my finger where a small shard of glass cut into the same spot as that day with the gate, the day my mother died.

Nik pulled it out and moved to heal it, but I pushed his hand away. "No, don't do it. It is a message. From whom, I don't know. It's the same spot where I cut my finger that day on the gate. This is magic." I closed my eyes to focus on the power that could be lingering in the room. A small sliver remained. "Nik, check the cameras. *NOW!*"

He lifted me into his arms and rushed me down the stairs to the office as he flicked on the screens. We searched through footage before a familiar face appeared, with the smug look on her face that I wanted to burn off. I wanted to kill her. The darkness wanted to eat her heart for breakfast.

"Stacey." I gritted my teeth, and my fists clenched. She had sent a message. Today was the day.

"Larissa, I will fix the security and find out how this happened." He touched my chin to look at him, and my heart sank. I grabbed his top, pulling his lips to touch mine. This feeling had deepened.

"I love you, Nik. It will be fine. I need to get to work." I took the stairs two at a time, knowing where I had to go and what I had to do. I stopped at the top, peering over my shoulder to see Nik deep in conversation with his guards on how it could have happened. They would never be able to fight with magic, especially magic as powerful as Stacey's. How did I miss that?

It was time to return home. To where it all started.

Chapter 30
DIVINITAS PORTUS

Nik

Flashback, January 12th, 2020.

Later that day, after I agreed to be the mascot for Duzi, it was announced to the entire world that we existed. This only seemed to heighten the fear that the end was near. Maybe this wasn't the best idea.

I couldn't feel Larissa. An odd sensation lingered between us through the bond. I focused my thoughts on only her, hoping that maybe she had shut it down slightly for her own benefit, but all I heard was silence. I dialled her number, and my phone beeped, revealing there to be no reception from the storm that thundered outside. The rain pelted harder against the glass windows as it hit me. This wasn't any storm. The clouds moved in directions that seemed supernatural, and my fangs elongated as I finally sensed the magic. The hairs on my arms stood up from the sudden drop in temperature.

"Larissa," I muttered. I had to find her. I sped from the office, scouring each floor for any trace of her. I could barely smell her signature scent anywhere within the office. I should have known the casual memo was nonsense. She had a plan since the glass broke this morning. Why did I push it away? I couldn't lose her. It wasn't today, it couldn't be today. I felt it last night, and the way she kissed me this morning. I believe she had the same thoughts.

I searched a few of my holdings and our penthouse, but still nothing. I could barely feel her through the bond. I had yet to suffer the unbearable pain, so I knew she still lived. But where was she hiding?

I reached our home. "Larissa…Larissa…Larissa!" I called out, only to be met with silence. "Larissa, where are you?" I muttered as I plonked onto our bed, wracking my brain for any idea of where she could be. I stood, making my way into the bathroom to the broken glass that still covered the basin. She saw something this morning. I raced down to the office, pulling up the footage from the time of the incident.

I contained my anger at Stacey being in our home, using magic to evade the guards. I would need Larissa or another witch to cast a spell of protection to avoid any further unwanted guests. I watched Stacey leave as Larissa entered, brushing her teeth before staring at the mirror. I noticed her eyes welling with tears, her face turning white. I changed the camera angle, going back a few seconds to see a mirage of images on the mirror, a message from Stacey, before Larissa broke the glass. She had gone home. We knew Stacey had been working with the gods, so I understood why she wanted her there. It was where Larissa's story began and where it could ultimately end.

"Roman, I need you!" I yelled into the phone, my stress levels rising.

"Who are we killing, brother?" His tone was serious but had his signature light-hearted humour.

"Meet me at *Divinitas Portus.*"

I was met with silence on the other end of the call. "Nik, I…I…"

"I know, Roman, I know. It is somewhere I never wanted to go again. I should have put it together earlier. Larissa literally lives close to it. Katrina was in hiding and tried her best to do it in plain sight. I am stupid for not seeing it earlier, but it's where Stacey has taken her."

"Fuck me."

"No, I will pass." I sniggered.

"Nik," he grumbled as I tried to lighten the mood after hearing his insecurities. I sensed his hesitation, he had too much to lose. So, I made the decision for him.

"Roman, just stay away. This isn't your fight, and do *not* bother arguing. You finally found your mate, and it's complicated enough. Go stalk her. I love you, brother."

"I love you, too, Remus."

I couldn't allow my brother to lose the most precious thing to him. It was selfish. This was my fight, and while he had been beside me this entire time, I would now take matters into my own hands. I was ready to take on the men who abandoned us. I would show no mercy.

CHAPTER 31
SPELLBOUND SHOWDOWN

Larissa

I CLOSED THE BOND BETWEEN US WHEN I SENSED NIK WAS distracted before sneaking to the penthouse and taking a car to drive home. Shaftesbury. The entire drive was filled with memories of Luce. The songs we sang, the jokes we made, and the excitement we had about the massive change to our lives. All of that had changed. I glanced at the ring on my finger, sighing at everything I had gained and remembering at what cost. The loss of those I loved, my two mothers and my sister. The pain made my heart ache. Why had Stacey decided that Shaftesbury was where it should start?

The town was quiet, desolate, not one person in sight. I parked the car, then opened the door, only to be hit with cold winter air. I reached over for my long black jacket, pulling it over my black jeans and green shirt. Nik had been suspicious of my clothes, but I told him it was casual dress day to lighten the mood at work. He didn't believe me, but he certainly didn't question it.

I walked towards the café and noticed a chain covering the door. I checked my watch; it was after eleven in the morning. I pulled my phone out, and it beeped from the lack of reception. This was incredibly odd. My stomach sank, feeling nausea and unease as I strolled further. No stores were open, and nobody was around.

"Hello?" I called out to the void. I noticed the trees still had their leaves, but were lacking their usual spark, almost like their life had gone.

"HELLO!" I yelled again, quickening my pace before stopping at the house that should not have been there. I pushed the gate open, my finger cutting on the rusty latch. I closed my eyes to focus and ease my nerves. Was this finally my time? Would I die where it all started? I walked up the stairs, listening to my boots clack on the veranda. I pushed that olive-green door open to hear the crackling of the open fire. Stacey sat in the red velvet chair, holding a glass of wine and reading a book.

"A bit early for alcohol, isn't it?" I asked her, leaning against the wall and crossing my arms.

"Oh, it isn't wine. It's vampire blood. I need to be juiced up to finally put you six feet under."

I rolled my eyes as she finished the glass. "So, you are basically a junkie, that's good to know. I am still honestly astounded that you started this over a boy. Isn't it a little preschool?"

She put the book down and stood, the chair falling backwards with the force.

"Oooohhh, I'm terrified," I said with a chuckle.

"He was mine first, and he will be mine again. It is what I was promised."

"Promised? Do you understand how fated mates work? Even if I'm dead, he will never even look at you. It's pointless. I had no choice, and neither did he. You need psychological help, girl. It isn't the end of the world that Nik doesn't return your affections. For all you know, he could be terrible in bed or have a bad attitude, but you still obsess over him. You know that isn't normal?"

"He is mine." She gritted her teeth at me. "I cannot wait to pulverise you into dust and take what is mine."

"Hey, Stace, just a question, where is everyone?" I wanted to throw her off balance, twist her thinking, so when I did attack, she would never see it coming. The hardest part was shielding my magic, I didn't want her to sense when or if I was about to touch it. I sometimes hated being this powerful.

Stacey stopped and moved toward the window. "You really have no idea, do you?"

"Please, enlighten me." I moved closer to her.

"This town pretty much didn't exist. Katrina built it as a protection for you with some help from the gods. All the people here were spelled to keep you safe, keep you protected from them. She did well, but ultimately, you cannot hide from them."

"How do you know this?" I queried

"Because I do." She turned back toward me with hate in her eyes.

"Talking time is over. Where shall we do this?"

"The place where it all started, the place where it needs to end."

"I'm not up to date with cryptic villain talk. A little more information, please." I jeered at her, my peppy attitude an attempt to cause her to slip up in some way.

"Walk with me," Stacey demanded as she moved toward the front door. She extended her hand in offering, and I slid mine in. I knew this would not change any outcome that had already been pre-determined.

She pushed the door open, and light burned my eyes as the scenery came into view. The smell of grass and trees filled my senses, a smell that was oddly familiar, but I couldn't place it. It took a moment to register where we had landed.

"We are at Woodhenge?" I questioned, wondering why we had landed here.

"You know, Katrina is quite smart. She cut pieces of this ancient site and put them inside the house for protection. You were always hidden. She even snuck pieces around Shaftesbury, creating a type of dome that they couldn't penetrate."

"Yes, I am aware of just how smart she was, but why are we here? This is where you want me to kick your arse?" I tried to sound cocky to hide the terror I felt inside, the brewing feeling that I was doomed to die today.

"Oh, Larissa, you truly are innocent in all of this. No, we want *Divinitas Portus*, otherwise known as Stonehenge. The portal to the divine. The portal to the gods. They want to watch me kill you, and then I will be given ultimate power and the love of my life."

I could see the location in the distance. The clouds seemed to keep the sun's rays beaming on the sacrificial circle as most people knew it to be. Nobody knew what it was for; there were so many assumptions, but now I knew. A portal to the gods, the location of my possible death. I stopped as Nik pushed through the bond. *'I am coming for you, my love.'* His voice was as clear as day. Stacey turned with a glare on her face.

"Hurry up, I haven't got all day. We need to be there before midday," she mumbled before she stormed away towards my doom.

I took a deep breath. I had to stop thinking this way. I would survive. I would beat Stacey. Nik and I would live happily ever after until the end of time. I had to hold on to that thought. Luce and my mothers gave their lives for me. I had to survive. I had to fight for them. I pushed the negative thoughts aside, filling myself with confidence as Nik doubled the emotion. The man who knew what I needed without ever asking. I walked faster towards our location, overtaking Stacey as I reached the stones. They buzzed with mystical energy, which thrummed in my ears. I could feel the gods as if they stood right beside me. I glanced up at the sky, holding my finger toward them.

"Hey, assholes, fuck you. When I kill Stacey, I am coming for you!" I shouted, knowing my threat would barely scare them, but I needed them to feel my rage at this entire fucked up situation. "Let's do this, Stacey. Are you prepared to die?"

The dark voices returned as I centred myself, focusing on love while I teetered on the edge of control and chaos. I removed my jacket, throwing it purposely onto the stone, believed to be used for sacrifices to the gods.

The fresh air hit me hard as my magic tingled with anticipation, building through my body, giving it the free rein it desired. The darkness grew infecting every part of my system. Stacey's eyes turned black as she waved her hands around in a circle, muttering a spell to herself. Her skin turned white with black poison, like lines carved through her skin.

"What have you done, Stacey?" I asked myself, staring at the evil creature before me, the human now devoid of everything that made her who she was.

She roared as she thrust a ball of light toward me. I pushed up a shield while the ball grew before it hit me. It sparkled with power as it bounced off my shield, barely causing me to lose my balance.

"Is that all you have? Going to have to try harder than that, Stacey. I have the blood of the gods, I transcended to High Priestess, the power from the Aqualis Coven is now mine. I have Nik's blood running through my veins. If you want to kill me, Stacey, it will cost you your own life. Do you understand that?" I wanted her to see reason, that this fight was senseless. I looked to the dark sky once more. "Are you enjoying this? You have manipulated an innocent person to attack me. Come down and do it your fucking self! Her blood will be on your hands!" I shouted to be met with no response.

"This is between us, Larissa." I shook my head. I didn't want to hurt her. She was unwell, her obsession had been twisted.

"Stacey, I don't want to hurt you," I pleaded. I couldn't bear the idea of taking another life. Too much blood had been spilt, and now another innocent person had been twisted for *their* personal gain.

"I was there that day when you killed Juliet. I walked away before you discovered who I was. The power you have shouldn't be allowed. It has to be returned to the earth from whence it came."

"I agree with you. I never wanted this." A storm burst overhead. Stacey's emotions were causing changes to the environment as strong winds tore through the stones, whistling sounds echoing all around. "Stacey, you don't have to listen to them. Just stop, look at what it has done to you."

A burst of lightning shot from her hand, the bolt hitting me in the shoulder, throwing me backwards. The dark voices grew louder, but I would not give them the blood they desired. I glanced at the wound on my shoulder, realising it was a spell to weaken me. I closed my eyes to let the tears fall. I had considered her a friend, and now I would feel her life leave her body.

"Stacey, stop, please." I stood, holding my shoulder as pain burst through my body. I gritted my teeth. She tried to hit me again, but I threw my arm up, blocking her shot. I walked toward her slowly, keeping the shield up as I gained on my enemy. I had to remind myself in this moment that that was exactly who she was. Stacey the friend had died, Stacey the enemy remained. Nik grew closer, his presence comforting through the darkness that wanted to throw its chaos around.

I dropped the shield for a moment, allowing her to shoot another lightning shot toward me. I grabbed it before it had the chance to sink its teeth into my power. I wrapped it around my hand, twisting the spell, and using it to weaken her magic. She dropped to her knees. She had been given all this power but had barely been taught how to use it. She dropped the spell, shooting a burst of water and wind toward me instead. It clouded my vision, and I struggled to see through the rain pelting against my skin. The force of it was like a flurry of tiny knives, poised to slice me open if I dared to let it in.

Fire burst from my hand, and I forced it toward the cloud hanging over my head, burning away the water, leaving nothing remaining before I spun it around Stonehenge, lighting the very space on fire. Flames surrounded me, not burning my clothes or my skin, a form of protection from my father. I stalked toward her as she backed away, trying to hide behind the neolithic stones for protection.

"You cannot hide from me now." My voice sounded demonic as it echoed through my head.

Stacey kept fighting, throwing whatever spells and power toward me, but they melted away before touching the surface. She was trapped. She surrounded herself in a shield, but when my hand touched it, it lowered slightly under the strength of my fire power.

"It makes me laugh, Stacey, that they wanted you to do this. They wanted you to kill me, but here we are." I poked my finger through her shield, watching it burst. "Is this enough to show you just how much they don't care?" I shook my head, taking a few steps back, hoping she would surrender.

"Larissa!" Nik roared befores he walked through the flames, running at me at his full speed. He pulled me into his arms as I placed a shield around us.

"I am here and I am fine. I won't apologise for my deception. I wanted to keep you safe. You can be mad, but I would do it again."

He chuckled, holding me tighter. "My stubborn principessa. I know, I know." He kissed my forehead, I turned back toward Stacey, her rage hanging in the air.

"If I can't have him, no one will." Her power burst toward us with a speed I had never seen before. Nik was thrown backward, hitting the stones, which crumbled from the force.

"Nik!" I screamed. He stood, blood rushing from his wound. "I'm sorry," I whispered to myself as I gave in to the darkness, letting it take over. I knew it wouldn't let me remember what it was about to do. She attacked my mate; she was no longer allowed to live.

CHAPTER 32

DEATH TO THE GODS

Nik

Flashback, January 13ᵗʰ, 2020.

"Do you ever wonder if they watch us?" Aurora asked as the world appeared to be collapsing around us.

"I doubt it. They only care about themselves. Did you manage to convince your parents?"

"No, I gave them until tomorrow. Then I will go and fetch them myself, with or without your permission."

I grunted, doubting she had the nerve to leave. She never had the nerve to do anything.

My lower abdomen ached from the burst of lightning. My back cracked as it healed instantly, but this wound was taking a little more time to heal. Larissa glanced at me, her eyes brighter than ever. She swore she would never kill another person since Juliet and the coven, but she knew in this moment that Stacey would never give up. Her obsession had taken over completely. I pushed through my love for her, hoping she would hold onto that tiny sliver as the darkness consumed her.

I watched her body rise in the air, flames erupting from her hands. The sky grew darker, and I smirked at how marvellous she appeared. I sat down on the ground to watch the spectacle that was my wife, my mate, my love. Stacey cowered as Larissa shot her flames, causing the rock to crumble into dust. Stacey was curled into a ball on the floor, sobbing as Larissa lowered herself and walked over.

"Stand up," Larissa ordered, her eyes flaring red with power. Stacey stood, nodding her head. She was accepting her fate. Larissa shot her hand into her chest, pulling her close before she ripped her heart out of her body, burning it to ash and watching it float away in the wind before Stacey dropped to the floor, the last moment of her life flashing before her eyes.

I stood, and my body ached as I walked over to my mate, taking her hand in mine. "I am here, my love, my light, my reason." She slowly turned to look at me, her eyes flashing before the familiar green returned, and her body relaxed. She began to turn, but I pulled her back. "No, it's not worth looking. It is done. She will never harm us again."

"Nik, will it never end? They want me dead." She pointed to the sky, knowing the gods above us would have watched the scene unfold. I kissed her forehead as the sky parted, and rays of light shot down from the heavens.

"Don't let go of me. Whatever happens, you hold onto my hand at all times. Do you understand?" Warmth surrounded us, and I felt lighter as our bodies floated in the sky toward them. The ones who had been pulling the strings for centuries, the ones we could finally confront.

"Nik." Her voice shook with fear as she tightened her grip on my waist.

"I love you, Larissa."

"I love you more than anything, don't you ever forget that." I moved the hair from her face, kissing her luscious lips, filling our bond with every inch of my love for her.

"Oh, here they are." A voice sounded as I allowed my eyes to adjust to the brightness of the room while Larissa buried her head deeper into my chest. We were in their temple. The familiar columns that Larissa had spoken about from her dream. The ethereal figures were covered in shadows as my eyes struggled to adjust to the brightness behind them.

"What do you want?" my voice bellowed as I portrayed strength to these vindictive creatures who had abandoned my brother and me.

"You will remember your place, son." The familiarity rang through my head. Centuries had passed since I last heard his voice.

"Hello, Mars," I quipped, not bothering to look at him as I searched Larissa's face when I felt her heart fill with sadness.

"I think I deserve a little more respect than that, don't I?" he asked in his deep voice as I glanced up to see the man whose seed had fathered Roman and me. The same dark hair and tanned skin, he appeared well over seven feet tall with muscles that defied belief. I had his face, while Roman had his muscular form.

"You abandoned me to a life of immortality. I begged you for help, and I heard nothing. You deserve no respect from me."

A signature laugh filled my ears as I noticed what Larissa had been fixated on.

"Oh, he has you there, Mars bar." Pluto chuckled as he popped a grape into his mouth, lounging on a golden chaise, looking every bit the god that he was.

"Shut up, peasant," my father snapped at him, which elicited a smile.

Pluto strolled over, taking Larissa's hand and running his hand over her face. She gasped. Devastation reverberated between the bond, a pain so extreme hitting my heart. I could barely breathe from the emotion that floated between us. Realisation covered her face as her father nodded at her. A silent conversation that I wished to know.

"Brother, remember your place. You are here out of respect in this situation." Jupiter's voice boomed over the whispers between the other gods. His golden hair was shorter than I remembered. I studied him while he watched the interaction between Pluto and my mate.

"Oh, shut up with your false niceties. We both know why I am here. Yet again, I get screwed by the lot of you, only this time my daughter is the one getting fucked over. She never asked for this, and yet out of the two choices that you have, you selected the one that ends with her death. You disgust me!" he spat at the ground, storming over to his best friend. "You could let her live."

The words filled my head. 'Death...Let her live.' Pluto argued with Jupiter as Larissa took my hands, forcing me to look at her.

"This isn't our end, Nik. Our story will have its happy ending, but that isn't today. Today...today is the day that I die." Her voice croaked as her heart beat faster, filling with an immense sadness that brought tears to my eyes.

"No, Larissa, we can fight this. We can do it tomorrow. There is nothing that we cannot achieve," I begged, my heart breaking. I didn't want to lose her. I would rather die fighting than risk her accepting her death.

"It was because of petty jealousy that my father was cursed, and now I am to be the sacrifice. You and I were but a pawn in their ridiculous game. Nerio was a vindictive bitch who did what she could to stay in power. She never cared for anything or anyone."

I pulled her into my arms. "Let's fight this together. I would rather die fighting with you than accept that we can't change our circumstances." She glanced over her shoulder at her father, who had tears in his eyes. He nodded with a small smirk as she grabbed my head, kissing my lips.

"One last stand." She cleared her throat as she took a step around me, my hand on her shoulder as she stood taller before the gods who had manipulated her entire life.

"You." Her finger pointed toward the goddess who started all this. Nerio. Jupiter moved to protect his son's wife.

"Brother, let it happen. We know it needs to end. This is justice. Her time is due for all the mischief she caused, for all the blood she spilt, for the treachery she brought upon us all by manipulating Katrina and killing my wife." I watched as his face softened at Pluto's words. He made sense; she had caused all of this, centuries of fighting, centuries of bullshit. All because of her.

Mars stood taller than ever, pushing out his chest to exert his power. I had to laugh as I held up my hand to clutch my chest.

"You think that will intimidate me? That shows just how little you know about me, Father. Your wife is dying today. I do not care for the consequences. Today, she dies." I moved to stand beside Larissa, my monster wanting to rip Nerio and Mars to pieces.

"We both know that you cannot kill a god." Nerio was beautiful, her dark hair down to her waist. With her beautiful gown, with golden threads on the bottom and around the waist, she had an otherworldly beauty. A serene look constantly graced her face, but hid her sinister actions underneath.

Jupiter walked over to his son, and Mars's face fell. He knew an order from his father had to be followed. He knew that he had no choice. He didn't bother to glance at his wife as he moved to stand beside Pluto, who pulled out a knife and sliced his throat within mere seconds.

"I have been dying to do that for centuries." He licked the blood from the knife before putting it back in his pocket.

"Brother!" Jupiter yelled at him as he rushed to his son's aid.

"We both know he will heal, and it isn't my fault he wasn't fast enough to act on my actions. The God of War, right? Maybe that should be changed to the God of Snails with his slow reactions." He chuckled at his own joke, and I rolled my eyes. "I am a little insulted. I taught him strategy and battle techniques. Maybe he needs a session in Hell." Pluto's eyes sparkled at the idea of torturing my father, and I would admit, even I liked that thought.

I turned my gaze back towards Nerio, the one whose presence had woven so much agony into my life. She stood there, her usually serene expression twisted, her eyes wide, her lips parted with a faint tremor. Her hands, which normally rested with quiet grace at her side, trembled, her fingers curling into fists with an erratic rhythm. The air grew thicker between us as I waited for her inevitable surrender. I took a step closer, her posture stiffening as her eyes darted around the room. I could see the panic in her face as she weighed the choices of running or staying. The mask she held on her face was cracking with each passing second. Her chest rose and fell too quickly, and I noticed her aura flicker, dimming as her husband and all other friends had abandoned her.

Sparks erupted from Larissa's hand as she rose in the air. I had to keep my head clear. I had to feel for her through the bond to ensure she didn't lose control, so her darkness would not take the last shreds of her humanity. Golden flames ran up her arms as Nerio took a step backward.

"Don't run now, you started this. Let's finish it. You are *the* Goddess of War, prove it." Her voice sounded thicker as Pluto walked over, his arms crossed, his lips turning up in a small smile.

"She is magnificent. I created that." He nudged my arm and I snarled at him. "Oh, grow up, Remus." He walked away, taking a seat to watch his daughter.

Nerio's body erupted in golden armour as a spear appeared in her hand. I rose to float beside Larissa, watching as she closed her eyes to centre herself. I pushed love through the bond, and she nodded. I could feel that she was crossing that threshold, so I had to use my powers to keep her in control. The power to affect a person's mood. It was only minuscule in comparison to my strength and speed, but it came in handy during times of negotiation.

I lowered myself once more and moved to stalk Nerio, making my way to attack her from behind. Her focus was solely on Larissa, who spun her hands in an intricate weave, making tiny knives take shape. Nerio created a shield in preparation. Out of the corner of my eye, I saw Mars move. He was up and awake, and I was ready as he charged at me. Of course, the man would attack at this time. Larissa pushed her tiny knives at the goddess, cutting through the shield and piercing her body, with some just slicing her skin. I spun around, grabbing my father around the neck and snapping it in seconds.

"You are right, Pluto, not that smart." I winked at him, finally in agreement with the god who cursed me centuries ago. He laughed which made Jupiter glare at him once more.

Larissa floated back to the floor with a look of satisfaction on her face.

"This isn't over, little girl," Nerio spat through her gritted teeth as the tiny cuts on her body healed. I wondered why she appeared so smug when she had barely caused her any harm.

"Oh, I am aware, but the best part is…" She moved her hand as Nerio's body flinched in pain. The tiny pieces of gold moving through her body glowed as they reached the surface. She snapped her finger as one of them burst out of her body, and she screamed. "You thought that was all I've got. That is funny. That is just my little torture. I see you have weapons, let me join you."

She snapped her fingers, suddenly holding a sword in her hand. It glowed red with a golden handle and sparked as she twirled it in her hands.

"I suppose the sword lessons from my father in Hell have prepared me for this moment. Didn't they use to name swords during your time? I think I will name this *Nerio Striker.*"

Larissa's eyes burned brighter than ever before, her power surrounding her. It almost appeared like wings behind her. My mate. I stood with pride before stepping forward, but her head snapped in my direction, and she shook it.

"This is my fight. I want to kill this fucking bitch for thinking she could meddle with my life and get away with it," she said, her voice deeper than usual.

"Larissa, hold onto love, don't give in to all of it. I am here with you." My voice was even and in control as I pushed a calmness through the area. Pluto stood beside me.

"You need to remember she is the daughter of the Devil, she will always have darkness. Where do you think the whispers came from?"

"I thought it was from you guys." I motioned to those around us. Pluto shook his head.

"No, her monster speaks to her as does yours. It is why you are matched so perfectly this time. We only whispered on a few occasions, but more often than most, it was her own evil. It spoke to keep her safe." He looked way too happy, and I was reminded that he truly was the Devil. He found joy in the darkest parts of the world.

The clouds grew darker as thunder bellowed, the air growing thinner as lightning floated through the clouds. I glanced at Jupiter, who shook his head. She was manipulating every part of the world around her. Rain started to pelt hard, but not on the area surrounding her, Nerio, and me. The remaining gods were not impressed, so Jupiter threw up his own force to protect the rest of them. With every strike of their swords, more lightning shot through the sky, and fire burst toward Nerio from Larissa's sword. She ripped another tiny knife from her system. She did this for another five strikes.

She laughed. "Not so tough now, are you? You were right to fear me, you were right to try and kill me, but ultimately, it is only going to end with your death." She threw the sword to the ground as she flapped her arms, conjuring electricity into her hands, rolling it into a ball. "I've had enough of this. I want you dead, and I want to memorise your screams before I take my final moments and break the curse that you selfishly helped to implement. All because you feared someone taking your power. Power that you didn't deserve." Her voice roared through the space.

She shot the bolt of lightning, and Nerio's body flew backwards as Larissa conjured more, standing over her, forcing the current upon her. It shot through her body as she screamed, the tiny leftover gold knives glowing before detonating in mini explosions under the skin. Nerio lay on the ground, black blotches appearing on her body, panting as her heart started to slow. Larissa waved her hands, and Nerio's arms were torn from her body, her legs next as she lay there, just a torso with a head. I walked over, thrusting my hand into her chest and ripping her heart out before handing it to my mate. She blew on the bloody heart in her hand, and it burst into flames. Nerio's entire torso and her scattered limbs were engulfed in the same golden flames. She *killed* a god.

I stood in disbelief while Pluto cheered before Larissa's body collapsed.

———

She finally woke after some time, her eyes back to their beautiful green, her hair with the same red tinge to it. I moved it from her face, pressing my lips to her forehead.

"Nik." I knew what was about to come out of her mouth.

"Larissa, you just murdered a god. We can beat this curse." I spoke softly, not wanting to admit defeat, however inevitable it seemed.

"It will never stop the reason this curse began, it will only postpone the inevitable." Her hand touched my face, a gesture filled with so much emotion and tenderness that tears welled in my eyes.

"This time is different, I know it." I had to look away from her. The idea of taking her life…It would destroy me. "We won, we beat Nerio. She was always against us."

"Nik, it *is* different. Out of all my deaths, we never realised the most important one, the only one to break the spell. With blood, the curse began, with blood, the curse must end."

"Larissa, I don't understand. What does that mean?" I couldn't understand the riddle.

She touched my face. "You sacrificed my unborn child; you sacrificed their blood. As their blood was linked to mine, it caused a loop of never-ending death. You have to…" Tears fell down her cheeks. "You have to end it, Nik. *You* have to spill the blood…" I shook my head, taking a step back. "My blood."

"*No!*" I shouted. "You don't know what you are asking."

"I know exactly what I am asking, Nik, but it has to happen, or we will never escape this curse. You have to…"

"Don't you finish that sentence, Larissa. Don't you dare say those words." I shouted, pointing at her in a mix of fear and anger.

"Whether or not I say them, they are still true. It has to happen, and I am so sorry that this is all on your shoulders. I wish more than anything to not put you through this, but it is the only way to move forward. I have accepted this. I don't want it to be true, but it *will* happen. The choice of whether or not…" She paused, steadying her shaky breath and wiping her tears away. She grabbed my handkerchief from my pocket, wiping the tears that fell from my own eyes. "Let him do it, Nik. Give him control and let it happen. I already forgive you because I know that you are doing this for our love to con—to continue, for us to…to finally have our happy ending…The one where we watch our children run around in a field…our son, strong and intelligent like you, while our daughter, fierce and beautiful, and both stubborn like their parents."

I leant my forehead against hers, the tears continued to fall as she wiped them away. "I fought for you for centuries, and this is how we end. This is how it has to end. I have to kill the only reason I had to live, the one who brought light to my world, who reminded me of who I am."

"I know it isn't fair, but it has to happen."

"How are you okay with this?" A pit formed in my stomach at the thought of taking her life.

"I am not okay with this, but I want us to have our ending, the one we deserve. The one they don't get to control, the one we were supposed to have from the beginning. This is all their fault."

"What? How?" I glanced up at Pluto, who nodded.

"Ask your father, it all started with him."

I pushed Larissa behind me, storming toward him. "Explain this now. Why do I have to kill the love of my life for you?" I demanded, my anger flaring as the sky darkened slightly. His eyes bore into mine, but I would not give up on this. I wanted to know why I had to lose my golden rose today because of the man who had left me to live this horror.

Pluto walked over, pulling me into his arms and holding me tightly. I closed my eyes, slowly accepting that in however many minutes, my heart would no longer beat. My soul would leave my body and float to Hell. Shouting erupted between Mars and Nik as my father kissed my forehead.

"I am so proud of you. So many would fall apart, but you stand here filled with pride, ready to tackle it all. You are your mother's daughter."

Tears fell harder and faster until I choked on them. "I needed to hear that. At least I might be able to see her soon. I hold onto the thought that I will not be alone in the darkness. I'm terrified of what it will feel like."

"You only need to focus on the love that you and Nik share, the love of your family. Push aside the dark thoughts and focus on the light that is within you. Don't give them the show they want. I love you, and I am sorry it has come to this." I nodded, sucking up the tears and stepping back and around him as I slid my hand into Nik's.

He paused, looking down at me, his red eyes flicking back to their beautiful blue as I squeezed his hand tighter.

"You are no different from me!" Mars shouted at him. "You chastise me for protecting my wife, but then she touches you and *you* back down."

"Because looking at her, I realise you aren't worth my time. I would rather spend the last moments I have with my wife, staring at her incomprehensible beauty, than argue with a man who abandoned me. A man who was too weak to take care of his mistakes, leaving my mother, brother, and me to fend for ourselves. Did you know she waited for you? She would pray to you every night, begging you to leave Nerio, to admit how you truly felt for her. I listened to her cry for you, and you ignored her. You kicked her out like she was a piece of shit."

"That is because she was. She dared seduce a god. She is lucky that she was allowed to live. Her curse could have been worse," Juno muttered.

"Worse? Worse? You truly are a fucking bitch!" I shouted at her. "Your and Nerio's pettiness cost so many people their lives, and you have no remorse. You manipulated whoever you wanted for your advantage. My mother asked for your help, and you twisted something so innocent when you discovered that Nik would be free. You set out to cause him continual harm. You want this power back. You won't get it. I will make sure before I take my last breath that I will make it hurt for you, for all of you." My emotions threatened to spill out, but I had to be strong. My father was right. Falling into a heap would do nothing. I spun around to Jupiter. "You are the worst of them all. You let this happen. You allowed this deceptive behaviour to continue, you allowed your best friend, your brother's wife, to be murdered, and you did not even think to punish those responsible."

"Careful, child, know your place," Jupiter warned as he stood taller than usual, his golden hair flowing down his back. The sky roared with thunder.

"Oh, I'm trembling. You have no spine. Your words mean nothing." Juno appeared behind Jupiter. "Stop hiding behind your husband! You also wanted me dead. You've done all of this for my blood. Come stand front and centre." She rolled her eyes, and I felt my darkness take over at the disrespect from her. She had been the cause of so many deaths, and she didn't care. I conjured a dagger, throwing it at her, and watched as it stabbed her directly in the womb. "Now that's fate playing her hand." Blood trickled to the floor as Jupiter rushed over to her, causing a fuss over a tiny wound that would heal in seconds. I turned back to Nik, touching his face and feeling his warm skin under my palm, the tickle of his perfectly manicured beard.

"Our words mean nothing to them. Save your breath and look at me."

He hung his head low. "Larissa, I don't know if I can do this."

"You can and you will. No matter what happens, I will always be right here." I pointed to his heart, and his hand clasped over it. "I'll never leave you. I'll be watching your every moment as you save the world and restore peace. Do me a favour, will you?"

"Stubborn as always, wanting something even after she has died."

"Take plenty of photos and videos for me. Imagine I'm right there with you. Share the experiences with me."

"What's the point?" Nik's voice was so deflated. Hurting him only made this so much harder, but it had to be done.

"The point is to be happy, to enjoy life. I'll never leave you because I'll be in every beat of your heart and every breath you take. Can you do that?"

"Larissa…"

"No, I want you to promise me that you'll do it. I know we will find each other again, if not in this life, then in the next, but don't wait for me. Don't search for me. Just live and be happy. You've spent centuries revolving your life around me, and it's time you did something for you," I blubbered, trying desperately to keep it together, but I struggled with the raw pain I could feel from him.

Nik dropped to his knees, crying and shaking his head. "I can't do this." I could barely breathe as my body registered how much this was destroying his soul.

"Yes, you can, I'm right here, Nik. In your arms, right where I have always belonged."

I wrapped my arms around his neck, my fingers trembling as he inhaled deeply, his breath warm against my skin. His lips brushed along my jaw to the crook of my neck, and then he groaned. The sharp press of his fangs sank into me, and my body shuddered in response. It was as if his love poured into the very bite that would take my life. Soft and tender at first, it grew more desperate, more monstrous. A guttural growl rumbled through his chest, vibrating against my body, pulling me closer, forcing my neck and body into an unnatural angle.

I closed my eyes, the overwhelming weight of memories crashing over me. I could feel everything—the sweetness of his love, the torment of his bloodlust. Every moment of our lives together flashed through my mind, vivid and raw, like a film reel spinning faster and faster until it blurred, then slowed. It began with *my* life, the one I had before him, before the curse. Then, like a tidal wave, it pulled me backward through time, through every incarnation we had shared.

My heartbeat slowed, its rhythm faltering as my breath became shallow. I clung to him, my body no longer my own, lost in the beauty and the agony of what we were, what we had been. His bite grew harsher, his desperation more frantic as I saw us, young and innocent, before the weight of this curse had consumed us. The first time I had laid eyes on him, the instant I knew my soul could never be whole without him. I had loved him then, and I loved him now. I would love him forever, even with what came next.

A soft smile curled at my lips, bittersweet, as the pull of death began to claim me.

With what little strength I had left, I whispered the words that felt both like an end and a beginning. "I return these powers to the earth from whence they came."

And as I spoke, my magic dispersed in a golden shimmer, cascading into the air, vanishing around us. And with it, my love, my memories, my very essence—drifting away like a final, fragile breath.

"No!" a scream echoed as my ears grew silent. Nik let go, his black and blue eyes staring at me, devoid of emotion, to stop his suffering.

"Thank you," I whispered, touching his monster's face and feeling myself fall, beginning my descent into Hell. "I...will... always...be...with...you.

CHAPTER 34

YOU WIN

Nik

Flashback, January 14th, 2020.

I watched Aurora fly from the balcony. She was stupid and rash, and refused to listen when I told her that the bomb would kill her, the radiation would melt her body. I flew after her, shouting at her. She blocked off the bond, and it remained silent as I watched her body fall into the ocean. My mate, dead once more. The snapping of our bond, gone in an instant, as if it meant nothing.

"SHE DIDN'T! NO WAY! THAT MISCHIEVOUS LITTLE WITCH. HOW dare she do that? She had no right!" Juno shouted as I held the love of my life in my arms, her lifeless body, her heart no longer beating. I could no longer feel her soul. My heart had been ripped from my chest, the pain indescribable, a crushing feeling of finality settling in. I had killed my mate. I killed the love of my life, the woman that I had sacrificed everything for.

I stood. Noticing the power of her blood flowing through me, I glared at the gods who took the most precious thing in my world. My senses were so heightened, I heard every shuffle of clothing and shifting of feet. I wanted to tear them apart, but I waited for them to move, any opportunity to take something from them as they had done to me.

A hand slammed onto my shoulder, and I spun, taking their neck in my hand, lifting them from the ground.

"Careful, Remus, remember who the enemy is," Pluto said, a hint of fear in his voice as he pointed to those behind me.

"Do not forget that it was you who cursed me from the start. If that curse never began, she would still be alive." I growled, bringing him closer, wanting to taste the power that flowed through his veins. My monster almost had total control. I didn't do as she asked. I wanted her to feel my love for her as she took her last breath.

"Without the curse, Larissa never would have been born, and you would be dead as all wolves are who find their mates. You know this. Once a wolf finds their mate, their immortality is gone. You would have lived a normal, human life. Did you ever stop to consider that maybe Larissa was your true mate? A mate is supposed to push you to be a better person. Did any of the others do that?" My head waged a war between logic and anger, one part wanting to listen, the other wanting to rage and kill them all. Pluto put his hand on me, twisting my fingers to let him go.

"Until the hour calls for it, do not seek her. Hold her memories, but let her go. Honour her words, Nik, live *your* life. Do what brings you joy. I am proud of you, and I am sorry for the pain that I caused you. It wasn't until her life that I realised my malicious ways had to stop. It was the only reason I brought her to Hell, to save her life. I hope one day you can forgive me." He walked away as her blood spilled onto the floor. Jupiter banged his trident on the ground as the last remnants of her body disappeared.

"It is done, Remus. We shall leave you in peace." His voice bellowed.

"What peace do I have without love?" I muttered as I was sent back to the stones. Stacey's body was still lying on the floor. I stepped over her, leaving her to waste away. I glanced over my shoulder, watching her body disappear into the ground, another sacrifice for the gods. They would enjoy that.

Larissa's magic pulsed through me, causing my beast to rage in my head. Every part of me screamed to numb the pain, to force away the grief that ate at my soul. I found it impossible. I *didn't* want to feel any of this. I wished to be empty, hollow, untouched by the pain that spread through my body like a poison. I could feel myself drowning under the weight of it all. **"You win."**

The words were barely a whisper. My voice broke as I closed my eyes, tears pooling through my closed lids. *I let go.* I let the beast inside take control, and with it, I knew the devastation that would occur. There would be no coming back from this.

CHAPTER 35

KEEPING THE PROMISE

Roman

I couldn't relax since Nik called me and asked me to meet him at the portal. I knew what it meant, but I hesitated. I left my brother in the lurch. I had never been terrified to run into battle, but knowing I had something to live for was what hurt more than anything. I glanced at Mimi, still asleep on the bed. She had allowed me to stay the night, but stipulated no sex. I had yet to question her motives on the night of the monster attack. I wanted her to trust me before I put another strain on our relationship, and I was slowly breaking down her walls. I had waited centuries for her, so I could wait a little longer for her to open up. My wolf grew eager to mark her, wanting to mate with her. I couldn't deny how much I wanted that life.

I walked through Mimi's tiny apartment kitchen. It was not designed for a person as tall as me. I flicked on the coffee machine, constantly checking my phone, hoping to hear an update from my brother. I watched milk froth and pour itself into the cup before making another. I returned to the bedroom, noticing Mimi had just woken, her thick caramel hair in a messy bun. A small smile spread over her face as I registered her joy.

"Did you think I had left you?" I asked, quirking my eyebrow at her.

"Ah…oh…no, I just woke up and forgot you were here." Her cheeks blushed red as I smiled and looked away from her to check my phone once again.

"What is it? You seem stressed." I peered up at her curiously as I took a sip of my coffee, her eyes watching my bicep move as she perved at my near-naked body.

"You seem to be enjoying the view. Why did you say no sex, again?" I quipped as I stood, making my way to the window and looking outside as my wolf grew suddenly alert.

"We…argh…just can't. You weren't that good, anyway." She pushed the blankets off her as I noticed the overcast sky. It wasn't abnormal for London, but the odd formation of the clouds was, and the lightning, too, that lit up the sky but did not touch the ground.

"Fucking hell, Nik," I muttered, closing the window and pulling out my phone to call my brother. It went directly to voicemail.

"What is it?" she asked, walking over and putting her hand on my bicep. My wolf moaned at the softness of her touch against my skin. The area tingled. I didn't answer, so she opened the curtains.

"That…isn't…normal." She hesitated between each word. "What does that mean?" she asked as the fear through our bond almost crippled me.

"Mimi, sit down." She ignored my request. "SIT. DOWN!" I ordered, and she stepped backwards till she dropped onto the bed. "The world is bigger than you know. Gods exist. That," I pointed to the sky, "is Jupiter. There is a disagreement between the gods and…and my brother and his mate."

"Larissa? She is so innocent, what could she have done against the gods?" she asked as I dropped to my knees before her.

"She was born, and it was never supposed to happen. Larissa's mother created her to break an ancient curse, but didn't realise what she had created in the process. The gods were not happy and, as such, planned to kill Larissa."

"What? We have to help her. She is not the person I expected her to be. She has a heart of gold, she…she…" I put my hands on Mimi's cheeks to stop her rambling.

"Mimi, I…" Blackness crossed my vision as searing pain tore through my chest. An intense pain I had never felt before in my life, the pain of a thousand deaths overwhelming me.

'Roman, take care of your brother. Don't forget your promise to me. I will see you again.' Larissa's soft voice echoed through my head before it disappeared. She was gone. She was dead.

"I need to go." I stood, holding my chest, grabbing my shirt and making my way to the door. My brother just killed his mate, the love of his life. I had to keep my promise to her, the last thing she had ever asked of me. I needed to stay true to her and her memory. She never spoke about the possibility of returning, but I hoped there was a way she could. I hoped this was not the end for my brother.

"Roman, stop! What the hell was that? You cannot just leave! You partially turned into a wolf."

"I'm sorry, Mimi. I have to go."

"Roman, is it Larissa?" I spun to look at my mate one more time, tears filling my eyes.

"Yes. I have to go to my brother. He needs me. I promised her. I'm sorry. I will call you soon. I love you." I slammed the door shut, rushing toward the elevator while I fastened the buttons on my shirt.

"I love you, too." Her voice was soft on the other side of the door, but I heard it clearly. "I wish I could tell you the truth. I'm sorry." I had to know the answers, but I knew Nik's monster would have taken over. He would have buried himself to hide from the pain of his actions.

I found my way to Stonehenge, my heart pounding in my chest, only to see a sight I never wished for. Among the ancient stones was what remained of my brother. His skin was grey with lines of black poison running through him, his features twisted by the monster that took control. His eyes, once filled with warmth, were now consumed with embers of fury. A rage that wanted to tear the world apart. His mate was dead, never to return, a curse broken. But his grief had been transformed into something far darker—something I knew deep inside. The anger he had now wasn't connected to loss, but more to vengeance towards any who caused him harm.

I hoped to contain the destruction that was coming for this world. But I knew some things would never be the same again. This world and Nik would never be the same again.

Chapter 36

THE TRUTH

Roman

A week had passed since Larissa's death, and I spent that time finding a replacement for her at Refresh Marketing. Nik had been hunting at night and staying dormant during the day. A typical vampire monster. I could still feel that last shred of his humanity holding on, but I had no clue how to bring my brother back. I spent most nights getting no more than three hours of sleep while searching for him. I had found him on a few occasions, but in this evil form, he was faster than normal. I knew that the more he ran from me, the more his monster knew I could bring him back.

I sat in Larissa's office as Mimi entered, and I understood the office flirtation that Nik and Larissa had. My wolf loved knowing Mimi was only a few metres away, wearing a tight skirt, and every time I walked past, I felt her desire increase. I really wanted to fuck her in the conference room, but I was here for my brother, not for my dick, as much as it ached to bury itself inside her. I busied myself in the finances, paying whichever bills I could in advance to keep the company afloat. I heard a commotion outside the door, and I stood, swinging it open.

I saw a man grabbing Mimi by the arm and pulling her toward him.

"You will come with me *now!*" he ordered as she tried to break free of his grasp. I watched with intrigue, neither of them noticing me. She kicked her leg out, connecting with his groin as I chuckled and beamed with pride at my mate. I admired her fierceness and her fight. I never had to worry about her. She knew how to protect herself. He stood, raising his fist, which I grabbed in a flash, my eyes flaring in rage.

"I think it is time that you leave." My voice strained as my wolf howled inside, wanting to rip the stranger to pieces for attempting to harm her.

"Roman, stop." I ignored her plea as I stared down at the stranger before me. "Roman, it isn't worth it. Just stop." It was absolutely worth it. He needed to learn his place, and it would be six feet under if he dared to touch her again. "ROMAN!" she shouted.

My head snapped in her direction. "He laid his hands on you," I said, tilting my head to look at her.

"I am fine, just drop it." She hung her head as I glared back at the mystery man.

"That's right, wolf. She is fine. Time to drop it." He wiped his nose, and I registered the cocaine on his sleeve. His cocky demeanour needed to be brought down a few notches.

I swung my fist, connecting to his nose. "I believe I just dropped it." I shrugged, spinning back toward the office to call security.

"I will fucking kill you. I don't care if you are the Alpha. The supernatural world is coming to an end, and I cannot wait for you all to fucking burn. The People's Revolution are coming for you all." I knew this to be true, but she had told me she left them. Mimi's gaze met mine, and I shook my head. "Yeah, you have been fucking the enemy. We have appreciated all the intel."

I roared. Screw the rules. "Leave this office now, or so help me, I will be the monster that you believe me to be. I cannot wait to see what you taste like." I licked my lips as the man grabbed Mimi's hand. "Let go of my mate." My claws and fangs extended as hair sprouted over my hands.

"She is mine," he snarled. "Why do you think she hasn't fucked you yet? She is getting the D from someone else." My heart ached, but I kept my monster present to avoid him thinking he had gotten under my skin. Mimi took a step back, putting her hands up. I felt the sadness that flickered between our bond. It might still have been the early stages, but I could sense intense emotions. "Tell him the truth, Mimi. Tell him."

She covered her face with her hands. I knew she had secrets, but I never expected it to be this. "You are relieved of your position, Mimi. Pack your things and leave." I didn't want to see her. I pulled out my phone, wanting to call the one person who would be able to perk me up, to help me see the brighter side or find a solution. He wouldn't answer. I needed my brother. I needed Larissa.

"FUCK!" I yelled as I threw my phone across the room, watching it break into tiny pieces on the wall. I threw the desk over, breaking the chair with a simple kick of my leg. I let this woman in, I had been inside her, I protected her. And this. I stormed from the office, locking the door behind me. "You are all dismissed, go home," I ordered as I pressed the door to the elevator. I drove home feeling detached from the world. My support system was gone.

———

When I parked the car, I saw Mimi sitting on the step outside my apartment. She raised her head, tears and smudged makeup covered her beautiful, soft features.

I watched her stand. "Don't, Mimi, just don't. I have lost enough this week, and I can't handle anything else."

"I know, it is why I am here. I have to tell you the truth…"

I pushed past her, ignoring her words as I slammed the door in her face.

"Roman, please," she begged through the door. "I love you. I can't explain what I feel for you. I hate it, but I love the feelings that rush through me the moment that I know you are near. I love the way my body tingles from your closeness, how my heart has never felt fuller. You are a monster, but all I see is you, Roman Silvia, the man who would never hurt me. The man that I have continually let down." She banged against the door. "Please, Roman, I love you, let me explain. Give me the chance to make this right."

I flung the door open. "For what? For you to betray me again? I lost my brother and my best friend while you used me. We made love, Mimi. I gave you a piece of me. How can I ever trust another word that comes out of your mouth?" My wolf whined when he saw her shaking from the cold, noticing she didn't have a jacket.

"Where is your jacket?" I asked, annoyed at this bond. Part of me wanted to hate her, but a bigger part wanted her safe.

"I ran from him. I told him the truth, that I love you, and I refused to be part of their group. Please believe me. I'm begging you to believe me. They will kill me." She fell to the floor, wrapping her arms around her body for comfort. I picked her up, carrying her inside and lighting the fire. I placed milk and chocolate into the microwave before handing it to her.

I removed my leather jacket and sat down on the couch near her.

She smiled. "How do you always know exactly what I want?" she asked as she took a sip, beaming with happiness.

"We are mates. I know everything that makes you happy." I couldn't be distracted by her beautiful smile and the way her eyes expressed her every emotion. She was my enemy. I kept my eyes focused on the flames to avoid her beauty or those hazel eyes that made me want to come undone for her.

"Roman, look at me," she pleaded. I shook my head and stood, making my way to the window. "I know I hurt you. I know I should have trusted you. I knew it deep down, but I...I have been hurt in the past, and sometimes, when something feels too good to be true, it normally is...but with you, it isn't. You are too perfect to comprehend." My body registered hers closing in, her arms wrapping around my waist.

"I want to know everything, Mimi. If you wish for me to trust you, I want every secret, every story. You are to give me every single part of you. Do you understand?" I turned to look at her, those hazel eyes with the smallest amount of gold flickering from the flames lighting the room. My heart melted for this girl as I pulled her into my chest.

"I swear it, Roman, I will lay myself bare for you tonight."

She sat on the couch and tapped the space beside her. I sat down, lifting her legs over my own. Her feet were frozen, so I rubbed them with my warm hands.

"I was an orphan. My parents were murdered by vampires. They had hidden me under the stairs in a panic room. I still remember their screams as they begged them to stop. My father pleaded with them to take him and leave my mother, but they drained them both dry. They never found me. I stayed there for two days. I was terrified to move, and I dreaded opening the door and seeing their bodies. I knew somebody would figure it out and come looking. I remember the officer telling me not to look, but I had to see it. I had to know just how dangerous these creatures were. We had always been told that humans were safe, but their bodies were ripped to pieces. I carried that hate with me for years before I ran into a man named Peter." The hairs on my body went up. "He told me there was another way. He showed me TPR, The People's Revolution. He told me their aim and how they had created a family within it." She sighed, shaking her head. "I didn't realise they were a cult, that they twisted everything to suit their narrative. I doubted them, but ultimately, we had the same goal. The destruction of vampires. It wasn't until Larissa that I knew the truth. I understood. She was no fool, and her love for Nik was endless. She had no fear or apprehension, and she would show just how human he was. When I saw you that day at the wedding, the tingle started. I asked what it could mean, and TPR warned me that I had been spelled, that the vampires were trying to turn me. The more you came around, the more I had to know you better. The voice in my head kept telling me not to trust you because I knew you were a wolf. TPR know all the supernaturals of the world, but your kind eyes and the way you always made me feel, you were never a monster. My heart waged a war; it wanted to listen to reason, but it could only focus on the way you made me feel. I had never felt that level of safety or calm before, but when I am with you, I feel complete. I feel whole."

"That doesn't tell me much about you." I got up from the couch, pouring myself a whiskey and finishing it in a gulp.

"I told you everything," she quipped back, standing up to confront me.

"You told me nothing about *you*, just some story of your parents' death and getting mixed up in that world. How old were you? What happened to other foster families? Give me something to make me believe that you want this, and it is not a trick because you were *fucking* another man while mated to me. Do you know what that does to a wolf? Do you know how much that *fucking* hurts that the woman I love has been getting it from someone else?"

She cried again, tears falling down her cheeks. "I never had a choice."

I threw my glass across the room. "Tell me why! I will protect you until my dying day, but I have to know why you deserve it because at this stage, I would prefer to reject you than deal with any more heartache. I have had enough in my long life." My anger rose at the very thought of someone else touching her, and the images in my head of her moans.

"Please, sit down." She didn't fear my beast. "Please, I swear it."

"I would prefer to stand. You sit and tell me all of it, or so help me. Mimi, I will…" I couldn't finish the sentence as it wasn't true.

"My parents were murdered when I was five, young enough to be manipulated. I was placed in the foster system, and I went through three different homes. Each one filled with different types of abuse—physical, emotional and…" She didn't finish, but I knew. "The last foster home is where I met Wade and Sandra. I knew them to be my parents from the age of thirteen, and they were picture-perfect. Everyone loved them. But they had secrets. Looking back now, I realise they were slowly grooming me to be the perfect soldier. They would manipulate my thinking of fellow vampires at school, telling me how dangerous they could be and reminding me of my parents' deaths. When I turned eighteen, I conveniently ran into a man called Peter. He had flair and big dick energy, and I fell for his charms. I was stupid and naïve when I brought him home to meet my parents. I discovered they knew each other, and they made it seem normal. I should have known back then. I should have run away, but it was the stability I craved. Peter spewed his hate towards all supernatural creatures before I had to…I had to kill one to be initiated into TPR. She was the same age as me. I remember her screams as I stabbed her through the heart. I washed my hands for days, still seeing the blood…" More tears fell, and my heart felt heavy. I wanted to hold her, but I needed more. She shook her head to compose herself. "I knew then that I had to escape, but Wade had resources, Peter had resources, they have their fingers in everything. After initiation, I was brought into their sacred space." She rolled her eyes. "It showed the vampire hierarchy. I remember it was the day that I saw your face for the first time. You were drinking a coffee with your brother and walking through London. Peter told me of your wolf nature, but you caused something to stir inside me. Your eyes. I became entranced by your strong jaw and how handsome your face was. I dreamed about you that night, and I pictured your hands on my body, touching me in ways that I had never experienced. I forced the thoughts from my mind and discovered their plans to kill all supernatural creatures. It started with Nik. They believed he was the beginning and end of it all. If he died, all would follow." I chuckled at the nonsense of their ideology. My brother was no ordinary man. "I was placed with Larissa to gain her trust and gather secrets from Nik and her. I portrayed the innocent, small-town girl, but guilt gnawed at me. Larissa is…was the kindest person I had ever met. Her huge heart showed me I could make the choice. She fought for her independence; Nik never had a chance to control her."

She was not wrong. Nik never could have controlled Larissa, she would always fight. I think this version of her was the one I loved the most. Her strength, even after being sheltered for so long, was something to behold. She refused to be that girl anymore.

"Then you started pursuing me, and my body wanted you beyond reason. It craved your touch, your warmth, and I hated it. How could a logical person be so attracted to someone that they just wanted them without explanation? You kissed me in the elevator, and my body felt alive for the first time in my life. You stalked me, and I knew it. My body would tingle, and sometimes, I would see you standing outside, just watching me. I felt so safe. You were my protector, and I slept better at night knowing that. I never feared that I would be hurt again, and the day at the ball…I knew about the attack. I planned the attack, but you…you looked so goddamn sexy, I found myself unable to stop wanting you. The way that suit clung to your muscular physique. Fucking asshole, nobody should be as hot as you. The way you touched me, the way you fucked me. The bond clicked into place, and I loved the sensations you brought to my body. I knew that day that I loved you and I never wanted to be away from you again, but I had to. Wade threatened to kill you. It is why Jackson was there. To take me. He was worried about your influence being so strong that I would turn on them."

She breathed out, looking at her hands and shuffling her bottom off the couch. I moved closer, still hesitant, but I had to hear her say those words. I needed her beyond reason, and I wanted her to say it.

"I had already started turning against them. I stopped doing particular tasks and warned vampires of an upcoming attack. I thought of Larissa, you, and even *Nik*, and how all of you wanted to bring the world back to peace. She is dead, and I want her dream to come to life. She sacrificed herself, and I want to be the person that she saw I could be. In her memory." She stood, walking over to me. "Roman, I will be hunted. They will try to kill me, but I don't care." Her voice was soft as she stood before me, and my chest grew heavy as my breathing quickened. "I just want you."

Her words were my undoing. I lifted her body, and her legs wrapped around my waist as I pressed her into the wall. I kissed her with a fierceness that would scare any other person, but she returned it, pulling me back by my hair and kissing my neck. She licked my ear, biting it with a force that sent electricity straight to my cock.

"Fuck me, Roman," she whispered, and I raced up the stairs, throwing her on the bed and removing my clothing. I grabbed her ankles, bringing them to me as I ripped her skirt, revealing her black, lacy thong. I groaned as I tore it in half, dropping to my knees at the sight of her dripping for me. I licked up her juices as my wolf howled.

"You are never leaving this bed. I will tie you down if you ever try. Do you understand me?" My voice was hoarse, and I struggled to stop myself from feasting on her and tasting her desire for me.

"Yes, I swear. I am yours until the day I die, Roman."

I plunged my tongue into her, licking up her sweet taste. Her moans filled the room as she grabbed my head, forcing it deeper. I smiled, knowing my mate would never be shy to ask for more. I brought her legs closer, reaching up to grasp her breasts. "Let me sit on your face," she said breathlessly as she rolled over. I lay down, watching her remove what was left of her torn clothing.

"Fuck yes."

She lowered her sweetness down, and I enjoyed every part she was giving me. My wolf roared, wanting to mark her, to make her mine in every single way. My fangs extended, and I had to do it. I bit into her leg, marking her as mine. A wolf's bite the final straw to solidify our bond. Euphoria spread through our bodies as she orgasmed with the sensation of taking her life into me.

"You are mine now." I licked her leg, flipping her over and thrusting inside. "Every single part of you is mine. You feel so fucking good."

"Yes, Roman. Give me all of it. I want to feel your cum dripping out of me. I want...oh, god...yes, harder." I thrust so hard, all I could hear was the sound of our skin slapping. "Roman, I'm coming, I'm coming. Yes, yes. FUCK!" she screamed as I unloaded inside of her. I stilled for a moment before pulling out and seeing my seed fill her tight little hole.

I grabbed her throat and lifted her up. "No more fucking lies, do you understand me?" My wolf took control, warning her not to cross us. I knew my eyes would be glowing golden in warning.

"Yes, mate, I am yours. You own my heart and soul, and I am so grateful you marked me out of sight. I hate seeing marks on people's necks. It's just weird." I chuckled as I moved my hair from my face, lying down beside her and pulling her into my arms.

CHAPTER 37
MOVE IN WITH ME

Roman

I ROLLED OVER TO FIND THE BED EMPTY, HER SCENT STILL lingering on the bed. I listened intently, hearing her footsteps below in the kitchen. I threw on a pair of shorts before sneaking down the stairs, the creak alerting Mimi that I had awoken. I froze in place.

"Don't try and hide now. I don't think you could if you wanted to. You are huge," she paused, "in every meaning of the word."

I entered the kitchen to see her wearing the black T-shirt that I generally wore to bed, her hair showing the amazing sex that we had just had. She spun, her eyes lighting up as she licked her lips.

"If you keep objectifying me that way, I will be forced to act on it." I crossed my arms over my chest, flexing my muscles as I did. Mimi clenched her legs, groaning as she turned back to the food. "Do I want to know what you are cooking and why? I generally like to cook for my girls."

"Oh, your girls, how many have there been?" She held up the knife in her hand with a cheeky smile.

"Trust me, none compared to how fucking sexy you are." I strolled over, spinning her around and bending her in my arms, planting a kiss on her lips. "And none as fucking delicious as you." She laughed as I nuzzled into her neck, enjoying the way our scents mingled. I had a mate, and she was mine, my mark permanently on her leg.

"Sit down, mister," she ordered, waving a spatula in her hands and whipping it at me. I moved to the stool as I watched her move around the kitchen with ease, like she had been doing this for years. I was the luckiest man in the world.

I wished to see this every day, to hold her in my arms and never let her go. I had never been happier than I was in this moment.

"Mimi."

"Hmm."

"Move in with me." I covered my mouth quickly as I registered the words that came out of my mouth. I was so enamoured by this woman that all reason had gone out the window.

"Ah…yes!" she squealed as she threw the spatula and ran around the counter, throwing her body onto mine and making us fall backwards. "Shit, are you okay?" she asked, rubbing the back of my head.

"Mimi, I have never been better. I honestly didn't mean to ask that question, it just came out as I watched you cooking for me. I am so deeply in love with you," I stated, using a serious tone as I moved a wispy strand of her hair behind her ears.

"You never need to explain anything to me, Roman. My heart, body, and soul are yours." I rolled off the stool, lifting the T-shirt, wanting some boob action. She pushed it down. "I want food. Sorry to say this, but I get hangry when I haven't had enough food. Like feral, almost animal-like. Maybe that was a sign from the start that I was mated to a wolf and destined to have his wolf babies."

She stood up as if her words held no weight. She spoke of babies. She wanted to have my babies. I lay back on the floor and covered my face. Was this real? It had to be a trick.

"Are you okay down there?" she called out before I sat up.

"Did you just hear yourself? You said babies. You want to have my babies."

"Yeah, it is so odd. I never wanted children before. The idea of nappies and continual crying is just disgusting. Why would any woman put herself through that? It is just torture. But I look at you and I just feel my eggs calling to me, saying, 'Mate me, mate me.'"

I snorted as I stood, lifting the chair back up. "That is because when women find their mates, their bodies go into overdrive, and all they want is to mate. Sorry, I should have warned you about that. My bite would not be helping. We should wear some protection to avoid a surprise pregnancy. I don't need any more stress right now with my brother being this way."

"That makes sense. Good thing I never stopped the pill. You won't need to wear protection," she quipped with so much happiness.

"Mimi, that will be totally ineffective right now with your situation. You may as well stop taking it. I will be sure to use a condom for now. I should have been doing it already, but you are so fucking amazing. I couldn't resist the sensation of your pussy clenching my cock with so much need." I looked down. "I'm hard again," I mumbled, readjusting myself.

"I can fix that." Her eyes were alight with desire and need. I held my hands up, wanting to fuck her as well, but needing to discuss our situation.

"Whoa, beautiful, we need to discuss a few things first. Like how to keep you safe and possibly moving in."

"Oh, right, yes." She finished dishing up breakfast and took a seat, handing me a plate. I sat down beside her. I watched her cut into the French Toast she cooked, carefully slicing a piece of bacon before popping it into her mouth. A small dribble of juice left her lips, and her tongue poked out to lick it up. Her brows knitted together, lips parting slightly as she tilted her head, uncertainty pooling in her hazel eyes. "Roman?"

"Sorry, yes, are you happy to move in here? I would be able to protect you from them around the clock. I don't need to work, I just do it for fun to avoid boredom. Nik is the workaholic." I chuckled as I checked my phone, seeing no new notifications.

"I had a thought, and to be honest, I haven't told them exactly about us or anything. I just ran away from Jackson in tears. They aren't aware of anything. I could tell them that you rejected me as your mate, and I'm still dedicated to the cause. I could be your sexy spy." She wriggled her eyebrows suggestively.

"Not happening," I answered, not allowing her any time to rebut my argument.

"Roman, you cannot stop me from doing it. I am with you, I am yours. I have to do this for Larissa. *They* are the key to bringing the world back to peace. *They* have contacts with the outside world." I noticed she avoided saying my brother's name. Her use of *they* showed her dislike for Nik.

"What?" I was stunned. How did they know more than Nik and me?

"We have people on the outside. They give us intel and send us resources and weapons. I need more information, though. Let me go back in."

"You want me to let my mate walk into a volatile situation and leave it to happen. Are you fucking crazy? I marked you. My wolf will never let you do that. I don't want you doing that."

"Roman," she put one hand on my shoulder and the other on my cheek, "it is happening whether you agree or not. I know what I am doing." Her voice was clear as she stood her ground, and I could feel that she wouldn't back down from this.

"You understand that I will be close by for anything, right? I can't just leave you alone with them." I took her hand from my cheek, bringing it to my lips to kiss it.

"I wouldn't have it any other way. We will come up with a system of signals then." She grabbed a piece of paper from my bench, writing down notes. I smiled as I dug into my food. She had no fear. Mimi was everything I could ever want. Utter perfection.

Chapter 38

Where Is My Brother?

Roman

Despite my grumblings about Mimi continuing to be part of that group, she went undercover and relayed whatever information she had discovered. She would return to her apartment every night, where I would be waiting in the dark. I searched it daily for any bugs to avoid them discovering our plan. As I had let her go, it made the lies easier for her. I set up interviews for her with businesses to keep up the charade that she was searching, but I knew Nik and Larissa would want her paid. She earned an income so she could pay for her apartment.

I sat in the dark, drinking a whiskey as I checked my watch for the tenth time. She was late. My wolf stirred with unease.

"She should be here," he growled in my head.

"I know, I know. She is coming. We created the system. She is only twenty minutes late. We said we would wait until thirty, at least. That was the compromise." He growled. "Oh, shut up," I muttered, finishing my drink and checking my watch once more. "Fuck this."

He was right, I had to know. As I moved toward her door, her soft voice echoed through the stairwell below. Her laughter made my heart feel lighter until I heard the voice of another man.

"*Let's kill him,*" my wolf snarled, and it was at these moments that I wanted to slap him. He had a rather murderous attitude since Mimi's arrival.

I snuck into her room, hiding in the robe, or rather, squishing in. I listened as the door opened, and she continued to laugh.

"Oh, Jackson, stop it." I could hear the unease in her voice. They had accepted her into their group. I had to be patient. I bit my hand to stop my wolf from telling me all the ways that he would rip Jackson apart. She came into the bedroom, flicking on the light and flicking it off again. Our bond tingled. She knew I was close. I exhaled in relief.

"How have you felt since you were rejected by that brute?" he asked her. I needed headphones to block this asshole out.

"It hurt, but I am grateful. I can't imagine being tied to a monster for the rest of my life. He was a brute of a man." She spat venom toward me, and I knew the mark would burn her for saying this. "Argh, did you want a drink or anything? I'm not sure why you came up tonight."

"I missed you, Mimi. I missed holding you. Can I have another chance?" he asked. I could hear the desperation in his voice. The pleading nature of this wimp. I bit my hand harder.

"Jackson, you are an amazing lover, but I just need time. After that rejection, it made my body feel foreign to me. Just give me some time, could you do that?" her sweet voice echoed. Must not kill, must not attack. I kept repeating those words.

"Yeah, I get it. Don't make me wait too long." There was a pause. "I should be getting back. Thanks for the hope, Mimi." I listened as her door closed, waiting a few moments to be sure.

"He is gone," she called out as I forced my way out of the closet.

My hand was bleeding, and when she noticed, she rushed over. "Roman, what the hell?"

"I had to stop myself, or rather my wolf, from killing him. Is the man fucking delusional? Also, he was a brute of a man?" I raised my eyebrows at her.

"Hey…" she pointed her finger, "don't start. You could have warned me about that fucking pain. What is that shit?" She applied a towel to my hand.

"Mimi, my love, it will heal. That pain is unfortunate, but you are marked. It's a way of telling you not to talk badly about your mate." She slapped the hand that was still healing.

"A warning next time." She rolled her eyes, taking the towel away and throwing it at me.

"Yes, ma'am."

"Does the wolf seriously have that much jealousy?" she asked, pouring herself a glass of wine.

"Oh, yeah, he became quite creative about ripping out his bowels and wearing them as a necklace with pride. With you, he is…he is…argh…very possessive." I rubbed the back of my neck. Admitting this to her was putting me in a vulnerable position, and I didn't like it.

"And you?" she questioned.

"Trust me, I know that you can't resist this. I am a fine specimen of a man." I flexed my muscles toward her.

She chuckled, walking over and wrapping her arms around my waist, her very touch calming my soul and my wolf. She buried her head into my chest as I held her tight against my body.

"I hate doing this, I truly do. The way they speak about Nik, especially on his rampage. You know my dislike of him, but he is dangerous. Roman, we have to stop him. He attacked three people last night."

I kissed the top of her head. "I know, Mimi, I know. I can't find him. There is one thing I can try, but it will also influence me," I whispered, never wanting to let her go.

"What is it? Something needs to be done."

"We used to be able to communicate with each other through our wolves. When he transitioned, we found it difficult, but when Larissa was taken by the witches, he broke through and found a way. We have only been successful a few other times in doing this. If I try it, the darkness inside him could...could seep into me. My wolf could grow agitated and..."

"I think it is worth the risk. I know he won't hurt me. Do it."

I huffed, sitting on her couch, closing my eyes. Her hand held mine, a comfort for what was to come. I focused on my brother, searching for him in all recesses of my mind before a brief glimmer appeared. I pulled on the thread as it fought against me. My hand gripped Mimi's tighter.

"What is it, Roman?" her soft voice called as I searched the darkness for Nik.

"He is fighting me."

"That won't be him, that is his darkness. His monster will fight you. He won't want Nik back. He will want to stay in control and revel in his bloodlust. What is the best memory you have of your brother? Push that into the darkness. Force him to see the truth, force Nik to come out."

I didn't want to do this. Nik had more mental strength than I. My physicality was the source of my power, whereas Nik's mind was his. Mimi's soft lips pecked my cheek, reminding me that she was right where I needed her. My heart and my soul, the girl this was all for. I had to keep going.

I remembered the time that our mother had left us in the forest to become men. We had to survive the night in the winter with no resources, her test to ensure we would survive the harsh reality of life. Our mother trained us for everything, stating we had to always be prepared. Nik and I huddled together in the cold, using our bodies for warmth as we managed to start a fire, knowing that it could attract any animals that were within our vicinity. I cut my hand on the twig, slicing it open. Nik took the same twig, cutting his hand and clasping our hands together. "Until death, brother, we shall *never* abandon one another. I love you, and no matter what happens, you will always be my family. We may find love and have our own families, but the only hand I want to hold when I die is yours."

A deep roar echoed through my head, his monster fighting to stay in control. Nik's warmth grew in the dark space as I saw visions of where he was.

"Roman. Leave me, brother."

"I won't, Nik, I am here."

"You should have been there for him when she died. When he felt his mate's soul rip from her body." His monster stayed in control. Nik didn't want it back. His pain tore through my heart, and I gripped my chest at the sheer weight of emotion that flooded through us. His heart was broken. Larissa had been different. She was his true mate, not a recreation, but a mate that brought out the best in him, and he in her. He taught her strength, and she taught him heart.

"Nik, I will never leave you in this darkness. We promised each other, remember that? Do it for her."

"*She's dead,*" his monster growled, forcing me out as I gasped, standing instantly. I had an idea of where he was hiding.

"What happened?" Mimi asked as she rubbed my arm, a slight comfort in the aftershocks of Nik's pain.

"He doesn't want to fight it, Mimi. I know where he is." I turned, kissing her full lips, nibbling on her bottom one. "I'll be back later. I have an idea." I walked out of the apartment in search of the area where all monsters hunted for fresh prey.

———

I walked through the dark forest, listening to all the creatures that lingered in the shadows. The vampires, the wolves, and the monsters who couldn't control their thirst. I could smell my brother, so I knew he was close. I removed my clothes in preparation for the fight that was bound to happen. The cool night air brought goosebumps across my skin.

"*You are brave to search for him. He doesn't want to be found, he told you this.*" The voice sounded like my brother, but dripped with evil.

"I will never give up on my brother. We promised each other. He would never hurt me." I scoured the darkness for the source of his voice. I could hear him running circles around me.

"*No, he wouldn't, but I have no care for harming you. I rather enjoy the spotlight, and I don't want you to take it away from me,*" he snarled. "*I should thank you. If it wasn't for you, I would still be trapped inside that ridiculous cage.*"

"What happened to Larissa?" I asked, already knowing the answer, but hoping it would trigger Nik to want to return. I wanted to trigger any emotions for him to feel.

"She's dead. We drained her dry. She tasted amazing, and her blood has given us so much power. I am enjoying this boost. I have never been faster or stronger. Just leave, Roman."

"I promised Larissa. I promised her that I would take care of Nik after she died. She knew, and she told…" A hand wrapped around my throat, restricting my breath.

"YOU KNEW!" it roared as my brother's distorted face was before me. His skin was grey, his fingers now sharp and black, his teeth covered in blood.

"Yes, she knew that Nik would need his brother, his blood, the one person he could rely on." I stared into the monster's black eyes. "Nik, I am sorry that I wasn't there for you. I should have been. I didn't realise that it was that day. If I could turn back time so I could have been with you, I would have held your hand as you listened to her heart slow, as you felt her love wrap around you. She loved every single piece of you, the monster and the man. She wouldn't want this, Nik. Come back. I am here now. Larissa wanted you to live your life. She would be so sad to know you were behaving like this. Take my hand and come back, brother. I need you. I need my little brother. I want to marry Mimi, and I need you beside me. I want you to hold our first ch—" He threw me against a tree, my shoulder blade snapping from the impact.

"LEAVE US ALONE!" He ran off into the darkness as my bones healed, fusing back to their original position. I fell to my knees, glancing at the sky and shaking my head.

"For once, Father, just once, give my brother something. He doesn't deserve this. Bring him back. If not for him, do it for me,

Father, please." I hung my head, glancing at the ground and wishing with everything that I had for Nik to return.

CHAPTER 39

STAR LIGHT, STAR BRIGHT

Nik

My monster had more rage since the confrontation with Roman. He was pleading for me to return, but how could I? After the death of Aurora, I was ready to give up. I couldn't take the loss of her again. Larissa appeared, and she was different. She became my life, my soul, my heart. She had warmth that none of the others had. She brought me back to life only to be taken from me again. The pain of feeling our bond being ripped apart shattered my heart into a million pieces.

I closed my eyes after my monster attacked another innocent, leaving her just barely holding onto life. His anger at losing our mate was killing him as much as it was killing me. We walked down another dark street in London, hiding in the shadows for our next victim.

The night was cold as the wind picked up, a sweet scent filling our nose as a small growl vibrated through our chest. It had another victim. It sped behind the poor, innocent girl, and she stopped, turning slowly to see the monster. She screamed and ran as my monster casually strolled after her until she tripped over something under the moonlight. He reached for her throat when I saw it, the same necklace, the same star. Her voice filled my head.

"What did you name it?"

"Solis—a star that shines as bright as the sun. As bright as all the women within the Solis line."

"Oh, Nik, it is perfect. I will never remove this necklace." Her arms wrapped around my neck, her lips crashing against mine. *"I will love you in this life and the next, Nik Dankworth. You are my everything. Never forget that."*

I shook him off, shaking my head and forcing my fist into the wall. The images filled my head, causing me to feel everything I had been burying. It grew harder to breathe as the thoughts of her returned, the emotions of losing her, the breadth of my love for her.

She lay in my arms as she played with the necklace, the biggest smile on her face. A smile that made my chest feel lighter.

"NO! We killed her, we deserve this!" the monster roared, not wanting to feel everything that I was forcing back into our lives. My fists clenched, feeling pain more than the love that she brought into our lives. His nails cut into my hand, blood dripping on the ground, but it only forced more memories inside.

"Not that it matters, but this moment is the one I want to remember when I die. Not from this curse, but rather when we are old and watching our grandkids run around while we rock on our chairs on the veranda."

"Get out of here!" I yelled at the girl, who watched the man before her fighting for control, fighting emotions that had been buried. I had to feel them. She wouldn't want this. We promised. We couldn't let her down. She deserved better than this. Larissa owned my heart.

"Take plenty of photos and videos for me. Imagine I'm right there with you. Share the experiences with me. The point is to be happy, to enjoy life. I'll never leave you because I'll be in every beat of your heart and every breath you take."

Her voice filled my head with every sweet thing she ever said. The girl who worked her way into every single atom of my body. *'Say my name, Nik. I am here.'* I searched around. It sounded as if she was right beside me. *'I never left you. I am right here with you, always and forever. Say it.'*

"LARISSA!" I yelled her name as relief flooded my chest. I collapsed to my knees, feeling the weight of it all disappear. She was gone. I killed her, but she would never leave me. A tiny spark lingered in my heart, the last piece of her that remained. I had a promise to keep. "Your time is over, monster. She didn't want this. She deserves better than the worst parts of us." He growled, not wanting to give back control, but slowly receded into the darker parts of my mind. I won. She would be proud of me, even if I had to live with the carnage that was left behind.

I pulled out my phone, listening to the dial tone.

"Brother." The sound of my Roman's voice almost broke me. I had hurt him. I heard the bones snap as my monster threw him against the tree. "I am fine, Nik. What happened?" he asked, his voice strained.

"Meet me at the penthouse." I dared not brave our home. I wasn't ready for those memories. I hung up the phone as I looked at the clouded but starry night. One star in particular seemed to burn brighter with a hint of orange to it. A small smile spread over my face. I kissed my fingers, blowing them towards the sky.

"I am sorry, my love. I will be better for you. I have a promise to keep, and we both know that you will hold me to it, whether in life or death." My heart grew, knowing she never lied. She was still with me and always would be.

Chapter 40

THE LETTER

Nik

I waited for Roman to arrive as I stood on the balcony. I feared walking into the living space and smelling her scent. I didn't want to disturb the area. I wanted to bottle her scent, to have it with me permanently, but I knew I had to move on. I had to live like she asked. I heard the elevator beep as I walked inside, and I froze, taking a moment as I looked around the space. I could see her everywhere, as if she were still here. Her smiling face in the kitchen wearing only a shirt, her messy hair as she worked on the kitchen table, her sleepy face on the couch before I would carry her to bed. She had ingrained herself in every part of this place. I smiled.

"Are you alright, brother?" Roman asked, disturbing my thoughts of her. I looked up at him and nodded. I wasn't, but I would be. Roman walked over, handing me a letter and bowing his head. "She asked, and words cannot express how sorry I am that I kept it from you, but we both know that you wouldn't listen to reason. Read her letter. I'll give you a moment."

My Dearest Nik,
Please don't be angry with Roman. I made him promise, and we both know his loyalty is unwavering. I've known about this for some time, ever since those words were revealed to me in Katrina's

grimoire. Pluto cast a spell on me to forget because I couldn't bear the thought of seeing you, of being near you, and hiding this truth. It would have shattered me.

Was I wrong? Yes. But would I choose differently? Never.

You would never have let me go. You would never have accepted that it had to end. The blood that was spilled needed to be undone—it was tragic, but necessary. I know where I'll end up now. At least it's warm, and Pluto will care for me there.

I made you promise, Nik, to live your life—to truly live it. I need you to honour that promise for me. It may not make sense, but please trust that I need this. You gave everything for our love— our love that spanned lifetimes, that crossed continents and centuries. A love beyond human comprehension. You were right about one thing, my love: this time, it is different. We are different. We are stronger. We are the versions of ourselves that we should have always been.

Liyana's fear carried through every reincarnation that we shared. But Katrina, she removed that fear when she created me. I am your true mate, the one destined to bring you out of the darkness and into the light.

So, please, do me this little favour: live, Nik. Enjoy the light. Don't search for me, don't look for me, don't wait for me. For I will always be with you, in every part of you.

My love for you has no limits. From the moment I met you, my life truly began. It may have been brief and filled with pain, but not a single moment with you was ever something I'd regret. The love you gave me is infinite, and I will treasure it always.

I love you, Nik. Never forget that.

Always and forever yours,
Larissa Silvia.

I scrunched the letter in my hand, wiping away the tears. She knew and made her final days happy to ensure that I finally got to live. I spun back to my brother as he waited, his forehead creased with anxiety, awaiting the anger that would normally follow. I strode over and wrapped my arms around him.

"I'm sorry, brother. I lost her and lost myself. There is no excuse for my actions, and I know there will be repercussions, which I will accept. I only hope the punishment is not too severe."

"Do you wish to talk about what happened?" he asked while he poured me a glass of whiskey. I took it, sitting on the couch as memories of Larissa in my lap resurfaced. Her smile, her laugh, the things I would never hear in person again, only through a phone recording.

Roman and I spoke at length about the events that surrounded Larissa's death and who was to blame. His wolf stirred, listening to the moments that she took her last breath, a reaction to the emotion I exuded. Wolves were responsive, with intense emotion, and despite Roman's wolf being thousands of years old, it didn't make him exempt. We discussed our father and how Pluto had never been the enemy. He simply wanted to keep his daughter safe from what fate had in store for her.

"We judged the King of Hell wrong. I mean, we could have never known." Roman shrugged, a sly cheek to his comment.

"No, but at least we know we have an ally if we ever need it." We both chuckled as I ran my fingers through my hair, standing and scanning the empty apartment. Despite Larissa being gone, I could still feel her presence here. I smiled before taking another sip of my whiskey.

"So, you wish to marry this Mimi. The one who has secrets and sees you as a monster." I put the glass down, picking up the photo from our wedding day, glancing over my shoulder at my brother.

"She is my mate." He beamed with pride at finally finding his girl. "There is no feeling like it. I finally understand what you mean by she makes me whole. As much as I loved Larissa, she never filled that small piece of me. Mimi is the puzzle piece that makes me stronger."

I tried not to remember those feelings of the day we met, the day we kissed, the day she finally accepted me into her heart and the day that we became whole. Today was about my brother and his happiness. My sorrow wasn't important.

"I would love to meet her again, the girl who makes your heart sing." I filled my glass a little higher this time, wanting to dull the ache that I knew would last—possibly forever.

Roman pulled his phone from his pocket, putting it to his ear and having a quick conversation with the girl. I glanced at the kitchen, remembering Larissa's face at the horror of discovering her young assistant had been mated to a man *a lot* older than her.

"She will be here soon." He stood up, fixing himself another drink. His hands shook a little from nerves, which was understandable considering our last interaction was not positive.

CHAPTER 41
WHERE TO NEXT?

Nik

Roman and I spoke more about how we might restore the world to its former glory. But where would we even start? We needed to get access to someone across the ocean.

Roman stopped, staring at the door. I watched him move slowly as his mate appeared. Her hair was in a messy bun, and she wore yoga pants and a baggy shirt. Her face lit up when she spotted the man who made her heart warm. I looked away as they interacted. I couldn't watch it knowing that I may never have that again.

"Lord Dankworth, it is a pleasure to meet you again." She bowed her head and offered her hand.

"Mimi, I see you have captured my brother's heart. Do I dare ask about your intentions?" I slid my own into hers, feeling her anxiety pulsing through the veins in her hand. Roman growled beside me, and I shot him a glare. "I have every right to ask this question. Is she not part of The People's Revolution? Was she not behind the monster attack that slaughtered my people?"

My eyes flared as I held her hand in mine, increasing the pressure. This human who had mated with my brother was also part of the group that wanted to kill me and my mate. Her throat bobbed as she stared into my eyes.

"Yes, I am. I apologise for my actions that led to the death of innocent people. I will not apologise for the truth in the fact that your kind are monsters."

"MIMI!" Roman shouted, abhorred at her statement.

"No, Roman, I told you that I could accept you. I know and understand that you would never hurt me and always protect me, but Nik has no such loyalty. He is a monster. We saw the carnage he caused when he lost his mate. He drained people dry, leaving them to die alone in the streets, gasping for their last breaths. I won't pussy-foot around and tell a lie when he can hear and feel it." She stared me dead in the eye. "I don't like you, and I won't pretend otherwise. You are the creation of monsters in this world. Your inability to let go of your lost love could have destroyed this world." She squeezed my hand, pulling it closer to her. "I will never forgive you for what you started." I glanced up at my brother, impressed that a girl as tiny as her stood before a thousand-year-old Vampire Lord and spat hatred at him.

In a flash, she pulled a knife, stabbing it into my chest. I stared at the object sticking from my chest cavity as blood pooled around it. Roman stood on alert as I slowly removed the knife, feeling the wound heal in seconds. My blood dripped onto the floor as I swung it in my hands. I chuckled, fixing my stare on Mimi.

"Nik," he growled in warning, "she didn't mean that."

I moved closer, holding the knife towards her. "Oh, Roman, if she wants to play with the big boys, she better accept the punishments." She had no fear, even if her actions now caused me to fear her volatile behaviour.

"Nik." His chest vibrated; his wolf close to the surface to protect his Luna.

"Enough, brother, this girl, no—this child—believes I am to blame for society's fuck ups. Tell me, Mimi, did I choose to organise actual monsters to attack human civilians within a safe environment? Did I bribe the human security guards to walk away from their posts? Did I allow humans to purchase guns to shoot my mate as she stood before me? Was I behind the bombing of the local private school last year that left hundreds of innocent humans dead or disabled? Do I need to keep going…?" I moved closer, holding the knife clearly in my hand, and her eyes registered that I had no issue harming her as she had done to me. "You speak of the plague that I created, but all I see is damage at the hands of humans. There has been blood on both sides, so do not speak all high and mighty when your race has done nothing but slaughter whoever they believe to be evil at the time. Or have you forgotten what the English did to the Irish? The Scottish? The Vikings? The Africans? Indigenous Tribes? I have a *long* memory, Mimi, and you would be wise to remember that my time on this earth, although long, barely measures against the bloodshed that your kind has done since the beginning of time."

Roman moved to stand between us, taking the knife from my hand. I licked my blood from my palm, turning away from the girl.

"What the hell was that?" Roman bared his teeth at her, his anger filling the space as she whimpered.

"I wanted him to know that…"

"He knows what he is. He has had to live with it for centuries. He knows the mistakes of his past. Do you, Mimi? He is my brother, and I will stand by him. We have stood by each other since we were children, since we created Rome and every single day since. Apologise to him, *now!*" my brother ordered his mate, his Alpha aura filling the room.

I chuckled as I poured myself a glass of blood. "Roman, leave the girl alone. I will never find myself in a dark room with her, but I admire her fight. She will need it to be mated with the Alpha. You know you need a strong Luna." Roman eyed me with suspicion. I rolled my shoulders. "I don't appreciate her words, but I think she should see that she needs to apologise to me first before forcing her to do it. Now, Mimi, would you mind telling us what you know of the outside world?"

I gestured for her to sit down at the dining table as I poured her a glass of wine while also making another drink for my brother. I could dislike the girl and still be polite. I sat the furthest away from them, crossing one leg over the other.

"How do you contact the outside world?" I asked her, taking a sip and feeling the rush of desire course through my body. It wanted to taste the sweetness of my mate, but registered she was gone. A pit in my stomach formed, another part I hated about losing her. My body had to remember that she would never feed us again, we would never taste her sweet elixir.

"We have to do it in parts. We use a two-way radio to contact a frequency that sits just off the island. He lives on a boat for this reason. It is his job to stay the middleman. Once he has been contacted, he will inform the other parties, who call us directly. The calls can never go for longer than two minutes, because if they did, the government could track us down. They tell us news and ask if we need anything. I didn't understand how they got things through to us, but a vampire was another middleman. I know they came from Ireland, but how they managed to get there…" She shrugged. "Wade and Peter refused to let a woman that deep into the organisation as *we couldn't be trusted*," she said in a mocking tone. I smirked before taking another sip.

"Do you know which coast, or have an inkling?" I asked, putting my glass down and staring out the window as more memories were brought to the surface. I remembered the time that I fucked her against that glass, her arse left an imprint on the window. I made sure it wasn't cleaned for a couple of weeks.

"Nik?" Roman asked. I looked back at my brother.

"Sorry, I became distracted by my thoughts, just remembering something. Sorry, please continue, Mimi."

"I pieced things together. I believe it is somewhere near Dover or Selsey. Selsey is more likely, as we always had an abundance of fresh fish."

I stroked my chin. "The area is a tourist location known for that. Did you want to check out Dover or Selsey?" I asked Roman, finishing my glass.

"Nik, we are not checking today. We need to sleep, it is late. Mimi and I will stay in the guest bedroom."

"NO!" I shouted, before taking a breath. "I didn't mean that to be quite so abrupt. Please, stay in the master bedroom. Roman, I cannot bear the thought of…" My voice trailed off as Roman stood, walking over to put his hand on my shoulder.

"Are the sheets clean?" I chuckled, nodding as he tried to bring some humour to the depressing situation. He had done this multiple times, and it had become the norm, but this time, it did seem final. I felt her soul leave her body. It didn't linger, it just disappeared, leaving no trace of her essence in sight. I used to be able to feel her for moments after, but this time, I felt nothing.

I trudged into the spare room, closing the door behind me. I sat on the bed, unbuttoning my shirt as more memories sprang to life.

Her soft kisses on my shoulder. "Here, let me help you with that." The cheekiness in her voice.

"Larissa, I am mad at you," I whispered back to her after another fight with her about refusing to transition.

"You can be mad at me and still make love to me."

I shook my head, pushing aside the feel of her soft skin and the way her body would respond to my touch as if it were the only thing that brought her to life. The idea of sleep seemed preposterous to me. There was so much to do. I listened for Roman, to finally hear his soft snores through the penthouse before I took off in the middle of the night. The cool air in the sky always brought a sense of refreshment, a sense of calm to the chaos inside my head. It took just over an hour to fly to Selsey. The town almost appeared derelict. I had been here a few times in the past with Aurora, and now there barely seemed to be any signs of life. How had a seaside town become so desolate?

CHAPTER 42

MY IMMORTALITY IS LIMITED

Roman

I heard Nik leave in the middle of the night, knowing he would avoid sleep for a few days. The same routine he always followed to avoid thinking of her and adjust back to a life without his love. Mimi snuggled up to me all night. I was unimpressed with her attack on my brother, but proud that she managed to stay strong against a fierce monster like Nik.

In the morning, I cooked Mimi some breakfast before I found Nik's keys for our drive. It would only take us around two hours to get there.

"Roman!" she called out, her mouth filled with food.

"What's up, babe?" I asked her as I grabbed a top of Nik's, looking it over and thinking of how tight it would be on my large frame.

"Wade wants me to come in for a meeting today. I just got a message saying, 'He's back.'" She held up her phone, showing me the text. They knew Nik had returned. My brow furrowed. How did they find this out so fast?

"Go, we need to know what they know, but…" Mimi stood, placing her hand in my own, her face showing exactly what I felt inside: *fear.* I wouldn't be near her, I would be too far to rush back and help her. It was dangerous, and I hated this, but we both knew that she had to go, or they would become more suspicious of her. The door to the balcony opened as Nik entered, wiping blood from his mouth.

"She can drink my blood," he said as if it meant nothing to him. I stood with my mouth open, waiting for an explanation on why the hell he was offering this. The mark on her leg was the same as Nik feeling her through the blood. "You will be too far away, and I have so much shit to catch up on. I will stay in the city, and if she is in danger, I can get there quicker than you." He rolled his eyes. "Trust me, I am not offering this for her. I am doing it for you, brother. I never want you to feel the pain of a lost mate. Your Luna needs protection, and I am offering my monstrous services." He shot a look at Mimi, giving her a wink.

"Nik." I growled in his direction at using his charm on her. I knew it wouldn't work, but my wolf had never enjoyed competition. My brother laughed, holding his hands in the air.

"Please, Roman, you know that my eyes have only ever been…" he paused, glancing at the ground and clearing his throat, "for her." His voice broke, still feeling all the emotions of his lost mate. A mate who broke the curse without knowing if she would ever return.

I walked over, pulling my brother into a tight embrace. He threw his arms up, pushing me away from him.

"Don't, Roman. Do you want her to take my blood or not?" He rolled up his sleeve, with a claw ready to slice it open.

"Fine, Mimi." I turned my back toward them as Nik groaned at the pleasure of another taking his blood, but knowing he would have preferred a green-eyed beauty to do it instead.

"You taste disgusting. I hated every part of that," she spat as I spun back around, seeing Mimi wipe her mouth.

"Now, head to Wade. Nik will come for you *if* you need him to." She stormed toward the elevator doors as Nik slumped onto the couch, his head in his hands. I waited for my mate to disappear behind the cold stainless-steel doors. I noticed the penthouse no longer contained any part of Larissa.

I sat next to my brother and waited for him to speak. We never pressured each other. We were close enough to know that sometimes, it was just being near one another that gave us comfort. I glanced at my watch. I didn't have time for this today.

"Nik, why did you remove all parts of Larissa from here?" I asked him, moving forward on the couch and staring at my brother's hidden head. He didn't answer as I stood up, moving toward the fireplace that had a photo of her yesterday. "Nik, where is she?" I said with more force.

His head snapped in my direction, his eyes red as he stood slowly. "Don't, Roman. Leave it alone," he warned.

"I won't leave this alone. You removed all reminders of her from your penthouse. You have never done that before. Why would you remove her existence?"

"SHE'S DEAD!" he shouted, his chest rising and falling as he panted. "I killed her. I took her life. I can't deal with the fact that I killed the most precious thing in this world. I destroyed her. I felt her soul leave her body. I listened to her heart stop beating. She had no choice. She was literally born to break this stupid fucking curse that I started because I refused to lose her because of her psychopathic husband and now…now she is never coming back. I drained her beautiful body dry. All that surrounded me was her love, her purity, her heart, and I can't handle it. I killed that. I took that away from existence."

"Nik, you have lost her before. Why is this different? She has died so many times in the past, so why is this time different? Where the hell are the pictures of her? Her clothes? Her shoes? Any part of her?"

"Every time I lost a version of *Liyana,* my heart would ache, almost like a knife had been stabbed and twisted. This time, I felt my heart break in half. I felt her being ripped away from me, the bond, the connection, the way she knew my soul and I knew hers. It was ripped from us, as if our entire lives meant nothing. That pain…I cannot recover from the weight of that. She is gone, and she is never coming back. I have to live the rest of my immortal days without being able to dig my head into her neck and smell her, to touch her soft skin, to connect with her through a bite. How do I…How do I move on? She asked me to go live my life, she asked me to move on, but how do I do that? She was my *everything.*" My brother sobbed as he dropped to the floor. I rushed over, pulling him into my arms and rocking him.

"She never questioned her choice. As soon as she discovered it, she didn't think about her loss. She only thought about you living. She saw it as a chance for you to finally enjoy life, Nik. You have been so focused on finding her, you would search for her everywhere we went. That's not living. She gave you the chance to live. She knew what it would mean for her, and she accepted that. Her love will always surround you."

"I heard her," he whispered as he moved out of my arms. "When memories came flooding back from seeing that necklace, I heard her as if she stood right beside me. She said, '*I never left you. I am right here with you, always and forever.*'"

I smiled, knowing that she would never abandon my brother, her love. "She will be with you always, Nik. She will be holding your hand in every step you take. It's time to live. Let's bring the world back to its glory and enjoy what we can. I marked Mimi, so we both know my immortality dwindles with each passing day. We promised each other that we would be together in the end. I want my children to know their Uncle Nik, the adventurer."

"Selsey was devoid of any human existence." He changed the subject. It was probably too much to remind him that I would be human in the next few months. I had accepted that I would finally pass from this world after growing a family with my mate. "Something happened there. I could still smell people, but they are either hiding, or there is a spell."

I cleared my throat. "I'll head to Dover today and search the area. If not, maybe we can send Mimi to Selsey. She is not a supernatural creature, so if any spell was placed on supernaturals, she would be able to see the truth."

"Yeah, I think that would be best. I will put my private investigator on it to see what else he can discover. Plus, we need to see Duzi for a proper interrogation." He stood, straightening his shirt and fixing his hair. Never a strand out of place, my perfect brother. The stoic creature who would bury and hide the truth of his pain.

"I will get on the road, then. I feel like letting my wolf out, though. He is hungry for some fresh air. Call me if anything happens to Mimi." I took a set of keys and drove to the outskirts of the city.

CHAPTER 43

A TWISTED INTERROGATION

Nik

I WALKED INTO WORK AS IF MY ENTIRE LIFE HAD NOT BEEN destroyed, as if I lived with no pain from her death. Travis, who would always greet me with a smile, hid his face as I strolled over.

"Hello, Travis and Alina." I had no idea why I wanted to speak to them. Was it some form of attachment to Larissa? To feel her beside me, to feel her essence in my life?

"Lord Dankworth, I…we are so sorry for your loss. Larissa was one of a kind. I only hope her death was…was painless." Travis's words were soft as Alina cried beside him.

"Thank you, Travis, it was. I only wish it had been me instead. If you guys need anything, please don't hesitate to ask. You lost two friends this week."

"Two?" Alina's tear-filled eyes looked up with confusion.

"Larissa and Stacey."

"Stacey is dead?" they said in unison. I nodded, and they both proceeded to cry harder. *Fuck!*

"Sorry to you both. I thought you knew. Stacey attacked Larissa, and she had no choice but to take her life. If you need to take the afternoon to grieve, please do so," I said, keeping my own emotions in check as I thought of our many adventures in the elevator together.

I rode in silence to my floor where Laura waited with sad eyes and a bloodcino. I noticed the packaging was from the same place Larissa frequented. She bowed her head as I took the coffee with a small smile.

"Hello, Laura, what is most urgent on our agenda for today?" I asked. Her heels clacked against the floor as she raced to keep up with me.

"Roman has hired a new Marketing Director for Refresh, and it is running smoothly. At this stage, he hired three more people to fill the immediate gaps in personnel. A vampire meeting is being held tonight to elect another leader to take Duzi's place. I am thankful for your return, as are Richard and Stuart. They were going to put in their preferences, but wanted you to return before doing that. There is a drug dealer who has been dealing vampire blood that was arrested last night, and you have been tasked with his interrogation to find the source of the blood. Plus, you have one thousand emails to respond to. Welcome back, Lord Dankworth, I...we have missed you."

"Thank you, Laura. Please only disturb me if you believe it to be important." I closed the door behind me and waited a moment before moving toward my desk. I clicked open the computer to see a picture of Larissa and me from our first ball together, her eyes bright with love and affection as I stared at my perfect mate. I right-clicked to change it before I stopped myself. Roman was right. I couldn't remove her entire existence from my life. She would hate me for that. I flicked through my phone, stopping when I found the perfect picture of Larissa. She wore my blue shirt, covered in a blood pancake, her hair in a messy bun with flour on her face. Her smile lit up the picture. This was my mate. Not the picture-perfect girl, but the one who never minded cooking in the kitchen for me. The girl who would yell at me for this. This was my Larissa. I transferred the file over as I beamed with happiness.

I managed to sort through my thousand emails and responded to just over half of them before I headed to the local police station to discover which vampire had been the source of this drug dealer. I brought Bodhi with me, as he needed to work on his compulsion skills. He slid into the car beside me as Andreas drove. The depressing energy in the car was almost suffocating.

"I know we all feel the loss of Larissa, and I apologise for my absence in this matter, but she is gone. She wouldn't want us to linger in those feelings. Do you understand?"

"Yes, Lord Dankworth," Andreas answered as his gaze met mine and he bowed his head in respect.

"Yes, Master," Bodhi answered, but he dared not look in my direction. I deserved the hatred. I had taken an angel from this world.

We arrived at the station and walked through the office area, with men gasping at my height. A sound I was used to, a sound I had lived with my entire life. The police chief stopped before me, performing a bow with peculiar flair. I held back a snort.

"Lord Dankworth, we are pleased to have your royal presence in our fine establishment. We would like to escort you to the prisoner." I listened to my surroundings; a few hearts were elevated, a few brows sweaty. I pulled out my phone, quickly messaging Roman to check in and ask whether he had heard from Mimi.

I followed the police chief, sweat pooling at the back of his shirt.

My phone rang. I noticed my brother's name and put it to my ear.

"Nik, it's a trap. Get out of there." I stopped, considering my next steps. I had to stay. I would survive, but if I left, Mimi would be outed as a spy if she gave the tip to Roman.

I turned to Bodhi. "Leave and tell Andreas to bring the car around the back. Don't question me, just do it." He dropped his lip in sadness. If only he understood that I just saved his life. I waited for this attack as I was led into the interrogation room. "Stay," I ordered the police chief, knowing they would not willingly harm another human on such short notice.

"W-why?" he questioned as his hand remained attached to the handle. An odd sensation coursed through my body, barely registering what it could mean.

"I may need someone to shoot me if I lose control." I smirked as I sat at the table, scanning the room, noticing the camera had no blinking light. I used my vampire sight to see that only one person stood behind the two-way mirror. The police chief stayed as I sat opposite the drug dealer.

"So, tell me, I find it interesting that you would deal in such a dirty crime when you are with a group who detests my kind." His tattoo peeked out from the bottom of his sleeve, the same one that all those connected to TPR had. The initials D2F inside a star.

"Huh?" he said as if he had no other words within his vocabulary.

"I am not stupid. Half the men out there were terrified, and the police chief is covered in sweat. His heart is close to stopping if he doesn't calm down soon. Also, only one man is behind that glass, and he is way too calm about it. Why have you gone to all this trouble for little old me today?" I leaned back in the chair, tapping my fingers on the table.

The criminal leaned forward on the table, his coffee-stained teeth, bald head, and bad body odour made the experience rather unpleasant. He pulled up his sleeve, revealing the tattoo I had already seen.

"You are no fool," he spat out as I waited for more intelligent words to reach my ears.

"I am thousands of years old, but you clearly are with your inability to form coherent sentences to answer my simple question."

"You murdered people," he snarled.

"I have in the past, I have never denied this. I was a monster, but I am no longer that man today. What is the point of this ridiculous line of questioning?"

"You lost your mate and killed. You are a monster, and we wanted to show others the truth."

"Ohhh, it makes sense now. Only need one of you to record this conversation and broadcast to the world. You should have simply asked." I stood making my way toward the two-way mirror. I waved with a charming smile plastered on my face. "Hello everyone, I am Nik Dankworth. I make no apologies for the blood that I have shed in the past. I regret those actions. As I regret my actions over the past couple of weeks, but I know for a fact that I never killed any of those people, wait, those human people. I killed two vampires, but they deserved it for their crimes against humans. These people want to portray me as a monster. I am. All vampires are monsters, but those who want to twist the narrative are no better than I am. They sold vampire blood on the street. All vampires know this is against our laws. We do not share our power for the carnage it can have on humans, the addiction that can destroy lives. I think I can confidently say that they have kidnapped a vampire to use his blood. This brings a whole lot of charges, as some vampire blood is tainted and can make humans sicker if they ingest it. I will never be a perfect man, but I know that I am better than those who fight to overthrow us. I have committed far fewer crimes, kidnapping for one." I gave a sly wink as I turned back to the drug dealer at the table.

"Is the vampire alive?" I asked him. He shook his head, and I listened to the outside go suddenly still. I moved to hide behind the door before it sprang open with force. I kicked it back, knocking the first intruder back. I heard a crunch, knowing that something had broken. I killed the lights with a clap of my hands. I could fight in the dark, they couldn't. I moved around the room, taking out each one slowly. I picked up the chair, throwing it through the two-way mirror, grabbing the mystery man by the throat. Only to discover it was not a man, it was Mimi. The sensation from earlier now made sense. I had forgotten what it did to my body. With no Larissa, I didn't entertain the thought that it could have been Mimi.

Her eyes froze as she held the camera, fear registering as I spun around, holding her neck tightly.

"Don't worry, I won't hurt you," I whispered into her ear, dragging her from the space and toward the back door.

"You know, I expected better. You know everything there is to know about me, and yet you brought five men. You are pathetic." I moved closer to her ear. "Sorry." I pushed her forward, speeding from the building and into my car. I slammed the door shut as Andreas sped away.

"What the hell happened?" he shouted at me as I ran my fingers through my hair. That was a good question.

Chapter 44
WHAT LIES BENEATH THE SURFACE?
Roman

My thoughts lingered on Larissa. I hoped she felt peace in those last moments. I had regrets about not being there for my brother when I should have been, but my fear of losing Mimi took over. How had a woman managed to infiltrate my entire life to the point where it was all I thought about? I shook it off, focusing on the changing scenery as I ran through the area, avoiding most eyes. People would see me in the daylight, but my speed would make it seem more like a mirage than the possibility of a monster so large running around.

I reached Dover in just over thirty minutes, my wolf enjoying the fresh air flowing through his fur. I shifted back to human, walking through the small town. This one was bustling with energy, people milling about. I kept searching the area for anything odd or out of place. We needed to know how they managed to contact the outside world. I stopped at the edge of the chalk cliffs, scanning the sea. It was devoid of ships, not one person on the water. I scratched my chin as a text came through.

MIMI

Tell Nik to get out of there, it is a trap.

ME

What?

MIMI

They are trying to kill him. Tell him now.

I pulled out my phone to relay the message before he hung up on me. Nik would know that if he left, it would only reveal a mole in their group. He had to stay, he couldn't be killed. He would figure it out. I spun around to look at the town, noticing a large telecommunications pole sticking out of Dover Castle. The family that owned Dover Castle were supposedly killed during the Great War in 1914, and it had since been claimed as an English Heritage site. Why would the government decide to deface a castle that was once considered the 'Key to England' during the eleventh century?

ME

We may have a clue here.

NIK

Busy.

I chuckled as I left the area, heading toward the castle. An energy surrounded it the closer I got. It was not magic, but rather the microwaves from the telecommunications pole. The door creaked as I pushed it open, listening intently for any noises. It was like walking into a time capsule. The Middle Ages were not a time that I wished to return to; the plague, those boils. I shuddered with disgust at the sickness that wiped out millions of humans from existence. Nik and I had found a rich family, and he compelled them to let us stay until it passed. Funnily enough, one of the maids was a reincarnation of Liyana. The times that she appeared and how they found each other were hilarious. She died from the plague before Nik had a chance to turn her. Their love was brief, but still magical to see.

I walked around the empty castle, which had become a tourist location, but nobody seemed to want to visit. I searched the kitchen, the many bedrooms, and the Grand Hall, but found nothing. I went in search of the dungeons under the castle to find the room locked from the inside. Why could I not hear anything?

I felt around, knowing that I could break through the space with ease, when I looked up to see a blinking red light, a hidden camera. I was being watched. I would have to wait for the cover of darkness to search further. I left the castle and strolled through the town like an ordinary tourist, purchasing items and making friendly small talk with the café ladies. I found a jewellery store that specialised in vintage jewels. My eyes lingered on rings. It was too soon, right? A bright light hit my sight, and I followed it to a pair of clip-on earrings. They were two-tone with tiny diamonds inside the gold centre and white gold petals. They were stunning and reminded me of Mimi. I purchased them and found somewhere to eat. I noticed a black four-wheel drive arrive in the town, stopping for food before moving on. They looked as if they did not belong. I watched them drive toward the castle. Bingo.

I waited for the cover of darkness, noticing the black car was still parked outside the castle. I shifted into my wolf, moving through the area with speed to avoid being seen by humans and the cameras. I would be a blur if they somehow noticed me. I found a dark corner near the dungeon and hid, waiting for any insight into this area. Voices grew louder as the door unlocked.

"Oh, come on, Jerry, we never had a chance against Dankworth. The dude is a legend. We were fools to think we could ever kill him." The men, both in their late thirties, early forties, laughed. One was balding, while the other had thick red hair and a beard. I watched them open a keypad, pressing the numbers: 1,

2, 4, 5. I rolled my eyes at the stupidity of that code. I knew how to enter now, but I wanted to see what else these gentlemen said.

"Yeah, I lost the bet. I wish we could kill him already. I mean, his mate is dead, and under suspicious circumstances. Did he drain her dry? We should investigate her death, and then maybe his own kind will execute him."

"Dude, that's a great idea, Jerry." Thwack, a smack to the back of the head. "You fucking idiot. She was killed by magic, not him. We already looked into it. He never killed any of the people he attacked. Our only hope is Duzi or Daniel."

"I reckon I could kill him and his dog brother."

I chuckled as I shifted behind them. "Oh, really? I would like to see you try. What are you, barely six feet tall?"

Their mouths fell open in shock. The redhead, Jerry, pulled a gun. I snatched it from his hand, crushing it in my hands with ease. I watched the men visibly gulp.

"Please, tell me more about your plan to kill my brother, which is comical that you think it is possible." They stood silent. "What's the matter, wolf got your tongue?" I snorted at my pun.

"Go away, wolf, this is private property." Jerry postured, though his face was pale and his hands trembled.

"Oh, shut up." I grabbed them both by the throat, lifting them from the ground. "Now, tell me, what are you doing here? And no bullshit." I tightened my grip as they gasped for air.

The balding man with no name broke first. "Alright, I'll spill." I let him drop to the floor while I threw his friend against the closest wall, watching his body slump to the floor as he fell unconscious.

"Talk, *now*," I growled, irritated that this even had to occur. I wanted to be home in bed with Mimi.

"Alright, lose the 'tude." His cockney accent annoyed my ears. "We use this base to contact various people within our organisation. We don't trust the phones because they are tapped by the blood-suckers." He lowered his voice, *"Death to all."*

"What was that?" I grabbed his shirt, bringing him closer to my face as my fangs elongated, wanting to rip his throat out.

"Nothing," he whimpered.

"What else? How do you contact the outside world? How do you get resources brought in?"

"I ain't sayin nuffin."

"You will tell me, or I will bite you and turn you into a monster. I am the Alpha, and I have no issues creating a pup to do my bidding." My eyes glowed yellow as my snout protruded from my face, fur breaking out over my skin.

"Fine, fine." Fear dripped from his words as his pupils dilated with terror.

"There is a submarine out in the bay. It constantly floats through the English Channel between here and Selsey. It brings in weapons and tech gear, whatever we want. Wait…you know about the radiation not existing." I nodded slowly. "You're not part of it." I shook my head. "But we thought that your kind were."

"Yeah, figures you would be that stupid. We only just discovered the truth, and we want to know how it all works. Nik went to Selsey, and it was empty."

"Only on top. We hid underground for that reason. Only a few know about that, those in the highest parts of our organisation."

He sprouted nonsense that didn't help. I needed to get into that room. I glanced away from him in the darkness, then punched him, watching his body fall to the floor. He would be quiet for over an hour. I moved back into the room, putting in the code as the door swung open. Only two people were inside.

"Jerry, Sean, took you long enough. Anything of import—" His voice stopped as his eyes found mine. His movements were slow as his hand twitched for the weapon holstered on his hip. The bullets would hurt and take a while to heal, but they wouldn't kill me. I growled as he ceased all movements, his eyes open in terror.

I walked around the room, inspecting the various computer screens and systems in place. It was far more advanced than we thought possible. I saw a picture of Duzi, Daniel, Nik, Larissa, Hector (a large red cross through it), and me.

I pointed to Duzi. "What do you know about this man?" I asked him, pulling his picture from the wall and scrunching it in my hand. I wished I could kill this pest, this piece of shit that had hurt so many since he was born.

"We discovered that he is behind the entire conspiracy. Nik, although the face, had no power to make the changes that Duzi had put in place. Nik has more influence, but he hasn't really used it for quite some time. The vampire community grew weaker, and this man took advantage of that. We don't know how he managed to produce the acid rain. We haven't uncovered that part yet, but we are close. A few humans who work for him have been slipping us intel."

"What are their names? I wish to speak with them as well."

"No way."

"We are on the same side, we want Duzi removed. We had him arrested recently. We are trying to undo what he did. We want to restore peace and bring the world back to what it was. Can we not work together?" I pleaded, hoping that in having a common enemy, we could undo the mistakes of the past.

"You are monsters. We will never work together." His hatred seeped into his words. I shook my head. Sometimes humans had no common sense.

"That is where your ideology is lacking. Tell your leader we want to meet. We aren't the enemy." I turned back toward the door, listening for any movement of a gun moving out of its holster. I stopped at the door. "Also, change your code, it is one of the easiest to guess." I chuckled as I left the dungeon, ready to shift and return home to my mate.

CHAPTER 45

ACCEPTING AN ENEMY

Nik

I sat around the penthouse, waiting for my brother's return, when the elevator beeped.

"Roman?"

I rolled my eyes and groaned. Mimi. She had yet to prove her worth in this spy business.

"I see you managed to survive today," she said upon seeing me, her dislike flickering through her blood. I could taste her hatred. A nicer person would thank her for the warning, but she didn't deserve it after stabbing me.

"Oh, please, Mimi, we both know that I cannot be killed that easily." I stood, making my way over to the kitchen and having another drink of blood. A human being around so close to my monster resurfacing was difficult.

"Where is Roman?" she asked, avoiding me and moving up the stairs.

"He went to Dover and hasn't returned yet. He told me he discovered something, but has been radio silent since."

"Did you not think to check on him?" she asked, horror in her voice as she dialled his number on her phone. It went to voicemail. "Nik, what if he is injured? How can you be careless? He is your brother."

"I think you doubt your mate's strengths, Mimi. He is built like a truck. He is fine. His immortality hasn't run out yet, either, so there is no need to worry."

"Immortality run out?" she questioned as her brow raised.

I spun with a smirk on my face. "He hasn't told you. That is interesting. When a wolf is mated, its immortality goes with it. He marked you, which means every day that passes, he becomes more human. It is the sacrifice of love."

"So we will live together until we die." Her heart slowed as her knees buckled. "Why didn't he tell me that? I thought he would live forever and hold my hand as I died. I have been struggling with this, and it was why I thought about rejecting him."

I walked over, helping Mimi to her feet and onto the stool, sliding her a glass of water.

"You are not destined for the same future as my own. You will live a long life together with children, no doubt. I know my brother has always desired a pup or two."

She laughed. "Please, he would have as many as possible, we both know that." I raised my glass to her as I quirked my eyebrow. I could feel her love for my brother. The way her heart beat faster at the very thought of him. I missed that sound from Larissa's chest.

"I am sorry, Mimi."

She glanced up from her glass, her forehead creased in confusion. I sighed as I took a seat beside her.

"I judged you harshly. I thought maybe you didn't have the right intentions. I am sorry. I was so focused on my pain that I didn't entertain the thought of you actually having a heart and not just being some *black widow.*"

"Oh, please, I am not that good at sleuthing. I am sorry for your loss. Larissa was one of a kind. Her love for you had no limits. She knew your faults and never made excuses for them. To me, that is love, knowing and understanding who your partner is. She made you...nicer." Her tone made it seem more like a question than a statement.

I smirked. "Huh. Here I was, thinking that I was still an asshole, but I can see the sprinkle of niceness."

She nudged me playfully. "Don't test me." Her face softened from our interaction, the crease around her eyes slowly disappearing.

Mimi and I continued to talk as we waited for Roman to return. I moved about the kitchen, cooking something for dinner. I had missed this. I barely noticed that Larissa had reorganised the entire kitchen without my knowledge. I chuckled at her ability to distract herself with menial tasks. I plated up a dish of paella as the elevator beeped. Roman looked pissed off.

"So, Dover Castle is home to those fuckers. There is a submarine offshore that communicates between us and the mainland, so to speak. Selsey is a base, but they are underground. Oh, and they are stubborn assholes in not wanting to work together to bring back peace. How was your day?" He wrapped his arms around his mate, kissing the top of her head as she tucked into dinner, her sense of love and fulfilment evident from the blood in my system.

"Interesting. We will visit Duzi tomorrow to get some more answers. I think a partnership between us could be advantageous, but I know it will cost us something. They will not do it without a benefit for them. Am I right, Mimi?"

"Yep," she quipped as I pushed a plate toward my brother. "I need to eat and run. Jackson asked where I stayed last night." She rolled her eyes.

"This Jackson visit you regularly?" I questioned, not liking the fact that another visited my brother's mate.

"Nik, it is fine. Trust me, there is no competition," Roman stated, moving a stray hair from his mate's face.

"I know, brother. She would be a fool to look at anyone other than you." I winked at him. "It was more, I wondered if I could compel him for more information to make it seem like he could be a mole. We need another member to infiltrate the organisation, but it will take far too long for them to climb the ranks."

"Nik, Duzi first. We will compel him for answers, then figure out our next moves. Leave Mimi to the sleuthing for now. She is building trust with Wade." Mimi yawned beside Roman, and I noticed the time had ticked past nine.

"Take her home, brother. She needs the rest. I will talk to you tomorrow. I have a scheduled interrogation with Duzi at eleven in the morning. Are you coming?"

He nodded, a huge smile on his face, filled with joy at wanting to take this man down. I only hoped I was able to contain my anger.

CHAPTER 46

HOW LOVE CAN CHANGE YOU

Nik

AFTER ANOTHER RESTLESS NIGHT IN THE SPARE ROOM, I WOKE AND walked into our master bedroom. Her smell still lingered as I sat on the bed, looking at the London skyline before me. Its cold appearance and modern architecture made me miss some of the older buildings. I showered myself as her vanilla-scented shampoo sat on the shelf. Unable to take my eyes away from it, I didn't have the heart to chuck it away. Part of me was holding onto hope that she would be back, that she could come back to me.

I shook my head. "You promised her, Nik," I whispered as I dressed myself in a blue shirt and black slacks, ready to take on the day. My alarm sounded as I made my way to Andreas, who was waiting with a car. Bodhi stood at the door, waiting for me.

"What is on the agenda today, sir?" he asked, bowing his head and opening the door for me. I knew Larissa would hate this.

I sighed. "Bodhi, you are not a slave. Please, I can open my own door."

"Sir, I do this out of respect, not because you are my master. You saved my life. I am grateful for any day to learn from someone as wise as you." His words reminded me of Larissa and her sarcasm. She would exist in everything, so how would I let her go?

"Thank you, Bodhi, we shall have to look for a permanent position for you later down the track. Let me know which one of my businesses intrigues you the most. Come, sit and let me know more about TPR." He nodded as he slid into the car before me. I followed, closing the door behind us.

Bodhi informed me of the hierarchy that had been constantly changing and the members who would go missing when they questioned how the system worked. Bodhi's family had been one of the original and remained that way. He spoke of Mimi's foster father, Wade, and what he thought about her. I wanted more intel on her actual role within this organisation. He told me nothing more than what I already knew. She had been marked by my brother, which made her unable to betray him, but something felt off with the whole situation. As if I was missing a piece of a puzzle. I pursed my lips as I watched Andreas pull up at the kerb. Bodhi and I exited the vehicle, heading inside and up to my office, where Laura waited with a coffee and her list of tasks for the day.

I noticed her eyes twinkle at my ward. I smiled at the romance blossoming between them. I wished for his happiness, as he had such a troubled life. The abuse he had suffered since he was a child…Some people should never become parents. Bodhi stayed outside the office with Laura as I worked through more of my never-ending emails.

"Lord Dankworth, Daniel is here to see you," Laura's voice chimed through the intercom, always so cheerful.

"Send him in." I pressed the button, not looking up as he entered and bowed his head out of respect. I disliked the way he did that, but he seemed adamant about doing it to show his respect.

"Lord Dankworth," his voice rang out. I rolled my eyes.

"Daniel, have we not spoken about removing the formality? You already swore your allegiance." He tilted his head at me. The words sounded foreign, even to me. I would never have said that to a former enemy, even if he swore his life to my own in a blood oath.

"Okayyyy." He dragged the word out. "Did you enjoy your break from reality? That is a question I have, actually. I've always been told that if we let our monster have control, there is no coming back. How did you manage to regain control?"

"I am the father of you all. I can do more than the lot of you. My monster and I are one, we are not separate. Do *not* forget that my monster was a wolf at one stage. We had a connection, and that didn't change. It was more of what he changed into. What news do you have?" I asked, hopeful to change the subject.

"As we know, Duzi is in prison, and he has not been allowed to contact anyone, even through his back doors. I have heard nothing from him. His various allies have been asking me what is next. They are freaking out. They are looking to me for support. What do I do?" he asked, the lines under his eyes showing the stress over this new responsibility.

I leaned back in my chair as I clicked the pen in my hand, checking my watch. I had to meet with Duzi and Roman in about an hour.

"What if you come and join us with Duzi? My brother and I are meeting with him soon. I'd love to see his face at your betrayal, and I wonder what his loose tongue will reveal before I compel him."

"Yes, I am there. I want this man to get his just desserts. He...he helped me into the virgin trade. I never wanted to do it, Nik—I mean Lord Dankworth. As much as they taste amazing," he cleared his throat, "they are innocent, and I hated how they were used for money and power."

"I struggle with how you managed to find so many and ship them around." He shifted in his seat. "Daniel," I growled in warning for him to reveal what was hidden just under the surface.

"They are brought in. I never questioned from where, but after I heard the rumours of the world being larger than just this island, I put it together. Girls were kidnapped and sent over here to be farmed for their blood and virginity." His voice croaked as he waited for the inevitable torture at my hands.

I shrugged. "We can discuss that later." I did want to kill him, but he was proving himself rather useful at the moment. I couldn't afford to lose the intel that he seemed to be providing, as much as he was a stain on the vampire community.

"That freaks me out even more now. Lord Dankworth, are you feeling alright? You always destroy without thinking. You are renowned for this."

I smiled as I shook my head. "Someone taught me to ask questions first. I need more answers before I decide what your punishment can be." I leaned forward in my seat, my arms resting on the desk, my fangs elongating. "And trust me, Daniel, there will be punishment. I feel like enjoying the taste of your blood, seeing as you revelled in those innocent girls." My eyes flared as he hung his head in shame. "Now get out." My voice grew deeper as the sleeping monster beneath the surface woke, thinking of the ways it would like to rip his body to pieces and feast on what was left. Daniel stood and left the office quickly.

I laughed to myself as I ran my hands over my face. "What the hell have you done to me, Larissa? The old me would have killed, and now here I am, letting the man, who openly admitted to his crimes, go. Fucking hell."

I stood, walking to pour myself a glass of blood to enjoy before joining my brother.

CHAPTER 47

ABOUT BLOODY TIME

Nik

At least I did not have to travel far. Being the Lord of the region allowed certain privileges, one being the ability to build holding cells within some of my establishments. I rode the elevator to the cells in the basement. Roman waited, his hands against the wall as if trying to contain his rage. I watched his back muscles flex and relax. Something pissed him off.

"What is it? Mimi? I haven't sensed her in danger." I stopped, standing beside him as his yellow eyes glowed.

"No, we had a fight. She wants to go deeper, and I told her no. My wolf is fucking livid. He wants to tie her up on the bed." His voice grew thicker and more monstrous as he spoke.

I quirked an eyebrow at him. "Roman, I have no desire to know about your bedroom activities, but tying down your mate seems a little excessive, and this is coming from the one who locked his inside a mansion." I winked at him as his shoulders softened, his entire demeanour changing in seconds as he relaxed.

"You are such a dick." He spun around, lightly pushing me against the elevator wall.

"You love me for it. Our ability to annoy one another so much that we just stop caring about the issues at hand. Now, hold onto that anger as we walk into that room. I'll need Wolf Roman. Push Mimi aside, she is safe. I can feel it. She is smart. Stop thinking otherwise. Also, Daniel is coming. I want to see Duzi's face when he realises I turned his second without him knowing." I beamed at the joy that it would bring, seeing those eyes fill with confusion.

"Fuck, you are a prick sometimes."

"One of us has to be. Why do you think I was mated to a bloody angel?" We both laughed. I wasn't wrong. Larissa was angelic in her thoughts and her purity. The pain was slowly subsiding, being replaced with an emotion that I had never encountered before. I was looking forward to exploring it. The elevator beeped as Daniel entered, his hands shifting into his pockets.

"Ah, Dan the man, the piece of shit who tortured innocent girls." Roman slammed his hand onto his shoulder. His entire body jerked forward as I stifled a laugh.

"Brother," I warned, not wanting to piss him off too much before he met his former partner.

"Alright, alright. I'll leave it alone for now. I wish Larissa hadn't destroyed that coven of witches. I would almost like to send him to them for punishment. Now we know how creative they can be." He chuckled, running his fingers through his hair and removing his leather jacket, wearing nothing but a white singlet underneath.

"The witches do still exist," Daniel stated, looking between us. "The ones that Larissa let go formed their own tiny group, and I mean, like, four of them. They have their own little coven, they just refuse to practice for anyone but themselves. When Larissa died, though, the magic that she stole from that coven returned to those four girls. They are quite powerful."

"You are holding out on me, Daniel. We need to sit down and discuss this more."

The guard brought Duzi over, iron chains on his feet and hands, as Roman and I smiled with glee at this man finally in a position that he deserved.

"Duzi!" My voice boomed in the small space as he registered Daniel near us.

"You *fucking* traitor!" he yelled, charging for him, but Roman pushed him against the wall. He fell to the floor with a loud crack, blood left on the wall behind him.

"Roman," I grumbled, not wanting to hurt him just yet, but his anger would be pulsing with the Mimi situation.

"Duzi, you are the definition of what a traitor looks like. You worked with the witches and the gods against your own kind, but the worst, in my eyes, is what you did to Valerie. I am just glad that Richard isn't here. I think his idea of your death would be infinitely worse than even I could think up," I said as I sat down at the table.

"Shut the fuck up," he spat in my direction. "Why is he in here?" He pointed towards Daniel, the man who had been giving me intel for months.

"Oh, Daniel, we are best pals and have been for a while now. Show him, Daniel." He held up his palm to reveal the blood oath scar. Duzi's reaction was better than I imagined. His eyes grew vacant, and his skin went pale as I listened to his heart beat faster.

"Why the fuck did you cross me? Do you know what I can do to you? You fucked the wrong man, Daniel." His words were meant as a threat, but I laughed at the comical side of it. "What the hell are you laughing at, Dankworth?" he spat at me.

"Oh, Duzi, you—"

"Lord Dankworth, may I?" Daniel asked, and I nodded, permitting him to speak. "Lord Nik Dankworth is not his birth name. You tasked me with discovering his secrets, to search his history for any information that could be used against him. It's safe to say that I discovered the truth. Nik is Remus, his brother Roman is Romulus. They are the wolf brothers who founded Rome centuries ago. Remus sold his soul for his love, Liyana. The cost was his destiny to become the father of our kind. The creatures who lurked in the night and drank the essence of humans at our convenience. He is the creator of our kind, he is older than you. Your words hold no weight against the son of Mars, the God of War. Look at them, Duzi, you were fighting against the wrong people, and you lost. I switched when I discovered the truth. I wouldn't go against the gods knowing they now existed."

"I don't care if he was the leader of the free world, he is a tyrant and deserves whatever comes to him. Know that when I get out of here, I will destroy you."

Roman and I glanced at one another before laughing. We couldn't stop ourselves from the stupidity of his threats.

"Oh, Duzi, you think you are getting out of here. You are not living past today, sorry. Your time has come to an end. The only choice you have today is to decide what information you give us willingly and what information I will force from you."

"Go to hell!" he shouted as he slowly waddled towards the door.

"Oh, I've been, and it is not that enjoyable. Rather red, filled with too much sorrow and carnage. I rather prefer Earth, to be honest." I stared at my nails, remembering how long it took me to get red dust out from under them when I saved Larissa from what I thought was her doom.

"I'm not telling you anything." He grabbed the handle of the door, trying to pull it open.

"Nobody is coming to save you, Duzi." Roman yanked him backwards, and he fell to the floor.

"Now, Duzi…" I let my influence infect his brain, taking over every single inch of it. His eyes rolled back into his head, fighting my influence. "Oh, Duzi, I can make this quite painful. Don't fight it. I think you will find that it feels quite nice." My voice was smooth and relaxing.

His body started to convulse.

"Nik?" Roman questioned.

"He is fighting me. I need his eyes. Grab his shoulders." Roman forced Duzi's head to look at me, and the compulsion locked into place. He would answer all my questions now.

"Alright, let us begin. How far does this control go? Where do I start to undo it all?"

"The military. I worked with them to stop communication with the outside world. I only needed to compel two people, and the rest all fell into place. They destroyed the towers."

"How do we undo what you have done?"

"You have to start with TPR. They kept the system crippled. I only sprinkled false truths in the media to keep people scared of the world around us. To stop the questions. They stayed in contact using resources to build their army."

"So TPR were part of it from the start?"

"Yes. I didn't realise who they were at the time, but now it makes sense. They manipulated the system, removing everyone from Selsey. They won't want the world to go back to normal until the eradication of our kind."

"Why did you try to destroy Larissa?"

A sly smile spread over his face. "Why wouldn't I want to hurt your mate? It was the only way to attack you. I only wish I knew the truth about the never-ending connection that you shared. When the witches told me about how she was always brought back to life, I wanted to ensure that I killed her every single time she came back. Some things are better left dead."

My hand grabbed his throat, tightening my grip as I lifted him into the air. My rage filled the room as Roman howled and Daniel cowered in the corner.

"Nik," Roman warned, "keep your head cool." My anger was suffocating the room and infecting him and Daniel.

"No, it is about time this man met his end."

"Oh, please, you won't kill me. Remember the day that you stopped Larissa from doing it? You knew my worth even before I was arrested."

I pulled him closer to me, smelling the stench of his breath on my face. "I stopped her because I wanted to be the one to kill you." I dropped him to the floor as he laughed, thinking he had won, but sadly, I was done with this man. I spun, forcing my hand into his chest and pushing him against the wall. "Let's see what other secrets you have lingering inside that head of yours."

I roared, sinking my fangs into his neck, feeling his sour blood fill my mouth. I wanted to rid the world of this poison, and I would. Images flashed through my mind, telling the story of his life from the moment he tricked Valerie through to now. I squeezed his heart as he squealed like a little girl in pain, unable to move. I loved this. I pulled my hand from his chest, ripping the chains from his hands and feet to make it an even fight.

"Come on, Duzi, show me what you got," I proclaimed, raising my hands in the air as I licked the blood that covered my mouth and chin. He charged at me, unable to move the mountain before him. He punched, barely managing to touch my skin. He attempted to kick next. The problem with Duzi was that he fought with words and had no idea how to actually win a physical fight. He had everything given to him, a real worm that fed off the weak and those who fell at his feet. He picked up the chair, throwing it at Daniel as I sped to stop it, breaking the chair in half to show him he would never win this fight. "What else do you have? You never deserved the gift of being a vampire. You are pathetic."

"I hope they kill you. I hope they figure it out and rid you from existence." His threats were hollow and filled with fear, knowing his end was near but not wanting to accept it. I admired him, if only for a second.

"Roman…Daniel." I looked at both of them as they nodded, ready for this to be over. We had what we needed. I sped, grabbing him, feeding on what was left of his blood. I waved Daniel over, allowing him to take what was left from his former boss. He growled as we ripped into his throat. More images flickered through my head when I saw one of Duzi and Larissa standing beside each other at Dover.

I froze, watching Daniel take more blood as I waved for Roman to finish him. Why had she met with the man who had worked so tirelessly to kill her?

Roman grabbed his head, ripping it from his body, and throwing it against the wall, the sound of his crushed skull echoed in the small space. I tried to hold onto that memory, to decipher whatever else his blood gave me. Roman ripped his arms from his body, clapping his hands together in a rather sadistic way. He plunged his arm into his torso, ripping the lower half of his body from his pelvis as his organs fell to the floor. Daniel took joy in the last part, ripping his legs in half and laughing like a maniac.

"That was euphoric," he said with glee as Roman came over, his hand on my shoulder, distracting me from my thoughts.

"What did you see?" His tone was soft as I glared at his bloody handprint on my shirt. He chuckled, looking at the mess he had made.

"Larissa and Duzi at Dover. Why would she go there? Why would she meet with the man?"

"I saw it, too," Daniel muttered as he wiped his mouth. "I never knew of any conversations that happened between them."

"I think we go back through his and her phone to find out what they both knew. She could have been possessed. It wouldn't be the first time it happened without her remembering," Roman said, moving toward the door.

He had a point, but it didn't stop the pit forming in my stomach. What else could she have hidden from me?

Chapter 48

Who Is Rory?

Roman

Nik could not bring himself to touch her phone. There were multiple missed calls, messages, and emails. I didn't bother with all of them. None seemed important when her death had been broadcast on the news a day after it happened. There was no explanation, just an announcement to say the Lady of Lord Dankworth had passed away suddenly. We put out notices to say that Nik would be in mourning until further notice, to cover his arse on his sudden disappearance. Nik put out a statement saying where he had been and what he had been doing. He thought honesty was the best choice and admitted to allowing his monster to take control in his grief. He apologised to his victims, paying for their medical bills and anything else they needed. He could certainly afford it.

Larissa had nothing on her phone linking her to Duzi, no hidden messages or emails. The phone contained photos of her and Nik, some of us, as well as some with friends. She made a huge impact, and yet her phone seemed devoid of anything. I opened another album named *Nik*. It had photos of places that she wanted them to visit. Various places around the world. I smiled. She never gave up the hope of having the life she dreamed of, even knowing that it may not end the way she wanted. I heard Nik shuffle behind me, and turned to see him leaning against the door frame.

"Anything on there?" he asked, staring at the phone in my hand as if it would bite him. True terror and fear of the item that belonged to his mate.

"No, but…" Was it the right time to let him know? I shook my head. "Nik, there is an album in here for you, I believe." I handed the phone to him, and I sighed in relief when he took it. "They are photos of places around the world. Places I think she wanted you guys to visit together, if they still exist. Her bucket list."

His thumb flicked through the photos as he ran his other hand through his hair. I waited as his eyes welled with tears before he sniffed them back in. I rolled my eyes, the stoic creature who could hide those emotions, but never from me.

"Thanks, Roman. I…I will hold onto these. I made her a promise and I intend to keep it as much as I can…for her." He exhaled. "Have you searched Duzi's phone yet?"

"Nope. That was my next task. How did it go with the council?" I asked him, knowing he would have had to justify his reason for killing Duzi. He sighed as I moved to exit the room that housed all the items he had packed away. I closed the door as he watched it intently. I listened to his heart. It was clear that it didn't beat the same. The pain tore through his chest with every mention or look at his mate. I put my hand on his shoulder to break the pain that floated through his mind. He smiled, but it didn't meet his eyes.

"The council are easy to manipulate. I brought Daniel along, who confirmed everything I said. The council were unhappy that I had brought it forward, as they agreed that his deception and treason were grounds enough to execute him. I told them that every day he lived was dangerous, and they eventually complied. My punishment is to pay the one million dollar fine, and I am not allowed to attend any court hearings for the next three months. I honestly think that is the best punishment. They are so menial and tedious, I am almost happy to be punished for killing a psychopath."

"What about your monster outbreak?" I queried, more concerned with this than our murder of Duzi.

"Oh, that. I never killed any of them, and I have compensated all the victims with money for therapy and anything else they need. As I said, easy to manipulate."

I snorted as I unlocked Duzi's phone. He had messages from Daniel, as we knew, and a few other people we knew were associates of his.

"Wait, who is Rory?" Nik pointed to a message chain from last week. I pressed it to open messages that went back years.

"I don't know any Rory, do you?" I asked him. Nik shook his head. We read through the plans for Dover to shut it down. They had overstayed their welcome, and Rory did not want them to use the space anymore. Duzi agreed. They wanted to destroy the technology, but Duzi was requesting that this Rory kill them all. Rory was a vampire, they deduced from the discussion between them. Nik pulled out his phone, searching the register for every vampire. There was only one Rory found. We nodded at one another. We would be asking this person questions today.

Nik and I drove to Northampton. He suggested that we fly and run, but I wanted to drive. It was time for Nik and me to talk if he needed. Nik opened the door to the Audi that he had gifted Larissa, and the car smelled of her perfume. My brother closed his eyes, inhaling deeply, and when he opened them, they were flaring red.

"I need a drink," he muttered as I handed him a bag I warmed before getting in the car. "Thank you."

We were silent until we left the city centre and found ourselves on the roads with little to see or distract ourselves with. My brother's shoulders were tense as his eyes darted around, like an enemy was going to jump out at him randomly.

"Did you want to talk about it?" I asked him, watching his body stiffen.

"Roman, this isn't the time for brotherly chats. I have no desire to speak of my loss any further. You have seen this before, it takes time."

"Yes, but none were Larissa, you said this. Can I do anything to make it better?" I wanted to ease his suffering, I wanted him to be happy. It had been so long since he had felt joy. Larissa changed that, and now she was gone.

"Unless you can think of a way to change the past, to bring her back, there is nothing to discuss. I did it, I killed her, and that lives with me every day. She filled her heart with love for me, so I wouldn't feel her pain. She pushed love to surround us because it was all she had for me, *love*. The one constant, even with the bickering and my inability to give her everything she needed, our love was…"

"Your love is what they write romance stories about. Love that is eternal, that lasts forever. I know she will come back. I know it."

"I cannot hold onto that hope, brother. She made me promise. The stubborn woman made me promise to never search for her, knowing that I would walk into Hell and pull her out."

"You assume she went to Hell, but she made the ultimate sacrifice. We know that means you end up in Heaven."

"It would never undo the evil within her blood and the fact that her father is the Devil. He would be fighting for her to join him. I wish I had listened to Pluto that day. He said he only wanted to protect her. He knew, and I didn't see it. I couldn't see past my own hate, and…" He punched the steering wheel.

"Hindsight is great, we know this, but it was her destiny to die. Even if she stayed, the gods would have figured out a way to draw her out. They are mischievous. Never put anything past them." I glanced up while speaking, staring at the clouds before us.

They would be watching us and finding new ways to test us. I stuck my finger up, making Nik laugh.

"We both know they don't care about us."

"They would care if I gave our father's spear to Pluto. What do you think about that? We know what it does. How would you like it if I gave Pluto the ability to walk the earth again? This is my way of saying fuck you."

"Roman, do *not* joke about that. You know they will find a way to punish us. Just don't get involved. I have done enough. I mean, Larissa killed our father's wife…" Nik froze for a moment. "What if Rory was Nerio?"

"No, they have been talking for years."

"Dammit, who is this Rory motherfucker? I want to kill him."

"Turn left and you have arrived at your destination," the GPS chimed. Where had the time gone? Even Nik's brow had creased, but we were here. It was never good when you lost time.

Northampton was a beautiful town. I had been here a few times for work. It was a mini-city that was known for its art and architecture. I used to work in construction, and was known for repairing that which seemed impossible. It helped to have super strength to do it. It allowed me to travel, which I loved, and Nik had connections. We had both made millions from working for so long and investing. Nik gave me the insider information on where to put my money, and he had never been wrong. My strategic brother.

"We are here." Nik unclipped his seatbelt and opened the door.

The house was quaint, a two-storey orange brick façade with white window trims and a red door. No garden other than shrubs in the tiny space between the road and the window. It was cute for someone just starting out, but I wondered why a vampire had something quite so small. Nik removed his jacket, rolling up his sleeves. I chuckled at my brother getting prepared to fight someone. He was out for blood.

"Shut up, Roman," he quipped as he rolled his shoulders. He wanted the fight to get rid of the anger he had inside. I would say he knocked on the door, but that would be an understatement. He pounded on the door until it opened.

The vampire before us was no older than twenty, with orange hair and freckles. His eyes grew wide as he bowed his head for Nik.

"L-L-Lord Dankworth, I was not expecting you." I glanced over his grey T-shirt, covered in food stains and the distinct smell of someone who had not washed in days. I wondered what the hell this vampire was doing.

"Move." Nik spoke with authority as he pushed himself inside. The vampire, Rory, stumbled, falling to his floor.

"What can I-I help you with?" His nerves were clear as Nik and I exchanged glances over the odd sight before us. The vampire seemed to live his life attached to a gaming controller.

"Do you know of a man named Duzi?" I asked as Nik searched the area for clues, his nose turned up in disgust. It was comical to see my brother being as judgy as he was in this moment.

"No, wait, no. I heard his name on the news, but I don't know him. Am I supposed to?"

"Where's your phone?" Nik was blunt, holding out his hand, and Rory handed it over. Nik flicked through it.

"What do you do with yourself, Rory?" I scanned the surroundings of utter filth.

"I play games. I am a game tester because I don't need much sleep. I just sit here all day."

"Isn't that a little boring?" I asked him, still confused about why there was so much filth for a man who stayed at home all day.

"No, I love it. I have a cleaner come in once a week. We have a deal. She cleans and gets a bite for her weekly fix, and that's it. I am happy with my life." He bounced on the balls of his feet as he watched Nik and me move about the room. I didn't care for the use of his vampire blood, but Nik might, depending on his mood.

"You are immortal and have the chance to do anything you want, and you selected gaming?" Nik's eyebrow curved upwards as he handed his phone back. Looking at me, his eyes told me the phone contained nothing.

"No, Lord Dankworth, I am happy. My life was turned to this at the beginning of our new era. There is nowhere to explore. This is it, and I am content."

"Interesting. Do you know of another vampire named Rory?" I asked him as I searched the room with my wolf senses, finding nothing of importance.

"No, sorry, I don't. I haven't encountered many with my name. What is this about?"

"We thought you were part of something, but it is clear that you don't have the intelligence for anything quite this sinister," Nik said as he turned toward the door, leaving the space he was clearly disgusted by.

"Thank you for your time, enjoy your game," I said as I left, seeing Nik with his hands on the car frame. "What is it?" I asked him, moving to the opposite side.

"Who the fuck is Rory? I was so ready, but it is clear that thing, he is not a vampire in my eyes. That thing just sits at a screen all day. He has no drive. It's rather gross, but anyway, we hit another dead end….*FUCK!*" he shouted.

"Nik, stop thinking you will get the answers straight away. They will come. Get in the car. We can brainstorm how we approach the general in the military. We know that is our next target. What ideas do you have? Because mine of bursting through the door will only get me killed. As much as I love smashing things." I winked at him as he rolled his eyes.

CHAPTER 49

HOW IS THIS POSSIBLE?

Nik

I sipped a glass of blood as I wracked my brain for any person that could be named Rory. It came up blank. I had a meeting with the general tomorrow. He agreed instantly, probably aware of Duzi's death at my hands. I hated sleeping. I stared out at the skyline, the only thing that gave me a reprieve from the guilt that crushed my heart on a daily basis. Her scent disappeared slowly each day, and I hated that I missed it. I didn't deserve it. Blood warmed my system as I took another small sip. My phone beeped, another message from my overbearing brother.

ROMAN

Are you sleeping?

ME

Go fuck your mate or something. Stop asking about my sleep.

ROMAN

Done that already but I don't need grumpy Nik, I need well rested Nik. You look like shit.

ME

Still better looking than you.

ROMAN

Yeah, keep thinking that. We both know I'm sexier and stronger.

ME

Maybe in your dreams. Goodnight, brother, I will see you tomorrow.

I turned it off, giving my brother the clear message that he needed to back off. I walked to the pool table, remembering how I spread her over it, feasting on her dripping pussy. Her body was a drug that I would never give up. I glanced down at my cock, now rock-hard in my pants. Shaking my head, I moved further into the penthouse, finding my way to the gym to work through my frustrations. I wrapped my hands, heading to the bag. I wished every punch would stop the pain, but it only made it worse, the feeling that I had taken such an angel from this world. My ears pricked up when I heard something. I stopped, looking around the room.

"Hello, Remus." I knew that voice anywhere, and I spun to see Pluto standing in the mirror.

"Hello, Pluto." I spat his name out as I crossed my arms.

"Nik." He said my name without a smirk, his face appeared genuine. He stared at the bench beside me, and I took a seat. "She is fine. I can assure you of that. Larissa is being looked after. She isn't mad at you. We both know she isn't capable of that. Let go of the guilt. It is actually hurting me to feel it." I peered up at him, "Yes, some of her blood is still in your system. I can still feel you as it dwindles daily. She doesn't want this for you. She made her choice, and she doesn't regret it. She wants you to be happy." He paused, looking somewhere I couldn't see as he smiled. "She has no pain. She is spending her time with her sister. They both seem to think they know better than the millennia-old god." He chuckled, and it appeared like his eyes almost sparkled. "We had our disagreements, I know that, but trust me when I say I've got her. Let go of the pain, Nik. You have more important things to focus on." He winked at me as a soft giggle echoed through the space.

I snorted as I glanced down. "Why are you…" I looked up to find he was gone. For some unknown reason, my heart felt lighter. I smiled as I moved toward the mirror, putting my trembling hand there. I closed my eyes, feeling a surge of warmth, a comfort, as memories of her flooded my mind. I knew once I opened my eyes that I had to move on and push forward for her. Our love would never die, an everlasting flame that would never extinguish. But hearing her laugh jolted something inside, pushing me forward. I owed it to her not to stay in the past, not to linger in the pain. With a deep breath, I opened my eyes, ready to face the future that I would create, no matter how much my heart ached. I walked up the stairs, lying in our bed, rolling myself in her scent and drifting off to sleep.

I woke the next morning refreshed, the best sleep I had had in a long time. I smiled, thinking of what today would bring, as I heard Roman call out. I glanced at the clock, realising I had slept in. Roman ran into the room, fear etched into the wrinkles in his forehead.

"What? You told me to sleep." He picked up the pillow near him and threw it at me, a scowl covering his face. I knew he would have thought the worst. "I had a visitor last night. No more brooding Nik. I heard her laugh. She is happy, Roman. It was almost like permission that I can live as she wanted, no more holding back. Let's do this!"

Roman crossed his arms as he pondered what I said, but didn't ask. I got up, and he covered his eyes, forgetting that my monster literally rolled in the sheets to cover himself in what was left of her scent.

"You are just jealous that it has always been bigger than yours," I jibed, looking down at my god-like body.

"Put some clothes on." He chuckled, closing the door. "I'm making you a coffee to go. We are going to be late!" he called out as I stood, dressing myself in black slacks and a black shirt. I expected to get dirty, and Maria had grumbled at me enough this week. I fixed my cuffs, rolling them up as I took the stairs two at a time. Roman held a thermos for me, which I gratefully took, opening and finishing the contents in a gulp.

"I feel like flying. Race you there?" I raised my brow at him as he smiled.

"There is something different about you, but if you want to start your morning with a loss, I'll see you at Andover." I opened the door to the balcony and took off into the sky, enjoying the cold morning air on my skin. The sounds of the world dissolved as I flew through the sky, twirling and feeling more refreshed than I had been in a while. I had a clarity that I missed. The smile could not be wiped from my face.

I landed, and as I waited at the gate, I thought about just flying on in, but I wanted to make a better impression. I looked at my watch as Roman appeared around ten minutes later, his face covered in spider webs.

I chuckled. "A little too much time with nature?" He pushed my shoulder as I dropped to the floor, chuckling.

"Sometimes you are an arse," he grumbled as he offered his hand. I took it, handing him a handkerchief to clean up the mess. I turned back toward the gate, and one of the men bowed their head.

"Lord Dankworth, Roman Silvia, it is an honour to meet you both." The other guard looked at him with confusion.

"I will never understand you supernatural creatures. Do you have a meeting?" he asked as he pulled out his clipboard, scratching his shaven scalp before returning his hat to his head.

"Lord Nik Dankworth and Roman Silvia to meet with General Chadwick." He scrolled down before the phone rang in the booth behind him. Roman and I exchanged glances as the vampire stared in awe at the gods before him. The other went to answer the phone, nodding before placing it down.

"You may enter, but you are not allowed to venture. You have strict instructions to head straight to the main building." His voice quivered slightly as Roman and I strolled through the base, watching the men complete their drills. Those who were vampires bowed their heads while the wolves did the same for Roman. The King of Vampires and the Alpha of Wolves. We stopped in front of the brick building with glass windows covering the front. General Chadwick stormed out of the building, a grumpy look on his face. His greying hair almost seemed to shine in the sun, peeking through the winter clouds. He was just shy of six feet tall with a broad physique. He wanted to appear intimidating, which would be hard against the two of us.

He held his hand out. "Lord Dankworth, Mr Silvia. It is a pleasure to meet you both. Come, let's talk in private." He motioned for us to follow, leading us to another smaller building. The room almost seemed like an interrogation as it was three by three metres with one table in the centre. Roman stood in the corner, appearing more intimidating as I sat at the table, lifting one leg over the other, one arm resting on the hard surface. The General sat up straight on the other side. It was clear who had the power this morning, even if he refused to see it.

"What brings you both here?" he asked as he squared his shoulders.

"Duzi informed us that you know the truth about the world. You or your superior helped him remove contact with the outside world. We want to fix that situation, to open up the United Kingdom to the entire world again. Let's get it started."

"Gentlemen, that is not happening. The world has been destroyed," he said it deadpan, without a hitch in his heart.

I glanced at Roman. "Compulsion," he mumbled as I stood, putting my hands on the table, bringing my eyes into focus and staring at the General as his body softened.

"Now, General Chadwick, let's remove that compulsion from other vampires and tell me what you know." I sat back down as his eyes rolled to the back of his head and back.

He cleared his throat and shuffled in his seat. "So that's what brainwashing feels like. I can think for myself again."

I pursed my lips. Duzi had been using this man. I wished I could rip him into tiny pieces for this…again.

"Lord Dankworth, Mr. Silvia. The world was nearly destroyed, leaving a lot of Europe uninhabitable. France was one of them. It is what destroyed our ships in the English Channel. Scandinavian countries are still around, Australia survived, most of Asia was obliterated, the Middle East is run by outliers, and there are no government systems in place. Africa did alright, but in South America, the vampires caused a lot of damage, which is shocking considering the power they gained from drug dealing in some of those countries. The West Coast of America was obliterated. The bombs set off an earthquake, which caused the collapse of California along the San Andreas fault. We predicted it for years, but I don't think we ever thought that bombs would do *this*. Before communication was cut off by that pig, we managed to let people know what had happened. The colder climate and overcast nature of the United Kingdom made it easier for your species to take control. To be honest, it wasn't as bad as many people predicted. There were a few deaths at the start, but the rules were clear, and *you* made sure that humans were protected at all times. The face of everything."

I smiled at Roman cockily as he rolled his eyes.

"What about The People's Revolution? How do they fit into all of this?" I asked him as I sat up straighter in my chair.

"They worked with us at the start, then suddenly, as if a switch flicked, they turned against us. They wanted the death of vampires. I am not sure what happened exactly, but they did the most disgusting things to vampires. I couldn't understand where the hatred came from."

"Who is their leader?" I asked him, stroking my chin.

General Chadwick pulled out a tablet, showing us different faces. "I am not sure entirely, but we have Peter, who is in custody, Wade, this girl, Mimi, Jackson, and many more. We haven't been able to figure out all the names. They seem to know when we plant a spy and kill them."

"Is Peter still being held here?"

He nodded. "Yes, for now. He is under twenty-four-hour guard. We only have those we trust the most watching him. Did you want to speak with him?"

"Not today, just double checking where he was located. I think that is all for now. I want you to call me if you remember anything else. We want full control of this. You will remove the blockages in place. Open us back up. I know there will be conflict, but I want to know everything. Do you understand?"

"Yes, sir, Lord Dankworth. I am happy that I no longer feel this cloud hanging above my head. I will do whatever is needed to bring about peace for our world." He paused as if unsure of his next words before he cleared his throat. "I am sorry for the loss of your mate. I heard she had a heart of gold. Did she...did she have a sister?"

It was a curious question. "That is complicated. Why do you ask?" She considered Luce her sister, but we knew that was not true. Cousin was a more appropriate title.

"I met this beautiful, and I mean gorgeous, vampire a couple of weeks ago. She compelled me to forget her, but I just remembered it when you removed that from my brain. Her looks reminded me so much of your mate, except her hair was shorter and her nose was a little bigger." Roman pushed himself off the wall.

"Do you remember the name?"

"Rory, I think she went by."

Roman and I exchanged glances. Larissa and I always wondered if there would be another. I shook my head in disbelief, not wanting to think of another version of Larissa.

"Can you show us the footage?" Roman asked as I sat still in my chair. General Chadwick flicked open his tablet, using his thumb as authentication before using a PIN and his iris. Plenty of security measures that he didn't seem shy to show us. He pressed into the files before opening his private office security.

"She told me to delete particular footage, but wasn't aware of the camera within my office." He slid the tablet over as Roman stood behind me. The face was unmistakable, and I dropped the tablet in shock. Roman grabbed it, watching it for a bit longer as I left the room to get some air. That body, the hair, the eyes, the movement. How was it possible? I pondered the thought when Duzi said that there was no nuclear blast effect, which is how she died, but she was alive and had been living in England this entire time. How had I not known? I bent down, my fingers touching the dew-covered grass as Roman came out, his silence speaking volumes.

"How?" he asked as I stood up, wiping the dew onto my pants. I looked at him, his eyes searching for an answer that I had no idea how to give.

"Honestly, I have no idea. I watched her die. I felt it in my heart. I...what the fuck is going on? Aurora is alive. Aurora is Rory, and she was working with Duzi. She knew the hate I had for that man, so why the fuck? Where the hell is she?" I growled, my monster stirred for the first time in a few days. My anger seemed to have awoken his need for blood. What had she done and why?

Chapter 50

UNINVITED HOUSE GUEST

Roman

It had been a few days since Nik discovered that his former mate still lived, that she had tricked him into thinking she was dead. Nik put a protection on the General's mind to ensure he could no longer be compelled by any other supernatural creature. If any tried, he was instructed to pretend and to contact him immediately. Nik hired his private investigator to find her. He wanted answers.

Stuart, Julian, Leo and Richard even reached out to their contacts while I alerted the werewolf community. I found the few witches who survived Larissa's attack, informing them of this vampire. Nik didn't dare visit them as they were still scared of what he could do to them. He had no care for their coven. Those who harmed his mate were dead. That was his only concern.

I returned home to Mimi's apartment. She had been working very hard at bringing information about TPR to us. They had been told about our move to open the lines of communication and were not happy. They were planning on attacking any form of telecommunications to stop our return to the rest of the world. I hated waiting for her. I missed her touch. It had been two days since feeling her lips, her skin, her everything. I just wanted to bury myself inside her and never stop.

I heard the door click as I hid from sight, only to discover she was speaking on the phone.

"Oh, Jackson, I know. The flowers are amazing, but I told you I am just not ready to take our friendship further...Yes, I am aware of what my father wants, but my heart just cannot handle another heartbreak."

She wore tight black pants that showed the outline of her perky arse, a white blouse that had her nipples poking through the fabric at the sight of me. I took her hand, dragging her to the bedroom, removing her top as I turned on the shower.

"Jackson, please. We have discussed this. I am going to have a shower. Enjoy your night." She hung up the phone as he continued speaking to her. Her eyes sparkled with desire as I removed my shirt. Her fingers tracing the lines of my abs, the touch sending tingles through my body as my wolf howled with need.

"I missed you," I whispered against her lips.

"Not as much as I missed you." My hands fumbled with her pants, letting them fall to the floor. Her phone buzzed, and I growled. She chuckled. "Oh, Roman, nothing could distract me from the need to feel you deep inside me right now. I want you to show me just how much you missed me."

"Oh, baby, be careful what you wish you." I lifted her up, walking into the shower set to the perfect temperature. She closed her eyes, letting it wash through her hair before flattening my own. I pressed her back against the black tiled wall with water that warmed the space for her.

She giggled. "You are always so considerate."

"Just wait for what is to come next. I am going to take my sweet time worshipping every single part of your body. I hope you are ready to be orgasmed out, my love." I handed her the soap to clean herself of the scents and smells of other people. I did the same before lifting her back into my arms.

"I am ready and willing for anything and everything that you give me." She moaned as I bit her nipple, loving it hard and rough. The perfect mixture of pleasure and pain. It was exactly how I liked it, letting my animalistic nature take over. I grabbed her breast before kissing her again. When she bit my lip, I groaned in response, tasting blood on my tongue.

"You are going to get it now." I kissed her harder, my fingers digging into her butt cheeks, bruising them as I thought about her giving me complete control. "Mimi, have you ever been fucked in the arse?"

"Yep, sure have. I hope that isn't a problem for you." She quirked her eyebrow at me.

"Oh, Mimi, you couldn't be more perfect for me. I don't care who you've had, I only care that I am the only cock that is to enter your three holes."

"Oh, really? Three, hey? Should I get started with my mouth tonight?" She winked, licking her lips at the thought of sucking me off.

"Oh, babe, you are going to be the death of me."

She laughed as I turned off the shower, keeping her in my arms. I dropped her onto the bed. Seeing her naked body on display, I pumped my cock in my hand, pre-cum beading, wanting and ready to be inside her. She scrambled to her knees, taking my hand and pushing it away.

"If you are going to stand there and stare, at least let me have some fun." Her voice was laced with desire, and she rolled her tongue over the cum and around my knob. I took a step back, and she almost fell off the bed. I snorted at her misfortune. "Roman!" she squealed as I lifted her back up, sitting her on the edge of the bed.

"Tell me, do you want to suck my cock or do you want me to eat your pussy?" My words were crude, but they only heightened her need. She was everything I had ever dreamed of.

"Eat me, baby," she whispered, and I pushed her back, lifting her legs onto my shoulders and bringing her closer to the edge. My tongue started with small strokes as she got comfortable before I opened her wider, letting my tongue taste her desire. A growl vibrated through my chest, my wolf wanting more. It wanted to just fuck her, but I also wanted to take my time. I wanted her to beg for it. I slid it up and down, burying my tongue into her hole as she squealed in delight.

"One," I mumbled before continuing as her body rocked, chasing the next orgasm that I could taste was close. Her juices covered my beard and face, but I didn't care. I just wanted to hear that sweet moan coming from that crude mouth. My mate, all fucking mine.

"Two." She slapped my hand as I continued to feast on her perfect fucking pussy. She was so wet, the idea of sliding right inside her was driving me wild. I held her tighter, pushing my tongue further.

"Three," I said cockily.

I stood, pushing her back onto the bed before dropping onto her and kissing her lips.

"How do you taste? Because to me, it's like fucking entrée, main, and dessert all wrapped into one."

She laughed as I lined myself up, thrusting inside, knowing exactly where that spot was located. Hitting it in just the right spot, her fingers dug into my shoulders, causing tiny speckles of blood to appear.

"Four."

I plunged myself deeper, putting a pillow underneath for the right angle, hearing my balls slap was musical. I needed this girl so badly.

"Five."

"Oh my god, stop it, Roman," she said breathlessly. I spun her onto all fours, pushing myself inside her again. She buried her head into the pillow as I stared at her perfect butthole. I wanted it. I was going to claim every single inch of her tonight. I sucked on my thumb before pressing into her tight hole. She groaned into the pillow, pushing her arse for more. I smiled to myself and let it move slowly before inserting another. Her body shuddered with delight.

"Six."

"Fucking hell, Roman, stop bloody counting." Her voice was a mixture of annoyance and pleasure.

I pulled myself out of her, seeing her wetness covering my erection. I ran it over her arse, lubricating it perfectly.

"I hope you are ready for me, baby." My voice was hoarse as I prepared myself for the sensation of just how tight her arse was going to be.

I was slow, not wanting to push her body too hard. She moved to get herself comfortable as I pressed in further, centimetre by centimetre, until she had swallowed me whole. I sat for a while, just waiting for her body to adjust.

"Are you alright?" I asked her as my fangs elongated. My wolf wanted to bite her, to mark her as his own as well.

She moaned as I picked up my pace. She kept moving.

"You are not comfortable." I could tell from her breathing, it was erratic and not from euphoria.

"No, just wait. Get on your knees."

I did as she ordered, watching her back herself up, lowering her arse onto my cock, as it slid inside her. She gasped as my hands ran up her soft skin and around to her breasts, grabbing them as she leant her head back. I kissed the crook of her neck. She was in charge of her own pleasure now, and I loved it. My mate, never shy of doing what she wanted, taking exactly what she needed and more from me. She forced my hand down between her legs, and I plunged two fingers inside. Her moans intensified, and it was like music to my ears, filling her tiny apartment. I could feel her getting close as her pussy tightened around my fingers. My balls were dying to explode inside her. I rolled my thumb over her swollen clit.

"Roman, I can hear your wolf." Her voice was light with a hint of laughter. "Let him mark me, please. Bite me. Do it!" she pleaded as I gave him control for a brief moment. He sank his fangs into her shoulder blade, and her body thrummed with energy and satisfaction. She couldn't take anymore, so I fucked her harder, chasing my final release. I groaned, pausing for a moment, licking the bite on her shoulder blade before laying her on the bed. I snuggled in behind her.

"I love you," she whispered. "It scares me how much my body feels complete when it is around you. Do you feel the same?"

"Yes, you are my home, and I knew it from the first moment I smelled your scent."

"I think I knew it from the day I saw you at the wedding, but I was too scared of what it would mean." She yawned as I heard my phone vibrate.

"Sleep, my love." I got up, cleaning myself and her before tucking her into bed. I left the room, grabbing a pair of pants on my way out. "Seven," I said, very proud of giving her so much pleasure.

I flicked open my phone, seeing a message from Nik. His investigator had found nothing about Aurora, where she hid or how she funded her life. Nik even searched his finances, finding no evidence of any money being stolen.

I pressed the dial button, and I heard it click before saying, "Nik, do you have anything with her scent on it? For the wolves to track down."

"Come on, Roman. You think I didn't try that already?" He scoffed, hating when I would show just how much stronger I could be.

"Wolves are better at scenting, don't forget that."

"Head to our old house, and you will find something there. I never got rid of that house despite what Larissa asked. I used it as a spare storage place. She would kill me if she knew."

"Yes, she certainly would. I will head there now to collect something and hand it to some wolves to search the country. We should have an answer within a day or two."

I shifted and ran to Nik and Larissa's old house, thinking about how they were barely able to enjoy their new one. The door creaked as I entered, and despite it being night, I could see light from upstairs. I slowly crept up the stairs to the room that used to be Larissa's. I pushed the door open, noticing a fire was lit and the back of a woman facing me. The figure was shrouded in darkness, with short hair hanging just to their shoulders. They held their arms around their legs for comfort. The smell was familiar as they turned slowly.

"Hey, Roman," she said, her voice registering as the person I had grieved all those years ago.

"Aurora?" I questioned as she stood, moving toward the light. Her features were unmistakable—the green eyes that could stop any man in his tracks, the olive skin, but her hair no longer flowed down her back. It was eerie to see her when Larissa had only just passed, as part of me wanted to run and hold her, while the other wanted to slap her across the face for hurting my brother.

"Yeah, I probably have some explaining to do. I will fix you something to eat. I remember the appetite you used to have." She strolled past me and down toward the kitchen. I followed as if in a trance. My pocket vibrated. It was probably Nik, seeing an intruder in his home.

"From memory, you didn't cook much," I said, watching her open the fridge that seemed to be filled with food. How had Nik not known about this? "How long have you been staying here?" I asked as she warmed a plate in the microwave.

"I think since Nik and Larissa moved out. It was really interesting how I was staying here at the same time as them. She was vocal in the bedroom." She chuckled as I cringed.

"But how didn't they know?"

"The staff only saw Larissa, and I kept out of Nik's sight. I wore Larissa's perfume to avoid being detected and only moved around when I knew they had left. Plenty of the staff were confused, but once it was announced that she was a witch, they kind of just accepted the weirdness."

She pushed the plate of spaghetti toward me as I smirked. It was clear she had ordered it from somewhere. I picked up the fork as she sat on the stool beside me. We ate in silence. I had so many questions, but I was terrified to ask them as my phone rang once again.

"You should answer that, you know he can be impatient and overbearing." It was strange to hear her speak of her mate with such dismissal. There didn't seem to be much love behind her words. I reflected on their relationship, remembering it had become quite toxic before the end.

I grunted, pulling it out. "Um, you should get here." As I hung up, I tried not to concentrate on the fact that the strange person, whom I believed to be dead, now sat beside me as if nothing had happened. Aurora and I never slept together. She found Nik first, and I believe they consummated their love that night. They met at Oxford and never separated.

"He is on his way."

"This will be interesting," she mumbled as she stood, pulling her hair into a ponytail and cleaning her plate. Her hands were shaking, clearly nervous over seeing her mate again for the first time in decades. I sat, watching her wipe down the bench and wash the dishes, drying them and placing them back where they belonged. She started the coffee machine, pulling blood from the fridge, and preparing a coffee for her former mate. I wondered if my head would stop spinning at the déjà vu before me.

Chapter 51

Broken and Mended Hearts

Nik

Stopping out the front of our old house, I stood there for a moment, preparing myself to walk in and see my mate's face. My former mate. I shook my head of the confusing thoughts as I headed inside, ready to see how the hell she survived. I opened, recognising her scent, which was different to Larissa's. Aurora did not smell as sweet as Larissa. I paused, watching her from the darkness as she moved about the kitchen, preparing a coffee. She didn't have the same grace or poise, and her hair was shorter. But the worst part—I noticed the ring that had stayed on her finger. She had tricked me and disappeared, but had the audacity to wear our wedding ring. Her head snapped up, smiling as her eyes locked onto mine in the dark. She sped over, wrapping her arms around my waist. I froze. I had killed my mate less than a month ago, and now here was another version of her, holding me. I couldn't quite comprehend what to do.

"Did you miss me?" she asked sweetly, batting her eyes at me.

I didn't answer. I walked to my brother, making eyes at him as he chuckled and shrugged. Picking up the coffee Aurora had made, I noticed she had remembered. She sat next to my brother, but I kept a distance, my brain and heart struggling to communicate with one another. I sipped the coffee, ignoring my monster, who wanted to feed from her. I couldn't, could I? She was no longer my mate. Larissa was. Aurora died. I felt it, but here she stood.

"I am sure you have questions, and I am sorry for deceiving you in this way. I discovered Duzi's plans, and I sought him out, trying to figure out what to do about it. He literally told me to fuck off and I did. The bombs started, and I flew to save my family. That was never a lie. I fell not because of the radiation but the…the rejection broke my heart. I knew that I couldn't reject my mate unless he wanted it too. I had to try. I said the words, and I felt it snap. Everything we had been through was gone, our love had dissolved in seconds, as if you never cared." I shifted on the bench as I remembered the discussion with Larissa that my relationship with Aurora had no love and was more like taking care of a shell. I accepted the rejection without even noticing. "I fell into the ocean, realising I meant nothing to you." I moved to speak, but she raised her hand to stop me. "I watched as you hovered in the sky for a moment before diving into the water to search for me. I swam out of sight before you could see. The pain was immeasurable. I found Duzi and explained the situation, and he was eager to accept my help. I stayed hidden in the shadows in one of his apartments, never crossing paths with you or Roman. I did his bidding, compelling and sleuthing to keep the country trapped. I followed him… more out of necessity than anything else. You accepted my rejection. It was enough to start a new life for myself. It hurt, but I did it. Katrina's plan to create the original version, that hurt even more. She was growing a new me. I protected her without her knowledge, keeping her safe with the help of…I shouldn't say their name."

I slammed my fist onto the bench. I was *not* about to let her keep secrets now. Aurora jumped, her eyes flashing red, and her fangs appeared suddenly with the fright.

"Aurora." Roman and I growled in unison, a warning that we wouldn't be putting up with any bullshit.

"Fine, your mother. Rhea helped me. She sought me out and helped me process the rejection and move on from you abandoning me."

I scoffed. "I thought you were dead. I had never been rejected before. How the *fuck* was I supposed to know that you were alive?"

"Don't speak to me that way." She gasped, horrified that I had raised my voice toward her. It wasn't something she hadn't heard before, we argued so often when the conflict began.

"I will raise my voice. I have just I discovered that you have been alive this entire time, and colluding with our *fucking* mother, who we also thought was dead from a broken heart."

Roman snarled as I threw the cup in the sink. The people I cared for the most had betrayed me in more ways than one. I stormed from the kitchen, leaving my brother to speak to the woman I barely recognised. The one who had suddenly grown a spine and a brain of her own. I moved to the bedroom, stopping in the doorway of what used to be Larissa's room before she finally accepted the connection we had. I sat on the bed, her smell filling my senses as I smiled at having her in my life rather than the thought of her being gone. I opened the bedside drawer, rummaging around before noticing Elizabeth's grimoire in a hidden compartment. I let the pages fall open to see her familiar handwriting. *How was Rhea involved?*

Larissa had been searching for answers, but always managed to come up short with any explanation. We knew my mother was involved when she told her to bite me, but why was she working with Aurora? Did my mother hate me *that* much, she wanted to break my heart continually, or was it something else that drove her? I heard footsteps, registering from the heaviness that they belonged to my brother. He sat beside me, not speaking as he put his hand on my back. We sat in silence for ages as I showed him the grimoire in my hands.

"This is so fucking messy." He closed it, standing and running his hands over his face. "I don't even know where to start. Our mother helped Aurora, she spoke to Larissa, and that message. I thought she was dead, like dead for centuries. Why the hell did she abandon us? I mean, we were little shits but what little kid isn't? She sent us into the woods to become men. I thought her heart broke from Mars staying with his wife even after all the love letters. My head hurts."

"That's because you're a wolf, an animal."

"Your point?" he asked as I chuckled to myself.

"You're an idiot." I snorted, unable to stop the laughter that left my mouth. Over the inability to understand what the hell was happening. Roman threw the grimoire at me, and I caught it, putting it down on the soft pink sheets. "Come on, we need to go back down and find out where our mother is. I want answers from her first. General Chadwick is already working on bringing back communication. We can't rush that, so let's figure out the *mum* situation."

Chapter 52

MOTHER'S DAY

Nik

Aurora told us where to find our mother, but knowing she would be pissed, chose to stay away from this confrontation. I sent Aurora to the penthouse. At least I knew the security would keep her somewhat protected from whatever could harm her. As much as my monster wanted to either kill her or fuck her, I took pity on her. Aurora stated that Rhea lived in Ireland, and she told her to meet her at the airport. Aurora chose to lie, saying she would be coming to see her. I hadn't flown in a plane for a while, and I had no reason to go to Ireland. I travelled sporadically at the start, but decided that the investments were better where I had control of the region of London.

Roman's leg bounced the entire flight while I sipped a glass of whiskey and blood. I had to stay in control of my rage. The woman who birthed us, the woman who raised us, she just left, dying in sadness. Or so we thought. The plane landed, and I buttoned my suit jacket and walked into the airport, taking our carry-on luggage with us. We walked beside one another, searching for the woman who gave us love but with consequences. I stood, seeing a tall lady with wavy brown hair down her back, wearing a flowing floral maxi dress. Our mother loved gowns, we knew that. She would twirl around, watching it spin with her. It brought the biggest smile to her face. She had never been given the chance to be more than a Vestal Virgin before she fell in love with a god, and her punishment began. Her only penance was the two boys who loved her unconditionally.

She stopped short, her one blue eye, one brown, finding me in the sea of people. Her eyes flitted to Roman as she covered her mouth with her hand, shaking her head. We walked toward one another; she was as beautiful as I remembered. Roman's wolf whimpered at seeing the woman who created him. My monster only saw anger for leaving us to what we had become.

"My boys." She held her arms out as Roman and I exchanged glances, wondering if we dared allow her to touch us. Roman took a step into her arms as they wrapped around his large stature.

"Mummy," he whispered, sniffing her neck and his body relaxed.

"Remus," her angelic voice called out, but I stood still. This woman made my mate bite me and helped another to stay hidden. She was standing before me as if she had done no wrong.

"Nik," Roman corrected her. My name coming out of his mouth seemed to snap me out of the brain fog that was filled with questions. I extended my hand toward her, it was the only source of affection she would be receiving from me. I wanted answers before giving her anything.

"I see you haven't changed, Remus, you—"

"My name is Nik," I snapped at her, letting go of her hand.

"Yes, I know. You changed your name after you were reborn as a monster for a girl." She rolled her eyes, and Roman snarled at her.

"Mother, watch yourself."

"Ah, the big brother always protecting his *weaker* little brother." Her words were filled with such hate.

"That's enough. You have no idea what Nik has had to endure. We need to talk. Lead the way. Aurora isn't coming." Roman shut her up, knowing I would happily snap her neck. She always looked down on me, always insulted me. She would make comments that I reminded her too much of our father. The way he spoke and the way he could manipulate through words.

Rhea showed us to a car and slid in, starting up the engine of the black Mercedes. It wasn't new, it had plenty of wear and tear, and the leather interior showed signs of too much friction in some areas. The carpet had indents and food wrappers. The woman birthed gods and lived like a slob. She drove for around an hour before arriving at an almost dilapidated mansion. The driveway was covered in weeds, the house was covered in vines that were dying from the cold weather. It had a bright red door and three chimneys. The large rectangular windows made it seem friendly, even with the dirt that covered them. It was situated on plenty of land with the smell of salt in the air and cattle mooing in the distance. I could see an old-fashioned butler's quarters that had no glass. The estate was barely being taken care of.

"Not impressed, *Nik?*" she said in a mocking tone, the disgust showing on my face.

"It is unique," I said, keeping my tone level and light.

"Don't bullshit me. I raised you. I know when you lie."

"Alright, fine, Mother. You live in a dump. Why are you staying here? If you were lacking in money, why pretend you were dead? I would have given you some."

"Your money comes from blood. Why would I ever accept anything from you?" Her words were filled with snark.

Roman grumbled and walked past her and into the house, pushing the door open. The interior was at least in better condition, with the carpets cleaned and the furniture up to date, and it smelled of freshly baked cookies. I moved around, holding my bag as our mother disappeared into another room.

"What is with the hate?" my brother asked, but I only shrugged.

"She started it."

"I'm finishing it. Stop. We need answers, not arguments."

I rolled my eyes as I walked in the same direction as our mother.

She was preparing something in the kitchen, the kettle boiling with its screeching noise. I sat at the tiny wooden table that could fit four people. She moved around with the same grace that I remembered, a smile covering her face as she put down the drinks with some plates.

"Thank you, Mother," Roman said with glee.

"Suck up," I mumbled as I reached for a biscuit. Our mother had exceptional cooking skills when we were younger.

"Nik, that's enough. You always were childish." Roman poked his tongue out as I motioned for her to look. She walked behind Roman, massaging his shoulders. "My big boy, you certainly filled out, and I heard you took your rightful title as Alpha." Roman all but purred at her words. The same shit, centuries later.

I pushed up from the table, needing some air. She had already started her crap, the same crap that caused a rift between us growing up. We constantly had to compete for her attention, but Roman always won. He was bigger, but I had the bigger brain. I walked outside to the nearest fence, seeing the ocean in the distance. Larissa would love this. I spun around, taking a selfie. It felt ridiculous, but it was what she wanted. I created an album, calling it *'Living my life'* and saved the photo inside.

"The promise, hey?" I looked over my shoulder to see my brother walking over.

"What do you want, Roman?" I asked, picking up a branch and snapping it into tiny little pieces before throwing them as far as I could. It stopped me from wanting to tear into someone's neck.

"I told her to stop, that we have been through enough. I said we were grown men, and we came here for answers and not to be compared to one another."

"How did that go?" I asked, throwing another stick, and watching it bounce off a cow in the distance.

"Nik, we aren't little boys competing for mummy anymore. We don't need her. We are here to see what she knows. We are here for us, not for her love, which we both know was devoid of any affection most of the time. You know this. Just block it off and view it as a business meeting. We need answers, no bullshit, let's find them out."

I rolled my shoulders and shook out my arms, knowing that my brother was right. We needed answers.

"Oh, here they come." Her hands clapped together in joy as we re-entered the kitchen.

"Enough, Mother, I want answers. Why did you tell Larissa to bite me?" I sat down, keeping my eyes glued to her every move as I listened to her heart beat furiously within her chest.

She laughed. "You are foolish. I never told her this. The gods tricked you, and I am sure you know which god was responsible. The one who hated me for supposedly ruining her life. But to answer your question, she had to. Juno told me that it had to happen. The curse that Pluto created was complex. She had to be fully yours for you to kill her and break it. You had to share an intense connection for her blood to be spilled. You should have let her die."

"You shouldn't have fucked a god, but let's not start," I snapped back at her. "Maybe you can explain to me why Katrina thought that if Larissa lived a whole life, never having known me, that it would break the curse? When I had to kill her to break it."

Our mother sighed. "If she lived, never having shared your blood and connecting with you, it would have been the blood sacrifice without you ever having known it. The moment she had your blood, that choice was over. The curse was always hidden within the *blood*."

My heart ached at the thought that she could have lived and been happy. It was my fault. Roman reached over, touching my arm. I smiled at my brother, knowing he wanted to comfort me from the thoughts running through my head. I shook it off.

"Why did you help Aurora?"

"She is a darling, I like her." The smile on her face was sickly sweet. "She doesn't deserve you. She needed support as she rebuilt her life. You made her so dependent on you that she had no idea how to do anything."

"I made her dependent? I didn't do anything. She moved in two days after we met, after we had sex, after she remembered her life, and she became a zombie. I didn't do anything to her."

"Nik, you cannot be that naïve. You were her everything."

"And she was mine. It was the same with Larissa, she chose to be more than just my mate. She worked so hard to prove herself. Aurora just wanted to be looked after. I encouraged her to work, but she didn't like it. I wanted her to try new things, but she said nothing interested her. Then, I discovered she had rejected me and had come to my mother. Why not tell her to come back to me?" I was exasperated that my mother thought it was my fault when I only wanted what was best for her.

"She didn't want that. She wanted to stop Duzi, and she wanted to do it for you. She wanted to show you who she could be. Aurora didn't realise that Katrina had figured out the curse. She spent every waking moment terrified that she would die from this curse, but it never came for her. She made the best possible decision in rejecting you. The day she removed her ties was the day that saved her life."

"Is that all they had to do?" I asked, feeling my heart breaking. My love for them killed them.

"I think she started the breaking of the curse. Larissa never would have let you go. Her love for you was on another level. Aurora had had enough of your cruelty and found it easy to let you go. Larissa had to die. She was the first, the blood that started it. She had to finish it. She accepted her fate and broke the entire curse. When you and Aurora solidify the bond again, she will never die. You can have long lives together." She spoke words that seemed distant to me. The idea of bonding with Aurora flooded my body with nausea. It didn't seem right. A part of me loved her, as I loved them all, only something was missing.

"It still doesn't make sense, why you left us. We thought you were dead. Why?" Roman asked as I shook my head to clear my thoughts.

"After Nerio cursed me to be a wolf, Jupiter took pity on me. He gave me the choice of accepting powers and disappearing, so I would no longer have to transform into a beast unless I made the decision to do it. I could be free. The idea sounded fantastic. I could live the life that I wanted. I did not have to worry about looking over my shoulder for the rest of my life. Mars told me that he would never leave his wife, so the choice was easy."

"Did you ever look for us or watch over us?" I asked her, hoping that she couldn't possibly be the monster that I had built up in my head.

"Yes, I watched you both grow, but some of your decisions disappointed me. I thought I raised you better, Nik. You became so selfish, so superior, that you never stopped to think of others." I glanced at my fingers on the table, looking anywhere but at my mother. Her words hurt.

Roman nudged me. "Until her."

"Pardon?" our mother asked.

"Until Larissa. She *changed* Nik. He became a better person. You would have liked her, Mum."

"I did. I met her twice. When she was younger, Katrina and I discussed what life would be like for Larissa. She needed my blood to cast the protection spell over the town. Pluto and I ensured her safety. It…It was the last time I used my powers. It drained them dry."

"We didn't even know you had any," Roman said, scratching his chin.

"As I said, Jupiter gifted them to me, but he told me they had limits. When Katrina selected where she wanted to live, being so close to the portal, we, Pluto and I, made sure she and Larissa were safe. We knew they would never think of her being that close."

"So you are a bitch with heart." I snorted, shaking my head at the woman who left us, but kept my mate safe until it was time.

"Well, I was a wolf, so I think it is appropriate, Remus." I shuddered at hearing my name and finished the cup of tea. "As much as I would like to sit and chat more, you boys have things to do. The world to fix. Aurora will help you. You boys will be tested, and, Roman, I would like to meet this Mimi, at least before you impregnate her."

My brother's face flushed with embarrassment. I wished she gave us more, but we knew our mother would never tell us the whole truth. That was her. We now understood that Pluto, Rhea, Juno, and Nerio were the ones who were complicit in the entire curse. Nerio was the only one who wanted to keep it going for her own personal torture because I was born. Gods can be as petty as humans.

Roman and I walked out of our mother's house. "Dare I ask if you are trying to get her pregnant?" I asked, not looking at him.

"Not yet, it is a bit early. I want my brother to have his happy ending before I focus on mine." I stopped before him, putting my hands on his shoulders.

"Roman, don't stop your life for me. You found your mate. Enjoy your life with her. I am starting to accept that I may never see mine again, and am destined to walk this world alone, but I will be the crazy uncle to my nieces and nephews. Do you understand?"

He nodded as tears filled his eyes. I pulled him into an embrace, realising I would have to say goodbye to him one day. Our promise to be together forever would never eventuate, but I would hold his hand as he took his final breath and look after his family line until I eventually found my own peace.

Chapter 53
You Are Free

Nik

The plane ride home was quiet. The realisation that our mother had been watching us and had done nothing stung. We had been abandoned by our parents.

I busied myself by checking my emails and responding to work issues while Roman just stared out the window. I think his understanding that we wouldn't be together at the end hurt him more than he would ever say. The sad reality of finding his mate and marking her. The plane phone rang, and when I picked it up, Roman froze as he registered an emotion from his mate. I didn't bother placing it to my ear, instead, I handed it over, knowing already that it was for him. Her blood had dwindled, and I barely felt her fear until seeing my brother react.

"What is it?" His voice was stern as his brow creased, showing his worry lines. "Where are you?" He paused, waiting for her answer. "Lock the door, we will be there in…" Roman looked at me as I checked our flight, spinning it around for him to see, "ten minutes. I'm coming."

He hung up the phone and then paced the small space, pinching the bridge of his nose.

"What happened?" I asked him, feeling his anxiety lessen slightly as we grew closer.

"She was attacked by Jackson. She has been telling him no, so he tried to force himself on her. I will fucking kill him. That piece of shit, I—"

"Roman, stop. Is she harmed?" I asked. From the emotions that I could slightly feel, it seemed unlikely.

"No, he tried, and she stabbed him in the leg. She is locked in her apartment now."

"Exactly, so stop worrying. She won't open that door, she is safe. Mimi is strong, she has to be, she is a future Luna. She just stabbed a man bigger than her. Tell the wolf to shut up and that you will see her soon."

He slumped into a chair opposite me with a small smile. I slid my glass of whiskey across the table for him.

"She *is* strong, isn't she?" He beamed with pride as my words sank in.

"Incredibly. The gods selected the perfect woman for you. They would not have paired you with her unless they saw that she would be suited to rule the wolves with you. Imagine her pregnant with your pup."

Roman's eyes glowed with glee. The idea of being a father was something he had dreamed about for years, and now it was so close to becoming his reality. I wanted him to have everything he ever wanted; I would fight to ensure that.

Roman ran to Mimi as soon as we landed, while Andreas drove me to the penthouse. I entered through the elevator and immediately poured myself a drink. I sat on the armchair, swirling the cubes in my glass as I pondered what the next move could be. I lifted the glass to my lips, letting the smooth whiskey run down my throat, when I heard her shoes clacking against the floor. Her wavy brown hair flowed to her shoulders, the same beautiful smile and green eyes, yet something didn't feel the same. I stood, not wanting to be in the room with her, and placed my glass on the table.

"Nik, baby, we need to talk about this." Her voice sounded almost broken at my sudden departure.

"I'm going to bed, Aurora," I mumbled. She had appeared back in my life as if she had never been missing.

"Nik." That voice, the way she pleaded. I closed my eyes, turning back toward her. "I love you and I'm sorry. How many times do I need to say it? The curse is broken, we can be together, we can have our life together." Her eyes sparkled with thoughts of our possible future. She walked over, putting her arms around my waist. She smelled divine, but it seemed to lack that sweetness that Larissa had. She placed her lips against my own, her warmth filling my body, reminding me of our love. The love that had spanned centuries, continents and curses. She licked my lips, wanting more, grinding into me. My cock barely stirred in my pants. It did *not* feel right.

I stopped, grabbing her shoulders and pushing her away as the realisation hit me. My heart ached while I shook my head, wiping my lips and turning my back to her.

"Nik?" Her voice was soft, desperate, and there was a question on those soft lips, a question I didn't want to answer. It would shatter her reality.

I closed my eyes to steady myself in preparation for what was next. "Aurora, I…you're not her." The words left my lips, and I spun back around to see her face.

Her lips parted, and her breaths became shallow as her eyes filled with tears that threatened to spill down her cheeks. "Nik, I *am* her. What do you mean? I love you, I never stopped." Her voice cracked as she clung to the hope that I would change my mind.

"It isn't that. You are *not* her. I didn't realise the truth until Larissa. She is my…my true mate. The one from the start, the one that connects to my soul. The one who made my heart beat again, every other version never compared to her. Katrina saw my devastation when you died, and I begged her to find a way to end my life or a way to end the curse. She told me she couldn't. I was distraught that I would be left to live this reality for the rest of my life. It's why Katrina fought so hard to bring her back, to bring Liyana back. She wanted me to remember that our love was worth the fight, to keep going even when I wanted to give in. She knew that better than I did, and it took me losing Larissa to realise that…" I held her face in my hands, moving her hair from her face. "She is my mate. I'm sorry, Aurora, but I can't give you what you need. You rejected me, and I felt it. We can't go back. I'm letting you go." I sighed. "Go live your life, do everything that you ever wanted. You are no longer tied to me, you are free." I kissed her forehead.

"Nik, I…I want to stay. I want to help you fix this. Please, let me do it." Her eyes pleaded to stay, begged for me to change my mind.

But I knew. Deep down, I knew. Larissa was the one. The woman standing before me, her eyes the same as my love's… She was the haunting reminder of a love I couldn't have. I couldn't keep hurting her. I couldn't say no to Larissa's memory, and I couldn't let myself destroy Aurora any longer. I backed away slowly, shaking my head, tears stinging my own eyes as I turned and took slow steps. The sound of her soft sobs echoed in my ears, but it was too late. My heart had already chosen.

"Fine, but you can stay in the spare room," I called out over my shoulder. I dreaded seeing her face.

I left the room, heading to the space where I stored Larissa's photos, which I put away to avoid the pain.

"Larissa," I whispered, picking up her engagement ring and remembering her vows. *'I will love you in every life.'* A single tear rolled down my cheek as I held our wedding photo in the other hand.

My phone began to ring as I put down the frame in my hand, keeping the ring in the palm of my hand.

"Yes, brother," I answered quickly.

"General Chadwick called. He has news and wants to meet."

"Where?" I asked, wanting this to be over. One step closer to bringing this world back.

CHAPTER 54

ATTACK AT ANDOVER

Roman

I met with Nik just outside the barracks at Andover. It was clear from the sweat on the General's brow that something had occurred. Nik and I exchanged glances. I scouted the surrounding area for threats while he sat the General down, using compulsion to calm the growing anxiety. His heart was beating so fast, we feared it would stop working. I nodded toward Nik, letting him know we were safe for now.

"What happened, General?" Nik asked, sitting on the log beside him. I stayed standing, watching the area. We were exposed and without magic to cover us, we could easily be attacked by anything, whether human or supernatural.

"They knew…they attacked…they…they killed some of my men…they took the vampires hostage." He held his head in his hands, his body trembling.

"Wait, you called us with news. What happened?" I asked him as a twig snapped behind me. "Nik," I muttered softly as his eyes turned red, using his supernatural gifts to see if anyone was around.

"Within ten minutes of talking to you, we were attacked. Why do you think I am meeting you out here? The place is covered in dead bodies. They want to stop you. They…fuck. My family.

I need to get to them. They told me they would kill them. I need to." The General tried to stand, but Nik sat him back down.

"You won't be going anywhere in this state. You are at risk of health complications, your heart is not beating properly. Give me your address, I will get them." His eyes flicked between my brother and me before nodding.

Nik stood, walking over to me. "I'll be back soon. Find shelter for now. I feel eyes on me." I nodded as I moved toward the General, offering my hand to him. Nik took off into the sky, gone within milliseconds.

"Come on, General." He stood as I put his arm around my waist, holding him up. He was weak and winced with every single step. "They kept you alive for a reason, I wonder what it is. Obviously, to send a message to my brother and me to stop trying. They are afraid, but of what?"

"Probably because of what you boys are."

"Sorry, General, I have not been called a boy in many years."

"You are younger than me. It is only normal to call you boy when you reach my age." I chuckled at his innocence in thinking I was younger than him.

"Oh, General, I fear with that analogy, I should call you boy. I am centuries old, I just haven't aged physically for some time." I chuckled, scouting ahead for a safe position.

"Oh, sorry, sir." There were rustles behind, and I turned to see four figures with guns.

"Fuck," I mumbled. "General, I am going to put you down for a moment. I need you to think of a building that would be safe for you to stay in while I take care of this." I removed my shirt and pants, standing before him in my underwear. I was ready to shift and tear them to pieces.

"The interrogation room that I took you boys to. It has reinforced doors, but it is too far away." He was right, I didn't want to run the other direction and have them escape. Nik and I would want to interrogate them.

"Alright, get inside the gatehouse. Stay low and whatever you hear, don't look, trust me," I warned him with a low growl before he ran.

I turned my attention back to the men who held weapons in their hands, noticing they had bulletproof vests and night vision goggles on. My wolf could feel something was off with one of them. Fur erupted over my skin, my teeth and claws extended, my back cracked, twisting itself as I dropped to my hands and knees before my wolf burst through my body. For any new wolf, it would cause intense and immeasurable pain, but after centuries, it barely hurt. My roar echoed through the still night air as the men raised their guns. This would hurt.

"You better run fast, bud," I said to my wolf as he took off like lightning, speeding towards the men. He slid on the floor, knocking all four men to the floor. I sensed one of them, their smell unmistakable. *Mimi.* My eyes found her as I picked up one of the men by the arm, throwing him in the air and catching him within my mouth. My teeth sank into his flesh, his screams filling the air, and I swallowed down his blood, enjoying the taste of victory. As I dropped him to the floor, knowing that he wouldn't survive that wound, I moved to the next, shifting back to human before grabbing his gun and snapping it in half. I stepped on his knees, taking away his ability to run. The last man pulled out two knives, holding them ready to attack. I smiled as I heard Mimi whimpering behind me. I didn't register that it was her, and my wolf retreated in sadness over hurting his mate. He moved quickly, swiping as I dodged him. My senses were on fire, especially hearing Mimi whining in pain. I hurt her. How the fuck did I do that? Her screams filled the air, and I spun to see the man with broken knees holding a knife to her throat. One of the knives was plunged into my back, and the other one into my side. I dropped to my knees, my body struggling with the sudden influx of pain.

"ROMAN!" My brother's voice echoed through my head. My eyes met Mimi's as I held the wound on my side that spurted out blood. He had clipped an artery. My healing ability had already begun to slow. Mimi's eyes filled with tears. I tried to stand, but a knife was held to my throat.

"Fucking wolf scum." He spat out hatred. "I will enjoy this, your mate watching you die. I can only imagine the pain you will feel. One less dog to take care of. Your brother is next."

My body grew weaker by the second, and he withdrew the knife in preparation, only it didn't come.

"You were saying?" Nik's voice was clear as day as I turned to see my brother holding the man's arm and knife in the air. "Nobody fucks with my brother and lives. *NOBODY!*" he roared as he snapped the man's wrist. I smiled as my body collapsed to the floor. "Hold on, Roman!" Nik yelled as I watched him rip into the man's throat, his blood spilling all over his clothes and face. His eyes glowed the brightest red I had ever seen before as he thrust his hand into his back, ripping his spine out. I watched the lifeless body fall to the floor as his monstrous gaze moved to Mimi and her captor.

"I would run if I were you," he warned as he walked over, but the man only pushed the knife deeper against Mimi's throat.

"Nik, I broke his knees," I whispered, fighting against my body wanting to fall asleep. It would heal, but it would take days. I had to stay awake. I had to make sure my mate was safe.

"Ah, that makes it complicated." Nik bounced into the air, grabbing the man's arm and forcing it from his body. His squeals filled the air as he looked at the space where his arm used to be attached.

"I'm sorry, let me go. I won't harm her," he pleaded as he scrambled, trying to get on his knees and beg Nik to stop, but unable to with his useless legs. He had one working limb left.

Nik looked toward Mimi. "What do you want to do? Shall I have the pleasure, or would you like it?" he asked, scanning her body for wounds before looking back toward me, his displeasure clear at me harming her.

Mimi held her hand out, and Nik bent to hand her a knife. My brother kept the man's body on the ground with his leg, his fangs showing his enjoyment at watching the torture this man was about to suffer.

"I thought you were a friend. I was wrong. This is for fucking with the wrong girl and harming my mate." She stabbed the knife into his leg on the femoral artery before moving to his working arm, slicing upward and finally to his neck. She thrust the knife inside as the man gurgled on his own blood and tears. Gasping for his last breaths.

"Enjoy hell, motherfucker," she snarled as Nik helped her to her feet.

"Damn, Roman, I think I got a little hard from that. Your girl is nuts." He licked the blood from his lips. She couldn't walk, so he lifted her onto his back. Mimi rolled her eyes.

"Alright, brother, what do we have here? This whole inability to heal as fast is really annoying. You are lucky I was already on the way back, but this just proves who is superior." He took a Superman stance, and I slapped his leg weakly.

"Stop gloating and heal me," I croaked as he bit into his wrist, bending down and forcing it into my mouth. I hated the taste of his vampiric blood, it tasted like burnt food and faeces. My wounds slowly closed as he inspected Mimi.

"It's a broken ankle." Nik turned it to inspect the damage, she reached over, stroking my hair. I lay back, allowing the last of the blood to heal the wounds before sitting up. I brought Mimi into my arms, holding her tight against my chest.

"I am so sorry. I didn't recognise you until it was too late. I was so focused on killing the men that I lost control of my other senses."

"I can heal her, Roman. Save your strength. We still have to talk to the General. Where did you hide him?" he asked, searching the area before nodding.

I stood up, stretching out my sore muscles as my body readjusted to its norm. I strolled over to the General, who was cowering in the gatehouse.

"It is all clear now, General, you can come out. I apologise for that, but it was necessary."

"Those noises were not for the faint of heart. Is my family okay?" he asked, finding his feet as I offered my arm to him.

"They are fine," Nik called out in the distance as he licked his wrist to heal the wound. "They are at Larissa's old apartment." Nik never told her, but he didn't have the heart to get rid of the apartment that she loved. He kept it under her name and paid the rent every month, hoping that one day she would be able to use it as a studio. He had installed state-of-the-art security measures for that day. Those ideas seemed so far away now.

"Thank you, Lord Dankworth, and thank you, Mr. Silvia. It is funny how you are portrayed as the monsters, and yet this…" he pointed toward the destruction of the army base, "was the work of humans. They killed twenty people and took ten vampires hostage. I heard some of them speak. They want you to come. They want to bargain with the vampires for something."

"What did you bring us out here for, though?" I asked as a reminder that was the point of the original phone call.

"Yes, I spoke with the outside world. They have been trying to get in touch with us for years. They said TPR control everything. They have people everywhere and want the United Kingdom to stay as it is. They want to kill the supernatural creatures first. They want to destroy all of you."

CHAPTER 55
WITCH'S TRUCE

Nik

Roman took Mimi home while I reunited the General with his wife and kids. I smiled at seeing them all happy to be together again. I crossed my arms as I leaned against the door frame, remembering an argument I had with Larissa.

In my frustration, I left, coming here to sit in the dark. It was the first time she saw me as something other than her boss, the first time she could picture a future with me. I sat on the floor until she called me in tears.

"Nik, I am sorry. I was unreasonable. I just feel like I can never give you everything that you want. I hate this bond, it messes with my head. I love you without any rhyme or reason, but when I see kids, it's like my heart and body ache to give you that."

"Larissa, as I said. I don't need kids. I only need you, Larissa Solis. I was born to love you, and I will die a happy man having been loved by someone as perfect as you."

"Come home, Nik."

"With pleasure, my love."

A hand touched my forearm as the General's wife smiled softly, her brown eyes showing her loving nature. She glanced back at her family, at the General holding his three children. She chuckled.

"Thank you, Lord Dankworth. I would like to show my appreciation. May I give you a hug?"

I stood up, opening my arms as she wrapped them around me. The touch of a woman made my heart jump a little. I yearned for the touch of my mate.

"I am in your debt, Lord Dankworth."

"No need for that. I am just doing my duty. I must keep—" She put her finger to my lips.

"Shh, we both know that Andover is not within your region. You did this because you are a good person. The General told me that you lost your mate. What do you know of death?"

I turned my head at her curiously. "That it is final. There is no coming back."

"I disagree. You die twice, once when your soul leaves your body, the second time when people no longer say your name."

"What is your point?" I asked her, unsure of the meaning behind these words.

"It means the more you speak her name, the more she will always be with you. I've heard that mates share an intense connection that words cannot describe. She may not be with you in the physical sense, but she will always be here." She pressed her hand to my heart. "She will never leave you alone. Have you ever heard her voice, smelled her perfume or just her presence in general?"

I thought of the day when my monster lost control. I heard her as well as on many other occasions when I felt odd, as if someone was near me, but I was alone. I smiled.

"I told you. She never left you. I know that you will be together again. Thank you for saving my husband and my family. I am forever in your debt, Lord Dankworth." She took my hand, placing a soft kiss against my skin.

I bowed my head before taking my leave, a smile lingering on my face. Roman's apartment was close, so I walked over in the darkness. My thoughts were plagued with everything that had happened since Larissa's death. I glanced up to see the moon bright in the sky, and I grabbed my phone, turning to take a photo. I held one hand up to catch the snow that slowly fell from the tree above my head, catching it and blowing it toward the camera. I saved the photo in her album.

The fresh air allowed me to think about what TPR could possibly want to bargain with. They had attacked with the purpose of getting ammunition. I searched my brain before I stopped suddenly at the realisation of what they wanted. I was stupid not to see it earlier. I needed a witch. I would have to speak to them about their support before I even entered into some type of agreement with TPR.

I stopped at Roman's door. I listened intently, hearing moans. I took a step back, leaving my brother to enjoy his mate without interrupting. I had to find the witches. I had to earn favour with those who remained.

———

I visited the old café that Juliet had chosen the times when we met. I could feel the magic brimming around the exterior as I entered. I smelled the air, taking in that maybe three of those around me were magically inclined. I listened to their hearts beating, noting one that sped up dramatically. I scanned the area, finding the face that matched the heart. Her doe blue eyes filled with terror as her hands trembled, holding the milk jug as she warmed it for a coffee order. I walked over as sweat beaded on her brow.

"I do *not* wish to harm you." My voice was calm and even to settle her nerves.

"How do I know you are serious? Juliet…I…your mate's sister."

"Just stop, that is in the past. I need your help. I have no desire for revenge. My mate let you go as she saw something inside your soul that indicated you were a good person. I trust her instincts, can you trust hers?" I asked her as I turned off the steam to avoid her burning her hand. She noticed as she put the jug down.

"I go on break in five minutes. Can you wait?" I nodded, ordering a bloodcino before sitting down to wait for my meeting with the young witch. She walked over, removing the apron around her waist. Her mousey brown hair was pulled into a tight ponytail with chocolate powder covering her black top and shorts. She sat down, crossing her arms over her body.

"What's your name?" I asked, taking a sip of the coffee that she brought over.

"Krystal." I extended my hand toward her, and she slipped her own inside.

"Please, call me Nik." I wanted to remove the formality to ease her apprehension and make me seem more human than a person of authority.

"Why are you here? Our kind want nothing to do with you, especially since your former mate outed witches. We are being hunted by those assholes now." I grimaced. "Larissa fucked us."

"That was never her intention or my own. We wanted to flush out the person who was keeping the United Kingdom trapped. We wanted to bring the world back together. I am sorry that it has caused disruption to your people. I can only offer you my protection."

She rolled her eyes. "In exchange for what? I know of your reputation. You only offer protection when you want something in return." She raised her voice, sitting up straighter, her confidence slowly growing the longer the conversation continued.

"Well, aren't you feisty?" I said with a small smile. I took another sip. "Yes, I want something in return. I won't lie that I have my own motives." She gestured for me to continue. "I need a witch to help me infiltrate TPR, some type of magical protection for my brother and me." I cleared my throat.

I wanted the protection more for my brother than myself. His healing powers dwindled with every passing day, and he almost died a couple of nights ago. I didn't want to risk his life again, not when his happiness was so close.

"How does your protection work?" She eyed me suspiciously as she played with her fingers under the table.

I flashed her a winning smile as her desire reached my nose, which was exactly what I wanted.

"You can either drink my blood or have my number on speed dial. The choice is yours." I pushed my card across the table toward her.

"If I drink your blood, does it affect my magic?" Her naivety was refreshing.

"Yes, it will be supercharged a little. You will be able to do more complex spells, but the trade-off will be that I can feel your every intense emotion. I mean *every*." I wanted her to understand exactly what it would mean.

She pushed an empty cup over. "Do it. I'll help with protection. They terrify me. What do you need me to do and when?"

"You will essentially be at my beck and call, you know that, right? Whenever I need you, I expect you to drop everything and come running."

She looked around the café, her eyes twinkling. "Fine, but I want better job security."

"Like what?" I grew tired of this girl and her sudden boost in demands.

"You have plenty of holdings. I want a job that I can pick up and leave and not worry about being fired. Do that, and we have a deal. The past is the past. My coven and I will do your bidding."

I gritted my teeth. "Fine, but that is it." I cut my wrist, letting my blood fall into the cup before I pushed it over to her. I watched as she drank it. I hated sharing my blood with others, but I needed this. She finished it, licking her lips as it dissolved into her system. Her sexual desire was intense as she reached over the table.

"Never going to happen," I said as I stood, buttoning my suit jacket and turning to leave.

"What did they do to you?" she asked. I stopped, turning back towards her.

"They have ten vampires and want to bargain for Peter's release."

"The man who attacked your mate?" I nodded. "I'll do what I can, but you have to promise that you will eventually kill that man."

"With pleasure, Krystal, with absolute pleasure." I smiled, and she reciprocated. "Stay near your phone."

333

CHAPTER 56

THE TRADE

Nik

I returned to the penthouse, listening to Mimi and Roman argue as the elevator beeped. I heard the smashing of a plate.

"YOU CAN'T DO THIS!" Mimi screamed as I ran over, catching the next plate.

"Do *YOU* mind?" I asked her, my eyes flaring as Roman crossed his arms. He was just as pissed as I was.

"He wants me to stay here. He won't let me out." She pointed towards her mate as she picked up another plate.

"Put the fucking crockery down. Roman, explain yourself." I kept my eyes trained on his mate with the plate in her hand and the broken plates that littered my floor. I would be making him clean this and pay for more. Roman walked away, but I followed, careful not to stand on any of the pieces. Roman rubbed his chin as he kept his eyes trained on his mate and her movements. Her heart was beating irregularly fast as she paced the kitchen counter.

"Nik, I heard something earlier, and I could be wrong. I hope I am as it is too soon, like way too fucking soon with all the shit happening at the moment. I was careful except for that…that first time and that other time… Maybe I haven't been that careful. She doesn't even know, and I…How the fuck do I tell her?"

I grabbed my brother's shoulders. "Roman, what the hell are you talking about?"

"Nik, listen, and I mean *really* listen to her body." I stopped, closing my eyes to focus on only her body, and my ears pricked at the smallest murmur. I sped over to Mimi, grabbing her and smelling the crook of her neck. She squealed but didn't fight me. She knew now that I meant no harm toward her.

I stormed back over to my brother. "Office. Now!" I shouted before moving back to Mimi. "Pick this shit up, Mimi, *now!*" I didn't need this. I didn't need another complication. I needed my brother's undivided attention, not a distraction like this. I slammed the door closed. "How could you be so fucking stupid? You know as soon as a woman finds her mate, her body goes into overdrive, and you decided to fuck her without a condom. You got her fucking pregnant before you even marked her. For fucks sake, Roman."

He hung his head in shame. I had never felt guilt like this before. The man found his mate. He didn't see reason, only a chance at happiness. Here I was, ruining what should be the happiest moment in his life. I sighed, walking over and grabbing my brother and pulling him into my arms.

"You are going to be a dad. Sorry, I shouldn't have jumped down your throat. It scares me. She…she is carrying your child. Does she know?"

He shook his head. "As soon as I heard it last night, I decided she is done with everything. She will stay here, where I know she will be safe. They cannot reach her here. What if something happened? I…I…Nik, what the hell?" He slumped onto the armchair as he ran his fingers through his hair.

"We will figure it out, but you need to tell her first. You need to explain the situation for her to understand, but I agree. She is done with TPR and sleuthing. She was done the day they attacked us, but still. No more. She stays here with your pup." The words were odd coming out of my mouth.

"Nik, I am going to be a dad." He cried happy tears over something that he had wanted for centuries. My heart grew heavy with jealousy, but happiness won out. My brother had everything that I ever wanted in life. I closed my eyes to the negative emotions, pushing them aside. If I couldn't have my happy ending, I would make sure that my brother got everything he deserved.

"I will tell her. Take a moment." I left the room, my hands shaking as I saw my brother's mate on the floor, picking up the pieces.

"Get up, Mimi, I will clean it. I need you to sit down."

"Nik, what is going on, and please, don't bullshit me. Just say it straight." Her voice and my fresh blood in her system alerted me to the worry she was feeling. I waited for her to sit down, and I ran my hands over my face before looking at her.

"You are pregnant. It is early days, and I mean like the heart just started beating. It is strong and we can hear it. As the mate of an Alpha, you must stay protected as you can be used to harm Roman and me. Trust me, this isn't ideal, and I know it probably isn't what you want right now, but that baby is growing and there is no stopping it." She dared not look anywhere but at my face.

"Fuck me," she whispered as her hands touched her stomach instinctively. "Are you able to tell me what it is?"

"Other than a baby?" I quirked an eyebrow at her. She rolled her eyes.

"I am going to check on Roman. I…thank you, Nik."

"For what?" I asked her, wondering what she could possibly be thanking me for.

"Giving it to me straight. I can always rely on you for that. You will be an amazing father one day, I know Larissa will come back, and you guys will finally have the life that you deserve." I bowed my head at her as I picked up the brush and shovel to clean the mess that she had made.

My phone rang and I picked it up without looking.

"Nik Dankworth," I said, placing it on the counter on loudspeaker.

"We have ten of your vampires. We want a trade." I knew that voice. I had heard it before.

"Wade, how are you?" I spoke with professionalism and a friendly tone.

"Don't sugarcoat me. I want a trade."

"Let me guess, you want Peter for the ten vampires."

"Yeah, by tonight."

"Tsk tsk, Wade, I am good but not that good. I am a little busy right now. I will see you shortly." I hung up, knowing that it would piss him off. He wouldn't harm any vampires, as I was known to be ruthless in negotiations. I would wait for my brother to finish his discussion before we thought of the next steps in this plan that seemed to be evolving daily.

Roman exited the room with Mimi under his arm. "We are having a baby!" he shouted with glee.

"I am happy for you guys. Mimi, write a list of what you want, and I will endeavour to have it arrive as soon as possible. Also, can you please let me know where exactly Wade hides during the day? I'd like to surprise him and disrupt his thinking that he is in a position of power."

Mimi smiled. "He will be at one of two locations. Either Victoria Street, in those old warehouses, or at Ranelagh Gardens. Today is Sunday, so I think it will be Victoria Street. Just make sure you are prepared. He is shifty." She snuggled into her mate before yawning. "I think I may go and take a nap." She walked toward the bedroom.

I laughed. "You are in for it now, brother. Do you remember how hormonal Liyana was? Constantly wanting sex, and the way she would snap at the smallest thing."

"Please, don't remind me. I am so not ready for this. What did Wade want?" he asked, changing the subject to avoid speaking about the stress that bounced around in his head.

"He wanted to trade Peter for the ten vampires. Part of me would prefer those vampires die rather than let that disgrace back out into the world. He shot Larissa, he kidnapped her, and turned her sister against her. He bombed a school. Do I need to continue? Even if I used my influence, nobody would agree to let him out. The only solution we have is to sacrifice the ten vampires or break him out."

"Which is why you want to go and meet him. You are weighing the choice of killing your own kind."

"To stop the criminal from getting out, yes, I am. I think that is more important. He murdered innocent children. I don't see an issue here."

"I do." Roman sighed. "We shouldn't be thinking about killing anyone. We should be focusing on no lives lost. I forget how heartless you are sometimes. Nobody dies. We break Peter out, we watch his movements, and—"

"And just hope he doesn't hurt anyone. Sometimes you have too much heart." We both paused, looking to the side where Larissa would often be standing, the sounding board of reason. The one who saw the grey instead of the black or white of us.

"You know what she would do," he said as he opened the bin for me to place the rest of the broken plates inside.

I sighed as I threw the brush and shovel to the floor. "Yes, I know. I hate this. They fucking win. They don't deserve to win. We will break him out, but I get to kill him when everything is finished."

"Done, as long as I can watch." He grinned from ear to ear as I rolled my eyes.

"Come on, let's go and scout out Victoria Street."

CHAPTER 57

NEGOTIATIONS

Nik

We ventured down the cobblestone region that smelled of chemicals and general human waste. The area had been cleaned up, but it still didn't remove the dirt that lingered from centuries of being a dumping ground. Roman and I split up, listening to the various sounds. Our witch, Krystal, was close by, keeping a protection spell on my brother. I didn't care so much, I would heal. It was eerily quiet. I could only hear my footsteps and my brother's. I stopped when I heard faint laughter. Roman appeared beside me, and I motioned for him to go around the other side. We moved with stealth as a door opened, and I sped out of sight.

"He will call. He won't let his own filth die." The man puffed on a cigarette. "Wade just needs to be patient, but I find it interesting that we haven't found Mimi's body yet. Do you think she is dead or ran off with that wolf?" He spat a lob of saliva to the floor, threw his cigarette down, and turned back to head inside as I ran to grab the door. I pushed it open, disappearing into the darkness of the warehouse. The noise increased, and I realised I couldn't hear it from outside. They had their own way to dampen the area. Interesting. I picked up the scent of a wolf as Roman appeared in his smaller version at my feet. He glanced up, his eyes glowing in the dark. Every step was tentative, and with apprehension that we would be discovered, I peered around the corner to see what was before us. The space had rows of computers and a big board with the world map, and various red lines were drawn through it. There were photos of different people, and I recognised Roman and I, Richard, Stuart, Duzi, Daniel, and Aurora.

I saw Wade come into view. I didn't realise when I met him decades ago that he was part of this group. I wish I did. His death would have been swift. He pulled out his phone, dialling a number before throwing it.

"Where the fuck is my daughter?" he shouted. "How the hell have we not been able to find her? A body just doesn't go missing. Jackson, if you say it is because she is with them, I will fucking kill her." Despite his age, he had taken care of himself. He appeared just under six feet tall, with thick black hair and broad shoulders. Roman snarled softly, and I hit his head to shut up. We had the one exit, and the rest of the space appeared locked down. It was smart, one entry, one exit. It would mean a huge number of people could die today if they failed to listen to reason.

"Shift," I said to my brother softly. He appeared before me again. "We need to stand united and not supernatural, as much as we want to rip them apart. Can you keep your wolf under control with Jackson and his attack on Mimi the other day?" His eyes glowed.

"I will try, but he attacked my pregnant mate. That is a little hard to let go."

"They don't know that, and it would be better if it stays that way. Now stand there and give people the angry stare while I speak, understood?" He saluted me with sarcasm.

We stepped out onto the bridge that led to the stairs. Our feet echoed through the space as Wade's head snapped in my direction.

"Hello, Wade, I told you I would see you shortly." He glared between my brother and me as we made the slow descent down the stairs. Men appeared at the bottom, holding guns.

"A little stupid to come here, isn't it?"

"A little stupid to think that we couldn't rip all of you apart in seconds before you barely managed to shoot us. Put the bravado away. I am here to listen to your terms before I get bored with your nasally voice." Roman chuffed beside me as I watched his eyes move around.

'The vampires are behind us to the right,' Roman said inside my head. I cleared my throat to let him know that I had heard him. I was wrong in assuming they would be underground at Selsey.

"Men, stand down. Nik, Roman, come and join me in my office. Maybe you can give some insight into where my daughter is," he snarked as we followed diligently.

As he closed the door behind us, I noted the space was larger than it needed to be with a bulky three-seater black leather couch in the corner under a window, a wall of books on the other side, and his desk sitting in the middle that could seat at least four people. He was overcompensating for something.

"Mimi is dead," Roman said completely deadpan, clearly not following the plan of not speaking.

"Did you kill her?" Wade asked. I knew Roman would not be able to lie about his mate.

"No, it was an accident. I was not aware of her presence until I tore her throat out. She died quickly and with honour. I apologise for this. As I apologised to my brother for taking away his mate, even though she rejected him."

"You come here to bargain? I should kill all your vampires for taking my daughter's life!"

"It isn't our fault that you sent her into battle against supernatural creatures. She was not prepared. Her blood is on your hands." I raised my voice at him, putting my hands on the desk and standing up.

"Sit down, *fanger*. You made your point. I was upset when she rejected you. I kind of hoped she would be able to use you further. It was entertaining to watch her toy with your heart." He wanted a rise out of Roman, knowing he had no ammunition to hurt me since Larissa's death.

"Wade, leave my brother alone. You spoke of wanting to trade Peter for the ten vampires. You are aware that no amount of influence will result in him being released. He bombed a school, he shot my mate and kidnapped her, plus there are so many more crimes. He has been sentenced to life imprisonment. How do you suggest that he be freed?"

He leaned back in his chair with a smug smile on his face, crossing one leg over the other as if he had all the power right now.

"That is up to you to decide. I have told you what I wanted. Get it done or I kill them."

"You know, Wade, your biggest mistake is thinking that I care for those vampires. I could just leave them to die, as you continually say. There are way too many *fangers* in the world. I am sure we could deal with ten less. Before I agree to this, I want you to stop blocking communication to the outside world."

"Or what?"

"Or I kill you right here and now and destroy your entire organisation? Sounds reasonable, right?" I turned to look at Roman, who laughed.

"You wouldn't dare."

"Wade, I have a few regrets in my life and one of them is not realising that you would be such a pain in my arse. I wish I knew it back then because I would have pushed you off the cliff to the rocky ground below, watching you bleed out while animals picked the flesh off your rotting carcass. It would have been a sight. Ah, anyway, let's stop with the blocking of communication or at least let me know what the purpose of it is. Why separate us, Wade? What do you gain?" I could easily have used my compulsion, but I wanted to avoid that, hoping the truth would flow from his mouth without hesitation.

"Nik, you forget that we aren't friends. I will *never* reveal my secrets."

I stood, walking around to the bookshelves behind him, scanning through the selection of books. Some of mythology, communication, marketing, and propaganda. It was an interesting selection, and I noted the lack of dust around one particular book.

"Wade, sometimes I think you need to use both sides of your brain." I pulled the book back, only for a secret door to slide open. "Oh, would you look at that?" He stood, but Roman forced him back to his seat. Wade reached for a gun, but Roman knocked it from his hand, making it clatter to the floor. "Now, Wade, I can search through here, I can compel you, or you can just tell me the truth. Which option would you like?"

Roman scrunched Wade's T-shirt in his hand, lifting him and baring his teeth and yellow eyes. A clear threat that we were done with his childish antics. I enjoyed these times with my brother, the brawn used as a threat to scare while I would use words to piss people off. I smiled as Wade glanced between us.

"I can call him off, but I rather enjoy watching my brother wolf out. It is magnificent to see him transform into such a mythological creature."

"Fine." Roman dropped him back into his seat. "We did it to stop *your* control and avoid your kind gaining more political control. The rest of the world fought and won. If you are able to get out, you would be able to spread your ideologies that we can live in harmony, and the benefits of living with *fangers.* If you have significant political or economic control, which so many of you have from your centuries on the earth, you would be able to gain allies faster. You'd be able to use your influence to trade resources and help destroy already fragile governments. If we isolated you, it would be a means of keeping your kind from using your influence on a larger scale."

Roman and I sighed in unison. "Why do you think of us that way? We have never wanted anything other than peace and harmony. We showed our existence to stop the eradication of human kind, we wanted the world to continue. You are speaking as if we want you all to die. If you die, we die. We have no food to keep going. We would become the monsters that you forced into my annual Christmas party that slaughtered dozens of my people."

"Yeah, they deserved it. Anyone who works for you deserves to die."

"Well, your daughter certainly did," I quipped as I let the door close again. He hadn't lied. I listened to his heart the entire time that he spoke. It was elevated. Not from lies, but more from the stress of the situation.

I sat back down at the desk. "I will break Peter out, you will let the vampires go, and you will allow my brother and me to leave the island and create a better future for everyone. That is the deal, take it or leave it."

"What do I get out of it?" He crossed his arms, unimpressed with the deal before him.

"You get Peter and your life." I knew that either way, I would be killing Peter as soon as I had my hands on him and possibly Wade, but I might leave that one for Mimi. She saw through his bullshit and might want to seek her own revenge. "What's your choice?"

He stroked his chin, "I want to come with you when you leave the island. Peter will obviously not be able to stay here. Safe passage to wherever you travel…to start fresh, ya know."

"Fine," I accepted begrudgingly. At least his death would be easier to blame on another. "But I would like something in return. You have resources, I assume. I want access to them, money, and a satellite phone."

"Then I want a million dollars as well."

"WHAT?" Roman spat out as I put my hand up to stop him from talking.

"Compensation for my daughter dying."

"Done," I agreed, knowing that if he thought she was dead, that was better for Roman and Mimi. I stood up, offering my hand. He slid his greasy hand into mine. "I will have Peter out in two days." He nodded as Roman and I made our way towards the exit, not daring to look behind us. We had managed to bargain without any deaths. I felt a small sense of achievement at that, even if I wanted to dance in their blood.

CHAPTER 58

PRISON BREAK

Nik

I walked around my desk, sipping my cup of coffee while scanning the map of the prison where Peter was located. Belmarsh Prison was renowned for being one of the toughest prisons before the end of the world, or what we thought was the end. I saw two weaknesses, but whichever way we picked, it would end with somebody getting hurt. I wanted to avoid this. Roman entered, slumping onto my leather couch. It made an odd noise as his jacket rubbed against the material. I raised a brow at him, and he snorted. He had dark rings around his eyes, and his hair, normally within a tail, hung over his shoulders. I wanted to grab the scissors and cut it off. A man should not have hair that long, but his wolf preferred the length.

He dropped his head between his knees, and as the temptation grew, a small growl filled the air. "Nik, don't test me."

I pursed my lips to hold in a laugh. "What is it, Roman?"

"Did you know what is involved with pregnancy and birth?" He sat up, leaning his head on the back of the couch with his hands covering his face.

"Yes, I helped a reincarnation birth her baby, remember? It is messy. Please tell me you were not unaware of the fun times ahead." I stifled my laugh at what he was about to go through.

"Fuck off, Nik, I knew about the hormones from Liyana but like, it opens up that big…" He held his hands up to show the size. "Like, wow, that—my dick hurts thinking about it. How the hell is that normal?"

"Well, I think Mimi may need to stretch a little more than that."

"What? Why?"

"Have you seen your big head?"

Roman threw a pillow at me, and I held my coffee up in the air to avoid it spilling on my clothes. I laughed as he stormed from the room.

"You can be such an arse, sometimes," he called back.

I left for a refill of my coffee when I saw Mimi looking equally tired on a kitchen stool. She moved her spoon around the bowl but barely ate. I cracked my neck as I watched Roman slam the door to their room. I took a seat beside Mimi, noting a tear sitting on her eyelid. I put my arm around her.

"A bit scared?" I questioned, and I kissed the top of her head. The girl stabbed me no less than a week ago, but she was carrying my brother's child. I would protect her even if I wanted to pay her back for it.

"I am terrified. I wasn't ready for this. I have no idea how to be a Luna, and now I have to raise a baby, a cub, a baby wolf. Whatever the hell you call it. Is it going to be a normal pregnancy? Will I grow hair in places I shouldn't? My head is swimming with questions." She paused for a moment. "Now I am wondering why you are being so kind to me? I stabbed you."

"Mimi, I would love to pay you back, but with that mark on your leg and that pup growing in your belly, all of that is gone. You are my brother's mate. You are family, and I will protect you as such. You are human, so the pregnancy will be shorter by two months. You will not sprout any hair, it will be normal, even down to the crying for absolutely no reason." Her hazel eyes looked up at me, and she buried her head into my chest. "Oh, Mimi. Did you know that the gods select who your fated mate is? Which means they saw the strength that you have inside, the power to rule over a bunch of powerful shapeshifters that have claws. You are destined to be with Roman. He loves feisty women. It has got him in trouble a few times, but he thrives off it. Roman is soft and gentle, and he loves a woman who can stand on her own two feet. He needs that person to rely on, to lay his head on their shoulder and get a combination of gentle love and tough love. You are perfect for one another. Stop doubting that you cannot do this. I will not have you harming the future Alpha." I kissed the top of her head once more as I stood.

I noticed Roman had returned, his scowl gone and replaced with a smile. Mimi turned around as if feeling his eyes on her. She ran into his arms, and he lifted her.

"My brother is right, you are perfect for me. We can do this!"

Mimi held him tight before looking up and kissing his lips. "I am scared."

"We can be scared together," he said, leaning his forehead against hers. It was a touching moment, a private moment, so I moved back toward the office. "Nik, I will be there soon," Roman called out without looking at me.

I waited patiently until the door creaked open. Roman entered, holding Mimi's hand. She was glowing already, even with the tiredness etched into her face.

"I want her here for advice." I noted the tone of his voice and the deadpan look on his face.

"I wouldn't have it any other way. Mimi, please sit down." I motioned towards a chair.

Even though our mother had been cold toward us, we learnt that women have heart. They build a home for you to protect. Which is why they must be protected at all costs. Mimi would be a queen among the Silvia brothers, and that wouldn't change.

"Alright, what plan have you concocted?" she asked, moving the papers around, making me want to smack her hand away. It was now time for Roman to laugh at me. I glared at him. He tapped Mimi's shoulder, bending down to whisper in her ear, and she let them go suddenly. She held her hands up and sat back in the chair.

"Thank you, Mimi." I cleared my throat. "The prison is impenetrable, and that design hasn't changed despite housing vampires. Even though we dry them out to avoid their ability to use their full strength. All the walls are reinforced, and guards are constantly stationed everywhere. The only chance we have is to break through this wall. It doesn't lead anywhere, but it is the weakest section of the building. If we compel the guard before his shift, it will make it easier. We can break through, but we need to make our way here. I will have to ask Krystal to come with us with some type of invisibility spell."

"No witches have those powers. Are you sure she can do it?"

"I gave her Elizabeth's grimoire. She will be able to master it."

"Wow, but—"

"She isn't here. She has no use for it, and after her support the other day, I could feel Larissa through the magic. I believe that when she sent it back to wherever it came from, the magic she took from Juliet's coven returned to her. She would want her to have it."

"Are you sure there are no protection spells on the prison?" Mimi queried as she stood, walking around rather than moving the paper now.

"Yes. I already sourced that information. The only problem is how many guards we might encounter once inside. Roman and I don't wish to harm any innocent people. We want to make it quick and efficient. We will leave within an hour to somewhere overseas to start bringing everything back together. I doubt Wade will hold up his end of the bargain, but we shall see."

"Did he ask about me?" Her voice was quiet and meek, something she wasn't.

"He believes you are dead. I think, considering the condition you are in, it is best if he believes that. I have paid him compensation of one million for supposedly killing you."

"Oh, right. Did he seem upset?" I glanced at Roman for help. What answer would be the best?

"He lost his daughter. Of course he was, babe," Roman answered, taking away the awkwardness of the situation. He rubbed her back, his touch a source of comfort for her.

"Good, I hope he rots in hell." Her head snapped back in my direction. "When does this happen?" She stood, shaking herself off as her skin turned grey. Roman stopped the motion on her back, keeping her upright and ready for anything. I kicked the bin toward him as she clutched her stomach. Roman grabbed it in a flash, holding it up to catch her vomit.

"Tonight, I need to go and meet with Krystal. I will see you both later. Roman, make sure you clean that up," I said to him as I walked from the room, holding my breath from the rancid smell.

I found the guards' schedule and discovered which were on duty. I visited their homes, compelling them to make themselves scarce between particular hours. Krystal had been supercharged with blood and had tested out the invisibility spell on various people and situations. I dressed in black pants and a black shirt. I wouldn't be seen, but I wanted to blend into the dark if the spell somehow stopped working. I stood at the wall with Roman and Krystal beside me.

"Are you ready?" Roman asked as I clenched my fist. I exhaled, shaking off the nerves, and nodded.

"Let's do this!" I clapped my hands together and bounced on the balls of my feet.

I braced myself as I punched the wall, breaking halfway through. I wound my arm up, ready. As soon as I broke through, Roman would run into the weakened wall to break it down. We only hoped Krystal could hold onto the spell for that long. My fist split through the last part of the wall as Roman charged. It collapsed with ease. We entered as alarms sounded. I took Krystal's hand to avoid her getting trampled by the guards who ran to the area. Her eyes glowed with the power she exuded, and I hoped her inexperience wouldn't mean the death of us. Peter was on the other side of the prison, so we sped in that direction. Roman and I saw our enemy, the man who had tortured someone we loved. A growl filled the space as Peter sat up, wearing the same disgusting white singlet with orange baggy pants. He had a smug look on his face.

"Hello, boys. How the tables have turned?"

Roman snarled at the cocky tone of his voice. He grabbed the bars, pulling them from their positions to allow space for Peter to squeeze between them. I nodded to Krystal, and she included him in the spell. She faltered. She wouldn't be able to hold on much longer. I swept her into my arms.

"Roman, we need to move quickly. Peter, keep up or get lost," I snapped at him as we started to run at a human pace toward the gap in the wall. We flew over the top of the guards, who were looking to see how the wall broke. I put Krystal down at a safe distance before going back for Roman, then finally Peter. Krystal, still sitting on the ground, panted at the amount of magic it was taking for her to keep the spell going.

"Krystal." I moved the hair from her face, her doe blue eyes looking up at me. "Drop the spell. We are far enough away now." She collapsed to the ground.

"Fucking witches." Peter glared at the poor young girl.

"That *fucking* witch just broke you out of prison. A thank you would be nice, or I will happily return you to that cell in seconds."

"Thank you," he mumbled as I threw a hat and fresh clothes at him.

"Get changed, we leave in an hour," I said, feeling my bloodlust rising at being near this man.

"Are you good, brother?" Roman asked, putting his hand on my shoulder.

"Always. Go see Mimi, but be at Heathrow in an hour, understand?"

"I won't miss it." He sped off into the dark as I stood with a man that I wanted to kill.

"How's your mate?" he asked as I turned my back toward him. I would ignore the question. He wanted to get a rise out of me, but he was not worth my time. I offered my wrist to Krystal, and she took it into her mouth. I would need to feed on the plane, as she gulped down more than I expected. The poor novice.

355

CHAPTER 59

DEVIL IN THE DETAILS

Roman

I ran into Nik's penthouse to find Mimi still awake, sitting on the couch and watching the obscenely large television on the wall. She ran into my arms, and I noticed how her scent had changed again from this morning. It was becoming a mixture of mine and the pup inside her. I had to leave her, but I wanted to be here. My mate was pregnant, and I had to bring peace to the world for our child.

"You are safe, thank God. Roman, I was terrified." I hadn't told her the truth yet. I knew she wouldn't let it happen, but I had to go for my brother.

"Of course, you know me. I will always come back for you," I said, kissing her lips. "Mimi, I came back to tell you goodbye. I am sorry. I know I said that we would be together every step of this pregnancy, but it was a lie. I didn't have the heart to tell you the truth. I have to go with Nik. I have to make the world a better place for our pup. You will be safe here. Bodhi, Andreas, and my pack will look after everything for you." I pulled out the special satellite phone, handing it to her. It had been coded to call only this phone no matter where we were. "I will call you on this daily and let you know where I am at all times." Her lip quivered, and I bit into my own. "Trust me, I want to be here to see those scans and watch your belly swell, but…I can't. I want you to remember one thing: I love you and you are my everything. You reminded me what true love is the moment I saw your hazel eyes. I was hooked. You are my everything and will be until the day we die together, old in our beds, surrounded by our children and grandchildren."

"Roman…" Tears covered her soft, white cheeks. "I…I understand, but I'm scared."

"Scared of what?" I asked her, moving the hair from her face.

"Scared you won't come back to me."

I chuckled. "Mimi, I have everything right here, waiting for me. I will fight tooth and nail to get back to you. I will crawl through the depths of Hell if I need to, but no matter what, I will be here. I am going to make you a promise. I will be here on the day that you give birth to our child. I will be holding your hand, dabbing your forehead, and listening to you yell and scream how much you hate me for doing this to you. I swear it."

She smiled and nodded as she kissed my lips. "If anything happens to you, just know that I will kill your brother and I will not hesitate."

"Trust me, he knows. I love you with all my heart, Mimi."

"As do I, Roman, as do I." I held her tightly to my chest, committing the feeling to memory. I would be back for this. I had so much to live for. It had taken centuries, but my life was finally beginning.

I left knowing that I had one more thing to do before meeting Nik on that plane. I ran to my apartment, breaking into the safe that housed my father's spear, the one our mother gifted to me. After speaking to Nik and hearing about the punishment that Malignus had been through for nothing, I knew what I needed to do. I cut my hand, summoning the Devil to the space. Larissa had given me the spell, as if knowing I would need it one day. I waited for a while before he stepped out of the flames in the fireplace.

"Now, I never expected to be meeting with…" He stopped, his eyes seeing the spear in my hands.

"Is that what I think it is?" he asked, moving closer, his eyes glowing the brightest I had ever seen them.

"Yes, it is, and I am willing to give it to you, but I have one condition."

"Wait, you want to give me the spear that I requested centuries ago before I cursed your brother and his love to torture for infinity?" He took a seat in my armchair, crossing his legs. "This should be good."

"Malignus…"

"You are holding something that belongs to me. I would prefer you call me by the name that I was born with." His tone was short and curt.

"Pluto, I wish to give you back the spear to use as you please, as is your right, but I must ask for one favour."

"Why the hell would I give you anything? You kept it from me." A small growl vibrated from his chest.

"Just shut up. I want you to set Nik free."

"I might need more than that because I hear that as you want me to kill your brother." He leaned his arm on the side, his finger running along the dimple in his chin.

"I want him to finally find his happiness. I want you to bring Larissa back. I want them to have everything that they ever missed. So they get to grow old together, have children, and live their lives as they were always meant to."

"What do I get out of this? You understand this is a big ask, one that requires sacrifice." His eyes sparkled.

"I am giving you the spear that allows you to walk the earth, the one that will allow you to collect more souls with every new deal you make. The one that will allow you to create an army if you wish. There is no need for a further sacrifice, as it is all right here," I said, banging the spear on the ground to remind him.

Pluto licked his lips. "That is a lot of power. You understand that they are watching this right now. You have just been given a mate and now a son, I believe."

"A son?" My knees wobbled. "A boy?" My heart ached to run back to my mate, who was carrying my boy, a son I would mould to be exactly as strong as his father and as fierce as his mother.

"Oh, yes. Sorry for the spoiler. Do you not fear their retribution?" he asked as I pondered his question.

"They made many mistakes, one of them causing the pain that my brother suffered for centuries. They can deal with this on their own. Nik and I deserve to be happy, and I want this for my brother."

"Bringing his mate back won't be that easy. If I do this, Nik would lose his powers, he would return to being a wolf, and his vampire powers would be gone. He has thrived as this monster. Are you sure this is something he would want? Can you live with making this decision for him? We know that Nik is not always forgiving. What if this breaks the brotherly bond that has kept you together for millennia?"

I breathed in and out. "Yes, do it." The words left my mouth without a care for the consequences. I only hoped that Nik would forgive me for giving him the life that he deserved.

Pluto stood, grabbing the spear from my hands, and twirled it around as it glowed from his touch. "Ah, I will enjoy this." The room filled with light and warmth. "Roman, I suggest you leave quickly. Unless you want to miss your flight."

"What is that noise?" As a sharp ringing filled the space, and I covered my ears slightly.

"Jupiter. Leave, Roman." He flipped the spear around his back, swinging with a finesse that I didn't know he had. I left the building as it shook.

I closed my eyes, running towards my brother and hoping that he would understand one day. I had unleashed the Devil on the world, but maybe it was time that he caused a little chaos. It might need it.

CHAPTER 60

WHO IS THE REAL ENEMY?

Nik

I waited with Wade and Peter as they bickered inside the plane at Farnborough Airfield. I grew impatient, my fingers tapping against the top of the door frame as I waited for my brother to arrive. I walked down the stairs to listen more clearly, hearing a small howl in the distance. I breathed out in relief. He was coming. I knew he planned to say goodbye to Mimi, but I wasn't sure whether it would be a long or short goodbye. I glanced at three hangars to my left. It was a tiny airstrip, but big enough to fly my jet in the middle of the night.

"Oi, *fanger*, how much longer?" Peter shouted from inside. The desire to rip his throat out grew by the second. I closed my eyes to focus my thoughts on peace rather than his untimely demise.

"However long I say, asshole!" I shouted back at him. I could hear Wade trying to calm him down. It was my plane, it was my plan, he needed to remember that. Roman's wolf came running around the corner, his eyes glowing in the dark. He shifted as I ducked in, grabbing him some clothes. He took them, dressing quickly and tying his hair back into a ponytail.

"Are we ready?" he asked.

I shook my head. I wasn't prepared for this. I had no idea what to do or what to even expect with the world that kept going while we stayed trapped within our little bubble.

"We will figure it out," he said as he zipped up his jeans and walked into the plane. I had a sense of dread at leaving, like something was missing. A figure appeared beside me.

"You forgot about me, didn't you, Nik?" Aurora's voice echoed in the dark.

"Yes, I did. I won't lie. I did. Sorry, please head on inside." She pushed her luggage into my arms with force. This would be interesting. She had made herself scarce since I rejected her advances the other day. She would be bitter, but nobody would ever compare to Larissa.

I placed her luggage into the overhead compartment, then took my seat, buckling in near the window as I crossed one leg over the other.

"Are we ready, sir?" The pilot popped his head out. He had been compelled to drop us off and return home without remembering who was on the flight. I couldn't risk being discovered as the person who broke Peter out of jail.

"Yes, let's take off, Greg." He closed his door as the engine turned over, and he proceeded to turn right toward the runway. He drove, increasing his speed before the plane lifted off the ground, and we were in the air. I had helped a dangerous criminal escape. What would people think if the truth was ever discovered?

Mimi, Stuart, and Julian had been placed in charge of various tasks to keep my holdings functioning and earning money. We would be in the air for roughly two and half hours, and I would be trapped inside a small space with two assholes for two hours. Roman appeared as Aurora joined me.

"What are you doing?" Roman asked, looking slyly to his side to avoid making eyes with Wade and Peter.

"I want to keep them near. I don't trust them. Would you?" He grunted with agreement, and Aurora smiled. It was odd to see her face, but it was more the short hair that seemed to confuse me further.

"Are you alright, Nik?" she queried, looking at Roman for support.

"I think he is just wondering why you cut all your hair off." Roman chuckled as he leaned back in his chair. He appeared to be enjoying this awkward interaction.

"I just found it easier to maintain. I do miss my long hair, though. Did you want me to grow it back?" Her voice had a new sense of hope to it.

"No," I answered bluntly, hoping she would remember that there was nothing between us anymore and stop thinking that way. I settled into my seat.

"Nik, have a rest. You look like shit," Roman said as he moved to sit beside me, his eyes trained on our enemy.

"But we should think about what we need to do when we land."

"Nik, sleep. I know for a fact that you haven't had much since she died. Just close your eyes. We will figure it out."

I knew my brother was right, so I allowed my body to rest. I had been taking a few hours every now and then, but I found the more I slept, the more my thoughts were consumed by her. I had to move on. I made her a promise, and I would fulfil it. I closed my eyes, seeing her smiling face, allowing me to sleep.

Roman woke me up a few hours later. I glanced out the window, stretching out my legs and arms. I could see the Colosseum, remembering it being built over eight long years. Roman and I even spent some time helping out at one stage for fun. In the intricate tunnels, we carved our initials. I wondered if they were still standing. It had started to fall apart centuries ago, and I wondered what it looked like after the planet had been ravaged by war.

"Home," Aurora said, as it was where she remembered her soul had been born. The place where our love story started.

"Beginning our descent, please ensure your seatbelts are buckled in as we make our way to the ground," Greg's voice called out through the intercom. It was a little bumpy as we landed. The airport had been modernised, as had the planes. They appeared sleeker, shinier, and less bulky. The world had certainly continued to move on without us. I half expected it to. I pondered what new technology would be around. Greg exited the cockpit, opening the door as the sun was beginning to rise. We left London at around three in the morning, and Rome was one hour ahead. The smell had not changed. I thought about how much of this place had changed since we founded it centuries ago.

Roman slapped my back. "Bringing back memories, hey?"

"It is."

It felt almost poetic to be here again. We had visited at various times in the past but had never stayed for too long. We moved on, and it never had the same feeling for us again. London became home. Police cars swarmed the area. We had been on a flight that didn't file a flight plan, as the communication was still spotty between us. I nudged Wade forward.

"This is where you come in. Double cross me and I will kill you right now." He rolled his eyes.

"Your threats are getting old, *fanger.*" He plastered a smile on his face as I attempted to appear as human as possible. Roman even managed a different look than his constant scowl.

The four cars stopped, pulling out guns and holding them up. The cars were small, white, shiny and sleek, and I noticed that they did not make a lot of noise. They were electric, still running, but I could barely hear an engine. The officer's clothes were dark blue with *Polizia* written across the front in shiny reflective material. Their guns were thinner than I remembered, with glowing blue handles where the bullets were located. They contained a serum of some type. The world had certainly moved on.

Wade stepped forward, holding his hands in the air as they yelled for him to stop. Part of me hoped that he would be shot and die. One of the officers walked over, holding his gun higher before lowering it and patting him down.

"Sicuro," he shouted, meaning it was safe, that he had no weapons.

"We came from London. We are here to speak to your leaders." Wade spoke as if they were stupid or had some type of learning disability. I rolled my eyes, stepping forward. This needed someone a little more intelligent than his meagre means.

"I apologise," I said clearly as I contemplated whether to speak Italian or not. "We have arrived to discuss the situation, and we want a resolution. We want to bring London back to join the rest of the world. We require a meeting with your world leaders. We are happy to be taken into custody, and understand that you may require proof of what we are saying before we reach the person who can help us to achieve our goal. We are willingly complying with any of your requests."

"Car. Now," the young officer said, and I moved toward it. The door opened, and I slid inside, motioning for Wade to join. I didn't want him and Peter together in the same car. Roman joined Peter while Aurora rode in a car alone. I kept my eyes trained ahead, not wanting to look out the window and have reminders of the past. I was here to fix issues, not to reminisce on what could have been.

"I had it under control," Wade whispered.

"You sounded like a moron. Excuse me for adding some intelligence to the mix. If we want to be taken seriously, we must sound like we know what the hell we are talking about. You spoke to these people before. I am beginning to doubt what you actually know," I retorted, a smile on my face as the young officer looked in his rear-view mirror.

We arrived at the station, where the glass façade made it seem cold rather than the old architecture that Rome used to be known for. We headed inside, each of us taken into separate rooms. I worried about this, about what hate Peter and Wade could spew. I had no idea about this society's thoughts on supernatural creatures, and being the King of Vampires would certainly not go down well. I had to avoid using compulsion as much as possible. The world had changed, but not as much as I expected it to. Time would reveal the fallout from the nuclear war.

I sat at the cold steel table, tapping my fingers as I waited for the inevitable interrogation that would surely bore me to death. I listened to the sounds outside, only to discover silence. I stood up, walking over to the walls to discover they had intense soundproofing that my superior hearing could somehow not penetrate. Was it magic or just new technology? We showed ourselves to the entire world, and they knew of our existence. I didn't sense any vampires among the men who took us into custody.

The door opened, so I sat down again to show that I was not a threat to the detective, who sat down on the opposite side of the table. He had his sleeves pushed up, not rolled. He was unrefined with very little class. His hair was balding, and he had dull brown eyes, greying hair, and a putrid smell that came from his mouth. I wondered if it was an attempt to throw me off.

"What's your name?" he asked, pulling out a notepad and clicking his pen. He didn't bother to look up at me. Almost as if I was beneath him. This interrogation tactic was intriguing. I stroked my chin as I leaned back in the chair, folding one leg over the other. I would play the same game as him.

"Remus." I wanted to avoid him knowing my real name of Nik Dankworth. It was a test.

"Remus, where did you come from?"

"London, England. I flew over with Wade, Peter, Roman, and Aurora." I purposely put those more important at the end.

"Why are you here? We know that the United Kingdom has been run by vampires for decades. How did you escape?" Again, he didn't bother to glance up when asking his questions.

"We wanted to bring the world back together, we want peace. There is no need for us to separate anymore."

He looked up, his dull brown eyes watching my every move. He clicked the ink, but tapped the pen on the paper, as if contemplating things. He cleared his throat as he waved at the two-way glass. Another man walked in, with a more refined look about him. His hair was slicked back like the eighties, but his clothes were different. He wore black suit pants with a leather-looking jacket, a material I had never encountered before. His shirt smelled like cotton, but the jacket plagued my mind with what it was made of. His skin was olive with deep brown eyes, and he wore an expression intended to terrify. The King of Vampires sat before him. I had no reason to fear a pathetic human who wanted to intimidate me. He walked around the room as I smirked.

"I understand this is an intimidation technique, but I find it to be a bore. I come in peace and have no reason to harm any of you. Please, just get this over with so I may go about the business that I set out for."

"You want to meet with our leader, but according to the men in the other room, you murdered his daughter and friend with no remorse. You are a vampire who has a mountain of bodies behind you. Your sole aim is to destroy the world and turn all humans into blood bags."

I kept my face stern, but I couldn't hold it for too long. I burst out with laughter, holding my stomach before I stood. The men flinched.

"Go back and speak to Roman, he will make a call to Mimi, the girl whom I supposedly killed. She is safe and currently staying in my penthouse. I have no reason to harm a pregnant girl. Go on, I will wait for your apology for believing the men who attacked, kidnapped, and tried to kill my wife. Who turned her sister against her with his manipulation. Peter and Wade are nasty people, and I brought them with me because I dreaded leaving them in London, where they could do more damage than good."

The man with slicked-back hair left the room before bringing Roman in and handing him the phone. Roman looked at me curiously as he took it.

"Call Mimi. Wade and Peter have spoken about my horrific crimes."

"Oh, yeah, I am apparently a werewolf as well. Did they have their meds this morning?" I knew my brother would keep up the charade of us being the better men. Roman pressed buttons on the phone, and it rang before he placed it on speaker. We waited, hoping that Mimi would answer.

"Hello?" her voice croaked, obvious that we woke her. "Roman?"

"Hello, beautiful, I am here. I just need you to tell me who you are. Wade and Peter have told the police that—" I cleared my throat. "Remus murdered you." We had our signals, and I was grateful for the centuries of knowing each other well enough.

"I am Mimi May Sullivan Silvia. I was not murdered by Remus. He saved my life, which was put in danger by my foster father, Wade Sullivan." Roman beamed at hearing her use his last name. He handed the phone to the men.

"Hello, Miss Silvia," the slicked-back-haired man said.

"It is Mrs. Silvia. Roman is my husband. Please use the correct title."

"Apologies, Mrs. Silvia. Are you able to confirm that you are pregnant? Is your husband a werewolf and Remus a vampire?" he asked, moving away from the phone.

"I am indeed pregnant. Around five weeks. It is early stages, with morning sickness and exhaustion keeping me in bed most of the time. My husband is not a werewolf, nor is Remus a vampire. They are both human, and any words that come out of Wade's mouth are preposterous. These men do *not* intend to harm anyone. They only want peace."

"Mrs. Silvia, are you under duress at this moment? Gold for yes, bronze for no."

"Bronze. If you are done with these questions, I would like to go back to sleep. I am growing a baby, and I don't have time for this bullshit." Roman and I smirked at the attitude of his mate. She played her role perfectly without even being asked to.

"Thank you for your time." He cleared his throat and placed the phone on the table. He ran his hands through his hair, but it failed to move. "Alright, gentlemen, I believe I have to apologise. Danilo, leave us," he said to the balding officer who peered at him curiously before looking back at my brother and me. "Yes, they will not harm me. Go, I wish to speak to them alone."

He left, mumbling on his way out, the sound hitting me as I focused on what was being said. "Ravon will be here soon. He wants to speak with the taller ones. He is not pleased about being summoned." Who was Ravon? I sat down as Roman stood and leaned against the wall.

"My name is Detective Filfia. You are quite intimidating, and we believed what was said. Our leader is on his way to speak with you. He is intrigued by what the world looks like. I suppose you have questions, so feel free to ask them."

"Thank you, Detective Filfia. What has happened since the bombs fell? We have been secluded for quite some time." I placed my forearms on the table, interlinking my fingers and hands together.

"Vampires revealed their existence, they showed their cruelty and manipulative natures from the beginning. We fought back. We did not wish to be ruled by monsters whose sole aim was to drink us dry. It took around a decade before we managed to find our feet again. Vampires are now secluded to the shadows, and we have a nightly curfew as they run rampant at night. If anyone is caught outside, they meet their end. We have enhanced soldiers, who search them out during the day to hopefully eradicate the remaining scourge on this earth."

"Enhanced?" Roman asked as he pushed himself off the wall.

"Yes, we were able to create a serum that gives humans the same strength as vampires. It enhances their hearing, sight, and smell. They have vampiric abilities without the bloodlust. It took a few trials before we found the solution that worked. The only negative is that those who take this serum are unable to procreate. They are informed of this when injected."

"Wow, that is intense. Do they suffer from the same rage and outbursts?" I ask him, leaning back in my chair, my grip tightening on the armrest. The words swirled in my head, heavy and wrong. Why had they twisted a monster's blood? My stomach churned with nausea. It shouldn't have happened. Those people sacrificed their lives to be lonely without the chance of a family in the future.

"Those who show those traits are…are executed. It is a risk that is explained in detail. They accept this, and still, we have volunteers."

"What about the rest of the world?" Roman queried as he sat down beside me.

"It is the same. Mr. Vexler changed everything; he is a billionaire with high intelligence. He has managed to get the world back on track. Of course, some fight against his ways. It will always be the case. Nobody is happy with anything. Mr. Vexler is a necessary evil to keep humanity thriving." I found it intriguing that he showed no emotion toward the man who apparently saved the world. *A necessary evil.*

"What of other countries? How many people survived?" I needed to know more about this world. A world that I thought I had saved, only to discover that nothing I believed was true.

"Asia was eradicated and is a fallout zone. Radiation still leaks through the area, especially from Japan and its nuclear power plant. We don't try to stop it, but we have managed to contain it for now. It isn't perfect, but it works. The west coast of America sank into the ocean after the bombs triggered an earthquake of nine on the Richter scale. South America had minimal damage but has dropped further into poverty. Africa has managed to find its stride and is excelling in mining and turning trash into clothing." He pointed to his leather jacket. It was literally trash. I had to hide my disgust. "They are now a stronger country than before the bombing. Australia has become a powerhouse. The small island that lingered in the shadows. As it contained no damage, it kept moving forward, creating inventions that have changed the world. It is where Ravon came from. Europe...we suffered damages. The northern part of Italy is a wasteland from the...the destruction of France. Germany also suffered. Scandinavian countries were fine, as are the Balkans. Spain and Portugal are no longer the same. They suffered losses, but the country is still survivable. When the first nuclear bomb was dropped on Asia and millions were killed, others criticised the United States for this and didn't entertain the idea of using those weapons in their arsenal. The bombs stopped the day vampires made their existence known." He sighed, hanging his head low, shaking it.

"Humans fought against their tyranny because we wanted freedom. They couldn't help us. So many people died in that battle, so many senseless deaths. We went from a population of seven billion to one, and we only hit that number recently, as people are starting to have children again without fear. It is going to change soon, though. Those humans who hide in the shadows, they want vampires to exist with us peacefully, w—they don't believe they are dangerous." His eyes met mine. I noted the way that he was going to say another word, was it 'we'?

"From what I have seen, they aren't. Vampires want peace. They don't want to hide in the shadows, which is what they have been doing for centuries. They aren't the only supernatural creatures, either," I said, trying to see what his stance was on supernaturals.

"Yes, we know about wolves and witches. We have heard whispers of demons, but they aren't able to walk the earth that easily. They influence weaker humans, those who allow it to happen."

Roman put his hand on my arm. "You don't seem convinced that they are the evil creatures humans say they are. I mean, in terms of vampires, werewolves, witches."

"I have seen the worst of humanity hating what they cannot understand. Humans have faults, as do supernatural creatures. Creatures that have had to hide who they are. I can only imagine how much it has twisted them up inside."

"You are a sympathiser." Roman and I nodded as he said the words.

Detective Filfia cleared his throat. "I will never admit to that."

"Detective, we want to bring about peace. Where would we start?" I queried, wondering if he was part of this group. It would be a good plant, an officer of the law, knowing about attacks before others. A spy, placed in a position of power.

A door creaked open, and he stood suddenly, bowing his head. Roman and I turned toward the man who had evoked fear from this detective. Fear from a human and not a monster.

Chapter 61

RAVON VEXLER

Nik

"Detective, I thought the common practice was not to be alone in an interrogation. This seems unwise." His accent was a mixture of Australian and Italian, an obvious twang with a hint of sophistication. I stood up, offering my hand. His cold blue eyes locked onto it as if it was beneath him.

"Yes, I apologise, Mr. Vexler, they aren't here to harm us. I thought it would be fine. Would you like me to stay?" Sweat beaded on his brow. He had been in the room with two monsters. Unbeknownst to him, maybe, but still.

"No, leave. Your Captain would like to speak with you, *now!*" His words dripped with disdain as he watched the detective leave before he locked the door and moved toward the glass, pressing what appeared to be a smoke alarm and opening it to turn off a hidden camera.

"Now that we are alone, let's remove the bullshit and bravado, shall we?" He unbuttoned his silky silver suit jacket, rolling up the sleeves on his blue shirt, revealing thick forearms covered in various tattoos. He purposely had a shaved head with no hint of a receding hairline. I noted the phoenix tattoo starting on his neck under his ear and moving toward the back. He was a businessman with a mean streak.

"I have no idea what you mean," I said plainly as I watched his every movement. My attention snapped when I heard my brother laugh.

"Oh, Lord Nik Dankworth and Roman Silvia. The brothers who founded Rome all those centuries ago, the men who hid in the shadows for millennia. It is quite an honour to meet the men who created Italy. What do you think of it now?" he asked as he stroked his chin.

Roman's mouth dropped open in shock, but I kept up my façade.

"Ah, Nik, showing his true colours, keeping everything close to the chest. Your wedding was beautiful. Larissa is…oops, *was* quite beautiful. Aurora, as well. Such a painful existence to lose the one you love over and over again." I wanted to rip his throat out, my eyes flaring in response to his words. "There he is! The powerful Lord. Which part triggered your monster, the mention of your dead mate or the curse that has plagued you for centuries? The curse that started the existence of the monsters who have infected our world."

Roman laughed louder, and I shot a glare at the man. He smiled as he moved to whisper in my ear.

"It is almost like looking in a mirror. Ravon is the human version of Nik. A sophisticated human who strategises and uses words to win arguments."

"Roman, shut your mouth," Ravon spat at him. "I am nothing like this thing before me."

I slammed my fists onto the table. "Do not speak to my brother that way. Why did you come here? To bring up the past? Or to threaten us into walking away? I think you underestimate us."

"Oh, Nik, you are quite simple, aren't you? Please, I am only here to get inside your head. You came to bring peace, but I don't think you are aware that I…" he leaned forward on the table, "own everything. I have my hand in everything. The world is mine. I control what people think. Vampires will die out, as do all creatures who do not survive evolution. Your kind will just be another blip in our history. Homo Sapiens are superior and will always be."

"I like him." Roman chuckled, shaking his head as he stood from his seat. "He thinks that we give a shit about his power. You know we could snap your neck right now. You turned the camera off, and it is two against one. You are in a room with two creatures that could tear you in half in seconds, and you think speaking to us this way will make us scared of you." Roman slammed his hands on the table. Ravon barely flinched. "It only makes us more determined to destroy the controls you have in place." I put my hand on my brother to stop him.

"Roman, he has had that serum." I saw the muscles in his arms flinch. Why wouldn't he take the serum? He would want the strength to scare people, the influence and power. It was my turn to stand as Roman took his seat. "I mean, why wouldn't you? Words can only strike fear in people's hearts to an extent, but power, true power, is what truly scares people. How much blood is on your hands, Ravon? How many have been killed under your leadership?" I queried as I stared at myself in the mirror, fixing my clothes before turning back toward my new enemy.

He raised a brow with a small smirk on his face. "Probably the same amount as you, Nikki." He relaxed in his chair, looking at his hands as if we were beneath him.

"Tell me, Ravon, are we under arrest?" He shook his head. "Good, we will be on our way. You have made your threats known, and I respect your need to keep your power. You think this world revolves because of you, but it is about to bend to my terms. Mark my words, my time is coming, and nothing will stand in my way. Not even a petty man who took a serum to make himself more powerful. Your clock is ticking, Ravon, and by the end of this, your hands will not be on the dial, making it move. They will be *mine!*"

I moved toward the door, opening it and leaving, only to hear the noise return. I nodded toward Detective Filfia, who held out his hand, and I purposely took whatever was lingering within his grasp. Roman followed as we exited the station. We had no idea what to do from here, but I now knew that this wouldn't be as easy as I thought. The world was broken, and a sociopath had taken control, worming his way into everything.

"We are out of our depth here, Nik."

"Come on, Roman, we always liked a challenge. Just think of that time in Rome when we established democracy. It doesn't take much to ruin a person's influence. We just need to find the weak link, and he will have one."

"He knew everything about you, though. How?"

"Peter. I could smell his scent on the man. They had embraced. Peter was his contact in London. I just reunited two psychos. Our first task: we have to find those humans who don't agree. They may not trust us, but we need to earn it. I have a feeling Detective Filfia will help us."

"I hope so. I am starving." He looked at his watch. "It is lunchtime. We have been held by them for over six hours. Food now, destruction soon."

Aurora stepped outside, joining us as she flicked her hair over her shoulder. I turned toward her.

"Aurora, I have your task. Watch Ravon. I want to know everything about that man, got it?" She nodded as she moved toward the shadows to watch from the darkness.

378

"Aurora, I have your task. Watch Ravon. I want to know everything about that man, got it?" She nodded as she moved toward the shadows to watch from the darkness.

CHAPTER 62

BUMPS IN THE NIGHT

Nik

Roman scoffed down his food at the tiny restaurant hidden down an alleyway, selected because I wanted to avoid the extra camera security. Ravon would be watching our every move.

The sun was warm today, and it irritated my skin. I could see why vampires weren't able to find their feet in this country. The climate made it a challenge. I needed blood, my irritation growing. Roman slurped the last of his food and wiped his mouth.

"Do you have to eat like a literal animal?" I said with disdain. Sometimes he could be a pig.

"We need to get you some blood. Just compel someone to take a drink."

I glared at him. "You know I don't really do that. It was only my mate or Maria that I have ever drunk from. Oh, and those that I kill. I need to keep a low profile here. Ravon is probably waiting for us to screw up. All he needs to do is put our picture on the news, and we won't be able to hide."

"They don't have phones like we do, so how would they know?" I had been watching the people around us, noticing that they were talking without holding a phone. Roman had never been this perceptive. This is where my strength lies. I watched, I observed, it was the only way I was ever able to beat him when we sparred. He attacked, I planned.

"Roman, look at their hands. Wait…" A young girl was walking past. "Excuse me, could you come here, please." I waved my hand, letting my compulsion flow freely. She obliged, coming over with a smile on her face.

"Ciao." Her Italian accent was thick.

"Come sta? Parla inglese?"

"I am well, and yes, I speak English. How can I help you two stallions?" Her eyes lingered on Roman's larger form, drifting down to his pants. Her desire filled the air, and I chuckled at her confidence in doing this with two strangers.

"Quick question, where is your phone? We are from somewhere else and have never encountered this technology. Could you enlighten us?"

"Si." She held out her hand, pressing into the middle of her palm, making it illuminate. "The chip here and just here." She pointed to a spot glowing just under her ear. "We don't need to hold anything now, it is just here. We hear it directly, and when we speak, they can hear us clearly. It is so convenient. No headphones and no actual phone. I cannot imagine living any other way."

"Thank you. Forget this conversation and have a beautiful day."

"Si, bello." She walked off, the memory slowly fading away.

"It's a chip. That's fucked, man. That cannot be good, having those metals inside the human body, surely."

"She smelled weird, did you pick up on that?" I asked him as I picked up a chip, putting it in my mouth and mashing the potato to placate the monster inside. It wanted blood, but it would have to wait. I wanted to see what happened when it got dark.

"Honestly, I couldn't get over her desire. It was incredibly strong. I swear, if I didn't have Mimi, I would have actually bent her over this table. How do you push it aside? Not that I would ever cheat on Mimi. She is perfection, but the smell is overpowering."

"I'm used to ignoring it. I have had a mate for centuries. We only see perfection in our mates, they are our other halves. The ones who make our hearts beat faster. They were created for us, and we feel complete with them."

"I miss her." He sounded sad as he put his fork down.

I picked up another chip, watching another police car drive past for the fourth time since we sat down.

"We will be home before she gives birth," I stated without hesitation. I knew that this wouldn't take long. There was always a weakness, and I would find it.

"I don't like his confidence. Can't we just kill him?" Roman asked as he slumped into his chair, looking at the scenery around us.

"You know that old saying: Cut one head off and—"

"Two more shall take its place. You are right, we need to remove the infection."

"Exactly. We need to move. That car has gone past five times now. I want to see how long it takes them to find us again. Let's go for a run to Tivoli. I wouldn't mind seeing Hadrian's Villa."

"You are keeping your promise to her, aren't you?"

"Of course. She would love to see it. I know she will be with me while I am there. Her soul might be gone, but she is still within my heart, and I will hold her there as I visit all the places I know she would have loved. Now, are you ready? It is a decent run. I wouldn't want you to get a stitch." I winked at him.

"Please, you could blindfold me, and I would still win." Roman scoffed as he stood up, stretching out his muscles, his eyes flaring in preparation. We found somewhere quiet for Roman to shift before we took off. I forgot how refreshing the Italian sun felt on my face during a run. I missed this. I saw a sign for Naples and my heart lurched, remembering the place where it all began. The place where Liyana died for the first time. At Castel Dell'Ovo.

It didn't take us long to arrive at Hadrian's Villa. I remembered when it was built all those years ago as a retreat from the stresses of being an Emperor. I found it humorous at the time that a leader needed a place to have a break. It was luxurious, for that time, with everything that people ever needed. I walked around the ruins, taking photos of the area as Roman spoke to his mate, calming her down from the conversation earlier in the day. I could hear her screeching from the other side of the Athenaeum. It amazed me that sometimes, from hundreds of centuries ago, structures were still standing. This villa had survived multiple wars, and yet it still stood strong. I took a photo, pulling a serious face next to a statue of a soldier. I walked around as I finally looked at the piece of paper from Detective Filfia.

Call me when you find somewhere safe. Don't feed from anyone.

There was a number attached, and I questioned why he had written not to feed from anyone. Was that prejudice or a legitimate warning? Roman walked over, shaking his head.

"Fucking hormones," he muttered as I chuckled, remembering Liyana pregnant, the highs and the lows. It was odd to have a mate pregnant with another's babe. He handed the phone over, and I checked the message board for anything from Aurora. She was still radio silent. I hoped she was alright.

I handed Roman the note from the detective, his brow creasing as mine did.

"Why would he say *don't feed?* That's a little odd, no?"

"Those were my thoughts," I said as I took another photo of Roman with that scowl on his face.

"Seriously, Nik? I am not in the mood. I hate being here. I am shocked you love it. You thought Hadrian was a dick."

"I am doing as instructed. I am enjoying my life, and how you looked then was priceless. Yeah, but he built a beautiful retreat. I often thought of running away here with Liyana. It was my first plan when I was trying to figure out how far I could run with a pregnant mate. It seemed the safest travel."

"Did she know?"

"No, I...I never told her much. I really am an asshole." I hung my head low. I should have been better for all of them. I didn't understand why it took till Larissa to be the person I should have always been.

"Yeah, but Larissa straightened you out. Liyana would have loved it here. You may not have always explained yourself, but your intentions have always been pure. Come on, let's keep exploring. We need to find somewhere to sleep." I stopped, looking around. There were no cameras here, and some buildings were still locked. Even if monsters did linger, Roman and I would be able to take care of that. "Why don't we stay here?"

Roman chuckled. "Brother, there are no windows. I am sure there will be a hotel in town. We know that nobody moves at night. They won't track us until then. It gives us time to speak to the detective about why he is so keen to help."

My brother was right. We made our way into town, finding a small hotel that had two king single beds. The sun was beginning to set when I picked up the hotel phone and dialled.

"It took you long enough. I have been waiting all *fucking* day." His tone was completely different to earlier in the day, his annoyance clear.

"Hello, Detective, we went exploring. I didn't realise that I was supposed to call you earlier. I will be more punctual to your needs in the future," I replied sarcastically.

"Funny one, aren't you? Anyway, where are you?" he asked as Roman and I exchanged glances. He shook his head, and I pointed toward the phone, which would ultimately reveal our location anyway. He rolled his eyes and ran his fingers through his hair.

"We are at Villa d'Este Bed and Breakfast." I glanced around the abnormally purple-themed room. The receptionist seemed to think that we were more than just brothers, and Roman rather enjoyed playing it up. His humour irritated me on occasions, but luckily, she listened to the request for two beds.

"Alright, good. You are out of Rome, good. I will come and find you tomorrow. Remember to stay indoors and don't open the shutters. The monsters look for any weakness to exploit for blood."

"Detective, it would be wise to remember whom you are speaking with."

"Oh, I am aware. Mr. V informed us of who you are. The King of Vampires and the Alpha. The twin brothers who founded Rome. You are exactly who *we* need." He sounded extremely happy, speaking about monsters and us being needed.

"Who needs us?" I questioned.

"Those who want to make a change and remove the dictator who currently runs the country."

Roman smiled and rubbed his hands together. Our suspicions were proven correct with his choice of wording.

"We shall see you in the morning. Can you explain why I cannot feed? I am hungry," I asked as the monster's irritation grew with every passing hour.

"I will in person. I will bring you some blood tomorrow. Do you have a preference?"

"No, as long as it is warmed to thirty-seven degrees. Thank you, Detective." Before I finished speaking, he cut the call short. It was barely a minute long. Roman timed it.

"He was worried about it being bugged. This is so interesting. I thought the stuff in London was interesting with the vampire sleuthing, but it is so much worse here. I wish I had some more wolves around. Actually, I thought about going for a run to check out this monster situation. What do you think?"

"No," I answered without hesitation.

"Nik, I am the Alpha."

"You are the Alpha whose healing powers are diminishing with each new day. No, I won't risk your life when you have a pregnant mate waiting for you at home. I have no desire to help Mimi raise that child if you die. She would surely stab me… again."

Roman laughed as he plonked onto my bed, watching the dust float in the air. The place was covered in filth, but we wanted to keep a low profile.

"Could you?" I rolled my eyes as I looked at my watch.

"Will you drop it if I do?" He nodded, and I left the room, making my way to the roof.

I sat out of sight on the rooftop, listening to the sounds of the night awakening. Screeches and howls. I hated the sound of the monsters that vampires could become. I dared not look at the sights below as I sat still, focusing on the creatures that terrified humans. I wondered how so many had turned into this. We had strength, compulsion. How had we fallen to our baser instincts? Roman snuck out to sit beside me. We sat in silence as he listened, his eyes glowing with every howl. I missed that ability to understand what my fellow wolf wanted. Vampire roars were nothing but that, loud growls. There was no language attributed to that. Roman put his head on my shoulder, and I chuckled as he sighed. He wanted to help his fellow wolf, but he knew that I was right. He had too much to lose. He couldn't make any rash decisions.

I looked at my watch, noting it was around three in the morning. The sounds were dwindling. We had no visitors on the roof and heard no screams from humans. Despite that, it was horrible. I understood why they had worked on materials to block out the noise. It was something that nobody needed to hear while they slept peacefully in their beds. Roman had fallen asleep on my shoulder, but suddenly, his head snapped up, and his fur shivered through his skin as his face protruded into a snout. I put my hand against his chest, his yellow eyes staring at me as I registered what had caused him to freak out. A wounded wolf was asking for help, and the sound of their howl showed their young age.

"Roman," I warned, but it was too late. He had removed his leather jacket and jumped from the roof. "Fuck," I mumbled as I jumped up, chasing after my brother through the streets. We sped past monsters lingering and listening to the same noises before following behind us. "ROMAN!" I shouted again, even though his wolf had taken over. He wanted to protect the young pup begging for help. When we found the wolf, she was surrounded by ten monsters swiping at her, trying to bite her. She scrambled away from every attack.

Roman roared, and I growled beside him. Their attention snapped to me over my brother, a fellow creature like them, standing with a wolf. My fangs ached to sink into flesh, my monster dying to rip them to pieces. So much for a low profile.

"Roman, get her to safety," I snarled at him. I could take these creatures on. Roman moved, flicking his nose under the young wolf. When she shifted back, her small frame was covered in blood. He grunted at her, and she jumped onto his back. Roman paused, and I nodded at him. I needed this. My monster and I would revel in this.

One monster charged, his claws moving to slice my throat, but I grabbed his arm, swinging him around with super speed, letting his body go as it flew through the air. Another pounced, and I lifted myself off the ground, watching three of them collide. I forced myself back down, grabbing one around the neck and jumping into the air once again. I squeezed his neck, ripping his head from his body as the lifeless body spasmed, falling to the floor with a splat.

I landed on the floor as they looked at their fallen comrade. They were organised, speaking to one another with small, almost alien-like twitters. "Come and get me." I baited them as a larger one appeared, pushing the others out of the way. He was broad and as tall as me. This was more of a fair fight. I waited for the first move, but he circled me, letting out an occasional grunt. He was sizing me up, trying to look for any weaknesses. My only weakness at this moment was dying of thirst, but being half a god, my powers and strength were untapped. The monster circled one last time before he grunted to his fellow monsters. They retreated as the tall creature smiled, running into the darkness.

I walked back to the hotel, jumping up onto the roof to see Wolf Roman licking the young wolf's wound to stop it from bleeding. She looked to be no older than sixteen. Her heart was frantic. I sat down, lifting her head and biting into my wrist.

"Drink," I ordered, and she flicked her gaze to Roman, who nodded before shifting back to his human form. He stood, keeping an eye on our surroundings as the young girl's wounds slowly disappeared. She pushed my wrist away. "Why are you out by yourself?" I asked as I removed my shirt, giving it to her even though it was covered in blood. She would at least keep her modesty.

"It was her first shift," Roman muttered as the sun started to rise. He turned back toward the girl, pulling his hair off his face. She nodded. "Where are your parents?"

"They are dead. The monsters killed them. I have been on my own since." She dared not look up at her Alpha, who pushed out his anger over the situation. I felt his aura. She fell to her knees in submission.

"How long for?" I queried.

I was shocked when she said, "A year. I tied myself up in the basement, but I broke free as soon as the moon hit its peak." She yawned, her body weakened. I scooped her into my arms.

"Let the girl rest, and we can talk to her more later. We have a visitor arriving soon, and I need a shower." I returned to our room, laying her in the bed and tucking her in. I moved the hair from her face as her brown eyes locked onto mine. "Rest, you will be safe here. Sleep as long as you want. I am sure it has been a while since you have."

Tears welled in her eyes, and I stroked her hair for a little while until her heavy eyes finally closed. Roman showered, and I entered once he was done. He sat in the chair, wearing a black tank top and shorts, watching the young girl sleep peacefully. He shook his head as I exited, pulling on jeans and a blue polo shirt.

"I now understand why you wanted me to come. I didn't realise that wolves would be suffering to this extent. She is a child and was left alone during her first transition. Don't start yelling at me for running off. He heard that girl and just took over. You know I was right to go. She needed help. Imagine if that happened to my child. What if he was alone?"

"He?" His face flushed as he registered that he had given away the sex of his baby, but even I knew that was too early to know.

"Krystal the witch told me. She said he would be super strong. It's nothing." He deflected, but we had more stuff to worry about at this moment, with the detective arriving soon and this girl asleep in my bed.

"We can discuss this later. I need food, mainly blood, but food will have to do. I have to tell you about the odd behaviour of the creature. I have never seen anything like it before." I scratched my chin, reflecting on the stalking nature of that thing. I couldn't classify it as a creature or a monster, it was not mindless like I originally perceived it to be.

Chapter 63

MORE SECRETS TO UNRAVEL

Roman

Nik spoke about the peculiar actions of the monster, how it sized him up before conversing with the other creatures to leave. I wonder if he sensed what Nik was or if he knew that he wouldn't win this fight. We hadn't encountered anything like that before. Nik ate more food than usual, his eyes flaring red continually. He needed blood, and he needed it soon. He stopped and sniffed the air as his eyes locked onto someone behind me. A bag flew over the top of my head, and Nik caught it, tearing it open and pouring it down his throat. He groaned at the taste.

"Detective, thank you for joining us. I hope you have more than one bag. Nik hasn't eaten in over twenty-four hours. He will need more than just that…" I lowered my voice. "He will need a throat to tear into, more than likely."

"That is the issue…" He took a seat beside Nik and me. He shifted, waving the waitress over for a coffee. "Yes, I have another two bags, that was all I could manage. In terms of eating a person, you can't. It will turn you into one of those bloodlust-filled creatures that plague our nights."

"Um, you need to explain a little more," I said as Nik grabbed another bag, pouring it down his throat like a man dying of thirst. I chuckled at seeing the intelligent strategist acting more like me as I took a sip of my coffee. It would be a long day of no sleep. Preparation for having a baby, right?

"Ravon created a serum that every person is injected with on the day they are born. It is a protein that messes with our blood but doesn't affect us in general. If any vampire drinks from us, they automatically turn into the monster versions of themselves. It is disastrous for vampirekind. I have been trying to figure out what is in it, but he keeps his formulas under lock and key. I think only he knows." His coffee arrived, and he rubbed his hands together in anticipation. "Grazie."

"Are you aware that he has taken the enhanced serum?" I watched as Nik tore into the last bag, seeming a little more like himself, his eyes no longer flaring red and his posture more upright than slouched.

"What? Wait, no. Are you sure?" He slumped back into his chair.

"Yeah, we could smell it," Nik said as he licked his lips and threw the final empty blood bag into the hidden satchel the detective gave us. He wiped his hands together and fixed the cuffs on his shirt, back to being more like my brother now.

"That *motherfucker.*" His accent sounded stronger than usual.

"What did you want to meet with us for?" Nik got straight to the point as he sipped his coffee with his calm confidence, assessing everything without giving anything away.

"Yes." He pulled out two tickets and slid them across the table. "You are going to an auction today. Wear a tux." Nik picked them up, noticing the names were different as he pulled out two licences with new names and faces on them.

"Dare I ask how you managed this so quickly?" I queried as I looked at my new name, Ryan Simina. Nik showed his, Noah Donati.

"I have my secrets, as do you. Don't be late. And look for the girl in the red dress. We will be in touch, gentlemen." He stood, throwing down some money to pay for breakfast. Nik looked abhorred at the action. I took the money, putting it in my pocket within seconds. I wasn't about to say no to free money. I moved to speak, wanting to ask him a question about the monsters from last night. Nik kicked me hard under the table, and I felt the bone crack from the impact.

"Tssk." I groaned as I glared at him, and he shook his head.

"Thank you, Detective. Let me know if you hear anything about Aurora's whereabouts. I have no way to contact her unless she makes contact."

"Will do." He bowed his head and left as quickly as he arrived.

"Why the hell did you not want to tell him about the monsters? And did you have to kick me so *bloody* hard? I think you fractured my leg." I tried to shake off the pain that still reverberated through my system. Nik pricked his finger, dropping a little blood into my coffee.

"You will be fine. I trust him, but not completely. We need more information from him before we give him everything we know. Let's see what tonight has to offer and check in with that girl first. She may have some answers that will help us further." I picked up the coffee, drank it, and felt the pain dissipate in seconds. He was right. I stood, flicking out my leg from the strange sensation that filled my body.

We entered our room to find the young girl still naked and asleep in Nik's bed. She was out cold, her soft snores filling the tiny room.

Nik cleared his throat. "I will go and buy her some clothing. Let her rest, and we can wake her when I get back." He spun back around, leaving the room.

I sat in the armchair, tapping my foot on the ground as I nibbled on my thumb. She was all alone during her first transition, the pain would have been horrendous. She tied herself down, not realising it wouldn't have stopped her wolf. Her human wrists were different to a wolf's. I stood, going to the window, watching the hustle and bustle down below. I would call Mimi later today to check in. I shook my head, remembering that I almost revealed my deal with Pluto to Nik. He must never find out. If he did, I hated to think of what he would do.

I heard the sheets moving and glanced over my shoulder. The young wolf stirred. It had been a solid five hours, more than enough sleep. She sat up and held the sheet to her body as she rubbed the sleep from her eyes. She glanced around the room, a look of confusion covering her face. Her brow creased as her heart rate sped up. Her eyes found mine, and she gasped, holding the sheet tighter to her chest.

"Everything is fine, we saved your life last night. We put you here to rest after you were injured." I had my hands up as I sat on the armchair, giving her a soft smile as she scratched her head.

"Th-thank you." Her voice was soft with an accent.

"Don't mention it. My brother has gone to get you some clothing. He should be back shortly. What happened?" I could feel my Alpha aura wanting to force her to answer, my wolf eager to know how she had been hurt. The door opened. Nik snarled at me, and I sank back into the chair. "She woke," I mumbled.

He handed her the bag of clothes and held the robe up for her to slip inside of as he looked at me. Giving her a small amount of privacy.

"Take your pick. We will be here when you get out." Nik's voice was gentle but stern. I watched her walk into the bathroom, closing the door behind her.

Nik threw the pillow at me. "I told you to leave her alone."

"She woke." I ran my fingers through my hair, standing up and putting the pillow back on the bed.

"You *should* have waited for me," he grumbled as he sat on the bed. I didn't need to ask him right now. "I did *not* think it would be this bad here. London was being held at the mercy of a tyrannical vampire while the rest of the world was going through the same, except theirs is a human who altered his DNA."

I opened my mouth to speak before closing it. The young girl exited the bathroom with her dark hair in a ponytail, her sleeves down, covering her hands as she crossed her arms over her body. I could smell her anxiety, so I moved toward her as she stepped backward. I didn't know what to do. I glanced at my brother, who nodded in our silent exchange. He stood, putting his hands up for her to see as he took a step towards her, shifting the aura in the room. Nik had retained that power since being born a wolf, but it never translated to other vampires after him. A calmness enveloped the space where even my wolf settled.

"We do not wish to harm you. What is your name?" His voice was clear and almost nurturing in tone.

"Dominica."

"What do you remember from last night?" he queried, keeping a safe distance from her as she played with her fingers. She avoided looking in our direction. I kicked a chair toward Nik, and he sat. I did the same further back.

"You saved me, I...I broke out. I under...underestimated my wolf's strength. She wanted to run free..." She shook her head.

"You couldn't have known. With the first shift, your wolf has more power because they are finally free. It wouldn't have mattered how much you restrained yourself, she would have always broken free," I said to her, leaning forward in my seat.

"Where are your parents or guardians?" Nik cleared his throat.

Nik pointed to the chair behind her, where she took a seat, her knees close together and her feet crossed over one another. The poor girl wanted to hide somewhere. Her eyes were sad, devoid of any happiness. I wanted to hold her and force her darkness away. She was a child. She didn't deserve this life.

"My parents were slaughtered by the monsters, they...they broke into our house one night. We lived further out, and we hadn't secured one of the shutters. They snapped it off. It almost felt personal, though. My parents, they locked me in the panic room, I..." Tears fell down her cheeks. "I remember their screams." She choked the words out. "I stayed quiet, holding everything in. The monsters tried to get to me, but the sun started to come up, and they ran. The police...they didn't help. I was left alone. I heard from family services that I couldn't be helped, that it was over their heads. It's long been known that Ravon doesn't like wolves. He has been trying to eradicate our kind for years. I think he hoped the same would happen to me."

"Are there other wolves in the area? Any other family?" I asked her, hoping to find her somewhere safe to land. I was worried sick about leaving this girl alone.

She shook her head as she glanced out the window, pulling her legs into her chest and crying. Nik leaned back in his chair, scratching his chin. I got up, lifting her and holding her against my chest. I hoped my Alpha aura would calm her inner wolf. Her tiny body relaxed.

"Why is my wolf purring?" She wiped her nose.

Nik laughed as he stood up. "I am going to get some food. I'll be back soon." He left the room as she glanced up at me with her hazel eyes.

"I am the Alpha, the father of all werewolves. Your wolf would recognise that. When she called out last night, I ran to protect you. I could feel your fear. I am glad you are alright." She licked my neck, which was common among wolves, done as a thank you, but the practice hadn't been used for some time, as it wasn't an act that could be done in public. I smiled at her and kissed the top of her head.

"What happens now?" Her voice was barely a whisper as she buried her head into my chest, my scent giving her comfort.

"I am going to go for a walk once Nik returns to see if I can smell another den close by."

"He smells funny, almost like death with roses."

I snorted. "He is a vampire." She sat up, her eyes wide. "No, not like those monsters. He tore them apart for you. He would never harm a wolf, much less a little girl. He is tame even if he smells."

"I would prefer to smell like roses and corpses than a wet dog." He winked at me as he returned, placing food down in front of her. She rushed to the table, picking up the food and stuffing it into her mouth. I watched her as Nik stood beside me.

"I have the auction to attend. Did you want to spend the day with her? See if you can find somewhere for her to stay."

I crossed my arms. "Yeah, I think I might."

"You know they will hunt her tonight as well. Their prey got away, they will want to try for her again."

He was right, she needed to be safe. We would have also been marked, so wherever we landed, it would need to be very sheltered. I looked at my brother as he nodded.

"I will see what comes from the auction. Maybe they can recommend a place to hide for the night. Don't forget to call Mimi. She will worry if she doesn't hear from you." He squeezed my shoulder before he walked into the bathroom to change for the auction.

CHAPTER 64

GIRL IN THE RED DRESS

Nik

I WALKED TO THE ADDRESS, CHECKING MY SURROUNDINGS FOR places to hide if the need arose. I hadn't been to this part of town for a while. The auction house was in an older building that looked more like an apartment building than a place to sell objects. I wondered why they wanted to meet somewhere so public. I adjusted my cuffs as I walked up the stairs to the brick building. The place was buzzing with noise as my new name was registered. I took my paddle, knowing I wouldn't be able to access the full amount of my wealth here. Luckily, Wade gave us cards so I could transfer some money to keep us going for a while.

I could smell that they were all human. Security was posted at the entrances, and guards tried to be intimidating with permanent scowls on their faces, but underneath, I could hear their hearts thumping rapidly.

I wondered if they had ever been around a vampire as strong as me in their life. I walked around, taking in the items that were for sale. Some were priceless while others were highly coveted, though none took my fancy. I planned to bid only enough to make my presence believable. As I took my seat, I unbuttoned my suit jacket and scanned the room for any sign of the mystery guest I was supposed to meet. I wished I had more to go on. I looked at my watch. A red dress flowed past my vision, and it took a seat beside me. Her potent floral scent assaulted my nose. I peered out the corner of my eye at the woman.

"Glad to see you could make it. I wondered if you would be brave enough to show your face." Her accent sounded more Spanish than Italian.

I cleared my throat. "I can see that you don't know of my reputation. Not much scares me, especially not a human requesting a meeting. You wanted to meet, talk. I have no time for bullshit."

She laughed as the auction began, the auctioneer speaking a million miles an hour. I put up my paddle to pretend that I was paying attention to what he was doing.

"Ah, there he is. I had to make sure I insulted your ego for a response."

"Sorry to tell you, but shapeshifters are not real. Vampires, wolves, witches, yes, but sadly, shapeshifters do not."

"We both know that demons exist, and they can shapeshift."

My head snapped in her direction, and I finally took in the beauty before me. Her thick black hair was wavy, down her back, and the red gown had cut-outs randomly across her body. All the important areas were to avoid nudity. Her figure was tiny. She had striking blue eyes and thick black eyebrows that made a statement. This girl knew more than she let on.

"I need a bathroom break." She motioned to the space behind her. "Meet me in five minutes. They won't break for another thirty."

She got up as I made another bet on an item that I had no interest in. I made eye contact with the elderly auctioneer, who nodded in appreciation. I made another bet before losing the item. I stood up, fastening my buttons as I made my way to the bathroom. I knocked, and the door opened. I walked in hastily.

"It's about time." She appeared flustered as she paced the room.

"Yes, dare I ask why?" I crossed my arms as I leaned against the door, waiting for her to calm down.

She took a deep breath before glancing back towards me. "I am Ravon's wife and also the leader of the uprising."

"Well, that is a difficult place to be. I now understand the guards and the need for privacy. I am curious why you are part of the uprising. To overthrow your husband?"

"Because he is an abusive asshole. I don't think I need to say anymore. I know you two met, and I am sure you have a few choice words to say about him. He is a prick, he is controlling, he is abusive, he used to be kind, but..." She paused as she put her arms on the vanity, swinging on them slightly with her eyes closed. "His parents were attacked, and it started all of this. He saw them torn to pieces when the world turned."

My ears pricked up, my brain calculating the dates from fifty years ago, and the fact that the man barely looked older than forty. A smile spread over her face as she nodded.

"Yes, I am sure you guessed it from his smell. He injects himself with a serum, and it essentially slows his aging process. It increases his strength and makes him superhuman. His temper, more than anything, and that is what scares me the most."

I cleared my throat. "If he adapted the serum from vampire blood, his temper would be triggered, almost like a bloodlust, and he can't be relieved. How is his sexual appetite?" I asked, even though I already knew the answer. Her eyes snapped to me, filled with fear, and that was when I noticed the bruise on her arm. This woman had a strength to her that had to be admired.

A knock at the door broke focus. I placed my finger to my lips.

"Esmeralda," the voice called out, and I motioned for her to answer.

"Yes, I am here."

"Why is the door locked? What is going on?" The knob moved violently as the man attempted to break in. My monster was ready, but she placed her hand on my chest. Her eyes closed as she exhaled.

"I was overcome with morning sickness. I need a moment to compose myself. I will be out soon. I promise, thank you," she called out before clearing her throat.

I took a step away from her, listening for any other noise, when the softest murmur reached my ears.

"We are done here." I moved toward the window to jump out and make my way around the building to avoid suspicion.

"Nik, wait, please. I didn't want this baby. I didn't think he could procreate. I need your help. I don't know what this is going to be. All I know is that it isn't human. It will be a literal monster. The ultrasounds don't look like a normal baby. His experiment has gone too far."

"No, I won't be part of this. I don't trust your alliances. You carry his child, and you want to destroy him." I raised my voice, running my fingers through my hair. I was stupid to agree to this.

"There is a serum. For all the vampires who drank from humans and were turned into those poor creatures, there is a serum to reverse it." She held up a syringe of a red blood-like substance. "Inject one of them tonight and see if I'm telling the truth."

"Why?"

"The only chance we have to survive is if we work together. The world deserves better than this."

"How will I contact you?" I asked her as I took the syringe.

"I will find you. I have more resources. Ravon forgets that. My bloodline is royal, and he uses that wealth to fund his experiments. I will speak to you soon, Lord Dankworth." She bowed her head out of respect before I jumped from the window.

CHAPTER 65

THE SERUM

Nik

I held the syringe tightly in my hand. I was taking a risk, and I knew it. There could be a tracker inside. I would certainly do something like that. I wouldn't trust me, but this woman carried his child. Her eyes revealed the scope of her fear. How did it even manage to be conceived? It was against the laws of nature. Vampires weren't allowed to procreate. It was part of the curse that started vampirism. We were literal demons on Earth. Ravon had found a way around it, though. I wondered how he had changed the power in our blood for this. I walked into the hotel room to find Roman showing the young wolf how to manage her shift better. She had warmed to him, it seemed.

"How did it go?" His brow creased.

"Interesting, she is his wife…his pregnant wife," I mumbled.

"How? You said he wasn't…" I watched my brother stare at the ceiling, thinking about how this situation had come about.

"That was my response. I honestly don't know if I trust her, but she has given me this." I held up the syringe. "Apparently, it is a cure for the serum that has turned them into those creatures. I don't know if it will work on a creature who turned into that through their own bloodlust, but I am sure we could tweak it. I will head out tonight and see if the theory rings true."

"Nik, what if she is wrong? You leave yourself open for an attack."

"It is worth the risk if it is true. Those things were organised the other day. One of them stopped me. He looked me in the eye, as if he was sizing me up before they ran away. Roman, that is unlike anything I have ever seen."

"I won't leave you out there alone. We are in this together, and I'm not about to leave you now. We will get this little wolf sorted somewhere safer, and I will wait with you." I wasn't about to say no, especially when his tone was more of an order than a request.

I pulled my brother into an embrace, needing to hear that. My big brother was my protector growing up, while I taught him how to manoeuvre and overpower people. He became a fierce warrior, while others came to me for help with strategy. I would always love him and protect him until my dying day, and I hoped that we would fulfil our promise to die together.

————

We dropped Dominica at a luxurious hotel for the night before we returned to our filthy hotel room. Roman and I watched the sunset, waiting for the monsters to appear. I was filled with anxiety, but also hope. Hope that this could bring us *something*, an advantage that would turn the tide in this world. Take back peace from the monsters who had plagued the world for so long.

Screeches echoed along the streets as the last of the sun peeked over the top of the mountains. We headed toward the roof, ready for the monsters' inevitable return.

"Here we go," I muttered softly as we stood on the edge of the building that we stayed in last night. They slowly crept out of the shadows, their fangs and claws shining in the moonlight. Their pale and hairless bodies slinked through the quiet alleyway. Roman moved to grab the first one, but I wanted the one I had encountered yesterday, the one I perceived to be the leader. I knew he would continue to hunt me down. I would do the same. A man who stood between me and my snack. I would dream of tearing him to pieces and dancing in his blood.

I heard the snarl behind me. I spun around, smiling at the creature I encountered last night.

"There you are. I have been waiting for you." He was around the same height as Roman and me, not as scrawny-looking as the others.

The creature growled as he stalked us, crossing his legs over one another as he circled. I handed Roman the syringe. I would attack and grab him while Roman stabbed him. Another four creatures joined him.

"Nik." Roman's voice was filled with worry more than fear. We knew we could take them, but it would hurt.

"I see them, just focus on this one." I crouched slightly in preparation as he roared and charged. I waited for the right moment before lifting off the ground and smashing my elbow into his head. He stumbled slightly as I grabbed his arms, tightening my grasp to hold him in place. Roman plunged the syringe into his chest, and I watched the liquid enter his body before I let him go. My brother and I ran backward and waited. The other creatures watched intently as the main one scratched at his chest, ripping into his body before grabbing his head and rocking back and forth. He threw his head back and screeched. We covered our ears, the noise piercing our eardrums before it slowly changed from a monstrous sound to something more human, that of a man yelling to the night sky. He dropped to his knees, naked before us. The remaining creatures stood still, yapping to one another before running away.

Roman and I walked over hesitantly, every step getting us closer as steam left his body. Small cries left his large frame as I grabbed the blanket from earlier, wrapping it around his shoulders.

"It's alright, I've got you," I said softly as he shivered.

"It has been so long. Thank you, Nik."

"You know my name. What is yours?"

"Paolo. Many of us know about you. I only recently turned into this beast when they stopped the blood flowing around five years ago. They wanted to eradicate us. Their solution was to inject everyone with the tainted blood to turn us into these beasts. It has been torture, with this monster in control of my every action. I have been screaming into a void for years. Thank you, I am eternally grateful." He wrapped his naked form around me, embracing me as he continued to cry.

"Let's get inside, shall we?" Roman suggested as we moved from the roof to our crappy hotel room.

I threw a bag of blood at him, which he tore into, his eyes flaring with joy.

"That yapping noise, it is how you converse with one another, isn't it?" my brother asked.

Paolo nodded. "Si, I thought that we were soulless monsters, but no, we are just trapped in our bodies. You can save all of us. Please, Nik." The man got on his knees, begging me for help that I had no idea how to give.

"I will certainly try," I muttered as I pulled him from his knees to sit on the bed.

He finally crashed as the sun began to rise, his body probably used to this sleep cycle. The phone in our hotel rang, and I picked it up tentatively.

"Well, did it work?" Esmeralda's voice came through the phone.

"Yes, but I still don't trust you."

"I respect that, but know the enemy of my enemy is my friend. I want a way forward where we can all live in peace and not within this tyranny. Work with me, let's build a better world together."

Chapter 66

Castle Ruins

Roman

We still didn't trust Esmeralda, especially with the devil spawn that grew inside her. Nik and I did discuss the same thing, that the creature mustn't be born, but the idea of killing an unborn child didn't sit well with us, even after Nik's sacrifice all those centuries ago. Esmeralda requested to meet with us a week later. Ravon was going out of the country, and she would have time to meet and work towards overthrowing him. We bided our time as we watched Ravon from a distance. I think Nik did this to search for Aurora, too, who still hadn't made contact. I believed her to be dead, but Nik had other ideas. His guilt ate at him for not being there to protect her and leaving her alone for so long.

We waited in a car as night started to fall, as Esmeralda instructed. It was easier for her to move about in the dark. She was tenacious and wasn't about to give up her mission of destroying her husband. Paolo came with us. He wanted to be a part of it, to help save those he considered friends, those who were also stuck in monstrous bodies. Paolo didn't want any more deaths.

"Where is she?" Nik asked, scanning the area. He didn't want another fight, especially since it had been a few days since he drank any blood. His monster was chomping for some action, and Nik struggled to contain him with the thirst of blood ringing in his ears.

"She is coming, relax."

"Don't tell me to relax! We are sitting ducks in the dark. There is nothing but this castle ruin before us. She set us up, the fucking bitch set us up!" he shouted as a screech echoed behind us.

"They are close," Paolo stated, looking around into the darkness.

Another car appeared beside us, and she waved sweetly. I understood why Nik didn't like her. She had an air of superiority to her, along with knowing that she was married to that asshole and carrying his child. She got out of the car with one of her guards as Nik jumped from the vehicle.

"What the hell is he doing here?" The frustration was clear in his voice at seeing one of her husband's men with her.

"We can trust him. He was one of my guards before I married Ravon. Come, let's get inside."

"You are the one who is late, and now we are out in the open."

"Oh, Nikki." She touched his cheek, making him take a step back as he growled at her. She pressed a button toward the ruins before us, and it morphed into something completely different. A massive castle appeared before us, lit up and protected by massive gates. "Quickly now, before they come. I would prefer not to kill any of those innocent people."

We walked in as I stared in admiration at the huge sight before us. "A bit overwhelmed there, Roman?" she asked. I nodded. "As I told Nik, I came from royalty before the world collapsed. We still have plenty of resources around the world. This is one of my family's castles."

"Which royalty?" Nik asked, clearing his throat. I wanted to know this as well. We had encountered many royals during our lives.

"Casa de Borbón," she declared with pride as she flicked her thick black hair. The mirage of the ruins came down behind us.

"Ah, the Spanish. I met King Felipe and his wife Letizia. She was stunning. We had adventures together. They were strong leaders."

"They were my grandparents. They were in France and didn't survive the blast."

"I am sorry for your loss." I voiced my condolences as we climbed the steps. "The House of Borbón had vast power and wealth. I can only imagine your resources. How many remaining royal families are there?"

"All royals were disbanded and told they were no longer important in the new world order. A lot of them didn't hide their money quickly enough, and Ravon managed to take it from them. Whether that was from compulsion or just pure manipulation, who knows? I missed a lot of his earlier tricks. When he found my family, he forced the marriage, presumably to get a hold of their money. I have a trust fund that I can access now under another name." She winked at us as she pushed the doors open, revealing the grandeur of the building.

"Holy shit," Nik muttered, his eyes focused on the massive golden dome ceiling and the ostentatious surroundings, dripping in wealth and opulence.

"Let's go down to the basement. That is where the magic happens." She waved for us to follow.

She led us down a corridor and into a study before being cliché and pulling out a book, *Pride and Prejudice.* Before stepping back, the case flung open to reveal stairs heading down.

"Careful, it is steep. Hold onto the rail."

"What, couldn't you afford an elevator?" I chuckled. Her eyes laser-focused on me, and I stopped instantly. Nik nudged me with a smile, and I rolled my eyes at him.

We made our way down the steep and winding stairs as it grew colder with every new step. It reminded me of an old medieval castle, leading the way to a hidden room or dungeon. We reached the bottom of the thick stone room. Computers were sprawled everywhere, with a mini science lab. Paolo walked over to the lab as Nik moved toward the computers, and I stayed near the wall. It was rather overwhelming to see this all set up with a world map and pictures of Ravon and his movements, another map showing the movements of the creatures in the night. I watched my brother point to areas and press buttons on the keyboard. He seemed to be making himself at home. He stood straighter before he looked back at me. I shrugged, but he motioned for me to come over.

I stood opposite him as he pressed a few more buttons.

"You seem to know this system easily enough."

"Most computers have similar programs. I am just flicking between screens and understanding what data they are collecting. Like here..." He pointed to a screen. "They figured out that there is a massive group of those monsters hiding here, while many others are spread out. Then," he flicked again, "this shows a system of spreading the cure by injecting some humans with this serum to slowly change them back and once turned back, if the newly cured are bitten, they will cure those and so on. Then..." I sighed at how intelligent my brother could be. "This is an atomiser that will slowly release the cure in certain areas and eventually cure all of them…even those who turned from bloodlust. Roman, this is what we wanted. We can take this back to the United Kingdom. Roman, we can fix everything." Nik's joy was contagious, but I still had one question on my mind.

"What do we do about Ravon? He won't just go quietly. He will fight you."

"I know, but we both know that we could destroy him in his sleep." He cockily rolled up his sleeves.

Esmeralda walked over with a bag of blood for Nik and a drink for me.

"I am glad to see you familiarise yourself with the system. Our plan is to attack this large group here and use the atomiser to turn them. Then we would work towards the smaller groups, who will need a leader to help them with the transition. You are going to need people to come and help. I can smuggle some support in if needed. Who do you know that would be able to ease people through the transition and back into the world as we know it? I can organise a plane tonight for you to go and pick up these people."

"You know that there will be speed bumps along the way." Nik crossed his arms, unimpressed with her statement.

"Oh, yes, absolutely, but we can finally work towards some peace. A world that is inclusive of all creatures, whether they are vampires, wolves, or witches."

It was a dream, one that I wondered could be possible. The world had always grouped the marginalised and placed them into boxes that generalised them. Could it be true that we might remove that forever? It was definitely not going to be an overnight fix. It would take years, and I yearned to be with my mate and raise our son. Did I want to continue to be part of this?

Nik put his hand on my shoulder. "If we fly over Julian, Stuart, Leo, and maybe Richard, you could go home to your mate. You go home and be with Mimi. I want you to enjoy the pregnancy journey and your future with her." I grabbed his arm with a smile and nodded. He understood me. It was my time to go home and be with her. Nik had it all sorted.

"May I ask one favour?"

"Always, brother."

"Make sure you record Ravon's demise." I squeezed my brother's shoulder.

Nik clicked his tongue and winked. "Always."

CHAPTER 67

TWO MONTHS OF SPREADING THE CURE

Nik

It had been a few months since Roman went home to his mate. I missed my brother, but it was the right thing to do, and I knew it. He yearned to watch her belly swell. I bet he probably wanted to avoid the hormonal changes, but that was his choice. Roman sent Richard, Leo, and Andreas over. Stuart and Julian had no interest in dealing with conflict. That was them, and I never expected them to change.

I stood in one of the bedrooms within a safe house that Esmeralda owned. We had been moving to different countries, providing the curse to large groups of those creatures. She stayed with Ravon, but we had received regular updates over the last month. We had cured around one million vampires, and when we flew over land, we dispersed small amounts into the air in hopes of helping others.

"Lord Dankworth." The door opened. "Esmeralda has another update. You are needed in the office." I nodded as I finished my bloodcino.

I walked down to the office, pushing the door open to see Leo already sitting at the computer with a smile on his face, his eyes twinkling. Leo had been a prince when he transitioned — the first human I ever turned. His family was considered royalty, and newer vampires often sought their counsel. Yet Leo would always come to me before making any major decisions. He once told me he never wanted to disrespect his elders.He enjoyed flirting, even though he was mated to Alina. I used to think my curse made my relationship complicated — but theirs existed on an entirely different level. The nature of their bond still baffled me. And yet, despite all the complexity, he remained fiercely devoted to her and the tangled chaos she brought with her.I remembered their first almost-date — Aurora and I had been there. I glanced at my phone for any new messages before looking back at Leo.

"Ah, he has graced us with his presence," Leo announced as he leaned back in the tall-backed armchair, a sly smile on his face.

"Shut up, Leo." I sat in a seat opposite him. "What's new?" I asked him.

"What, don't I get to see your face, Nikki?" Her fake voice rang in my ear.

"I've told you not to call me that," I said through gritted teeth. "Stop bullshitting," I warned her.

"Fine, it is going very well. The cure is spreading like we anticipated, and the numbers are far better than predicted. The vampires are starting to band together, which isn't what we hoped, but we know that once you return, that will get sorted out. Ravon is...well, his temper is getting worse. He is not impressed with what you have done and has ordered a hit against you and whoever is within your vicinity."

"Pfft, that is nothing Nikki can't deal with." Leo snorted and wriggled his eyebrows at the nickname. Leo enjoyed baiting me, he had since the beginning. I think it was why I kept him around.

"Fuck off, Leo. What of Aurora?" I asked as I stood up, wanting to be out of this room.

"Aurora is coming to you. She has insight about Ravon. I found her and told her about your worries. She should be there before nightfall. How is Australia?"

"Hot. Summer here is ridiculous, and the way people speak is incredibly odd, with their slang and shortening of words. Are they unable to speak normal English?"

Leo chuckled. "Does it insult your precious ears?" He batted his eyes at me.

"Leo, keep going, and I will rip your heart from your chest and throw your body to the wolves," I snarled, annoyed at his bravado for Esmerelda's sake. "How is your mate going?" I quirked an eyebrow at him.

"Thank you for the update, Esmerelda. We shall converse again soon." Leo replaced his wit with professionalism at the reminder of Alina. He would be furious, but sometimes he acted like a child.

"Sometimes you are an asshole."

"Yes, but you knew that before you transitioned. I think I explained that to you in detail." We snorted.

"So much has changed since those days, you had just gained control of your vampirism and were coming to terms with your loss of Liyana. You were so young. I am glad you finally managed to get some style."

"Just remember that I can end you as quickly as I turned you."

"You wouldn't. You would miss me too much, especially with Roman..." His voice drifted.

I left for the kitchen, not needing the reminder that I wouldn't be alive without my brother. I wanted some food. I moved about the white kitchen with soft wooden benchtops. I grabbed out the bread and eggs, warming the water and placing vinegar inside. I added the eggs and swirled them, making them perfectly poached. I smiled, knowing Larissa would love the adventures we had been on lately. We visited various parts of Europe and some regions of America before moving to Australia, and will be finishing in Africa. I flicked through my phone at the photos I had taken. I was living my life—with a set mission at the moment, but I was living. The most I had done in centuries. I wasn't searching for her like she asked. I didn't look over my shoulder, hoping that maybe her father would bring her back to life or the gods would let us finally have our happy ending.

I sat down to eat when I heard shoes on the tiles. Aurora entered with her short bob of hair, wearing denim shorts and a white tank top. She seemed to fit in with the attire that Australians liked to wear.

"You arrre only missing the thongs," I said, trying to emulate an Australian accent.

"I heard you were looking for me." She moved closer, making herself a coffee before sitting down opposite me on the island bench.

"You didn't check in. What have you been doing?" I asked her, reaching over for her hand. I had to know she was alright.

"You were worried. That is sweet. You rejected me, but you were worried." She sighed. "I was doing as you asked. I was watching Ravon. By the way, the more I watch him, the more he reminds me of you. A less brooding and more human version, but literally the same cocky attitude and those blue eyes. He is a sexy piece of arse."

"Aurora!" I said, abhorred at her statement.

"Leave it, Nik, it has been a while."

"Anyway, what else?" I cleared my throat.

"He keeps to the same routine. He doesn't alter it. Either he is arrogant, or he has no fear, and from what I have heard, I believe it's the latter. I have seen him inject himself with a serum once a week. He always does it at his facility, the entire building is covered in glass. I sneak in and remain hidden, just watching."

"Whereabouts is the drug?"

"Behind the picture frame in his office. It has a code, but it changes every week. I don't know when, but it is handed to him by his receptionist. His wife is beautiful and deserves a medal for dealing with him on a daily basis. I would have killed him by now, but I hear she is pregnant. I wonder what that child will be. Certainly not human." She was rambling.

She reached over, grabbing a piece of toast and dipping it into the egg yolk. "What about you?"

"We have cured more than we anticipated and hopefully plenty within Australia. It has been marginally more successful than we planned. I am rather pleased, and I am looking forward to my next meeting with Ravon sometime soon and putting everything back together. Are you coming to join us later with the dispersing device?"

"Yeah, I would love to see it in person." Her excitement bubbled as she bounced on the barstool. It squeaked against the tiled flooring.

"Sounds good." I nodded, pulling my plate closer to avoid any more food getting stolen.

———

Night grew closer as Leo, Aurora, and I ventured toward the largest congregation of these monsters. We snuck in through a gap in the door. The theatre hall was exceptionally quiet as we moved in close, knowing that we had to turn on the device as close as possible. Aurora had requested the honours, as she wanted to make a difference. Her feet were light on the floor as they all stood facing one another in the darkened space. A few were moving. I motioned for her to hurry up. It was too close to nightfall, and they would wake soon.

She placed the device on the ground, then turned her back to the monsters. She pressed the button, but it jammed. "Fuck," she whispered, which was loud enough for one of them to wake. The leader in the centre of the group opened his eyes and scanned the area, searching for the source of the noise. Aurora kept trying, pushing another button, making it beep open. The remaining creatures growled, and when she looked behind her, arms stretched, grabbing her and pulling her into the group.

"No!" I shouted, moving to save her.

"Nik, you can't. It's too late." The space filled with her screams as they tore into her body, ripping her arms and legs before feasting on her limbs. The rest of her fell flat on her back as their claws ripped into her flesh, her torso covered in blood. Leo was right, it was too late. The device started as smoke dispersed, filling the room with the cure, keeping her obscured from view. I waited as the screeches died down, the people all on their knees and panting. I rushed in, finding Aurora's lifeless body. Someone had torn her heart out. I saw it lying beside her body. She didn't deserve that end. I wanted her to be happy because she had suffered enough. I moved over, closing her eyes with my fingers before kissing her forehead.

"I am sorry, Aurora. I hope you find peace, whether in this life or the next. I love you," I whispered, hoping her soul still lingered. I wanted her to know she was cared for.

Leo helped many of the transitioned vampires in a daze to find their feet and handed them some clothes. I couldn't bring myself to move as I stared at my former mate.

Leo's hand squeezed my shoulder. "She is gone, Nik. We must move on, and you know it. We have done what we needed, and Esmeralda organised a flight over the east coast to disperse more of the cure. We are done here. Time for us to move on." His words made sense, but I couldn't leave her there.

"Do you have a lighter or some matches?" I held my hand up expectantly, knowing he smoked the odd cigar. He reached his hand into the inside of his jacket and pulled out a lighter. I stood in search of an accelerant before finding some methylated spirits. I poured them onto what was left of her body before lighting it on fire.

"May your body and soul rest in peace." I bowed my head, waiting a few moments before leaving. Leo stood outside, staring at the sun making its final descent below the mountain ranges.

"It is a beautiful sunset. She would have liked that." He wasn't wrong, she would have. I only wished her death had not been so violent.

Leo smacked my chest. "Come on, let's go before it gets any darker."

I nodded, pausing to look back at the building that was beginning to glow. She had helped save around seventy people. I hope she held onto that wherever she was going.

"Where to next?" I asked as I joined Leo. He handed me a cigar as we found our way inside with our newest liberated vampires.

"According to Esmerelda, as Africa's population of monsters is tiny, she will organise for planes to fly over to scatter the cure rather than heading there. I honestly believe the next stop is to go home. Time for you to meet with Ravon and find a peaceful solution." He snorted. "We both know that it is not going to end well."

"Yeah, I am not too worried about him. I am sure logic will overcome ego," I said.

I noticed that Leo had stopped walking, so I spun to look at him. "Of course, the man who is pure ego would say that. Sorry, I am flabbergasted. You have enough ego to fill a room."

I walked over, tilting my head as I placed my hand on his shoulder. "Leo, you know my secret. I am a god. It is written in the rules that I must have a big ego." We both laughed, then turned to rest for the night. Leo was right—it would be a battle of egos, but the question was, who would fold first?

CHAPTER 68

GIVE ME MY BROTHER

Nik

I MANAGED TO SLEEP THE ENTIRE FLIGHT BACK TO ITALY. SINCE Larissa's death, sleep had eluded me. My thoughts were constantly plagued by thoughts of her and whether I made the right choice. I discovered that the more I thought of her, the less it started to hurt. She would always hold a piece of my heart, but I had to learn to live without her. An announcement came through the cabin, alerting us that we were to land shortly. I sat up straighter, looking over at Leo, who stared pensively out the window.

"What is it?" I asked him as he stroked his chin.

"We have been gone for months, travelling for months, and getting our updates from Esmerelda, but it doesn't feel like it is enough. We have barely touched the surface of stopping Ravon's evil plan. He had this serum that we have managed to counteract, but it isn't going to stop the hate or the prejudice toward our kind or any supernatural creature for that matter. Tell me, what was the point of all of this?"

Leo had a point. I sighed. "Leo, I don't think it matters; there will always be prejudice. If it isn't directed towards us, it will be some other minority. There will always be people who cannot see past hatred and lack empathy to understand. We have seen it before we took control of the United Kingdom. If it wasn't vampires, it was ethnicity or religion. Humans are inherently judgmental, and that will never change. I only hope that I can convince people of the truth, that we have never wanted to harm humans." Leo cleared his throat. "Well, not all of us. See, that is exactly the problem. There will always be those who create a poor image for the rest of us."

Leo tilted his head in agreement. The next step, I feared more than speaking to the masses. I would be the face of everything again, only this time, I knew what was happening. I had pushed aside my doubt about Esmerelda and discovered that she truly was a beautiful person without any prejudice, except for her husband, which I understood. The plane bumped, signifying its contact with the ground. The pilot made his announcement and thanked us. Leo stood and made his way to the door, but I waited for a moment, checking my phone to see multiple missed calls. I opened a text.

MIMI

He knows, Nik. He took Roman. I hope you get this soon.

Dread filled my heart. I would kill Ravon for this. Nobody but me could harm my brother. I pressed dial, placing the phone to my ear.

"Ah, Nik?" Leo's voice was hesitant. I stood and made my way to the door as Mimi answered. I hung up the phone only to be met by the man who took my brother.

"The man of the century. I don't believe *hour* truly represents the way you fucked up everything for me." Ravon stood before me, his arms crossed, as multiple armed men surrounded us.

I pushed Leo behind me as I sniffed the air, noting that the bullets in their guns smelled strange. As I tried to decipher the peculiar smell, I realised these bullets were created to inflict pain. Leo took another step, hiding inside the plane.

"Ravon, it is a pleasure to see you. Wait, scratch that. I am going to remove the formality. Give me my brother, or I swear I will draw your death out, slowly pulling you to pieces and thriving off the sounds of your screams." I didn't want to placate this man. I wanted this to be finished because my brother had his happy ending to get to.

"I see, straight down to business. I have it from here, men, you can leave," he ordered.

"No, wait, I want them to stay. What do you have to hide? I don't care what they see from me. They will only see a man wanting to protect his family from a manipulative monster who has twisted facts to suit his narrative. To keep the world scared of a creature that doesn't exist. Men, stay," I ordered, standing my ground against him.

He gritted his teeth as they looked back at him, and his face changed. "I am not worried about the men being here. I just believe their time would be better spent protecting the world from the creatures that you all inevitably turn into." His words were smooth as he nodded and waved for them to leave.

I took a step down, moving closer to him. The men looked nervous—I could hear their hearts beating faster, their hands shaking above their weapons, their eyes darting between Ravon and me. But more than anything, I could smell their fear permeating the air. My monster was loving this. He wanted to snarl in hopes of a few running away. They had probably never seen a vampire quite like me.

"Oh, please, you say words that have no meaning!" I shouted at Ravon before speaking to the innocent men. "The purpose of the serum Ravon created was to turn vampires into those creatures. The ones who run rampant at night. Leo," I called out for my friend, listening to his approaching steps. "Would you be a willing participant in this experiment? I have a spare cure. All you need to do is feed from one of the volunteers below." Leo nodded as I turned back to the men before me. "Who would like to volunteer to be bitten to prove the words that I say are the truth? I will heal you instantly, but if Leo takes a bite, he will transform immediately." I put the proposition forward, hoping that one would be brave enough to accept the challenge.

I stared the men down as they glanced anywhere but at me. I softened my eyes, hoping at least one would agree.

"I will." A man raised his hand, removing his helmet and walking over. Leo gulped, and I squeezed his shoulder as he walked past.

I watched Leo bite into the man's throat, my fangs extending as the smell of fresh blood hit my nose. It took a few seconds before he pushed the man away, his screams turning into monstrous screeches. I charged at Leo, tackling him to the ground and holding him as his skin changed colour. The men around gasped. I had to wait for the full transition before injecting the cure, or it wouldn't work. He stopped thrashing, his eyes closed, and his breathing normalised. I pulled off the sheath protecting the needle as his red eyes sprang open, glaring at me. I stabbed him directly in the heart, pushing the serum into his body. He pushed me off before jumping up and collapsing onto the ground again.

I could hear the whispers as doubt travelled among the men, who slowly looked to their leader. The man who had tricked them.

"You are dismissed. Please tell others what you saw today." I helped Leo to his feet as he gripped the pole connected to the stairs before he finally sat down. It had taken it out of him. I paused for a moment before remembering that keeping an eye on my enemy was more important. Leo just needed a second to find his feet. Two guards stayed behind, and I listened to them talking.

"I didn't see anything, did you?"

"No, Ravon would never lie to us. He tricked us with some compulsion nonsense. He is dangerous."

"You are right, gentlemen, I am dangerous. I am the son of Mars. I am a demi-god. I am a weapon, but I can assure you that although my powers are vast, I did *not* compel you. What you witnessed was Ravon's manipulation. Well, one of them. Tell me now, this man currently has my brother, he is being held against his will. What reason did he state? I am intrigued about what my innocent brother could have possibly done to be taken by this peasant before me." It was an old-fashioned insult, which was the complete opposite of what he was, but from what Esmerelda said, he did not like to be reminded of the fact that he was born into poverty.

"He…he was accused of working with the creatures." One of the men trembled as I kept a close on Ravon's position in the crowd.

I held my stomach, laughing at the comment. "He was accused of working with creatures who cannot speak. I know you are smarter than that. This man has you fooled. He isn't the protector that you think."

"And let me guess, you are. They all need Lord Nik Dankworth, the man who sold his soul and sacrificed an unborn child for a girl, which created the plague that is the vampires." Ravon finally spoke after fading into the background, watching the scene unfold before him.

I paused. He wanted to hurt me, but there was one problem. I had accepted the mistake I made. I looked at the ground before glancing up.

"He is right, I did those things. The very thought of not being near the love of my life tore my heart into pieces. I was born a wolf. So she was my fated mate, and she was taken from me. The one who made life worth living. The thought of every day without her made life seem pointless. Nothing made sense without her. I had been alive for centuries, barely living life, just taking it day by day. Then I saw her, a beautiful woman who took my breath away, living perfection. I sold my soul to save her in exchange for becoming this creature. I have often wondered if I would do it again, and you know, after seeing what it has done, my answer is no. My selfishness has caused so much pain. I was wrong, and that is why I want to fix this. I have to. This all started because of me." The words didn't sound like me. They almost reminded me of my old self, the man I was before my actions ripped my soul in half.

Ravon looked murderous, his pointed glare unwavering. Any mortal man would be scared, but I felt a small amount of joy as I contemplated the ways to destroy this man who had kept an entire world underneath his thumb. He twisted everything for his own agenda. He and Duzi were the same, the only difference was that one was an immortal and the other a human. The men still looked unsure.

"No, the human race doesn't need Nik Dankworth. They need someone willing to sacrifice for them, not one who expects the sacrifice. Humans deserve someone who cares about them and not as a science project. I started this plague, but I am here to end it and create peace once and for all."

I listened as the men's hearts started to beat slower. I watched as their weapons lowered marginally with every passing second.

"What are you doing? This man is a monster! He will kill you and your entire family!" Ravon shouted. He grabbed the men's guns, lifting them up. His actions were desperate, knowing he was losing this battle.

"I am a monster. I have never denied my faults." I smirked as I thought of Larissa and how I worked with her to understand that having a monster inside doesn't make you evil. "I have flaws, I have issues, I have a temper, but at my core, I care for people." I pointed towards Ravon. "He does *not*. You saw the truth in your blood. We may never understand what it has done to your biology." It didn't bode well for vampires in the future, but Esmerelda explained her solution for that.

The men shrugged and walked away, leaving Ravon with Leo and me. He punched the window on the car beside him, making it shatter.

"You made an enemy," Ravon snarled.

"You already considered me one before I arrived. Please, don't bullshit me. I see through your façade."

"You will get back on your plane and go back to your shithole of an island. This is your final warning."

"Or what? You have my brother, so I won't be going anywhere until he is returned to me *unharmed*." If Roman had been harmed, I would rip him apart slowly, starting with his fingers and toes before moving to the larger body parts.

"Roman will be delivered to you once you are gone."

"Ravon, in the old-fashioned way of saying this, I don't negotiate with terrorists. Hand my brother over *now*. This is your final warning." My monster itched to attack, my claws slowly extending with anticipation.

Ravon laughed as he walked closer, clasping his hands behind his back. He strolled as if he had no care in the world, as if he didn't fear the god in front of him. He stopped before me, his eyes bright but filled with anger at somebody having challenged him.

"This is your final warning, Lord Dankworth. Leave, and I will return your brother. Stay, and I will ensure his death while taking his pup from his mate's womb. I think I would like to understand more about wolves and what they can offer humans." He pulled out his phone, showing a split camera—one of Roman chained like an animal, and Mimi on the other, lounging in the penthouse. "I can make people hurt anywhere, anytime."

I recognised the room that Roman was being held in. I nodded before spinning on my heel and making my way back into the plane with Leo.

"What are you doing?" he whispered as he motioned to the door closing.

"Take off. Do we still have those parachutes?" I asked the pilot, ignoring Leo's questions as his brow creased.

I sat down, staring out the window at the man who thought he had won this round. If only he knew the truth, that there would always be two things that I would protect more than anything. The first was my mate, the second was my brother.

I SAT IN THE CAR, RUNNING MY FINGER OVER MY CHIN. Esmerelda had confirmed where my brother was being held. I knew what I had to do, but I needed to avoid harming any innocent people. They weren't the intended targets; it was only my brother. Ravon's men were doing as instructed. Leo sat beside me, tapping his fingers on the edge of the door.

The phone rang, and I glanced down to see Mimi's name flash across the screen. I knew Roman should never have given her a phone to contact us. I sighed before answering,

"Hello, Mimi."

"Don't hello me, Nik. Where is my Alpha? I can sense that he is in trouble. I have been sensing it for a while now, but when Roman said he had to go dark, I avoided contacting you guys." Her voice filled with anger and worry.

"Mimi, I am handling it."

"Don't *handle it* with me, Nik. He is my mate. I can't lose him. You promised me that you would protect him."

I suddenly registered what she had said. "Wait, what do you mean go dark? I sent Roman home to you around two months ago." I sat up straighter as my monster snarled.

"He called to tell me he was coming home. A few hours after that, he called back and said that he had to go dark to help you out."

"That motherfucker. I am going to fucking destroy him. Mimi, I have to go."

I hung up the phone, turning towards Leo as my eyes flared, and soft snarls echoed from my chest. A wave of nausea washed over me. I had never had this sensation before. My body felt heavy, my chest constricted as if a weight sat atop it. How could I let this happen?

I stepped out of the car, slamming the door behind me. I had no care now, only one singular focus—saving my brother. Leo scrambled to join me as I slammed my hands into the elevator doors, forcing them open as the alarm rang. I didn't care. Nothing would stop me from getting to Roman. I stepped into the elevator, pressing the button for the basement. Leo joined me, and I cleared my throat.

"I thought we were going for stealth." Leo quirked an eyebrow at me.

"That went out the window when I discovered that my brother has been held captive for *months*."

"But we spoke to him. How?"

"I know. Ravon is dying today, I don't care. Today, he meets his *bloody* end. You can kill anyone, but leave him for me. Do you understand?"

"Gladly, also, now that I cannot be turned again, it's making me excited for the taste of fresh blood."

I nodded. The one benefit to the cure was that they would never turn back into those monsters.

I had spoken to Esmerelda about my concerns as I planned my brother's rescue, and we discussed the idea of her taking over as leader when I tore her husband's heart from his chest. She only had one request—she wanted to be there to watch it happen. I had it all planned. Break my brother out, drive to an empty sports field, and finally kill Ravon.

Leo and I hid behind the panels as the doors opened, knowing they would be waiting.

"Come out with your hands up and we won't fire," a man shouted.

I scoffed. I would enjoy this. "Stay," I ordered Leo as I took a step into their view. I assessed the ten men before me, all holding a new type of machine gun that glowed green. I fixed my sleeves, rolling them up my forearms. I loosened up my neck as I took a step closer. "Gentlemen, I told myself that I would spill no blood today. That was before I knew the truth. I will give you the option to walk away now because…" My eyes flared red, and my fangs elongated as I growled, "I won't be holding back."

Four men remained after the others scampered away. I heard the click of the safety and knew it was going to hurt. I squared my shoulders, ready for the impact.

"Leo, hold position." I watched their fingers touch the triggers before sounds exploded. Bullets flew through the air, hitting my torso and body all over. The pain was minimal as I watched blood slowly falling from the holes. I took a moment, but the bullets pushed themselves out, and the wounds healed slowly. I smiled, glancing up.

"*Run*," I warned, as the men scrambled away. I chuckled, straightening up as Leo joined me.

"Why are you taking all the fun?" He looked at the pool of blood, his eyes flaring at the sight of it. Leo knew the truth, and though many young ones would be eager to taste the blood of an older vampire, it would kill him. I shook my head as a reminder. "I know, but it does intrigue me. The power within you would be delicious. I mean, I was your first, should I not be immune to it?"

"That is not something I want to test out. You are my oldest friend. You were there for me when I lost her countless times. I can't lose my mate, my brother, and my best friend in one day."

Leo gripped my shoulder, "Are you going soft on me?" We laughed together.

"Let's find my brother. Esmerelda believed that he would be near the back, hidden away, where many of the tortured prisoners are kept." The words made another wave of nausea overtake me. Stupid technology had deceived me with the use of AI to change someone's voice.

I directed Leo to take the corridor to the left while I took the right. I looked inside every single window and smelled for my brother. I hoped I wasn't too late, especially since Ravon had him for so long. His wolf would be murderous, so I hoped he hadn't lost his sanity. I moved faster as my ears pricked with movement upstairs, the sound of more men advancing on us. I tried to tap into our link, but was met with silence. The need to find my brother grew stronger, and I started to become frantic. I stopped, taking a deep breath, separating the smell of human urine and faeces before scenting my brother, the wet dog smell that irritated me.

"Roman," I whispered as a small bang echoed further down. I ran faster than ever, bursting through the door. My brother was tied to the floor with welded chains. Chains that wrapped around his wrists in a room that stank of wolfsbane. My brother had been poisoned. It would never kill him, but it made sense why he had been stuck here for so long. He never gave up. I yanked the chains, burning my skin, and I noticed they had been engraved with ancient mythological symbols. Ravon was smarter than I predicted; he had thought of everything, but he had a source constantly feeding him information: Peter and Wade.

"Roman." I rolled him onto my lap, moving his hair from his face. His breathing was laboured, his wrists covered in tiny burns thanks to the wolfsbane within the engravings. It constantly poisoned him. I slapped his face, and he groaned. "Brother, I am here. I'm sorry. I'm so sorry."

Voices were growing louder as Leo rushed into the room. We didn't have much time, so I slapped him harder.

"Roman, you need to snap out of it. Think of Mimi, think of your son. Get up, brother." His yellow eyes snapped open, and he bared his teeth as fur erupted through his skin. He would be too weak to transform, though. "I don't need your wolf, I need your feet to work. Either drink my blood or stand the fuck up."

I knew saying that would piss him off, with our constant competition over who was stronger. A small chuckle met with a coughing fit. Specks of blood came from his mouth, and without thinking, I bit into my wrist. He could hate me if he chose to, but I wouldn't let him suffer any further. This was my fault. I dragged him here. He gagged on my blood, eventually drinking some of it. I stood, holding out my hand for him until he latched on, pulling himself up. He looked me over, my shirt covered in blood.

"I know you like blood, but bathing in it seems a little excessive." I snorted as I threw my brother a shirt to wear.

"Nobody needs to see a hairy beast roaming the halls. Cover up." He pulled it on as Leo glanced behind us, his eyes filled with sadness.

"Nik." His tone was a warning that we were running out of time.

"Leo, get to the car. We will meet you there!" I shouted as I squeezed my brother's shoulder. He pressed his forehead to mine as we took a moment. I found him. I saved him. I would get him home.

"I'm sorry, brother."

"Save your apologies for later, Nik. We need to get out of here. Have you encountered any super soldiers yet?" he asked, pulling his hair off his face, extending his claws, and preparing himself. "They are ruthless and lack humanity. I hope you are ready to tap into that monster inside because they are just as bad."

We left the cell as more men arrived, holding up their futuristic weapons, only these were red and not green like the ones earlier. Curious about what the difference was, I watched as one flicked off the safety, and a small flame burst out. This was going to hurt. Why couldn't our father have been the God of Water? I looked behind me at the wall of reinforced steel, containing more mythological symbols.

"This was made for us. He knew he would have our company one day. Which means that he has something planned for our exit. Are you feeling strong enough to shift or anything?"

"I want to rip some of them apart."

"Good, take the top back off. I won't have you rip something you just put on." He rolled his eyes at me as I took it back, tucking it into my back pocket.

"Nik," he held out his arm, and I took it in mine, "we are in this forever, as we have been since the day we shared that womb. If this is our end, I am honoured to have made it this far with you."

I slapped him hard. "We are not dying today. Shut up, Roman."

I charged, ducking under the flames and destroying the guns by ripping them in half while Roman ploughed into the other men, throwing them around as if they were toys. I didn't want to cause harm, but circumstances had changed. I tore their limbs off, others, their heads, and some, just a simple punch to the right area to paralyse them. Plenty of men ran, heeding the warnings, while others still lingered. The car was in sight, but two men stood before us, built a little bigger than the others. Their eyes were lifeless and grey, and they showed no emotion as their hands clasped together in front of them. They appeared to be mindless creatures.

"You don't get to take what doesn't belong to you!" the taller, dark man shouted as his eyes fixed on my brother.

"My brother belongs to no man. Ravon knows this." The alarm sounded, and the room filled with red flashing lights and a blaring noise. It seemed a little excessive if somebody was already in the building.

A faint thud echoed, and I saw a door closing before us. I quickly glanced at Roman, who nodded. We charged the men, knowing that we had limited time before we would be locked inside with no idea of what technology they had to torture us with. Ravon had far more resources than even I could comprehend. The men braced themselves as we scaled their heads. One caught Roman's leg, bringing him to the ground with a hard thud, his jaw shattering in the process as Roman and his wolf howled in pain. I had never moved so fast, forcing my hand into the man's chest and pulling out his heart. I threw it at Roman, knowing a fresh heart would help his wolf heal him quicker, especially with my blood still lingering inside him. The second man, the one who spoke, fired his weapon, the bullet landing in my chest. Warmth filled my body, and I looked down to see it glowing, small flames coming from my chest. I snapped my fingers, distinguishing the flames.

"You are going to have to try a little harder than that to kill me," I said as the man flicked a switch, changing the colour of the gun to gold. "Roman, get the car and start driving." He didn't question my order as he scrambled into the car, slamming the door behind him. I moved backward slowly, unaware of what could be expelled from the gun at any moment. I remembered the small knife that I had tucked away in the back of my pants. Leo handed it to me 'for luck' as he said. The knife had saved him on many occasions. I moved at a glacial pace to avoid the man recognising my movements. I fastened my grip around the handle before throwing it with all my strength and speed. It lodged into his throat, and he stood stunned, moving to grab it. He yanked it out, and blood began to spurt from the wound as he clutched his throat. "Looks like that serum doesn't give you any more brains." I turned, opening the car door.

Leo sped from the building. I knew we would have a tail and that it would be Ravon. I hoped he would follow as I shot a quick text to Esmerelda, alerting her of our upcoming arrival. I noticed a large black SUV forcing the other police cars out of its way.

"Ravon," I whispered as Leo planted his foot on the pedal. This car had a turbo like I had never seen, and it sped through the city of Italy. Ravon smashed into any object that dared get in his way while Leo avoided creating any further carnage. I heard a faint buzzing noise and peered up to see a drone following us. I prayed it would have a camera to show the people of the world Ravon's lack of humanity.

CHAPTER 70

THE DEATH MATCH

Nik

Leo tore into the stadium, scraping the side of the car. The screeching noise would cause any human's ears to bleed. We all covered our ears from the sensitive noise piercing through. Leo letting go of the wheel had disastrous effects for us. The wheel popped, causing the car to jolt and spin out of control as we tumbled through the stadium's entrace to a field. I punched the door open before inspecting the small scratches on my body from the broken glass that were healing slowly. I reached down for my brother, helping him up as he shook it off before seeing Leo crawl out. He stayed on the floor for a little longer before we heard the sirens stop as Ravon drove into the field.

"Let the games begin, gentlemen. You know what you need to do."

"Wade is *mine*," Roman snarled as fur sprouted over his body, his wolf ready to tear his mate's foster father to pieces. I watched my brother's eyes glow yellow and his claws extend. He was ready for battle. Wade and Peter stepped from the car, smirks on their faces as they pulled guns from behind them.

"I'll take the weak-looking one," Leo said as he bent down in preparation, his eyes focused on his target. Leo was a fierce warrior when I encountered him on the battlefield. We bonded with our strategic minds, and he has been loyal since his first transition. I would forever be grateful for his friendship over the centuries.

I stepped forward, staring Ravon down as he tore his shirt from his body. We walked toward one another, every step wanting to quicken, to bring this man to his knees, to make him eat the dirt beneath my feet. I wanted to remind him that he had no place in this world to treat people the way that he had. We stopped before one another. I could see hell in his blue eyes. A darkness that seemed to take hold of him, a demonic element that seemed supernatural. The sight, although not unfamiliar to me, took me by surprise. He *was* human.

"I see you've had a little upgrade," I commented as I observed his muscular physique, his tattoos on display, each a dark element, and others depicting horrifying scenes. I saw significant dates that humans would rather forget. He was the definition of a sociopath. I wondered about the rings on his forearm, if they were tokens from his victims.

"Admiring the view?" He quirked his eyebrow and flexed his bicep.

I scoffed. "No, just staring at the stupid in front of me. Why any person would inject themselves with a serum containing supernatural elements is beyond me."

"I thought that at first, but I discovered the benefits without the downside. Once I had your brother's Alpha DNA, that was a whole other thing. His blood has so much potential. It contains so many hidden elements. I cannot wait to unravel them all. I already had a little bit, and I have noticed a difference. I did have one question though, is it the god blood that stops you from not turning into one of those creatures?" He sprouted his words with so much pride as if I should admire him.

I laughed at him. "Clearly not all the benefits if you ask stupid questions. I see that your bloodlust is hidden within that temper. You just can't see beyond the power you have inherited. The mood swings are your body trying to regulate because of the serum, which is not normal. I am honestly shocked that you managed to conceive a child."

His eyes flared brighter, and I noted that slight yellow tinge on the inner iris. Pieces of Roman had already interacted within his system.

"Let's end this, Dankworth. I have plans for later tonight, like killing that pathetic wife of mine, as she has outlived her purpose."

As Peter and Wade walked past me, Peter hocked up a chunk of saliva, spitting it in my direction. I waved at him with a cheerful smile and a small wink. I clenched my fists as Ravon charged, his fists connecting with my jaw.

"Strong, but not enough to hurt me, it seems," I taunted as I clicked my jaw back into place. "Oh, look, one less man for you to worry about." I pointed toward my brother.

Roman had already taken care of Wade. The man stood holding his intestines in his arms, his legs shaking from the trauma to his body. Roman transformed into his wolf, roaring at the man who had harmed his mate, who raised her to be an evil creature when her heart had nothing but purity and love. His jaw launched at his throat, his teeth snapping around his neck. A gurgling scream left his throat as Roman removed his head from his body before feasting on the corpse before him.

I turned my attention to Leo, who picked up Peter by the shirt collar, spinning around before letting him go. He soared through the air and landed on the scoreboard, his body convulsing with sparks of light as the power spread through him, charring his flesh. Peter shrieked, the last moments of his pitiful life. The power shorted the rest of the lights, leaving the area in dusk and smoke. I spun back around to Ravon and shrugged.

"Once upon a time, I would have given you leniency. Larissa probably would have convinced me to do that, but I am standing here right now, and I have no sympathy for what is going to come your way." I allowed my monster a little grace to take over. We had to be one.

I listened as Ravon's heart beat faster, his fear increasing with every beat. He was alone with only one other man to back him up. A guard lingered close to the car, sweat beading on his forehead, and his hand shaking. He had no intention of helping his boss. I assumed after witnessing Wade and Peter's gruesome end.

"I'm not scared of you."

"Absolutely not," I said smugly as I glanced at my hands, letting him know that I had no care for his words. I wanted this over. Ravon charged, pulling a knife and thrusting it into my side. I stopped, the wound burning.

"Poison, really?" I raised a brow at him.

"Aren't you all powerful? You'll be fine."

I pulled the knife out, throwing it to the ground as I sped towards him. Despite his enhanced eyesight, he never saw me coming. I punched him in the knee, shattering it before sending another blow to his torso. He landed on his knees, screaming in pain as I lifted my fist for one final move. I almost wished it had been more difficult, but this never would have been a challenge; he was, after all, just human.

My fist froze in the air as the ground started to shake, and lightning struck the earth around us.

"Nik!" Roman's voice came as a warning for what was coming. A high-pitched whistling noise screeched above us, and I looked up to see Jupiter's pet eagle. I stepped backward, moving towards my brother as we got on our knees, bowing our heads to avoid being seen as disrespectful. The gods hadn't come to Earth in millennia. This wasn't good.

"Rise Romulus and Remus, you may be half-breeds, but you are still worthy," his deep voice boomed as we stood, seeing the god before us. His long beard and intense gaze explained the pet eagle.

"Holy fucking shit, what is that thing?" Ravon asked, his voice trembling. His eyes were trained on something behind us. Roman dared to look.

"Pluto and Cerberus," Roman whispered, almost in awe of the creature before him.

"Did you think you could have all the fun without me, brother?" Pluto asked his oldest friend.

"I did give you the message, didn't I? This Ravon is responsible for a multitude of vile acts against humanity. He colluded with The People's Revolution with Duzi, and even the witches. If your daughter hadn't shown her true strength, she might still be alive." Jupiter bowed his head slightly in Pluto's direction, a silent apology.

Cerberus snarled as Pluto patted one of the three heads on the rottweiler-type animal. The King of Hellhounds and his creature who came to collect souls.

"Easy, boy, trust me. We will have our revenge. Thank you for the invitation. I just want to point out the cameras watching us right now."

"I'm aware. Why do you think there is currently an electrical storm?" he said, rather chuffed with himself. Pluto tapped his nose in a peculiar way. "Roman, Remus, how are you? I hope you don't mind the intrusion, but this one messed with god blood when he took from Roman. We will take care of this the old-fashioned way. I'll make sure the footage shows your amazing battle." Pluto laughed.

"Do you ever stop?" Jupiter asked, rolling his eyes.

Roman and I stared in disbelief as we listened to the banter between these two ancient creatures.

"What…what…" I stumbled over my words.

"Spit it out, boy." Jupiter rolled his eyes.

"Why?" I finally managed to sputter.

Jupiter's eyes softened as he took a step forward, lowering himself to eye level and putting his hand on my shoulder. The touch was warm and brought a comforting sensation through my system.

"Good question. We thought, after losing your mate and all of your efforts in making things right, that you deserved a reprieve. You are trying to change the world. We appreciate your efforts, and this is your reward. Unless you have other ideas?" His eyes fell on Ravon.

I looked at the man on his knees, trembling in fear. "Nik… please," Ravon begged.

"Nope, don't talk to him. We will be sure to torture him very well. He hurt a demi-god, after all." Jupiter scowled while Ravon whimpered, I could smell his fear.

"Oh, trust me, why do you think Cerberus is here? He needs fresh meat. Let's go feast." Pluto winked at me.

I stepped backwards as Leo appeared, white as a sheet, his finger pointing to the gods.

"Is...is that real?' He stumbled over himself. Roman and I had never had that moment of *holy shit the old stories are real*. We knew they were, we lived them, but for Leo, it was something out of this world.

"Yes, it is, very much so," I mumbled.

Roman and Leo spoke quietly, my brother filling him in on who the men were. I turned back towards Ravon, wanting the satisfaction of watching his death. It almost seemed anticlimactic as I observed the eagle peck at his eyes before tilting its head back and swallowing the flesh. While Cerberus feasted on his organs, tearing them from his body, Ravon's scream echoed through the field. He felt every bit of his torture as Jupiter and Pluto spoke to one another, allowing their pets the satisfaction of killing the man.

Chapter 71

Time for Change

Nik

Esmerelda stood in the player's box that looked out over the field, barely flinching as I entered. I saw the spare clothes on the table. She appeared in thought, her breathing even as her hands held her belly. I could smell her anxiety but not her grief. She truly didn't care for the man who fathered her child.

"I suppose thanks are in order." Her tone was curt as she turned around. I stood before her in just my drawers. Her eyes lingered over parts of me in a way that I would generally enjoy, but not today. Her desire brought a sense of unease, but I shook it off, trying to dress myself faster.

"I am unsure what is with that tone. You wanted his death, and now you seem displeased. Did you have second thoughts?" I asked her, straightening the cuffs on my shirt before sitting down.

"I wasn't expecting it to be quite so…well, vulgar. I thought for sure you would have just snapped his neck, but the whole blinding him with your thumbs before ripping open his abdomen and ripping his organs out for all to see. A little over the top."

I smiled, remembering Pluto saying that he would make it look good. "I have a flair for the dramatic, what can I say? The man is dead, and you are free. What happens now? There is a lot of disharmony between vampires and humans, and there will be those who cannot accept the changes. What do you plan on doing?"

She sighed as she took a seat opposite me and ran her fingers through her hair. "I think the truth is in order. I believe I need to show people proof of Ravon's deception, show his death and…and," she cleared her throat, "I will need you beside me. A face for vampires. You are the father of them all, so they will trust you. I need you to stand beside me and show your support for all supernatural creatures. I might need Roman and any witches that you know to also be there. I want to show everyone that we can survive this and we can thrive. This war started with power hungry assholes, so maybe it is a time for a female to rule."

"I think the appropriate word is princess or queen, if you rather. You are not just a female, you are the heir to the Spanish throne, if it still existed. You told me that many don't know of your true heritage. I think it is time to stand up and accept it."

Roman and Leo entered and quickly dressed before Roman slumped beside me.

"I will stand with you, but Nik has a point. They will not just accept you because you are Ravon's wife. They will need a reason for it. Show them the strength in your bloodline, show them what you are made of. The vampires, wolves, and witches will be there with you."

"I appreciate it. I shall inform the news tonight and set up a podium outside Town Hall for the speech." She walked over, offering her hand to me. I slid mine in as I stood. "Thank you for having faith in me. I appreciate it from a man such as yourself, Nik. I know taking a chance on me would have been against many of your morals, considering how close I was to the entire situation. I saw your position change that day in the warehouse when you saw who I truly was. I thank you from the bottom of my heart."

"No need. I look forward to seeing what you are made of." She rubbed her belly, glancing down at the possible monster that she was growing. I just hoped that peace would last. "May I?" I asked. It had been centuries since I had touched a baby belly. She took my hand, placing it in a particular area. I could feel the child move as I closed my eyes to feel its nature. The child had its mother's heart and soft disposition. I smiled, knowing my anxieties had been eased. This world was in good hands.

———

Esmerelda had set up the stage, and we stood behind the doors, waiting. The people had been informed of their leader's death and his treachery. She paced the room, her heart thudding hard as Roman and I watched her.

"Do you think she's got this?" Roman asked as I looked over the suit that he wore. He kept pulling at the collar.

I chuckled. "Missing your leather jacket, brother?"

"Shut up, and yes. What are your thoughts?" he pressed further, wanting to know.

I scratched my chin. "In all honesty, I had my doubts. She had so much to disclose, so many secrets, but honestly, she is what the world needs, with her heart and her compassion. We have seen enough devastation in the last fifty years, and I believe she will lead the world out of it. She will be tested, she will stumble, but ultimately, who doesn't? Those who are known as the greatest leaders in the world all have skeletons in their closets."

"She really did change you," he mumbled as Esmerelda walked over. The Larissa effect would be lasting, and I would be thankful every day to her for bringing me out of the darkness and finally seeing the light.

"Are you guys ready?" Her hands shook, so I took them in mine. She settled instantly, her body relaxing as her eyes locked onto mine. "If only you weren't mated. You certainly have an effect on my body that I rather enjoy, Lord Dankworth."

"You've got this. Let's do it," I said, tapping her hands as she pulled them away. She made her way to the door as a local witch joined us. I handed Roman a pair of glasses to cover our eyes from the bright sun, and he chuckled at my ability to be prepared for anything.

We stood behind as Esmerelda stepped up to the plate, ready to deliver the performance of a lifetime. The people were either ready for it or they were not. Only time would tell. She cleared her throat and drank some water before pulling her speech from the breast pocket of her two-piece navy suit.

"The people of the world, I stand before you today not as the wife of the man who led us down a dark path but as a sign of the future and what we can achieve. We stand upon the broken shards of a world that has been torn apart by mistrust, by fear, and the refusal to see the beauty in our differences. But I tell you now, as the winds carry the whispers of hope across the lands, that the devastation we have endured is not the end of our story. It is the beginning of a new chapter, a chapter that we will write together."

She paused before continuing, "The time has come to remove the prejudices that divide us. Yes, we are different, but it is in those differences that our power lies. We have centuries of knowledge and strength from the vampires, the wolves, and the witches. They can help us rebuild humanity. We can form a force that no destruction can overcome, that no darkness will be able to swallow. We will never be able to undo our past, but we can shape the future. Let us move forward not as separate tribes or warring parties, but as one united world. Let us build a future where children are not taught to fear what they don't understand, but to embrace it by learning and celebrating our differences. I understand that old wounds take time to heal, but with courage and compassion, we can rise above them. We will prove that from the ashes, we have bloomed into a new era, a time for peace. Let us create a world that is not just rebuilt, but reimagined—a world of peace, of unity, of acceptance. Together, we can heal the scars of our past. Together, we will light the way for our future generations. Together, we will prove that love and understanding are more powerful than any force that seeks to divide us."

The crowd erupted with cheers. Many people nodded and clapped at her words. It was a moving speech. She knew the right words to say, never mentioning her husband, but rather focusing on the way forward. I had not written a speech. I wanted to see what she wrote before deciding what the supernatural creatures would want to hear. She turned around, holding out her arms for an embrace, which I walked into before she planted a soft kiss on my cheek.

I stood at a podium, my fingers tapping against the wooden grain as I stared out at the expectant faces before me.

"I am speaking to all those who have doubts, all those who think that Princess Esmerelda's words carry no weight. We find ourselves at a crossroads. Our past has covered us in shadows that seemed to only grow with every passing year. But we know the truth that the smallest light can bring the biggest changes." I turned back to Esmerelda, pointing toward her. "She is our light, a light of hope. A hope carried by a leader who dares to dream of something greater than what we have now. I stand before you not as a Lord or the Father of Vampires, but as a man who has witnessed the power of resilience. Esmerelda's vision is not just about resilience but about hope. The world we knew is gone, but from the ashes, we will build something stronger, something better. Her call for unity is not her being a naïve princess, but rather a challenge born to signify her strength. She has asked us to embrace the uncomfortable truth that we are all different. We have different stories, histories, and ways of life, but it does not mean that we have to remain divided. I have been around for millennia. I have seen cities rise and fall. I have seen the best and worst parts of humanity. Through this, I have seen the strength of the human spirit."

I cleared my throat, taking a moment to think of what to say next. "The princess is right. We cannot focus on the past. We must look forward. We must grow together as a new world. It is going to be difficult, and we may begin to falter and have our doubts, but if we truly work together, we can achieve the impossible. For this reason, the Alpha, the High Priestess, and I have pledged our full support behind Esmerelda's vision. This isn't because it is easy or just to make people happy. It is because it is necessary, a change that must happen, a change that will benefit each and every one of us. This is not just her fight, it is ours. We are fighting for a world where our children can grow without fear and know the best parts of this world. A world where peace is not a fleeting dream, but a lasting reality. Together, if we do this, we will triumph."

The people erupted, and many began to chant,

"Esmerelda, Esmerelda, we are behind you."

She smiled as she waved to the people around her. I joined my brother and the witch as we watched the people cheer with delight over what would be their future.

"What happens now?" Roman queried as we re-entered Town Hall, the doors closing to the madness outside.

"I do what I promised," I said with a smile.

"What's that?"

"I enjoy my life as Larissa would have wanted me to. I will see you soon, brother. I am off to explore the world and see the sights as never before." I squeezed his shoulder, and he smiled as I spun and walked away. It was my time to enjoy the world.

CHAPTER 72

FULFILLING MY PROMISE

Nik

I had lived for so long, but I had never seen the true beauty in everything around me. The beauty that she forced me to see, the world that she saw. I had travelled so many paths over the centuries, but I never experienced what it was like to be a tourist. I had learnt countless languages, but this time, as I travelled and explored, I tasted their life. The best part was knowing that Larissa had created an album of all the places she wanted us to visit. I had a map in my mind to honour her memory, to do exactly as she asked. I planned my trip and hugged my brother goodbye, knowing that I would miss the birth of his first child.

I knew where I had to start, the place where it all began, the city where I first met her. I walked through the streets, remembering when I first laid eyes on the beauty who changed my life forever. Her green eyes that reminded me of a rainforest, the eyes that stopped me in my tracks. Every life, she kept her eyes. It was always a small freckle or dimple, anything that made her slightly different to the past, but never her eyes. The streets that were once cobblestone and sand were now concrete. I sat in the space where she was stabbed thousands of years ago. If I knew now what I knew back then, I wouldn't make the same mistake. It only prolonged my torture, a torture that was handed to me from the gods' petty behaviour. I kissed my hand, placing it on the ground,

"It is all for you, my love. I made you a promise and I will fulfil it. I will love you every day of my long life until we meet again. You are the reason that I breathe, my reason for everything. Goodbye, my love," I whispered as my voice croaked, taking one last moment before standing and moving on.

I travelled through Europe, seeing the beauty that I missed the first time, visiting the old historical buildings and experiencing life. I took photos and videos as a daily journal, sending them to my brother. Once I had completed Europe to my satisfaction, I visited America, Africa, and smaller islands that were filled with so much life and love. I met with celebrities and lived my life for all to see as the man who only wanted to bring about peace.

I created a social media presence for myself, showing the world what exciting places still exist. I chose not to hide anymore. I had once lived within the shadows and refused to be part of the limelight. Now, I spoke about real issues and made my opinion known on important matters. I refused to stand by. My follower count went from one hundred to over a million within twelve hours. The stroke to my ego made it more entertaining, especially with the thirst trap pictures that I would post. I knew it would make Larissa laugh.

The best country that I visited was Australia. The beaches were by far the most beautiful. The sand and atmosphere were peaceful. It reminded me of our honeymoon, just pure tranquillity. If Larissa returned, I promised myself that this would be the first place I would take her. Despite her multiple lives, we had never been to Australia. She believed it was full of savages after what the English did to the Indigenous Australians.

I fulfilled my promise to her. I took her with me in my heart. I returned home after a year, holding my nephew in my arms. He was the image of my brother.

"Isn't he perfect?" Roman asked, staring at his pup with adoration.

"I believe the only perfect specimen is me. I mean, he is yet to be toilet-trained." I winked at my brother.

"Nik!" He held his chest as he laughed.

Something about that name seemed wrong now. I was no longer reborn. I didn't feel like the same person that I was three years ago, before she stepped back into my life.

"Roman, brother, call me Remus." I didn't hesitate or question this. It just felt right. I was no longer the Phoenix, Nik, I was the man I should have been centuries ago, before I lost my humanity for the sake of a girl. Larissa showed me the path to being a man, one she would be proud of.

My brother smiled as I stared at the precious baby in my arms. Roman had everything he wanted. I couldn't be happier for him. Even if something was still missing from my own life.

Mimi walked over, kissing the top of my head as I held her son. "I know she will come back to you. Give it time. Your story is too epic to be left with such a tragic ending."

"I am at the mercy of the gods, Mimi, but I appreciate your kind words. Now, sit down and hold your child, and I will cook some food for you."

I stood and made my way around the kitchen, preparing a feast as Mimi and Roman stared lovingly at the child they created.

I sold the company, but I made sure to keep Refresh Marketing. Larissa would want to continue working for a little while if she returned. I no longer had a desire to rise the way I once did. I had enough money for this lifetime and the next. I wanted to focus on the time with my family and helping those in need. I volunteered at homeless shelters and tried to help people in any way that I could. Larissa would be proud.

CHAPTER 73

FIVE YEARS LATER

Nik

I STOOD IN LINE AT THE CAFÉ, WAITING TO ORDER COFFEES FOR Roman and Mimi. It had been five years since we cured those who had been turned into monsters. Ravon was dead, and Roman had his four-year-old son. He was the image of his father, and as intelligent as his uncle. We were celebrating Marcus's fourth birthday, and Mimi was terribly sick with her second pregnancy. She had become a fierce Luna and never let Roman get away with any nonsense. They were well suited to one another.

"Next, please," the young waitress called out, her blonde hair plaited down her back with makeup a little too thick around the eyes. "What can I get you, handsome?"

I ignored the flirtation. "A bloodcino, a latte, and a tropical juice." The latter was the only thing Mimi could keep down.

"A name for the order?" Her words caused my body to tingle, almost like it was telling me to accept something.

I paused and smiled before saying, "Remus." Saying my name was still surreal, and changing it within the business world was an interesting feat. Maybe it was from knowing that I was free from a curse that tore my heart out every couple of decades. I enjoyed my life, living up to the promise I made her. I took plenty of photos and visited so many places. I stood, checking my phone as another sensation shook my body. My phone buzzed in my hand.

"Where are you?" Roman huffed into the phone.

"I just ordered. I will be there in ten minutes."

"Yeah, I don't think I will survive that long. I got the time wrong, and Mimi is pissed."

I chuckled. I could hear her in the background, yelling at my brother. "Tell her I'm coming."

"Have you ever had a party with twenty four-year-olds? I almost wish to be tortured again," he mumbled down the end of the phone to avoid his mate hearing.

I winced, remembering that time I failed him. "As soon as my name is called, I'll speed there and entertain the little ones. I promise."

"ROMAN!" Mimi screeched in the background. I hung up, trying to avoid being the next victim of her hormones. She was worse than any other pregnant woman I had encountered.

"She didn't sound happy. Wife?" The man beside me chuckled as I stood there, holding my phone in my hand.

"No, luckily, my sister-in-law. My brother is the one in trouble." I spoke with a small smile. Watching their relationship develop and grow had been amazing. They were perfect for one another. She would tell him when he was being an asshole, and he just listened with a smile. It infuriated her further, but she knew him well enough that she didn't care anymore.

"Ah, women, they drive us mad, but we couldn't live without them." I nodded in agreement.

"Yes, that's true," I muttered.

"I see you're not married. A handsome lad like yourself. Haven't found the right one?"

"No, I did, she…she died."

"Oh, I'm sorry, mate. I can see so many women eye-fucking you right now. You've sure got your pick of the litter when you are ready." His accent was different, but the way he spoke almost seemed familiar.

"Yeah, I know now that nobody will compare to her, but I'm open to finding happiness." It was true. I never knew if she was coming back. She told me to let her go, and I had.

The stranger slapped me on the back. "What about her? She is stunning." He pointed to the brunette outside, her long hair cascading down her back in soft waves. She wore a black skirt and a blue shirt, and though her face was obscured, there was a glow about her, something radiant.

"Yes, she is." I noticed my heart no longer ached for Larissa. Maybe it was time. Not today, though.

"Remus." I heard my name called.

"Thank you for the conversation to bide the time. Enjoy your day."

"Same to you," he called out as I rushed to the door.

Holding the drinks and texting Roman, my body shuddered again, and I stopped to look around. What was this intense feeling? I couldn't place it. I opened the door, stopping suddenly and lifting the drinks above my head to stop them from spilling on me and the woman who bumped me. My phone crashed to the floor, and she bent down to pick it up, glancing up as her green eyes sparkled. Warmth filled my heart.

"Almost like déjà vu." She chuckled, sliding the phone into my chest pocket.

"Yeah, lucky it wasn't coffee." We laughed together as I took a step aside, letting her pass.

I watched her arse sway as she took her place in line. I couldn't be late getting to Roman and Mimi, so I walked away. I noticed the warmth in my body dissipating with every step I took. I stopped, spinning around to look at the coffee shop as realisation dawned on me. The brunette beauty was gone, nowhere in sight. I spun back, seeing her leaning against my car, speaking to Andreas.

I moved hesitantly, my breath catching in my throat. It couldn't be. The one who had made my heart feel lighter, the girl I had loved more than anything in this world. My heart pounded in my chest as I watched her, standing there as if no time had passed, as if all the pain had been nothing but a dream. She pushed her brown hair from her face, and her green eyes locked onto mine—those eyes that could brighten my entire day.

"Larissa," I whispered, my voice thick with disbelief. A smile spread across her face, and I felt my world shift on its axis. I dropped the coffee in my hands without a second thought, my heart racing as I watched her laugh—a sound that filled me with warmth, joy, and a sense of peace I had been missing. Slowly, we walked toward one another, and with each step, I was overwhelmed with a rush of emotion I couldn't contain. I had to touch her. I had to see that she was real. My heart beat faster, and my body tingled with a feeling of love and longing.

She was here. She was real.

When I reached her, I couldn't hold back any longer. I pulled her into my arms, burying my face in her hair, feeling the softness of her skin as she melted against me. Her smell, sweet and familiar, flooded my senses, and her touch ignited something deep inside me, setting me on fire in the best possible way. I squeezed her tighter, afraid that I might lose her again.

"You're here," I whispered, my voice trembling with emotion and my eyes welling with tears.

"I never left you," she mumbled into my chest, and I could feel her smile against me. I pulled back slightly to regard her, searching her eyes for any sign of doubt, but all I saw was love, pure and unwavering adoration.

"Tell me this isn't a dream, that this is real? I'm not hallucinating, right?" I asked, my voice cracking. I needed to hear it from her, needed her to assure me that this wasn't some cruel trick, that we hadn't been torn apart by fate forever.

She shook her head slowly, her gaze steady and filled with warmth. "I'm here, Remus. And I remember everything."

A weight lifted from my chest, but it was quickly replaced by a new kind of fear—fear of losing her again. "No more curse? No more tricks?"

She smiled softly, the kind of smile that only she could give me, full of warmth and certainty. "Nope. This time, it's forever. This time, we can be who we want to be. No more waiting for something to happen." Her voice dropped to a whisper, her hand reaching up to gently caress my cheek, her touch causing my body to burn with need. "The question I have for you, Remus, is, are you willing to give up your immortality? To live the life we always deserved? The one that we always dreamed of?"

The question hung in the air between us, but there was no hesitation. I knew what my answer would be. I looked at her, my hands cupping her face as I leaned in closer, my forehead resting against hers. I had to keep touching her. It didn't feel real.

"A thousand lifetimes, yes," I said, my voice thick with emotion, with the weight of everything I had ever wanted. "There is no question. You are my everything."

And in that moment, I knew. No curse, no immortality, nothing could keep me from the life I had always dreamed of, as long as she was with me.

CHAPTER 74

THE LIFE WE ALWAYS WANTED

Larissa

I ROLLED OVER IN OUR BED, MY HANDS SEARCHING FOR REMUS before I noticed he wasn't here. I shot up, listening intently. Even though Remus had to give up his vampirism to return to his wolf—and in return, he became human like his brother—I still had access to my powers, although not the full extent. I was just a simple witch. My father had one stipulation. When my mortal life ended, I was to take my rightful place next to him in Hell and rule in preparation for taking over one day. I negotiated in return that Roman must not be harmed for his deal with him. Remus wanted his brother to be happy, and there was no more need for sacrifices, especially after all they had endured after my death.

Pluto showed his heart by giving Remus and me a chance to be together, even though he was the Devil. He had a heart, but I suppose Luce had something to do with that. The gods would always squabble. They were so old that everything seemed massive to them, even when I believed it to be trivial. Pluto and Jupiter were on speaking terms since Roman gave his father's spear to Pluto, allowing him access to the world if he wanted it. He had enough souls that he didn't care to tempt any other humans in the future. Unless he suddenly grew bored and wanted some entertainment, which, knowing Pluto, seemed likely.

I heard the soft giggle of laughter coming from the kitchen, and I smiled, knowing they would be running amok. I pulled on my robe, wrapping it around my growing belly as the little one kicked my hand away.

"No need to be feisty, thank you." I chuckled as I descended the stairs, the railing wrapped in tinsel. It was Christmas, and I was hosting. I loved having everyone who was with us on this journey. Our lives were complete and made better by the people in them.

I snuck around the side to the dining area that linked to the kitchen. I peeked through, seeing Remus mixing pancake batter, his hair covered in flour, as was our little girl. She was just over two years old, her dark hair wavy like mine, with darker olive skin like Remus's. She also shared his crystal blue eyes. My heart filled with warmth, and as if sensing me, she spun quickly, almost falling. She was clumsy, but Remus caught her.

"Mumma!" she screamed as he put her down, her little legs running toward me. I lifted her into the air and held her tightly.

"Hello, my beautiful girl, are you making pancakes with Daddy?" My heart swelled. The fact that I could call this sexy man Daddy, the man who fathered my children, brought so much happiness to my heart. I could not love the man more if I tried.

"Alessandra has been an incredible help," he said, shaking his head of the excess flour. I snorted as it floated in the air a little.

"It is a good look on you." Alessandra and I giggled as she touched my face, flour now covering my cheek.

"Same as you, Mumma." He winked as he took Alessandra from my arms. He didn't need to be a vampire to know that I struggled to hold her while pregnant. He kissed the top of Alessandra's hand as he buckled her into her seat. He walked over, rubbing my tummy and bending until his mouth almost touched my belly button.

"I hope you are taking care of your mummy in there, little man. I cannot wait to meet you." He kissed my stomach as I ran my fingers through his hair. He stood up, bending me over and kissing me.

I squealed in delight, wrapping my arms around him. He kissed me another four times. Despite reverting to a wolf, his inability to keep his hands off me hadn't changed.

"Why did you let me sleep in? I would have liked to have joined in on the pancake making." I pouted at him. I enjoyed the moments with our family.

"You needed your rest. You stayed up all night cooking for Christmas lunch today. Plus, you are growing a human, and... you looked incredibly beautiful with your hair sprawled over the pillow. You made my heart stop for a moment at how devastatingly gorgeous you looked." I rolled my eyes as he tapped my bum. "Go and sit down, please."

I handed Remus a present before sitting down with Alessandra and her favourite teddy—a fluffy bunny she named Benny. She waved it around excitedly, and I watched her with so much joy that it felt like my heart might burst.

"Larissa." His eyes were filled with tears as he looked at the heart necklace I ordered before my death. It had been engraved the year that our love story started. "This is perfect." He pulled it over his head before setting plates in front of each of us, his movements easy and familiar. We laughed, and as I watched him, I couldn't help but reflect on all we had been through together. From the kidnappings by psychopaths to encounters with gods, being tortured by witches, hunted by wolves, and finally, finding a moment of peace. Through it all, we had survived, and we did it together.

"What time is your brother arriving?" I asked him as I moved Alessandra's thick hair from her face. She needed another haircut.

"Around eleven, I believe. Did you want him earlier?"

"No, no, it's fine."

"Leo and Alina aren't able to make it."

"Oh, what?" I gasped, looking up at Remus and perving on his sexy arse. He purposely shook it for my viewing pleasure. My cheeks burned, betraying my dirty thoughts that I dared not speak in front of our daughter.

"I will never tire of you blushing."

"Mummy purtee," Alessandra said in her baby talk.

"Yes, Mummy is very pretty and you will no doubt be the same."

"Ooft," I said, holding my stomach.

Remus rushed over. "Is everything alright?" he asked as I stroked his face.

"Nothing could be more perfect. Your son is very strong, and I do not doubt that he will be running amok with his cousins when he arrives."

"I cannot wait to help them during their first transformation into their wolf form." His excitement brought warmth and desire to my body. He sniffed the air, his eyes glowing yellow. I wouldn't lie that I missed his red eyes, but I truly didn't care what he was, as long as he was mine.

"No, we don't have time."

"I can make time." He winked before he nibbled on my neck.

"Later, I promise. I want to enjoy breakfast with you both."

Remus disappeared for a moment before returning with a present. I slid my finger into the paper, ripping it open to reveal a beautiful emerald necklace, surrounded by diamonds."

"Remus, this is stunning, thank you."

"I bought it while in Africa. I almost forgot about it until you mentioned our next family holiday and found it."

"Watching your smile during that time made hell bearable, especially with Luce and Pluto." I shivered, the idea still didn't sit well with me, but I had never seen my sister happier, nor my father.

Roman walked in for Christmas lunch as I rushed around the kitchen to get everything perfect. His three kids were hanging off him as he spun them around, pretending that he didn't know where they were. Mimi glowed as she stared at her mate. Remus and Roman chased the four kids around as Mimi sat at the counter, and I slid a glass of wine over for her.

Bodhi and Laura entered. She held out her hand, showing off the impressive ring as we all swarmed her with a tight embrace. Bodhi had never been happier. The best thing for him had been becoming a vampire.

Andreas, Stuart, Julian, Richard, and Valerie arrived next. The house became louder, but I smiled at the family we had created. All these people had been with us since day one and supported our story in one way or another.

Alina and Travis arrived next, and I noticed the eyes that Andreas and Travis made toward one another. Remus nudged me when I motioned for him to go and do something about it. I mixed the potato salad dressing through before putting the last bowl on the impressive dining table.

James came in next. Remus got over his fear that he had been part of it all. It was purely a coincidence that James looked like my first husband. He was a genuinely nice guy who just got screwed around a bit.

The room was loud and filled with laughter as I wished that those who had passed could be here. We couldn't always get what we wanted. The flames in the living room grew brighter as the last guest joined us.

"Father!" I shouted as I rushed over. He had taken advantage of the spear, and Jupiter allowed it. He said humans deserved whatever was coming their way, considering how they handled the vampire, wolf, and witch situation. Alessandra had magic, but I rarely used mine. Remus was no longer immortal, just a simple beta under his Alpha brother, Roman. Who looked older than his brother now with his greying hair. But he was still as handsome as ever. I sat back down and watched Pluto sit beside James.

"Long time no see." He winked at him, and James fainted, falling off the seat.

"Pluto," I growled in warning as he chuckled.

"Fine, I will leave him alone, for now." His eyes glowed with mischief.

"Did you need anything else?" Remus asked, taking my hand and bringing it to his lips.

"I have everything I need right now," I said with a smile.

The world still had its struggles, its imperfections, but perfection was a fleeting dream—utopia was a fantasy that could never truly exist. Pure peace, it seemed, was an illusion. Yet, for now, in this moment, the world was as peaceful as it could be.

Our house was filled with laughter and love. This was the life I had always imagined, the one I had fought for—and finally, it was mine. Or rather, ours.

The End

The Heirs trilogy

After the initial release of my debut novel, 'The Hidden Heirs', in 2023, we finally get to see what happens next for Faith, Annie and Harley after being thrust into the mystical world of Zilanta. Faith has to navigate the treacherous world controlled by men to ensure her survival, all while trying to resist Sebastian's proposition for marriage. Aleksander must do what he can to protect the girls from the tyrannical leadership of Sebastian, as well as those who wish to harm them.

Book 1 will be re-released in late 2025, with Book 2 being released on the same day, and Book 3 coming at the start of 2026.

Eternal Flame

If you enjoyed the sneak peek of Leo, be sure to stay tuned. Eternal Flame is set before the bombs fell, where he discovers his mate, Alina. Vampires are not known to exist within society, and Alina has to navigate the world while being a single mum and falling for the handsome Prince Leo. This will be a duology.

Daniella and Drake's story

This story focuses on the underground witch coven, think magic with mafia. Every person within the coven has access to one of the four different elements of magic: air, water, earth and fire. Daniella is a feisty teacher who ran from her life within the witch coven after falling pregnant to a man outside of the coven. Drake is the High Mage, in need of a wife; he has his sights set on Daniella. This will be a duology.

Whispers of the Damned

This will be a novella that focuses on Pluto and his life struggles before and after the arrival of his daughter, Larissa.

ACKNOWLEDGMENTS

To my betas — Dani, Coral, Steph, and Michelle — thank you. This series, this whole journey, wouldn't have even started without your belief in the story and in me. You pushed me to hit publish when I wasn't sure I could, and I'll never forget that.

To my amazing street team — your support has meant the world. You've shown up again and again, and I've felt every bit of it. Thank you for sticking with me.

Em — I gave you a chaotic, half-baked design brief and somehow, you turned it into something absolutely stunning. I honestly don't know how you pulled it off, but I'm so damn glad you did. Your talent blows me away — truly phenomenal.

Laura — thank you for being there during the moments I thought I wasn't good enough. You've pulled me through more "I can't do this" spirals than I can count. Also… sorry for all my spelling and grammar mess. You're a champ for putting up with it.

Josie — my longest supporter, my dear friend. I'm so grateful we met. You've lifted me with your words during some really dark times, and I'll always hold that close. You mean more to me than I can put into words.

Krystal — you are the light on the days I can't find my own. You've stood by me through everything, and I honestly don't know what I'd do without you. You're one of my best friends, and your love and support have gotten me through more than you probably realize. Thank you. Truly.